Mystic Tea

a novel by

REA NOLAN MARTIN

ISBN 13: 978-0-9910322-1-1 (Paperback edition)
LCCN: 2013954288

WIA**W**AKA
PRESS

*In acknowledgement of her heroic outreach
to the underprivileged, as well as the countless
testimonies of miraculous healings and ensuing
conversions that followed her death,
Saint Grace of Syracuse,
"the Saint of Many Miracles,"
is hereby appointed the official patron
of the lost and abused.*

— Official Record of American Saints 1955

PROLOGUE

1940

Augusta rushes across the field of ankle-high timothy, hiking up the skirts of her new white habit as she charges through the spring air like a colt. Every step a winged prayer, she lands deftly on the slate stepping stones that forge a path from the back of the farmhouse to the shiny silver trailer where Mother Grace lies dying. There's no time to consider how Augusta feels about their beloved founder's earthly departure. If she stops to take it in for even a second—the unthinkable vacuum of Grace—she will lack the breath it takes to get to her friend on time. And Grace will die alone.

In her left hand, Augusta grips the cruet of holy oil Grace asked her to sneak from the chapel sacristy. "No one must know," Grace had whispered—her voice a holy ember. "Only you. All I ask for in the end is a peaceful death in the presence of the one human who understands me best. You, my dear scribe. You!"

How Augusta deserved this honor, she will never know. She is one of fifty novices at this rural monastery where, thanks to Grace, miracles and novitiates abound. The Most Holy Order of Divine Grace thrives where other Orders have failed heartily. It is filled with life, faith, and most of all Grace, whose brilliant spirit is legendary in sacred circles. So how is it that this exceptional woman chose the young, inexperienced Augusta to care for her in the end? It is as mystical an alchemy as Augusta has ever experienced,

5

as if Grace had been waiting for her all along. As if they'd known each other across eternity.

Augusta stills her breath as she steps inside the trailer. She must be calm; she must not alarm Mother. In the tiny bedroom, she opens the cruet, leans down and blesses Grace's forehead, moving aside strands of her long, thick wavy hair. Augusta marvels at the volume of hair on this tiny, ancient creature—hair that still casts a dim halo of the wild titian red Grace was known for in her youth. At Augusta's gentle touch, Grace's milky azure eyes slowly open. "Thank you, dear," she whispers.

"But don't you want a priest for your final blessing?" Augusta asks eagerly. "I can call the Bishop. The Cardinal. Even the Pope would come to you!"

"What for?" says Grace quietly. "Do you think their blessing means more to God than yours?" She waves her bony hand. "Bring me some more of that tea you made, child, will you? The one that helps me see through time?"

Augusta steps into the tiny kitchen and warms the tea cup over the gas flame. Back in the bedroom, she cradles the cup for Grace to sip. "Oh, that's good," Grace says. "I see it now; I do. The next world. Though not as clearly as you do, dear. You see it all." Her head dips slowly back into the crushed feather pillow and she holds a crooked finger to Augusta. "Trust the darkness, child."

Augusta's eyes widen. "The darkness?" she repeats. "Not the light?"

Grace shakes her head. "God plants his strongest seeds in the darkest soil," she says. "Be open to it, Augusta. In times of trouble, things are not always as they seem. Trust what others do not. Trust yourself." A labored sigh escapes. "I will not abandon you even when you think I have." The words catch in her throat.

Tears bound down Augusta's cheeks. The absence of Grace is right before her. If she reaches out, she will touch it. "But how will I know it's you, Mother? How!"

A deep quake erupts in Grace's chest. Her beseeching eyes widen knowingly and then close. Augusta watches in awe as a great burst of incandescent white flame rises from the sacrum of her beloved friend and disappears.

What will become of them now is anybody's guess.

PRESENT DAY

GEMMA

Today is Gemma's thirtieth birthday. Not that there's much significance to the date or that anyone but Gemma even knows about it. This is how she wants it; business as usual with as much normalcy as humanly possible. Normalcy is underrated, she thinks, underappreciated. There are people who have so much of it they throw it out. If Gemma had normalcy she would shove it in drawers, pile it on shelves, deposit it in her savings account and spend it only on her worst days. And even then, sparingly.

In the meantime she stands on the old wooden ladder in the musty stacks of the church library focused on the only job she's managed to keep for more than six months. Out of nowhere the vision unfolds—the same vision that has haunted her for thirty years. She sucks a breath, leans hard against the shelf for balance, and prepares herself as familiar spirits surround her in curls of violet mist. Beneath them in the vision, Gemma lies listless. The spirits urge her to leave their realm—to die, she supposes, but as a spirit too, is she not already dead? Or is there more than one kind of death? Though she vaguely entertains these questions, she doesn't torture herself; she doesn't have the luxury. She is tortured by too much else.

As is her nature even now, in this vision Gemma is reluctant to leave but stoic in her resolve to cooperate. Anyway, what choice does she have? She'll do what she's told. She is aware, as all the spirits are, that her Earth mother is in labor. Her young mother lies in clear view somewhere in the ether beneath them all, curled in a suffering ball, soaked in sweat, moaning as she hugs her huge belly. "Get this child out of here!" she demands. *It is time for Gemma to go.* In dying to the spirits, Gemma will be born to the Earth. Or at least that's what appears to be happening—or have happened. Or maybe this is just the story she tells herself to make sense of it all.

As the soft spirit voices whirl around her, *"Leave. Leave!"* she steadies the library ladder against the shelf, tightening her hold on the fat pile of Thomas Merton books in her arms. She feels dizzy; takes a deep breath; refocuses. *"You can go now,"* the spirits chant, passing an unprecedented streak of magenta smoke before her eyes. In her shock at this new special effect, Gemma's arms drop; books tumble; and she clings to the edge of the library shelf to steady herself, barely. The loud crack of the bindings against the stone floor jars her. *"You can go now,"* they say. *"Leave!"* She curses the vision, focuses hard, and places her worn black sneakers one rung at a time down the library ladder.

Gemma is not afraid of these voices or this memory per se. Historically, it recedes on command. It's the other, more eager, relentless voice at the far end of this memory that haunts her. *"Come on, Gemma,"* that voice says. *"Let's get out of here! We're going to have so much FUN down there!"* Fun, Gemma thinks. *Ha!* For Gemma so far, this life has been anything but fun. And as far as she can tell, the difficulties have not been of her making. The struggles she's endured can be blamed first on her deceased mother, and next on the damnable voice that obeys no one but itself—the voice that tortures her. The so-called 'fun' voice that calls itself *Maya.*

A shadow darkens the already dim stacks. "Gemma?" says Deacon James. His substantial frame eclipses the single shaft of filtered light. "Are you okay?" His head tilts in a kindly, paternal expression of concern and he steps toward her, reaching.

She backs-up and clears her throat. "I uh..." Because of the memory, perhaps, she is so flustered she can't speak. Had she spoken aloud? Had he heard her? She stoops to gather the books, but can't follow through. Deacon James steps aside barely as she squeezes past him and moves swiftly toward her desk. "I'm sorry," she mutters. "I have to go."

"But are you okay?" he asks. "Why are you leaving? Because you dropped a few books? Gemma, we all make mistakes."

"I don't," she says. "I can't afford to."

At the reception desk, she squirms hurriedly into her navy quilted jacket, the pockets stuffed with personal items—glasses, an old coin purse, a cell phone and a half-eaten tube of mint lifesavers. "I'm sorry," she repeats, tucking her long thick braid of gold hair into the back of her coat. She walks down the hall through the vast oak doors of the old library. Waving awkwardly behind her, she wonders if she'll ever see this place or Deacon James again. Maybe not, she thinks. Probably not. No, in fact—she won't.

Realizing that at this very moment something essential within her is changing, shifting, *ending!*—she charges across the alley, down the river road, and keeps on running against the strong March winds to the river path where she stops breathless—head down, strong slim body bent, hands leaning hard against sore bony knees. For a moment she hears nothing but the hum of bridge traffic above, and beneath—waves slapping shore. She sits on a stone slab stacked on the river's edge, the Hudson River which she has called *Henry* since she was two years old. Since she could talk. Her eyes well up. "Help me, Henry," she pleads. "For God's sake, help me."

She knows it sounds far flung—the river helping—but it isn't really. Gemma Sinclair was born to Henry the way others are born to an ocean, a city, or a majestic mountain range. He is her métier, her vital ether, her River Jordan. Holy things happen in lesser places. Over the years she watched his every ripple from her crib and later from her bed in the old rotting cabin she still calls home. Henry is possibly the only thing left in her entire life that still makes her smile. Not that he has any competition; he doesn't. No family or friends, a few incidental acquaintances are all. Deacon James maybe, but not anymore. And then of course, Maya.

Henry kicks up some froth from the wake of a passing tug, and for a moment, she's hopeful, because this is how Henry talks to her. How he communicates. *"Don't give in!"* he pleads. *"Don't let Maya win!"*

I won't, she resolves. And again aloud, "I won't!"

The shrill voice of her nemesis intrudes, *"Stop the meds!"* it says. The memory—the vision—has predictably awakened Maya. "You don't need the meds," it continues. "And anyway, as you can see, I've figured out how to get through them. All they do is mess up your mind. There's nothing wrong with you! We have work to do. We need clarity. *Stop the meds!"*

"You're the one who messes up my mind," says Gemma.

"I aim to fix that," says Maya.

But Gemma knows better. She's older now—three decades! It's about time she seizes control. This is the day she will transform into something so radical that even Maya will be unable to hunt her down.

"Get lost, viper!" Gemma screams into the wind. She stands, walks back up to the river path under the palisade cliff toward the home she inherited from her long-gone mother, the mother who was no good whatsoever in helping her figure things out. The alcoholic mother who was as fuzzy and confusing a figure in Gemma's life as Maya-the-Voice was and still is.

In the periphery, a beam of light catches her eye and she turns. What? she thinks. What's that in the water? She raises her hand like a visor and squints into the glaring light. Currents gather north and south, east and west, morphing midway into a steel-blue whirlpool. Henry appears to be confused, and like Gemma, unsure of his path. Or maybe he's trying to tell her something? Something dramatic, she thinks. Yes, something of monumental import. She leans in; the river speaks. She is all ears.

"Don't listen to the damn river!" the voice interjects. "Are you crazy?! It's a *river!* Listen to *me!* Time is running out!"

In a moment of frustration Gemma throws her head back, raises her arms and howls to the wild parrots nesting in the pin oak above her. The emerald and yellow birds scatter uniformly and in layers, like a grand feathered kaleidoscopic image.

"Oh that's effective!" says Maya. "Seriously! We have work to do.

You need clarity. Get off the damn pills!"

"Shut UP!" Gemma screams. "And get out of my head! It's my head, not yours!"

"For God's sake," says Maya, "if I had my own head don't you think I would use it?!"

Gemma is startled by a rustling sound behind her and turns. A young, rugged, dark-haired guy jogging in place says, "Hey! You okay? I heard you scream."

She freezes, fixated by the unexpected intrusion—as if from another dimension—then forces herself to say, "I'm fine."

"You sure? Because…"

She turns and walks rapidly back toward the water, speechless, nodding. She stands on the edge, looking down until she's sure he's gone, wondering if this might be the final humiliation—if she should just…climb the stanchion. *And jump!* But there are guards there now, so even that desperate act would be impossible. Untimely. She would have to wait.

And she does wait, thinking, wondering, staring at the myriad reflections of vibrant life on Henry's slick surface. People survive, she thinks. All sorts of people survive.

In time, silver clouds reel in and there is a holy speck of silence even from the voice. No traffic, city sirens, helicopters, ferry whistles, nothing. A rare void. Gemma is drawn to the cascading whitecaps from a downstream tanker. She would like to vanish into the vortex of its wake. More accurately, she would like Maya to vanish. She imagines the voice getting raspy and broken-up like a bad cell signal. "You're breaking up on me!" she screams in her head.

She stares at the shimmering surface and the distorted reflections of the golden monoliths that loom across the river from the city's west side. What a vision! The buildings share a blaze of copper light that draws her further in until she is staring at—*what?!* She rubs her eyes. In the glistening whirlpool is a—*huh?* A face? She squints hard. By God, yes it is—a kind of, well—face. Wait, not a face. A building, she thinks, but no. If you look deeper, if you stare into the light, it's clearly a face.

There they are: the eyes, the nose, unmistakable lips parting. Calling out. All at once and for no apparent reason she is reminded of her old friend, Sister Michael Agnes, her third grade teacher at the now defunct grammar school of Saint Grace. Not that the face looks exactly like Sister Mike, as she was called. It doesn't. The face is distorted, more abstract or cubist, but still. The hard features and right angles call out to her in a familiar way she can't dismiss. Another vision, she thinks. But no. *It's more than a vision!* It's her future.

Gemma is flooded with memories of the stern nun. How she filled in so many times for Gemma's derelict mother. How for years, eight or ten, she brought Gemma to the convent for meals and the occasional overnight when she discovered Gemma's mother had been drinking and cavorting with the longshoremen at the Downriver Saloon. How Sister Mike, before she moved to the monastery in upstate New York told Gemma to call her anytime. She still remembers the number; how could she forget? Sister Mike now in the middle of the Hudson River in full Technicolor focus, yes—*and no!*—how strict she was, but how loyal.

The face in the river reaches out to Gemma with those determined gray eyes. Draws her in. Whether the image is intentional or even real is immaterial, because what choice does she have? None. It's either this face, these knowing eyes, a life in a monastery, or…Maya.

She turns and climbs the hundred granite steps through the wooded park to her cabin. It's clear to her now. She knows with certainty that something good can still come of her life. As she lobs home, she chews on the ends of her thick gold braid—another bad habit she will break in the monastery. She'll break them all! Anything to banish Maya. After all, isn't that what monasteries are for? To become good? Holy? Gemma will follow the narrow path exactly, whatever it takes to regain herself. To seize control.

She returns to her old shack on the Palisades overlooking Henry, tosses a few belongings—underwear, t-shirts, a crystal talisman from the good witch who, years ago, tried to dispossess her of Maya—into Grandma's faded carpet bag. Other than Henry, it's the only vestige of a family she has. She plods resolutely to the top of the hill and heads left to the bus stop where she will catch a bus to the city. And from there to her freedom—to Sister Mike and the monastery of Saint Grace where she will commit herself to orderliness. To penance. To sanctity, even. To sanity.

She has been called!

She has sensed for some time now—since the astrologer, the exorcist, the witch, the naturopath, the Ph.D. shrink—all of whom have failed her, that God is her only remaining hope. She will surrender herself to Him in exchange for her right mind. She isn't crazy. *She is not crazy!* At least not yet. And some day, one way or the other, if Gemma follows every rule to the letter, exceeds every expectation of God and Sister Mike, this blessed truth will be made perfectly clear. *Gemma Sinclair is not crazy!* And the voice will finally be laid to rest without a funeral. *You can't bury a voice!* It's nothing really—a genderless piece of cosmic trash! A fragment of disconnected copper wire in an overloaded universe.

All it's ever done is ruin everything.

As the bus pulls alongside the curb, Gemma turns and smiles at the sliver of silver water still visible between the trees. "Goodbye for now, Henry," she mutters. "Catch you upstream!" She climbs the steps, pays the driver, and blows the voice to bits with a mental bazooka as she slides into her seat.

"By the end of the week," she tells Maya, "you won't even know who I am."

ARIELLE

Arielle Santos hardly knows herself anymore. She's in-body, out-of-body and everywhere in between—the ceiling, the floor, the cinderblock walls. Her brain buzzes; her eyes sting. Her tongue is a switchblade. Don't provoke her; she'll cut you down. How did she get here?! She can't remember. It's been sooo long—hours or days. Up to a week seems possible. Was she ever anywhere else? She doesn't know. Detox is a time warp.

She bangs her head on the loose center rail of her jail cell. "I don't deserve this!" she screams. "I'm a good girl!"—which is true. She's a damn good girl. Just ask her mother if you can find her. Once upon a time, Arielle did everything for her so-called mother, e-v-e-r-y-t-h-i-n-g. She could not have done more. *Name one thing!* So where is her mother now? Or anyone, really. Anyone at all.

She paces back and forth, back and forth, then gives up and drops down on the rancid cot. Her ass is killing her because she has no ass, just bones. Bare bones on cot springs covered with a disintegrating orange yoga mat. *Why orange?* Not to mention joints made of burning, grinding metal. And a brain, ohhhhh my GOD, a pounding brain made of—*name something explosive*—a brain made of that.

She's dizzy for a minute, gets ready to collapse, but instead is inexplicably overcome with a burst of the highest octane energy she has ever felt without a needle. Going completely with it—*you could absolutely not resist*—she rises up, grips the cold steel bars and releases a

15

piercing aria of obscenities that she hopes will unhinge the deputy, or whatever he is—the gum-snapping hayseed jackass. In a cow-tipping town like Hebronville, New York, the jackass is probably sheriff, judge, jury and hangman, she thinks. Probably so many things he'd be illegal in a civilized place, like Albany or even Fort Ann. *Who put him in charge?* He couldn't be much older than she is—no more than twenty, twenty-one. He barely has a beard. And from the way he's able to sit for hours staring at his own muddy boots, he must smoke weed for breakfast, lunch and dinner. Either that or his brain's been dipped in fertilizer. *Fertilizer—yes!* Isn't that explosive?

"Get me out of this filthy bullshit torture chamber, you frigging asshoooole," she screeches. She's way beyond the flirtatious approach. Fuck the flirtatious approach.

When she gets no reaction, she belts out another minute-long howl until her head, her heart, and her lungs hold hands, close their eyes, and jump off a cliff. God, this is work! She needs a hit of cocaine, but no, no...X. Ecstasy. Hell, even a bottle of witch hazel mixed with marmalade would make her happy at this point. Isopropyl—*isn't that explosive?* It sounds explosive. After 24 hours in jail her veins probably contain nothing but blood. How will she survive? Can you survive on blood? She forces a cough. "I'm dying," she says to the jackass. "I need Robitussin. Get me Robitussin. Grape or orange. Extended release."

The deputy trades his gum for chewing tobacco. His silver badge catches the sun as he shifts his impressive weight.

"Hey, Captain Cud," she wails, "your two-cent tin foil badge is blinding me!"

He rises slowly and marches like Frankenstein, opening and closing his hands like he's going to wring her neck. So what, she thinks. He can't intimidate me! His fat fists can't fit through the bars anyway, and if he opens the cell, I'll dart like a lizard. That fat lard can't catch my bony ass.

Napalm! *That's it!* The terminal explosive for industrial-sized headaches like hers.

Oh God, she is so hyper, and yet, so exhausted and just...crazy.

Crazy! She might go out of her mind if she can keep it long enough. "Seriously," she says, "how long do you think you can hold me in this monkey cage? I have rights!" But she wonders if she does have rights. She's a 3-eyed alien in an Andy Griffith jail cell. Do aliens have rights?

The deputy finally comes alive, lunges at her, then shakes his cheeks like a plate of jello jigglers and storms out of the room with his hands in the air. His underarms are soaked. Ten minutes after he's gone, she gets the shakes again. The shivers and shakes. That's it, no more drugs. They weren't her idea to begin with—just a little birthday gift from her mama, Willa. *What to give an eight-year-old? Geez, oh, I know...dope! And for your ninth birthday...cocaine, LOL!* Thoughtful gifts from her no-clue mother and the long list of skeeve daddies that kept them in ganja.

The napalm headache returns for a command performance. *Pow! Pow!* Where's the jackass now, she wonders. She thought she would feel better without him around, but she doesn't. She feels worse. Worse than the time in high school it took her 28 hours to have the baby she had to turn around and give up. *She would have kept it! She wanted to keep it!* Worse than her 24-hour marriage to Lucky. Her skin itches and crawls like snakes. Maybe she's allergic to cinderblock. *Or orange!* It's so fucking bright!

"Help!" she screams, jumping up and down. "For God's sake, somebody help me!"

She hyperventilates for who-knows-how-long, a minute or an hour, and then drags herself to the decrepit cot and rattles the springs. She has the heebie jeebies, but no it's worse than that. She's getting ready to remove her jeans and hang herself from the window bars, when some kind of magic spell runs through her cell and over to Captain Cud's desk. She squints, tries to focus. *Huh?!* A thousand Tinkerbells shimmer over the desk in waves, but that could be her own dementia. She rubs her eyes. Blinks. Shakes her head. She can't believe what's materializing.

She needs cocaine...no wait...angel dust. Definitely angel dust, but then she thinks—I will not allow myself to cave into this delusion. I'll stare it down. I'll go straight. *I will go straight!* Make something of my life for once! No more drugs for me. Not even rubber cement, though the memory of those fumes makes her nostalgic for fifth grade slumber parties at the trailer camp.

"OK," she says to the sparklers, "I'll go straight. I swear!" And she means it. She does. She orders the sparklers to leave, squeezes her eyes shut and flicks her fingers twice. "Poof! You're gone!" Opens them. The sparklers remain, consolidate, and take form. Oh my god. Oh my god! She screams for the jackass, "Help! Help!" But he's history.

She backs-up to the wall, jerks a fistful of her sweat-drenched hair to make sure she's alive, and refocuses. It's an electrical fire maybe, or an asteroid, but no. Before her very eyes the thing grows wings, a Hollywood face and a Vegas robe. Oh god, no, she thinks. "Not an angel," she says out loud.

"Yes," it says kindly. "An Angel of the Lord."

Arielle and the Angel of the Lord stare at each other for a while, before the Angel tells her she can be freed from her addictions right here and now if she simply chooses a life of holiness and prayer. It's all Arielle can do not to burst out laughing, since she's barely heard a prayer in her life that wasn't the punch line to a dirty joke. This angel has the wrong jail cell.

The Angel directs her to a what? *Are you kidding me?!!* A monastery? "The Sisters of the Most Holy Order of Divine Grace," it says, "on the farm in the high hills on the outskirts of town overlooking the river. They are all holy women, but they are in turmoil. They need you as much as you need them. You're the answer to their prayers."

Arielle is trying hard to snap out of this hallucination, but something tells her it's real as skin. Even though she's having a hard time believing that her sorry life could be the answer to anybody's prayer, something inside her changes just like that. Sits up and takes notice. Knows that her entire life was headed like speed toward this very moment. She can't explain why. The intense withdrawal from the toxic shit of a lifetime…just floats away with the angel. *Poof!*

It's gone.

MIKE

Sister Mike stares at the packet from *The Vatican Congregation for Institutes of Consecrated Life and Societies of Apostolic Life* and thinks—could the title be any longer? The content any more absurd? So the Vatican is investigating women religious in an effort to what? To divert their attention from the clear and present danger of the male religious? What do they expect to find? She pushes the tedious pile of information aside; can't read it one more time. Can't decide at all whether or not she'll resist or cooperate with a Jurassic papal administration she could not feel less connected to. It's an acute dilemma on top of a host of chronic dilemmas. Dilemma upon dilemma. The refuse is piled high.

She stares out the window of her untidy office in the rambling thirty-room farmhouse of her monastery...or convent, really, for there is little any of them still follows in the way of monastic routine. Not enough communal prayer, for instance, or contemplative practice, or any other ritual for that matter. So much has fallen by the wayside. An abbreviated daily Mass in the open chapel, yes, offered by Sister Mike, herself—the consecrated Eucharist supplied by the sanctimonious Father Kevin on his monthly visits. But because of the uneven chapel attendance of the "townies" as Father Kevin likes to call the parishioners, the supply is often inadequate.

There aren't enough priests, of course, especially up here—one for every seven parishes in upstate New York. So the nuns are left to figure things out for themselves. Or more precisely, Mike, as Prioress, is left to

19

figure things out, and the others follow suit. They're used to it. It's not as if any of them has ever relied on a man.

Father Kevin, in spite of his overly vast pastoral domain, could unquestionably provide better service to the nuns. For one thing, he could give them what they ask for—a larger supply of hosts and holy water. And for another, he could stay long enough to register their needs and complaints. But the townies wear him out, he says, so after hearing a dozen or so of their hair-raising confessions, he heads for the hills. Not that the nuns want to see him more frequently; they don't. At least Mike and the old hermit, Augusta, don't. Every month Augusta says, "Who does he think he is—the Pope!?" The others, well…they cater to Kevin out of pure medieval conditioning. Undeserved hero worship, shall we say.

It's not about the religious details anymore, the spiritual filigree, Mike supposes. It's about survival. About how to survive an undernourished religion. Maybe at this point instead of a monastery or convent, it should be called what it really is—a broken down retreat for outcast middle-aged and elderly women who don't have much stamina left for exhausting farm work, or if she's being honest, for a rigorous religious life in general. With the exception of Gemma, of course. A sincere girl, yes—so endearing as a child—and still stunning now in an eccentric kind of way with those eyes—the one ice blue, the other sienna brown. So bewitching!

Mike was so surprised to see her when she first arrived at the monastery two years ago, so desperate to join. "I felt you calling out to me," Gemma had said.

An odd remark, since even if Mike believed in such things as mental telepathy, thoughts of Gemma hadn't entered her mind in years. There had been no "calling out."

"I'll do anything you need done," the girl had said, falling to her knees. "I've been called to this," and then like an afterthought—"by angels!"

And though by twenty-first century standards Gemma's dramatic behavior was extreme, how could Mike have turned her away? Maybe she *was* called! Only time and the harsh realities of communal living on an isolated upstate farm would tell. And anyway, the nuns needed all the help they could get! Gemma was strong, and in time proved to be a dedicated worker.

Still, Mike wonders—why the shaved head? And why so obsequiously anxious to please? A bother, really, in the way ascetics can be. Or maybe just plain crazy, who knows? Let's face it, even the hallowed Desert Fathers were arguably extreme, anti-social, and quite possibly borderline personalities. There was no such thing as psychoanalysis back then.

Mike shuffles some papers around without much luck; just not into the paperwork today. Or anything else. She removes her reading glasses and stares out at the pond where the weeping cherry is dropping its last spring blossoms into the reflective water. Spectacular! She loves this place; she really does. But how will they keep it? They've run through their financial endowment and they're too old for hard labor. Except for Gemma, of course. But the girl can't work fifty acres of farmland on her own.

In general, Mike tries not to think about Gemma, but that tack isn't working today. Gemma is simply on the mind. The truth is, in some ways her eccentric behavior is intensifying. Mike barely knows what to make of the girl's insistence on *being* the essence of the Order. The next saint, for God's sake. It's not a competition! She wears the full habit even when weeding the flower beds or hoeing the potatoes; recites the entire *Prayer of the Hours*, broken into seven sessions, and including Matins at 3 AM. Mike is surprised she doesn't say it in Latin.

The truth is, Mike would actually applaud this effort to reconnect to their monastic roots, were it not for the fact that Gemma broadcasts the prayers full blast and directly outside Beatrice's bedroom as if to make a holy example of herself. As if to intimidate the others. Something wrong there, Mike knows. She knew it when she went through the discernment process with Gemma. A classic search for approval that Mike simply cannot endorse. And it wasn't just the derelict mother, the near accidental upbringing, no. Something else less obvious or at least better hidden. Mike will have to bide her time on that one.

She stares down at the dreaded mail; the dreaded bills to be exact. What will she do? What will she do? What *will* she do? Other than Gemma, there hasn't been a novice or even a postulant for over twenty years—another reason she's reluctant to bear down on Gemma's scrupulosity. And although harvests have been adequate for their own needs, they have not had great luck producing enough fruits or vegetables to bottle, can, or even sell fresh, except at their little farm stand.

And now *this*. This investigation of women religious by the Vatican! Mike runs her fingers through her short, coarse gray hair. Don't they have enough to do, she thinks, dealing with the priest abuse? She swivels the chair to the back wall dominated by a portrait of their founder, Saint Grace of Syracuse, otherwise known as the *Saint of Many Miracles*.

Looking squarely at Grace's sweet oval face framed by her famously long, titian-red hair, and directly into her azure blue eyes, Mike says, "Where are the miracles now, Grace, hmmm? We could use one or two, you know."

If this investigation is real, Mike knows, they'll shut her down and sell the farm. Squeeze them all into a two-bedroom condo in Albany if they're lucky. Hand them the *Want Ads* and a three month deadline as happened to Mike's old pal, Celeste. Oh Mike could probably find a job in clinical psych or social work; she has a Ph.D. But at this point no one else could generate significant income, including Gemma. Mike has no idea in the world what would become of Gemma, or any of them, really, outside the walls of this ramshackle sanctuary.

She lifts the devastating financial report of the just dismantled Mother House in Syracuse and presents it to the portrait. "We're all that's left of you, Grace," she says. "We could use some help from that angel of yours." *In case you didn't hear me the first time.* God, she's getting hard and cynical. Well, she guesses that's what happens when you're sitting alone on the high seas in a row boat waiting for a cyclone to cut you in half. You get cynical.

A growing part of Mike wonders where Grace really is. Dare she think it—if she was ever here in the first place. She means this little heresy in the spiritual sense, of course, because Grace was definitely a living person. Mike's own Mother Superior, Augusta, knew Grace—took care of her for years. The Mother House in Syracuse was Grace's own home. She was real—Grace—a lovely, shiny-eyed little woman with a halo and a pocketful of miracles. When Mike came on board...when she was drawn to her vocation...it was really Grace she'd been drawn to in the first place. Not a life of abstinence at all, but a life of abundance. A life of miracles, for heaven's sake. That is the only thing this ragtag group ever had in common. Each and every one of them believed in Grace and her miracles.

Mike tries not to show defeat, but she feels it. It doesn't pay to be dishonest with oneself, or for that matter, with God. Maybe it's that time of her (or anyone's) life when the spiritual path is in need of an overhaul—riddled with frost heaves from a winter of doubt. Or maybe it was all just a wonderful tale. The miracles, that is. Though no one can deny they happened, right? In 1935 when the wandering carpenter built the dormitory addition, and disappeared before they could pay him? In '65 when they had their highest yield amidst a spring soaked with floods and fungus followed by the worst drought in history? In '70 when the raging barn fire spontaneously extinguished before the fire truck even arrived? To name a few.

And then of course, there was Gemma who claimed that Grace—or Mike herself, or *something*—appeared to her in the river—or through the river—or rising up from the river. The story morphed so many times it was impossible to track. At any rate, she'd claimed that Grace had in some manner inspired her to enter the monastery and become a nun. For Mike, however, Gemma's so-called mystical intervention was, and still is, less a miracle than another dilemma. At this point, at least, Mike will not be recording it in the *Chronicles*.

So excluding Gemma's questionable claim, there hasn't been a miracle in decades. Maybe what Mike thought was faith, was just innocence. Or ignorance. Or wishful thinking. An over-eagerness to participate in a life of miracles, as Grace had. Miracles that were possibly misconstrued in the first place. After all, was it really an Angel of the Lord who saved Grace on that dark day in 1910? *She had servants, didn't she?*

Mike hates herself when she gets like this, so despairing, really, so unfitting for a nun, a woman of God. But is it really despair, or just practicality? Somebody has to be practical; has to pay the bills; mediate the disputes; maintain a semblance of order. At any rate, when faith runs thin, there's really very little one can do about it, is there? Just ask for a renewal and wait. And in Mike's case, wait and wait and wait. And wait some more.

Sister Beatrice pokes her round little potato face in the door and knocks unnecessarily since they have already made eye contact. "Good afternoon, Mike!" she says.

"What is it, Bea?"

"Oh well, you know, Constance is pushing for a schedule change. Not feeling up to the housework again."

Mike drums her fingers on the desk.

Beatrice advances. "And so, well, I just…can I sit down?"

"No need," says Mike. "You think Constance is faking it and you want me to intervene."

Beatrice pulls her bold flower-print jersey self-consciously over her substantial hips.

"Constance is seventy-five-years-old," Mike says.

"Yes, but I'm sixty-two, and as you know, I have the hip problem…and my neck has been…"

"We're all getting up there," says Mike. She herself is fifty-nine. She stares absently for a minute and inadvertently says, "In truth, I can't say how this aging group of women is ever going to be able to keep this place together."

Taken aback by her own words, Mike shakes her head. She can't believe she actually verbalized this thought. *Losing her filters!* This won't do.

Bea is bug-eyed. "What?!" she says. "Saint Grace will come through, don't you think?" She narrows her eyes. "Don't you?"

Mike stands up, smoothes the static from her long black pant legs, and says, "Yes, of course she will, Bea. But for now, please perform Constance's chores for her if you can manage. I have an appointment."

She slips the Vatican letter into her back pocket, shoos Beatrice out of the office and up the stairs, and exits through the back door.

The crisp spring air enlivens her as she strides earnestly past the newly seeded gardens. The women have done a decent job, she thinks, until she trips over a cast iron garden rake in the path and catches herself against the potting table. Breathing deeply to temper her annoyance, she continues across the pasture to the rusty trailer where Mother Augusta lives in her self-fashioned hermitage. Augusta can't stand people anymore, and this is the real reason for her almost comical exile—too much communal living. But Mike doesn't blame her.

Standing on the top step, she hesitates, then raps on the aluminum door. She hates to bother Augusta, she really does. But she must. No one else would remotely understand the significance of this letter from Rome. An investigation of their practice! To see if they are conforming! *To what?!* They are all that remains of the Order. They make their own rules.

Minutes pass. Where is Augusta? *Sick? Fallen? Dead?* Mike dreads the day she loses her old friend. Augusta gives her purpose; reminds her who she is.

"Who's there?" Augusta finally says. "Is somebody there?"

"Yes, Mother, it is I, Mike."

"Oh, Michael Agnes! Do come in."

Mike swings open the door and searches for the tiny nun in the mess of books, sacramentals, quilts, dishes, and tea concoctions. "Over here," she says from the corner chair. She is covered in blankets and petting one of the patchwork farm cats she calls Assisi. Tolstoy's *War and Peace* is open midway on her lap.

Seeing her like that, blended into the soft textures and muted colors of her surroundings, Mike is stunned by her appearance. Her endearing face is a shrunken apple, a leather trophy to the glory days in the hot sun working the land and praising the Lord. Mike's heart aches for those days, those miraculous, euphoric days when Augusta was Prioress. When the spirit of Saint Grace lit up the community like a solar flare. Tough old bird, Augusta, to be truthful, but also honest, inspired, and wise. Mysterious—in the ways of a mystic. *That inner knowing.* When Mike became Prioress, she had tried to fill those shoes, but in her own estimation, she has not even begun to measure up.

"How are you today, Augusta?" Mike says.

Augusta strokes the cat. "I'll do." She purses her lips. "But don't send that Sister Gemma over here again. She's a trial."

"So you sent her away?"

"I can handle my own housekeeping."

Mike sighs as she collects dirty dishes, napkins, cutlery and other kitchen debris. She detects the sour odor of urine and hopes it's the cat. "Can you be more specific about Gemma, Mother? I can't act on generalities."

"I can't abide her manner," says Augusta. She scratches the raw pink scalp beneath her scarce, pin-straight, white hair. Her crooked fingers point in so many directions, they look like ancient cuneiform symbols. Maybe they are. "The girl's not right," she says.

Mike folds blankets, fluffs pillows, tosses towels into a laundry pile by the door. Housekeeping triage. She knows she won't get more information than that, but she wants more. She wants specifics so she can help Gemma grow in the spiritual and the communal sense. So she can figure out what's wrong—the girl has made too many enemies too fast. "Nothing then?" she says. "Because I'd like to help the girl."

"Oh well, just bad energy," says Augusta dismissively. "I did the purification on her, but anyway, it did no good. At least not enough; nothing lasting. She walked right through the smoke and came out the same way she went in. Something tough and sticky about her." She leans forward and makes circles with her hands. "Something all around her that won't leave."

"Purification, Augusta?"

"Yes."

"So, you lit the myrrh?"

Augusta nods. "To purify her energy."

"I know about your purifications." Mike doesn't want to say this, but she does anyway, "I thought I asked you not to use matches."

Augusta leans on the pull-down table and lifts her bent little body upright. "Would you like some water?" she asks Mike. "I'm going to get a drink."

Mike sighs. "Here, let me help you up." She has every intention of pursuing the interrogation, but gets a close look at Augusta standing, and is distracted by her appearance. What is she wearing?! It looks like a motley collection of housecoats, one on top of the other, some snapped, some zipped, and some open. There must be five.

"Oh I'm fine," says Augusta. "Fine, fine, fine." She shuffles a few feet in her woolen slippers to the kitchen where she pours herself water in a used glass. Just as Mike decides to give up on the interrogation, Augusta says, "I'm perfectly capable of lighting incense, Michael Agnes. When I'm no longer capable of it, I'll stop."

Mike bites her bottom lip.

"If you're wondering what to do with me," she continues, "you can just forget about it. I know I'm useless, but I'm not going anywhere. This trailer is my home."

"No, no, not that, Mother. Believe me," says Mike reassuringly. "I've given you my word on that, and I'll keep it. I was just…wondering about…your clothing," she says. "If you need some help changing." Oh God, she hates this; she really does. Augusta deserves more.

"Not at all," says Augusta, but I could use a clean dress if you don't mind."

"But you're already wearing …"

"I know very well what I'm wearing," she says pointedly. "I'm cold. And I can't reach the closet bar, so I can't fetch things and I can't hang anything up." With her chin in the air, she waves her arm like royalty. "Thus the piles. There's got to be a clean dress in there somewhere."

Mike surveys the entire trailer. What piles? Is Augusta going blind?

Finding no obvious stray apparel, she instead strips the dirty bed linens in search of another housecoat or nightgown or any other form of clothing that might be hiding around, something easy to put on and take off. But before she was dismissed, Gemma must have gathered whatever she could and taken it to the laundry.

Once she remakes the bed with fresh linens, Mike turns around to find her old friend settled in the corner chair, nodding off—Assisi purring in her lap. She washes the dishes, sweeps the trailer, and collects the pile of laundry near the door. Forget the Vatican letter, she thinks. Augusta's life is too hard as it is.

As she reaches for the door handle, Augusta says, "What's that in your pocket, Michael Agnes?"

Mike hesitates. "Um…nothing," she says. "I'll be back a little later with your clothes, Augusta. And your dinner."

"Don't send that girl," says Augusta.

"I won't," says Mike.

"I haven't the countenance."

"Yes," says Mike softly, "I know."

As she squeezes through the door with the pile of laundry, she thinks there's something very different about Augusta this time. She's not the same woman she was even a month ago. And it's not just her age. It's the malaise. The malaise, thick as mayonnaise, has permeated everything. *Everyone.* Except Gemma, that is, but she's a separate issue. The truth is, like Augusta, Mike would like to curl-up in a big crazy trailer of her own and never come out. Depression? Oppression? Take your pick.

She crosses the pasture deep in thought, watches absently for stray tools, enters the farmhouse at the lower level, and deposits Augusta's laundry in the basement bin. Sister Rose will have to be reassigned to Augusta's housekeeping duty, she supposes. But no, that won't work. Even though at fifty-two, Rose is the youngest next to Gemma, Augusta finds Rose too timid and simple-minded. Well then, Sister Gabriella, but…no. Augusta finds Gabriella too talkative, and in truth, Gabriella does waste so much time. Constance is difficult, too, and never healthy, really. Always tired.

Mike takes the stairs to the main floor and wanders down the hall toward her office to force some paperwork out of herself. She supposes she should send Constance back to the clinic for a more thorough set of labs. After all, what if she isn't just a hypochondriac as the others always complain? What if she has Lyme Disease? Or an underactive thyroid? Or some kind of auto-immune disorder? You can't chalk everything up to old age.

At any rate, Constance is out, so that leaves Beatrice to clean the trailer. Not that Beatrice will be co-operative; she really is overworked. Not to mention overweight and still gaining. And here Mike is a psychologist, for heaven's sake, and she can't figure Beatrice out! Or any of them, for that matter! Not that she's been in a professional clinical practice, but over the years, the Sisters have brought her enough lunacy to make her wonder if she was tending a monastery or a Star Wars bar. But back to Beatrice. To be truthful, Mike wonders if Bea can even fit through the trailer door. Can she? She tries to imagine this.

Oh for God's sake, she'll just clean the damn trailer herself. At least for the short term. She enters her office and closes the door, thinking, *short term? Ha!* Are you kidding? As if there will ever be a long-term! Barring an outright miracle, that is. She plops down on her desk chair, exhausted. Those Vatican investigators won't make it through one day here before…

Her thoughts are interrupted by a sharp knock at the front door, fifteen or so feet from her office. Someone's on call—but who? Whoever it is doesn't answer the door, because a second knock turns into a persistent set of knocks— *rat-a-tat-tat,* and then pounding, really, *bam bam bam,* followed by one continuous, two-minute door bell ring. Perturbed to the point of suicide, Mike reaches for the intercom to rally the assigned hostess, when she thinks, oh hell, why bother, and yells "Just a minute!" in a throaty scream. She's a one woman show.

Crossing her office in long, annoyed strides, she enters the wide vestibule, looks here, there, and anywhere for one of the nuns to deal with the visitor. But no one; nothing. Where are they?! *How will she ever get any work done?!* She grabs the brass doorknob and pulls open the heavy oak door, ready to sign the receipt, receive the package, accept the unprecedented donation, *whatever*! But instead she just...stares. The door is wide-open, and she is looking out and her mouth is hanging open. She tries to speak, but just...cannot.

"Oh hey!" chirps a tiny, unkempt woman—or girl, really—a teenager no bigger than Augusta, and so packed with kinetic energy that she's practically dancing to keep herself in place. On her back, and strapped across the front of her *Earl's Barbeque* t-shirt, is a worn-out, red-plaid backpack, half the size of her entire body. Her long, tangled, titian-red hair frames an oval face marked by wide, azure blue eyes, an impish smile, and a radiant pink complexion.

Mike steps back involuntarily. "Grace?!" she says. "Is that you?"

The girl looks behind her. "Um, no? I'm Arielle?" she says. "Arielle Santos?"

Mike blinks, rubs her eyes, and reopens them. This is no Arielle Santos. This is Grace Gannon. It most definitely is Grace—a messy little disheveled version of the great saint, but still. It has to be Grace— it looks *exactly* like her. Mike feels a little dizzy. She backs into the vestibule where she accidentally knocks against the bottom step of the staircase and lands on her backside.

The girl follows Mike in, and says, "Hey, are you okay?"

Mike nods her head like a bobble doll. "What are you? What do you..."

"Oh, well, I've just come to join the monastery?" she says, or really, asks. "I was sent here by an, uhhh...I don't know, angel, I guess? An 'Angel of the Lord' it said?" She shrugs. "But like, that was before rehab, so..."

GEMMA

Gemma arrives at Sister Mike's office slightly winded and bleeding at the knees from embedded gravel—her secret, forbidden penance. She is breathless just thinking that, minutes from now, she will finally be face-to-face with the new candidate. The girl had apparently arrived at the monastery a few days ago, but was sent directly to a friend of Sister Mike's in Albany to get talked out of her decision. "A questionable fit," they'd said. At least that's what Gemma overheard Sister Gabriella telling Sister Beatrice the other day. But why should she believe them? They don't belong here either.

Gemma has lived on this farm for two years as a postulant first and now as a novice prepared for her final vows at any time. Being completely honest, it isn't the sanctuary she thought it would be. Unlike the other nuns, she has lived her life to the letter of the monastic law and beyond. She has been a true and faithful witness to the sacrifice of the Cross. As with many saints who have pursued this path, she has become a near outcast in this unhinged community that seems to have forgotten the sacred seeds of its own origin. What they need is new blood—blood so foreign and challenging in nature as to be nearly unrecognizable to the spiritual complacency that has beset them.

The very appearance of this new girl is noteworthy. Who is she? Where did she come from? She is the only candidate to cross their threshold since Gemma joined the Order two years ago, so what lack of discernment would it take to send her away? Assuming she stays—

assuming the others don't discourage her—it is Gemma's intention to draw the girl in. To lead this young innocent down the righteous path before she is seduced by the lazy Vatican II liberties of the older nuns.

She checks her pocket watch—2:00 sharp. Where are they all? Late as usual. She wonders why Mike puts up with them—their stubborn disorganization and just...outright defiance of authority. She searches the starched white folds of her habit for the oversized beads to begin a rosary in the void, to use her time wisely and for the good of humankind. But then, even through the closed office door, she can't help overhearing the deep, resonant voice of her Superior. She steps gingerly around the coat rack and leans in discreetly.

"I want you to feel free to ask me anything, of course," says Sister Mike to the candidate. She clears her throat. "However, I find your first question altogether puzzling and not at all of a spiritual nature. Not that issues like this aren't raised eventually, but not at first. Usually the vocation is first."

Gemma visualizes Sister Mike staring with her unblinking translucent gray eyes. How intimidating they are, like a cat's. How they bore into you.

"Oh sorry," says the girl, "I'm not overly familiar with, you know...nuns, and how they live all together like this. But with a name like Mike I just assumed you were gay."

Gemma's eyes widen. Can she be hearing things? As shocked as she is by this naïve blurt, she is also more than slightly thrilled. Mike has been tough on Gemma since the day she arrived. Testing her vocation, perhaps. And as grateful as Gemma may be for the spiritual opportunity to withstand this condemnation, she feels highly over-criticized for her strict attention to the letter of the law. After all, isn't that what they're here for? To live the monastic law?

"Well I'm not gay," says Mike evenly. "My full name is Sister Michael Agnes, in honor of my parents, as was the tradition when I took my vows. Mike is simply my nickname. Not that anyone's sexual orientation should play a role in a monastery. It shouldn't. We're committed to celibacy."

"Hooray for celibacy!" says the postulant, clapping. "I've absolutely had it with men, believe me. I never intend to get pregnant again. You can just count on me being celibate every day, I swear."

At this, Gemma is knocked off balance, catching her wimple and veil on the coat rack. She takes a minute to carefully extricate herself before the whole thing collapses. By the time she's finished, she can hear nothing else except the thunderous pounding of footsteps from the herd of nuns descending the front staircase. Do the ladies know *nothing* about propriety, she wonders? Even Gemma's drunk mother taught her more than this.

At the head of the herd is Beatrice followed by Gabriella, babbling as always, followed by Rose and Constance. Except for Constance, who is dressed in a hideous, yellow-striped Simplicity pattern shift of her own making, they are all wearing unflattering jeans and preposterous flea market shirts. Buttons popping. This includes Beatrice, who suffers a "glandular problem" that is apparently getting worse by the day.

Gemma tries hard to suppress her frustration that these stout women don't understand the value of discipline and just…fasting for the salvation of souls. Or even the value of wearing the habit as witness to God! She bites her tongue. No amount of effort on her part will make the slightest difference, she knows. What was the word Beatrice used to describe Gemma? Oh yes, scrupulous. As if scrupulosity were an insult. Wait until I become Prioress, she thinks. And she will in time, she's certain, because no one else here is qualified for the task of reviving this freak show to its rightful honor as a divine oasis on the road to Calvary. Even Mike is completely burned out.

All are present now except Augusta, who will not be joining them, no doubt, because she hasn't attended a meeting in three years. Other than the fact that Augusta is an unbearable crank, she is the only nun here whom Gemma truly admires. The crankiness is probably due to body aches and pains and the mental frustration of living in a monastery that doesn't live up to its purpose. But Gemma has had the privilege of witnessing firsthand the hermit's prowess, the fruits of her obvious holy spiritual gifts. The woman is a mystic master and there is much to be learned from her.

In fact, though Gemma need never admit it, Augusta's secret little incense ritual a few days ago banished the voice right out of Gemma's head. No more Maya. Not even a whisper. Because of this, when Mike told Gemma she was being removed from trailer duty, she was devastated—depressed for days. But she won't give up; she'd done nothing wrong. The hermit has moods, hates visitors; they all know that. She's a hermit! Gemma will bide her time, do anything to get reassigned to the trailer. Anything.

Not that she can appeal directly to Augusta. She can't. At the advanced age of ninety-five, Augusta, though hearty enough, is unlikely to leave her trailer for anything less compelling than her own funeral. But Gemma will ingratiate herself to Sister Mike by offering to train the candidate, a task she wants anyway because the girl needs to be trained by somebody with a shred of holy discipline.

The Sisters smile politely to Gemma and file into Mike's office. One-by-one they glance at the girl, clearly surprised by her appearance in general (she looks like somebody, but who?!) and her tattoo in particular. Two tattoos really, but the tiny purple dragonfly on her right upper arm pales in comparison to the pernicious rattlesnake that circles her neck like a noose. For this girl, the room is as warm and welcoming as a crypt.

A little sparrow of a thing with tumbling laser-red hair, messy and unkempt and dressed like a sidewalk sale—she wiggles nervously. Gemma performs a mental makeover, dressing the girl in full formal habit right up to her ears and over her head, obliterating her tattoos and her siren hair. All will be made new in the Lord! The picture is so satisfying, Gemma nearly sighs out loud.

The other Sisters are not so charitable. They study the girl with what Gemma can only interpret as ridicule or contempt—wide flaring nostrils, squinty eyes, and open jaws. Well, good for them, she thinks. Let them spurn the new girl as they spurned me. Gemma won't judge the girl. The little mongrel is quite possibly her ticket to canonization.

Sister Mike smiles reservedly and announces, "Sisters, I would like you all to meet our new resident, Arielle Santos."

Arielle continues to wiggle, her shoulders shifting constantly up and down. Her eyes wander all over the room, and she smiles at something—the nuns or the ceiling—who knows, she is so unfocused. "Hey," she says with a shy grin. "I know this might seem a little, well…weird to you, that I'm here and all, but like, it's a lot weirder for me, so."

Mike stands, walks around her desk, and places her hands on the girl's shoulders with enough authority to stop the constant pumping. She raises her chin and says, "Arielle has requested residence in our monastery. She wishes to explore the religious life as a potential postulant."

There is general murmuring.

Arielle says, "A postulate is fine. Or whatever. You can make me whatever you want. I'm a hard worker."

"Postu-*lant*," enunciates Gabriella.

The older nuns stifle a collective giggle, which is so rude Gemma can't believe it. She will suffer their rudeness and offer it to God on behalf of the mongrel.

Mike paces thoughtfully then says, "But under the circumstances, Sisters, our new friend, Arielle, will require some extra preparation before vows of any kind. So she won't be a postulant right away. She will first be properly educated in the Catholic faith and baptized accordingly."

Practically jumping off her seat, Beatrice says, "What?!" then retreats quickly under the power of Mike's evil eye.

But Gemma can't believe it either—*not even Catholic!* Why is she here?!

"I know a few things about Catholics," Arielle says hopefully to the dissidents. "One of my stepfathers was once a Catholic. He told me about Christ on the cross and his suffering wife, Mary." She shakes her head. "I can relate to it because my life has been pretty crazy, too."

There is dead silence. Finally Gabriella raises her hand.

"Yes, Gabriella?" says Mike.

"May I ask our new, uh, what do we call her?"

"Arielle," says Mike.

"No, but I mean…what is she?"

"For now, she is a catechumen—a student of our catechism."

"Ok, well, I would like to ask our catechumen why, if you know nothing at all about our religion, are you the least bit interested in our Order?"

Arielle shrugs. "An Angel of the Lord suggested it?"

Beatrice draws in her breath. "An angel?" she says. "Really? What did it look like?"

Mike steps forward. "It looked like an angel," she says dismissively. "Now, we have some business to attend to before dinner."

"I can draw a picture of it if you want," says Arielle. "I'm pretty good at drawing."

Gemma would very much like to see a picture of this angel, as a matter of fact, since Mike had also ignored Gemma's angel story completely, as did they all. She would be very interested in seeing if they give any credence whatsoever to Arielle's story. What is Mike so afraid of with the angel, anyway, she thinks. Hadn't Grace herself been saved by one?

Arielle grabs a pen on Mike's desk and a piece of paper to draw her picture, which Mike quickly retrieves. "Perhaps later," she says. "Right now we need to make accommodations." She points to Beatrice. "You will be in charge of Arielle's catechesis. She will be in class with you from 9-12 daily until she is able to recite and fully understand our beliefs."

Beatrice's face drops as her chronic rosacea rash creeps up her neck and cheeks. "But…with all due respect, Sister Mike…can we share that task? I've got the gardens this month and the kitchen prep, and…I've been working on this, well, quilt."

"Never mind about the gardens," says Mike. "Consider them reassigned to Gemma for now."

What?! Gemma has to practically swallow her tongue to be quiet. She has just finished a grueling schedule of spring garden duty that began in March with soil overhaul, which she accomplished almost single-handedly and finished just a few weeks ago with the Holy Week plantings. She stops these thoughts in their tracks, however, and reminds herself that this is simply one more opportunity (out of the thousands that present themselves in this asylum) for penance. She bows her head reverently. "Yes, Sister," she says. If she can just zip-it, the new girl will see that Gemma is the obedient one who sets the holy example. Who respects her vows. The girl will want to follow Gemma's lead.

"And because of our financial plight, Sisters," says Mike, "the dormitory must remain closed-off. As a result, Arielle will be rooming with Sister Gemma for the foreseen future." She raises her chin. "And Sister Constance will be in charge of Arielle's orientation in monastic philosophy and procedure."

For God's sake, Gemma thinks, Constance doesn't do a damn thing but worry about her health! The girl will be a hypochondriac by September! "But, Sister Mike!" she says. "If the new resident will be living in my room, might you not give the duty of her orientation to me?"

"Thank you for offering," says Mike. "But the orientation will be Constance's job. As the weeks go on I will revisit this plan and adjust accordingly. And let me say also, that since we are in a period of evaluation, nothing should be discussed with outsiders." She blinks. "Or…should you run into her…Mother Augusta. At least for now. This wonderful news is something I myself will tell her."

Break to her, she means, Gemma knows.

"Is that understood?" says Mike.

They are a sea of bobbing heads. "Ok then, let us all join hands and invoke the Lord to bless our growing community."

ARIELLE

Arielle's first overnight at the monastery is a nightmare. After barely laying her head down on a rock hard pillow, she immediately dreams about Lucky the Loser, of all people *not* in her life. Next, thanks to Sister Rose's greasy undercooked goulash, the horror show continues with enough intestinal gas to fill a black hole. Try holding that in. And as long as all this is driving you crazy, why not invite a chorus of screech owls, bullfrogs, coyotes and what-have-you, croaking, babbling, prancing, flying, and slamming right into your window with a death wish. *Where am I—Amityville?* And now she is waking up to a mad woman swinging her arms in the air chanting what sounds like a foreign language. "Something something something, Jesus!"

Or maybe Arielle can't make sense of it because of the Kleenex balls she shoved into her ears in the middle of the night when the same madwoman was chanting something else. Or maybe it was the same thing, how would Arielle know? She's not a nun. It was no Lady Gaga tune; she knows that much. The madwoman was standing in the center hallway where everyone could hear her high holiness, except maybe Mike whose apartment is on the other side of the kitchen. Arielle doubts that's an accident.

In spite of her frustration from no sleep whatsoever, she actually wants to learn about Jesus. She wants to know what all the fuss is about. Why so many people in the clinic thought he was the greatest, and why Mama Willa never bothered to teach her anything about him or anything at all really except how to nurse an overdose. According to the angel, she was brought here to help but also to learn. In honor of the angel, she unplugs her ears.

"Deservedly did the Prophets announce that He'd been born; the Heavens and the Angels that He'd been born," says the roommate, or as Arielle likes to think of her—*the saint*. She's basically dressed in a burlap bag with a hood, eyes skyward. "He lay in a manger, and yet the world rested in His hands," she reads.

Arielle sits up and swallows a huge yawn so she can listen to the drama which, so far, reminds her of rehab—just the fervor of it. After making it through that carnival, this place should be easy. After rehab, she should be able to take a nap in the middle of a buffalo stampede.

"O sing unto the Lord a new song; for He hath done marvelous things," the saint continues. "The Lord hath made known His salvation; His righteousness hath He revealed in the sight of the heathen."

Arielle raises herself on one elbow. "What heathen?" she says.

Gemma moves her spacey eyes—the one brown, the other blue—in what appear to be different directions. Arielle is mesmerized.

"What did you say?" Gemma chokes.

"Which heathen? You or me?"

Gemma grits her teeth. "Every heathen," she says. "A heathen is someone who lacks knowledge of God. I don't exactly think of myself as a heathen, but I suppose even my knowledge of God is incomplete." She closes her eyelids. "May I continue?"

"I'm a total heathen," says Arielle, yawning.

"Yes you are," says Gemma. "And do you know how I know that? Because only a heathen would interrupt a person in the middle of Laudes. It's extremely bad monastic form. Remember that because you won't learn it from Constance. In fact everything she tells you should be double-checked with me immediately after you learn it so you don't go around half the day with the wrong idea. Constance hasn't followed monastic form since I've been here."

"What are Laudes?"

"Morning prayers from this…" She pulls a little black book from the dresser. "We're all supposed to be saying special prayers at designated times of the day and night. It's what nuns do." She sighs. "I'd like to continue if you don't mind."

Arielle says, "Fine, but can I see that book?"

"I'm sure you'll get your own book once you've learned the fundamentals of our religion," says the saint. "Until then, however, I don't really think it makes any sense to parrot words and concepts that are beyond your understanding."

Gemma finishes her prayers and Arielle tries to ask her a question or two, but every time she tries, the saint purses her lips and sticks her finger over them, so Arielle goes back into voyeur mode. One thing the saint doesn't seem to mind is being watched.

Here are a few things Arielle learns from watching Gemma: when she removes the burlap bag and head wrap, she's…*bald!* She kneels and prays before she puts on each piece of clothing, which is a lot of clothes and a lot of kneeling. First there's a white dress made of something that looks very warm and goes all the way to the ground; then separate skirts and bigger sleeves that go over the other sleeves, as if two sleeves are not enough. Next comes a white piece of fabric that covers her neck and squeezes her cheeks forward like two crab apples. This is followed by a stiff cardboard hat that has a veil attached, also white. Then a belt. Around the belt are some gigantic wooden beads.

Arielle thinks the beads are fierce, not to mention the huge silver cross around the neck, which makes the costume look so official. There are more parts to the saint's get-up that are not worth mentioning though, such as the black witch shoes there are just no words for.

"I thought you were working in the gardens today," Arielle says pleasantly. She wants to get off to a better start with the saint.

"That's true," says Gemma as she gathers her prayer books and other unidentifiable objects.

"But won't you be a little, you know, hot out there in that outfit? And won't it get dirty?"

Gemma's big-lidded wicked crazy eyes shrink fast into glaring marbles. "I'm going to give you a piece of advice," she says. "This is a hard life of commitment and sacrifice. You get out of it what you put into it. Got that?"

Not really.

"I'd advise you to get ready, Arielle," she says, "since Mass begins in 15 minutes."

"Mass?"

"Yes, Mass."

When Arielle still looks confused, the saint says, "Church."

Arielle jumps. "Oh! I'll get dressed right away."

Gemma nods approvingly. "That's good, Arielle. Very good. Remember always to be prompt around here, no matter what sloppy behavior you observe from the older nuns, and believe me, what you don't see, you'll trip over. They're not your best example. God expects more of us."

"Okay," says Arielle.

"And today is a very holy day," she says, "so reverence is in order."

When the saint sees that the holiness of the day isn't registering with Arielle, she says, "It's the Feast of the Ascension of Our Lord into Heaven."

The only word Arielle can think of to cover-up the mile-wide gap in her education is, "Cool." Not exactly genius, but.

"*Body and soul!*" emphasizes the saint, all worked-up.

"Wow! What a trick!"

"Ascension is not a *trick!*"

"Double wow!" She is definitely up for a life where ascension into heaven is a normal occurrence.

Gemma raises her chin. "Well, see you in chapel then," she says with an almost-smile or possibly a twitch, hard to tell.

Arielle is a speed demon brushing her teeth, combing out her forest fire hair, washing her underarms over the sink since there's no time for a shower. She wants to make a good impression. She throws on her jean shorts—not the short-shorts, she isn't stupid. It's a holy day. The ones with the fewest rips and tears, followed by her only fresh t-shirt, *Madonna at the Palladium*, and a beat-up old pair of Frye boots left by Mama Willa before she split to Splittsville somewhere in Montana or Iceland, Arielle can truly not remember which. Anyway, the Frye's were a fair exchange if you ask Arielle, nicely broken-in, cowgirl cool. Perfect for a farm, even a farm with nuns.

Arielle's already decided that if she's forced to wear Gemma's get-up at some point, she'll still wear the Frye's. Her personal touch. She will absolutely not wear the black clunkers. She'll tell Mike—who does not wear the costume—that the Frye's mean something to her. That on the rare occasion when she misses her mother, she actually sleeps with the boots on, and it helps. This has only happened twice in the three years since she last saw Willa, but that's irrelevant. To her these boots are guide dogs; she'll take them everywhere, even to church. They're her only reference point in the whole wide world. She can't live without them. She grabs her backpack and charges downstairs.

Surfing across the polished, wide-plank pine floors on a worn area rug, she hops off at the doorjamb and sprints outside under the sturdy barn-wood canopy in search of the nuns. The canopy has a trellis on top that crawls with vines and tiny purple flowers—romantic in an old-time nostalgic way. It's hard not to slow down and appreciate this little spring treat of flowers and such, not to mention the swimming pool sky and the rippled pond to the left and the lilacs and wild dogwoods. This place is prettier than she remembers from yesterday, but how could she remember anything from yesterday? Yesterday was like a former life altogether when you think about it—a blur of a movie starring crazy characters with the real Arielle in a minor cameo walk-on role. Or walk-on-by is more like it. She was so disoriented she barely recognized herself or her surroundings. *Where am I!* Not that she feels at home now; she doesn't.

Arielle spots activity ahead and hurries toward the small stone chapel where Beatrice is huddling with Rose and Gabriella in a busy little cluster that reminds Arielle of a hive. Constance, on crutches, slowly rounds the corner from the kitchen. Arielle slows down, because…*why hurry?* No one else is.

As she gets closer to the hive, Arielle suddenly feels naked, like in one of those dreams when you're about to take a test in school and just as you pick up your pen, your clothes vanish. The possibility that this actually happened is so real that she yanks on her Madonna t-shirt to make sure it's really there then pulls on the ragged bottom of her denim shorts. Intact.

Of course, the nuns give her the once over anyway, a genuine technique she remembers well from high school on the days she managed to get there. On the days when her mother wasn't crying in a corner of the trailer and begging her to stay home. The principal said, "Girls! Cover yourselves up right now or you'll get into all sorts of trouble and deserve every bit of it." The principal was right about the trouble. Now Arielle lives on a farm full of principals.

"Sorry about the shorts," she says, "but this is all I've got." *All they let me keep when I got out of jail!*

Rose narrows her eyes and pulls her lower lip into a point. Constance frowns; Beatrice stares wide-eyed. Gabriella folds her arms in a huff. How many shades of disapproval are there?

In what Arielle doesn't mind calling a stroke of sheer genius, she says, "If you have ideas for outfits I could borrow, or like…make myself, I'm open to it."

Constance comes to life. "You know how to sew?" she says.

"Um, no, not really," says Arielle. "Not at all, actually. But I could take a class. I'm willing to learn."

"I could teach you," she says.

Arielle drinks in this picture of Constance rocking back and forth on her crutches, the shoulders of her dress pushed way up against her ears. She's not exactly a You Tube video of someone you would pick to teach you to sew. The straight shift on her lumpy little body looks exactly like the yellow one she had on last night, except today's version of the same pattern is red-plaid. Instead of saying, "*Where are the bagpipes?*" Arielle says, "Wow! You would really teach me?"

Beatrice snaps, "Don't play with Constance. She takes her sewing dead seriously."

This attracts some hardy sniggers from the Bea-hive.

Arielle turns to Constance and says simply, "When do we start?!"

"You'd be interested then?" Constance says a bit suspiciously.

"Don't waste her time, young lady…" says Gabriella, arms still folded. "If you're not being sincere, then drop it."

All at once Mike appears at the door of the chapel. She's dressed like a funeral director again in an all black suit. Arielle thinks there's a good possibility she's a man. Not that Arielle is hung up on the idea of a man posing as a Prioress in a women's monastery. Why not? It's no weirder than anything else in her life. A person can get used to anything.

"We could do with a little less chatter, Sisters," says Mike, "and a little more respect."

The nuns bow their heads and file in past her, but Arielle says, "Feast of the Ascension, right?!" She points up and nods knowingly. "Sign me up for a front seat!"

Mike scowls.

"I'm gonna like, sit in the back," says Arielle. "If you don't mind."

"Whatever you feel comfortable with," says Mike. She checks Arielle's outfit up, down & sideways which, though Arielle hates to admit it, is disappointing since it's not like she came with a wardrobe trunk. But whatever. She slinks into a pew in the back.

Throughout the readings, the chants, Mike's little talk about "rising up to your spiritual potential," the constant kneeling and the standing, Arielle squirms like a garter snake. She can't stop the thoughts parading around in her brain, and just the distractions of a brand new environment. First, there's the rustic beauty of the stone walls—the stained glass windows and the gold touches on the statues that catch the sun from the one skylight. And there's the singing, which is very pleasing and harmonious. Then there's the completely different distraction of the local people who look like farmers. There's one old redneck Arielle thinks she recognizes from the post office in Fort Ann where she went to high school. And then there's all the old-time language from the prayers, like poetry—not Lucky's limericks, but more like the Romeo and Juliet days when everybody talked in rhyme. All in all it has a surprisingly deep effect on her.

With all this going on, Arielle suffers a little flashback to a day when she was about four years old and Willa's parents, Gram and Pa, brought her to church one Sunday in her favorite Cinderella dress, which was a hand-me-down from a cousin. She can't remember what religion the services were, but it was somewhere in New Hampshire and it looked a lot like this church. So maybe she is Catholic after all, or would have been if her mother had been capable of keeping a commandment. Seeing as how Willa hated her parents (because they wouldn't put up with her shit), Arielle didn't see much of them after that.

Then it hits her—maybe they're still alive? If they are, they must be as old as Constance or older. Maybe they're on crutches, too. She gets the idea to look them up if she can get hold of a computer, not that she's seen one for a while. At least not since the sheriff confiscated the Mac and iPhone her dealer bought her, ugh. With all her contacts on it, double ugh. But wasn't there a PC in Mike's office? She performs a mental inventory. Pretty sure there was. Later on, she'll take a look.

MIKE

The Cardinal was pleased to hear about the wholehearted and genuine responses of many congregations to the Questionnaire. However, I also shared with him my sadness and disappointment that not all congregations have responded to this phase of dialogue with the Church in a manner fully supportive of the purpose and goals of the Apostolic Visitation. He encouraged me to ask those who have not yet fully complied to prayerfully reconsider their response." —*Office of the Apostolic Visitator on the Investigation of Women Religious*

Back in her office, Mike stares at the letter from the Apostolic Visitator for the umpteenth time, and in a moment of sheer madness, dangles it over the wastebasket. Why not? she thinks. *Throw it out!* If they want to show up anyway to evaluate the merits and viability of their Order, well...let them. It's fine with her. Let a posse of four Vatican-sponsored interrogators take up residence in the nearly condemned old dormitory, walk around all day with clipboards and pens asking questions, checking off all the insubordination—all the unorthodox, nonconforming, nearly heretical situations that occur at this monastery all day long. Let them report it all to the Mother Superior in the Office of the Apostolic Visitator and put them out of business. What kind of word is 'Visitator' anyway? It isn't even English.

But let them visit. Let them witness the disorder, the slovenly form, the dearth of faith. The televisions! Not that the original Charter expressly forbade TV's—they hadn't even been invented. But it does imply—well, specify—that a nun's free time should be used for work, prayer, and charitable efforts. Still, after 9/11 Mike felt that the women should be better informed, better prepared for any emergency—to house travelers, for instance, in the event of a mass exile from New York City. Not that this reasoning would necessarily hold sway with the interrogators.

But she will not remove the televisions or the radios. No. She will not enforce rules that have been senseless for decades just to please an out-of-touch and imperious ruler from a far-off land. Instead, she will watch with satisfaction as the invading "visitators" are sucked into the magnetic vortex of confusion and indecision that she and her Sisters have been experiencing for years. Confusion and indecision about what in the hell comes next when no one in Rome or Albany seems to care one bit about the wellbeing of their dwindling Order or their monastery. You can't force women to become nuns. Maybe their time has plain run out.

Mike continues her fantasy with the visitators, watching in her mind's eye as they cross the patchy fields and spot the unsanctioned trailer. *Check!* They move up the steps and inside the door where they are greeted with the acrid fog of Augusta's exorcising sage or myrrh. *Double check!* Coughing and clutching their throats for oxygen, they come to the end of the smoke cloud, only to find the hermit queen herself dressed in a half-dozen housecoats and perched on her worn wingback throne. And what is she doing? Not reading Melville today, no. Not curling up with a calico cat and Faulkner, either. Or Agatha Christie. Today, in front of her Vatican visitators, she is instead consecrating a chalice of unleavened wafers, transubstantiating them from ordinary bread into her very own Eucharist as she so enjoys doing. *Too many checks to count!*

"I'm not waiting around for Kevin to bless my Communion, anymore," Augusta told Mike last year. "I have asked the Lord to ordain me, and He has obliged. It's done. His hand came down upon me, Michael Agnes." She pats the top of her balding head. "The heat was searing and the light blinding—I was a burning bush. It's a miracle I survived."

And Mike believes her. Why not? Why would God or anybody choose as pedestrian a man as Kevin over the glorious and mystical Augusta to administer his sacraments? He simply would not.

So now, in her continuing visitating fantasy, as long as they are infinitely checked for their misdemeanors and most likely full-bore excommunicated, Mike, in the spirit of complete transparency, will advise the surveillants to troll the halls at night so they can witness one of Gemma's sanctimonious 3 AM rants. Not that Matins at 3 AM is incorrect form; it isn't—unless you do it at the top of your lungs with the intention of intimidating others. And truly, as far as form goes, anytime before daybreak will do. Mike says her Matins at 5 AM. The others are on their own. Do they say it before daybreak? Do they say it at all? Mike doesn't know. This is not a prison. It's a home.

And after the alien envoys apprehend (or join) Gemma in her prayers, they can observe one of the many forbidden penitential cuttings Mike strongly suspects she performs. And if they miss those, (she's very covert), let them examine the laundry and observe the streaks of blood on the inner sleeves of her garments. The thorns in her stockings. The nettles in her rain boots. The girl is disturbed, but ingenious.

And after that, let them close it all down.

Let them pack up Grace's dream and sell it to Exxon for the reported abundance of shale and natural gas that runs beneath the soil. Or if they prefer, let them sell it to IBM instead, or any other sanitized corporate sponsor. Who cares? *What a relief!* Mike releases the letter and watches it fall into the wastebasket. Plunk.

She reaches in and pulls it back out.

On the other hand, there's the girl. It's really impossible for Mike to believe that the girl's sudden appearance at the monastery, not to mention her resemblance to Grace and the very specific angel reference, has absolutely nothing to do with a…dare she think it…intervention. Intervention of a miraculous nature. It has to. She shakes her head. Still, they've been through so much, and why…*WHY!*…she feels herself building up a good head of steam…*do you*… she raises her eyes to the wooden crucifix on the opposite wall. "Why do you always have to wait until the very last suffocating minute?"

There, she said it. She can't help this thought; it's called honesty. And at any rate, nothing is hidden from the Lord. So she might as well go ahead and say it. Everything, *everything!* is a last minute bail-out it seems. Even Grace. She spins the chair around to face Grace's portrait. "Do you ever think about that, Grace?" she asks. "The fact that the Angel of the Lord waited until you, in your utter despair, plunged the knife into your chest before saving you? Why? Why not gently remove the knife from your hand in the first place? Why not console you in your utter misery leading up to that despairing act?" *Why not prevent the act?!*

Why?

So in an act of overarching hope, or stubborn stupidity—take your pick, Mike will bring the damn letter over to the trailer and see what's up with Augusta today. Maybe Augusta will be spry and coherent and helpful. Maybe she'll know exactly what to do. And while she's at it, she'll tell Augusta about Arielle before Augusta spots the girl in the field sunbathing in a bikini. *Or buck naked!* Or smoking dandelions in the potting shed, who knows? Of course she dreads telling Augusta both bits of news; one is no worse than the other. Both represent the sheer desperation of their circumstances. A non-Catholic, for God's sake! *A hillbilly!* What next?

She walks out of her office with a renewed sense of something— purpose or confusion—and then hears the hysteric, Gabriella, screeching something unintelligible from a distance. Anywhere inside the house the pitch of her shrieking voice would be shattering glass, so she must be outside. This woman, well—all of them, really—are so out-of-synch. When did it deteriorate so badly, she wonders? Nothing like the presence of a stranger to highlight one's family weaknesses.

As Mike gets closer to the door, she sees Constance leaning on her crutches beside the pumpkin patch next to the trailer. Mike can't make out what's being said, but wishes like hell she were not headed in their direction. She has really lost all patience for Gabriella's constant babbling nonsense. Or anyone's for that matter. She hopes no one puts a pitchfork in her hands.

Once outside she hears, "Are you crazy, Connie?"

She can see Gabriella's arms in the air, her head jutting forward at an obtuse angle about three inches from Constance.

"Mother will have us hung!" shrieks Gabriella. "From our toes!" She steps back and kicks a hay bale, which causes her substantial loose flesh to bounce beneath her waist-high dungarees and striped short-sleeved jersey. "If Mike doesn't behead us first!" she adds.

Mike feels like beheading them.

At this point, Rose chugs out from the dormitory about 100 feet away at an impressive clip. "What's going on?" she shouts. "I can hear you over the TV!"

Constance turns her head. "I thought Beatrice was teaching her!" she says. "I thought she was in catechesis with Bea!"

So now Mike knows the lunacy involves Arielle. But why can't the Sisters handle it? The girl is not rabid! Sometimes Mike can't suffer the stupidity. She crosses the gardens, marches around the sprouting sunflower field and passes the potting shed.

The women spot her and play a game of statue.

"What's going on here?" says Mike.

"Constance was out checking on the seedlings and she saw Arielle wandering around the trailer," says Gabriella, suddenly able to speak in the voice of reason.

"Around the trailer?"

Gabriella blinks rapidly. "And then she just…well, we tried to stop her, but…"

"She went inside," says Constance. "She opened the door and went inside." She sighs. "Walked right in."

Mike serves up a good penetrating stare.

"She's been in there twenty minutes," says Constance. "She hasn't come out. We thought she would be out in minutes…seconds! I mean, what is she doing in there? Mother Augusta hates company!"

"And who is she, anyway?" says Gabriella. "She's nobody! Nobody…bothering somebody!"

"Enough," says Mike.

Rose just stands there with her eyes to the ground—the usual, irritatingly submissive posture she saves for Mike.

At that, the trailer door opens; the girl exits and jumps down the cement steps as if they are made of rubber. Without a care in the world.

They are all mesmerized. Her robust energy is as foreign to them as Times Square, hip-hop dancing, or a first class cruise to the Italian Riviera.

As she approaches, Arielle greets them with a big smile, thumbs-up. "Cool old lady," she says. "She like, sees the future and stuff?"

With her index finger, Mike traces a line back and forth in the air from Arielle to Constance. "You—," she says to the girl, "are supposed to be in class with her. Got that?"

The girl grins. Beams. She raises her arms above her head and performs a charming little shimmy dance that leaves them all slightly stunned.

"You bet," she says. "And right after that..." she eyeballs Constance meaningfully, "with any luck, I'll get me a sewing lesson, right?"

And then something unfamiliar happens—Constance smiles spontaneously. Then Rose smiles, then Gabriella. It's clearly infectious, so before it reaches Mike, she bears down harder. "You're not to go into Mother's trailer again," she tells Arielle. "It's completely off limits."

"Oh," she says, "Sorry. I didn't realize she was your mother."

Rose turns away. The others cover their mouths, giggling.

"She's not my mother," says Mike. "She's the mother of the monastery."

Arielle ponders this. "Wow. All of you?" She shakes her head. "You're like real sisters? But I guess by now nothing should surprise me."

"Go on," barks Mike to all of them. "Get on with your day. Constance, I expect you to clarify this situation with Arielle."

Constance nods, biting her bottom lip.

"And turn off the TV, Rose," says Mike. "If you've got time on your hands, do some laundry for God's sake. Or help Beatrice in the kitchen."

She marches up the path to the trailer, takes a deep breath and walks inside.

Augusta is up and about, humming an indecipherable tune. She turns when the door opens. "Is that you, dear?" she says, shielding her eyes from the glare.

"Yes," says Mike. "It is I. I'm here."

"Oh," says Augusta in a rather dull tone. "It's you, Michael Agnes. I thought it was the girl. What's her name again? Arena?"

"Arielle," says Mike. She leans down and picks up a sopping wet towel, then notices a number of them on the floor in front of the bathroom. "What happened here?"

"Oh, nothing. The sink overflowed," says Augusta as she steeps a hand-fashioned cheesecloth tea bag up and down in an ancient Limoges cup from Grace's collection. "Our new friend got a wrench from the shed and fixed it. Isn't that grand!"

"She fixed it?" says Mike.

"She fixed it perfectly. She said she knows everything about trailers. She actually lived in one herself. Isn't that interesting?"

"Very interesting," says Mike. She kicks the heavy towels into a pile and examines the bathroom. Spotless. Arielle must have cleaned it, too.

"Then she made me a lovely egg sandwich," says Augusta. She cradles her cup with two hands and lifts it.

"Let me bring that cup back to the chair for you," says Mike.

"No need, Michael Agnes. I'll be fine, fine, fine." Augusta shuffles back to the chair. "Let's have a little talk, shall we?"

Here it comes. Beauty into Beast. Daisy Mae into Granny McCoy.

She sets down the cup and settles her tiny, floral-fabric clad body into the cavernous chair. "There, now."

Mike watches nervously as Augusta covers her lap with a large pink crocheted blanket from the day when crochet was the rage. Back when the Sisters crocheted every imaginable thing to death—shopping sacks, toaster covers, tea cozies.

"Well, then…" says Augusta. "Well, well, well."

Heading a lecture off at the pass, Mike says, "I'm sorry, Mother. I really am. I should have consulted you. The girl…"

"…is Grace," says Augusta. "She's back."

Mike rubs her forehead. "No, no. I mean, there's an undeniable resemblance, but…"

"Look at me, Michael Agnes," says Augusta.

Mike can't look at her. She looks down.

"Look me in the eye."

Mike tries to look into the old sunken baby blue eyes, but she can't.

"It. Is. Grace."

"No. No, Mother," says Mike. "I thought it was, too, but…"

Augusta slices her crooked little wrinkled hand through the air like a knife. "It *is* Grace. It's Grace Gannon—founder of the Most Holy Order of Divine Grace, and that's the end of it. I of all people would know."

"She has a mother," says Mike. "She has a mother and a birth certificate."

Augusta sips her tea. "Oh? And where is the mother?"

"Somewhere. Arielle doesn't really know where."

"I want the girl to be assigned to my trailer," says Augusta. "Is that clear?"

Mike frowns. "I need to…vet her, though," she says, almost apologetically.

"I'll do the vetting."

Mike sits there for what seems like an eternity. She doesn't really know what to do.

Augusta shivers. "It's a little chilly in here, don't you think?" She tries to get up. "Let me get you some tea."

Mike shakes her head, no. "There's something else, Mother," she says. She reaches into the pocket of her suit jacket and produces the letter. Just holds it in front of her old mentor waiting for her to bite.

"Let me see that," says Augusta, and she plucks it from Mike's hand. "The official seal," she says, frowning.

"Yes."

"Are they closing us down?"

Mike shrugs. "They might as well be."

Augusta sits back in her chair, reaches for her glasses and reads the letter, the tip of her crooked index finger at a right angle, slowly following the lines. When she finishes, she looks up.

"I don't know what to do," says Mike. "A part of me wants to just let them take the farm. Be done with it."

"Oh, they won't take the farm, dear," says Augusta. "What the hell would they do with it?"

This makes Mike laugh, just the way she said it—reminds her of the good old days when she and Augusta were compadres—confidantes. "Sell it to the bank?" says Mike. "Mine it for gas? I don't know."

Augusta sips her tea and calls Assisi, who jumps off a wall shelf, alarming Mike.

"Good Lord, Augie," she says. "You and your cat."

Assisi pounces onto Augusta's lap, and is rewarded with long, deep strokes. "You have nothing to fear," she tells Mike. "Grace is here. She will guide us."

"If Arielle is Grace than she has a few manners to brush up on," says Mike. "She's not even Catholic, Augusta. She thought Mary was Christ's wife!"

"Ohhh, ha ha ha ha!" laughs Augusta. "Ha ha ha ha ha! That's just what we need around here, Michael Agnes—some fresh innocence! Someone real for a change. Grace is a genius to come disguised as a little hippy runt!"

Mike sighs.

"And anyway, the older I get," says Augusta, "the less I really know. Just because the girl is unsophisticated doesn't mean she doesn't have a great deal to teach us. Many of the great saints were vagrants."

"Were they also drug addicts?" asks Mike. "Because to be completely truthful, she came to us from rehab, Augusta. Just in the interest of full disclosure. And before that, the county jail. All we're doing right now is educating her in the faith. I don't even know if she'll stay…if we'll keep her."

Augusta is unimpressed. "Just think of Saul," she says. "Think of Augustine—my own namesake. Mary Magdalene. Profligates, all! When the Lord renders a conversion, the hows and whys are not our affair."

Mike is too overwhelmed to humor Augusta any longer, and she doesn't want to burden her with the details. "I have to go," she says. "I'll be back later."

"Don't try to control everything, Michael Agnes."

"I'm not trying to control everything, Mother. Just the monastery, which is my job."

"Surrender."

Mike nods uncertainly.

"And send Grace over with my dinner," she says as she buries her face in Assisi's fur.

Mike retrieves the Vatican letter from the end table and returns it to her pocket. "Fine, but I doubt she can cook. Though she did claim to be an expert at hamburgers."

"Hamburgers suit me fine."

"But you need more than…."

"The girl makes me happy."

Mike nods.

"And I haven't been happy in a very long time."

"So be it," says Mike.

"Nor have you or any of us," says Augusta.

"I know," says Mike as she picks up the pile of sodden towels and lumbers out under their weight.

After crossing the back fields to the farmhouse, Mike deposits the heavy towels in the basement bin. She encounters Gemma there, who is leaned over the laundry sink scrubbing her tunic with enough intensity to wear a hole through the dense serge fabric. She's muttering something; Mike listens. A rosary.

"Hello, Gemma," Mike says quietly, not to alarm her.

Gemma jumps back and screams, "Aaaaaaaaaaa!"

"Good grief!" Mike's right hand leaps to her chest. She waits as the girl collects herself.

"I'm sorry," Gemma says, turning her head toward Mike. "You startled me. I was all in my head—fourth sorrowful. The Cross transfixes me."

"I can see that."

The girl drapes the garment on the lip of the sink behind her and turns fully around to face Mike.

"Why are you scrubbing?" says Mike.

"Oh…just some…garden dirt from the sleeves and knees."

"May I see?"

Gemma frowns. "I'm perfectly capable of cleaning my garments," she says.

"I'm sure you are," says Mike. "But I've seen blood."

Gemma's eyes move rapidly left to right and back. "Well, just from time to time with the pitchfork, you know." She looks at her feet. "Garden work is grueling. A few nicks can't be helped. And all the scrapes from the brambles…"

"As long as that's all it is."

"Of course. What else?"

"Physical penance is forbidden, Gemma. You're not at a spiritual level to even consider it."

Gemma's face screws up in confusion or defense, Mike isn't sure which.

"You have nothing to tell me then?" says Mike.

"I just…work very hard. Maybe too hard, I'll admit, but who else is going to do this work?" She hesitates. "Actually, if it's possible, I'd appreciate some diversions. I don't know…maybe the trailer. Perhaps you could talk to Mother again?" She looks up eagerly. "I'll continue my other chores, don't worry, but I'd also like to tend to her. I know she's cranky, but I just love being around her. I can't explain it."

Mike sighs. "I'm sorry," she says. "I'm afraid that's impossible."

"Impossible?" says Gemma in astonishment. "Impossible?! Who

else will do it? You can't do it forever! Why is it impossible?"

"Mother Augusta has requested the new girl."

Gemma squirms around trying to contain what Mike can only interpret as hysteria. She can't even look at Mike. She jumps around like a bullfrog that's swallowed a swarm of crickets. "I'm sorry," she says. "May I leave? I have more gardening."

Mike nods sympathetically. "Don't take it so hard," she says softly. "It's nothing personal." Although Mike knows it's everything personal.

Gemma wipes her eyes with her sleeves, nods to Mike, and charges off. Her footsteps pound the tile and echo through the cavernous hall. The screen door slams.

Mike stares at the garment, tempted to examine it, but in the end, does not. The girl has had enough trauma for one day. And anyway, what proof is Mike looking for? She already knows the girl is disturbed. The question is, how much? And who would have guessed the attachment to Augusta? The girl has exhibited attachment to no one and seemingly nothing since her arrival—operating at such a purposeful remove from the others for years. So maybe her attachment to Mother is a good sign?

She shakes her head as she drops the towels into the machine. No, probably not, she realizes. Probably anything but a good sign. Just one more thing to worry about. She promises herself she'll face this situation head-on as soon as she gets Arielle settled.

Rose appears in the doorway, her curly gray hair windblown and wild. She's carrying an armload of kitchen towels and aprons. "Oh, um, sorry," she says, immediately lowering her eyes.

"No problem, Rose. Are you on laundry duty today?"

"No, Ma'am," she says, eyes lowered again. "I'll be happy to do the laundry, though."

"Can I ask you a question?" Mike says.

"Yes, of course."

"Are you afraid of me, Rose?"

"I just…um, no disrespect intended, Sister." Still no eye contact.

No use, Mike thinks. She's either a simpleton, crippled with devastating shyness, or sanctified with genuine humility. What Mike really wonders, is why she is suddenly so determined to figure everybody out. Why? What's the difference? She shakes her head. Maybe because it's all coming to a dead end, she thinks. Maybe it really is.

"No disrespect taken," says Mike. "Carry on."

GEMMA

Gemma frantically finishes spreading the fertilizer on the lower gardens, the perfectly neat little mounds of rich black soil hiding nascent lettuce, kale, spinach, and zucchini—the miraculous products of nature and her own sweat and blood. God's work and hers; a perfect partnership. Under her heavy garments, her neck and chest are soaked. Sweat runs freely through the grip of her tight cowl and down her face like rain. She's invigorated from the punishment of it all and the fact that she was able to say sixteen complete rosaries without interruption in spite of the horrific disappointment, the out and out rejection of Mother Augusta and the new girl. The vulgar new girl assigned to the trailer! *What?!* Gemma can't get over it.

She wipes her forehead with the terry hand towel that was tucked into her belt, and stops to survey her good, hard work. Such elegant, even rows of sheer perfection. The crop will be unsurpassed this year, praise the Lord! She will punish the devastation away. She will drive it like a serpent from her spirit.

Good God, she is so dehydrated and just so desperately thirsty! She could drink from the hose for ten minutes nonstop, but instead reaches for the thermos she'd hidden in the bushes, screws off the cap and sips the bitter white vinegar, coughing and sputtering as it burns its way down. She tries not to spit it out. Vinegar, after all, was the last taste in Christ's mouth before his surrender to the Father. She's proud to replicate His final earthly act. She sips some more, savoring the razor burn of the acid on her tongue and throat. *The hell with the hermit!*

"You need water," says someone, somewhere, and Gemma's head flies around left, right and up the hill to identify the source. "Your body needs water, not vinegar," it says.

This freaks Gemma out, because even if someone were there, that someone would have no idea what she was drinking. She caps the thermos and hides it behind her back. "Who's there?" she says.

"You can't hide anything from me."

Gemma shudders. The great void of silence is apparently over and done with. It's filled with the voice. She gathers strength, grabs the hoe that leans against the tree stump and hurls it in the air like a javelin. "Shut up," she barely mutters, because she's been in the hot sun most of the day and her strength is waning. How much can she really take? How much more is expected of her?

"You can't run away from me," says the voice. "And you shouldn't want to either. I'm your protector, your friend. Your *sister.*"

Gemma drops the thermos, lifts the skirts of her habit, and runs down the hill, periodically tripping on an imbedded rock or gopher hole. Her white habit is filthy and her hands are scraped and bleeding. "Get out of me," she screams, still running and running until she reaches the grassy knoll above Henry's northern shore at the bottom of the hill. On the bank, she drops to her knees, covers her face with her hands, curls up, and wails…*keens*…at the utter injustice of it all.

The wailing takes time. The sniveling torrent of tears drains her of the little fluid she has left. She has no idea how long she cries. *Weeks!* All she knows is that during the wailing, Maya's insistent speech grows quieter and quieter until it's completely hushed. Realizing this, Gemma slowly uncurls her body and rises, woozy, unsteady. She leans against the huge oak and looks ahead where Henry sparkles like a diamond. With Maya out of the way, she can focus on him.

"Henry," she says, mesmerized, walking toward the water.

Here on his northern shore, Henry is even more beautiful than in the grand city. Here he is wilder, more fecund, more expressive. Teeming with life. As far as Gemma knows, none of the other Sisters ever comes here to this very spot. Or even cares about Henry at all. They're far too lazy to take a walk this far, anyway. To them he's just a piece of the landscape. Backdrop. A decorative shade they can draw up or down at whim. Gemma's room—well now, Gemma and the vagrant's room—is the only one that overlooks his shores. The others couldn't care less.

Gemma checks her pocket watch—4 PM. No one will be looking for her for hours. She removes her heavy oxford shoes and elastic tights, raises her skirts and holds them in a ball by her left hip. This is an indulgence she needs, she tells herself, although the biting, icy water could most certainly be incorporated into her punishing routine. She eases down the embankment and dips one foot in. *Brrrrrrrr!* Freezing! Then the other.

"Take off everything!" says the voice.

Gemma gasps, startled. "That's indecent," she says.

"Indecent? No way! Liberating! And no one's even here. You belong to Henry!"

"I belong to God."

"You belong to Henry and Henry belongs to God," says the voice. "Take off your habit and get in."

Gemma is confused. Does Henry belong to God? And God belongs to her? *What did the voice say?* Was the voice making sense? Should she get in? Is she *supposed* to get in?

"Just take off your veil," says Maya. "Just do that one thing."

Gemma is disoriented from thirst and heat and from the shock of cold water. She removes her veil.

"And the cowl," says the voice. "Remove the cowl. Let our head breathe, for God's sake!"

Gemma removes the cowl. The warm breeze feels amazing against her bare, shaved head.

"Now the scapular," she is told.

She lifts the weighty fabric over her head. It feels so good.

"Now the tunic."

She removes it.

"The under dress."

She's practically naked.

"The damn burlap."

She pulls the cord and lets it go.

"I'm not removing anything else," she says. "The underwear stays!"

But oh, it feels so good—so refreshing and punishing at once. Her chilled feet wrap around the smooth stones, and she feels her way slowly across the beginnings of the muddy bottom until she is mid-calf. Her body shivers with relief, delight, and biting, icy pain. She feels she's being called upon to submerge completely in imitation of Christ's baptism in the River Jordan. She leans over, dangling her long thin arms and hands above the crystal clear water, ready to dunk.

"Far fucking out!" says the voice, puncturing the atmosphere between them. Gemma is startled. This is as loud as she has ever heard it. She hears a thudding in the distance and her eyes are drawn to a flash of scarlet between the cedar branches on the hilltop. She freezes.

"I knew there had to be a swimming hole around here!" says someone somewhere. *Not the voice?*

Wrapping her arms around her nearly naked body, Gemma looks toward the flash and recognizes the catechumen who is practically flying downhill. Practically opening her arms and hang-gliding down as if it were utterly possible for a human to fly. Her long tendrils of flame red hair spread behind her like kite tails in the wind. As she gets closer, she removes her ridiculous Madonna t-shirt, whips it around in the air, curls it into a ball, and chucks it all the way past the broad, flat rock near Gemma. Revealing nothing at all underneath. *No bra whatsoever!* Not that she needs one.

Mortified, Gemma trudges out of the water, up the embankment, collects her garments and begins redressing.

"Oh hell, no, don't do that for me!" says Arielle. "I just want to take a dip with you."

"No one can know!" says Gemma anxiously as she slips back into the sackcloth and underdress. She grabs the tunic and pushes her head through the opening, her arms through the sleeves.

By now, Arielle has removed her raggedy jean shorts. No underpants—not even a thong! Completely naked—*completely naked!*—she climbs on another rock against the shoreline, grabs an overhanging branch and swings.

"Wheweeeeee!" she screams, releases, and disappears into the river.

Gemma can't believe this. The girl is out of her mind! She didn't even bother to test the depth of the water! She could be lying still under the water right now, completely paralyzed or unconscious for all Gemma knows.

Instead, what seems like a full minute later, she breaks surface, laughing and gasping for air. She continues to laugh, hugging her scrawny ribcage as she struggles up the embankment. She can't get out fast enough.

"Oh my God!" she says. "It's a glacier in there! *Brrrrrrrr!*" She cackles with laughter. "I thought this place would be such a bore, but instead I might be having the trippiest day of my entire life! The most fun ever without drugs! First the old lady…"

"The old lady?!" says Gemma. "You've already seen Reverend Mother?" Gemma had been counting on Augusta tossing the girl out of her trailer like a cockroach. "Bring Gemma back!" she'd fantasized the hermit demanding. "I need Gemma!"

"Yeah, oh yeah! The cool old prophet in the trailer," says Arielle. Shivering, she plops her naked body on the hot flat rock by the garden, spreads her hair out like snakes, and clasps her hands behind her head like she's posing for Picasso.

Embarrassed beyond belief by this exhibitionism, Gemma quickly covers her head with her cowl and veil. She has dressed herself frantically, out-of-sequence, and without prayer. She lifts her scapular from the high grass and holds it tenuously, unsure of her next move.

"Get naked," says Arielle. *Or is it the voice?*

"What?!" says Gemma. "I most certainly will not!"

Arielle raises her head and turns. "Most certainly will not…what?" she says, but doesn't wait for the answer. She lies back down, melting into the heat of the rock, sighing. "You don't know what you're missing," she says. "This rock is hot toast and I'm a hunk of butter, ha ha! Bye!"

Gemma is confused. Does she want to lie on the rock, too, or is somebody trying to make her? Is Arielle trying to make her? *Who said what?* She can't keep it straight. She is soooo tired! And the rock looks so inviting. Is the voice here? Is Arielle? Does Arielle hear the voice? Does the voice hear Arielle? *Is Arielle the voice?* Her head pounds.

"Whatever," says Arielle. "Do what you want. More rock for me." She raises her legs and crosses them at the knees. "Does everyone come here? I mean, is this like…the spot?"

"Cover yourself!" says Gemma with near hysteria as she throws her scapular on the girl.

"Get naked!" says Arielle, or not? *Not Arielle?* Gemma's head is a ping pong match.

"Get naked! Get naked! Get naked! For God's sake be freeeeee!"

Gemma pounds her fists in the air. "I absolutely will not get naked!" she screams. "Do you hear me? I will not not not not not not not…get naked!" Lying on the rock is one thing; getting naked another thing entirely. She moves back from the rock into the heather, hunches over and lowers herself into a squat. Her face is a clenched fist. "I will not do what you say!" she screams.

Arielle sits up and tosses the scapular back to Gemma. "Whoa!" she says. "Did you just shoot a speedball or something?" She scoots to the edge of the rock. "Cause I know a thing or two about drugs and I can help you come down."

Suddenly, Gemma sees herself haphazardly dressed, curled in a cannonball position, and rocking in the middle of the heather. Even in her state of anxiety she's able to ascertain the lunacy of this. She rises slowly. "What did you say?" she asks Arielle.

The girl grins. "You were just like…going on and on about not getting naked." Her eyes widen playfully. "As my fourth stepdad Jehovah used to say, 'Thou doth protest too much'!" She shrugs. "Like, if you don't want to get naked…don't get naked! It's a free country."

Gemma blinks.

Arielle jumps down into the heather and retrieves her t-shirt. "If you protest too much…" She slips on the shirt. "…it means…"

"I know what it means!" Gemma snaps.

"So then, why'd you say it so many times? 'No no no no no no no'…like that?" She hops into her tattered little jean shorts one obscene, skinny leg at a time.

"I don't know," says Gemma, and then she feels it all erupting like one giant volcano of fear. She came to the monastery on the promise of a new life. A new sane life. And then…and then…she heaves a sob of complete and utter grief and cries so hard she can't stop. Before she knows it, the urchin is holding her, stroking her head and telling her it will be alright.

"What will be alright?" cries Gemma between scoops of air.

"Whatever's wrong!" says Arielle.

"I'll tell you what's wrong," says Gemma. "I wanted to clean the trailer. Cleaning the trailer was my job."

"Well hell, you can clean the trailer," says Arielle. "I'll just visit the old coot from time to time. I don't need to clean the trailer! Is that all?"

Gemma raises her head, wiping her nose on her inner sleeve. "She's not an old coot," she says. "She's a spiritual master! She entered the monastery when St. Grace was still here. She *knew* Saint Grace! Grace was her teacher! That's why you don't belong in that trailer—you wouldn't know a saint if you cleaned up after one!"

At this, Arielle jumps to attention, snaps her fingers and says, "A saint is a very holy person who loves God perfectly and is now in heaven." She eyeballs Gemma intensely. "I learned that from Bea-bop today!"

In spite of the absolute abject horror of her own breakdown, the return of Maya, and just the entire traumatic day, Gemma is totally disarmed. "Bea-bop?" she says.

Arielle says, "Ha ha, yeah, Bea-bop!"

"Did you call her that to her face?" Gemma asks in astonishment.

Arielle shakes her head dramatically. "Noooo! I was tempted to, though. The whole time she was teaching me, all I could picture was Bea-bop from those mutant ninja turtles, remember?" She shrugs. "I don't know. Seemed funny, so. I don't know what comes over me sometimes."

Gemma feels her edges thawing. She half-smiles. "Me either," she says. "I don't know what comes over me either."

They're quiet for a few moments, as the burnt-orange sun sinks lower in the sky bleeding violet clouds and a sunset of hot, steamy color. "Time for Vespers, right?" says Arielle.

Gemma nods slowly, surprised. "Time for Vespers, yes," she says.

Arielle offers her hand to help Gemma up, then brushes the dirt and grass from the back of her tunic. "You wear too many clothes," she says. "You could suffocate in this heat. It's not good for you."

"These are the rightful vestments of our Order," says Gemma. "You'll wear them too, one day if you're lucky. It's an honor!" She walks a few steps. "I need water. "That's why I got confused. I forgot to drink water."

Arielle walks her to the hose, turns the spigot at the pump house, and lets the water run cold. She holds the hose in an arc while Gemma drinks hungrily.

"That's better," says Gemma.

As they walk companionably up the hill, she says earnestly, "Don't tell anyone, Arielle, ok? Not a single soul."

Arielle shrugs. "Tell who? What?"

ARIELLE

It's already the end of June, which so far has been a hot, rashy, back-sweating, humid and rainless month. Not that Arielle gives a compost heap about the weather as a rule, but this month she's been in charge of watering the gardens, so. And it's not what you'd call a sophisticated sprinkler system, unless you call dragging miles of soaker hoses all over creation and turning them on one at a time, a sprinkler system. Arielle calls it slave labor, not that she minds. What else is she doing, anyway? She's not exactly turning down dates. She lives in a monastery.

So anyway, here she is on the longest day of the year in the longest year of her life. She falls dead asleep at the stroke of midnight only to wake up as usual at 3 AM to the buzzing and screeching of her obsessed roommate reciting Matins in the hall. After six weeks of living in this medieval sideshow, she's getting used to it all—the order in the chaos. Or is it chaos in the Order? Whatever. She's getting used to people living together without fighting or getting along, either way. Or else getting along for a miraculous shining moment only to remember that they don't get along and then walking away all pinched-up and pissed-off. After a while, this business of not getting along moves to its own beat—a spiky rhythm, not without purpose—like Velcro ripping apart to rearrange a seam. Or a life.

Still, some days Arielle wants to grab that Angel of the Lord of hers by his see-through throat, shake him, and say, "What in the hell were you thinking?!" Not that he's given her the opportunity; he's been AWOL since he packed her off to the monastery. And she must admit he's made good on his promise to detox her head—she hasn't had a single craving for chemicals since she got here. And also certain days have been really worth the trip—for instance, last Wednesday. That was the day Arielle raised enough Cain to force a full-throttle laugh out of a dead-serious stiff like Constance—*oh, the joy!* Even now just thinking about that afternoon makes Arielle nearly pee laughing. And it was so simple! All she did was secretly plop a decrepit old rubber rattlesnake (that she'd unearthed in the tool shed, no doubt a long ago effort to scare rats and gophers) into Bea's toilet bowl, close the lid—and forget about it! Out of sight, out of mind.

An hour later, Arielle is standing in front of Beatrice and Rose, modeling her new creation—a sensible box-shaped summer shift sewn under Constance's demanding supervision. *Designs by Gestapo!* In truth, the purpley dress is freakishy long (to her knees!), and loose enough to hide a humpback whale, but so what? She likes the bright color and the totally unfashionable, out-of-touch zigzag pattern, *who would wear this?!* But when she's got it on, she feels like a nun—like she's one of them. Like she belongs somewhere besides Narcotics Anonymous, a loser trailer park, or jail.

"Oh, it's lovely, dear!" squeals Bea-bop. "A decent church dress for you! Great job! Now we can throw away those obscene little hippy doll clothes of yours."

Rose raises her index finger. "One more thing," she says. She opens a drawer and pulls out an old gray chiffon scarf that she ties around Arielle's neck like a bandana. Goes good with the Frye's.

Arielle checks it out in the mirror, and rather likes the effect. Even though she knows the scarf is meant to hide the serpent tattoo, she doesn't mind one bit because the damn snake is beginning to bother her too. After all, how stoned do you have to be to allow some jackass to jab you a thousand times with a needle in the jugular? To make a snake! Get real.

"There," says Rose shyly, which is the only way Rose can say anything at all. She lays her hands on Arielle's shoulders approvingly.

Minutes later, Gabriella strolls into the Bea-hive. "Why hello," she says, nodding admiringly at Arielle. "Very nice effort. Connie must be pleased!"

"I guess," says Arielle. "Not before making me rip out every seam and start over a dozen times, but whatever."

Gabriella snorts like a pleased pig and swats the air. "Well, Beatrice and I never got the hang of it at all, so don't let that worry you, right Bea?" Without waiting for Bea to answer, she says, practically singing, "OK, I'm here for our quilting session, Beatriiiiice!"

The hive is convinced they can save the monastery's financial ass by selling wedding quilts, as if nuns know a thing about weddings. Rose does all the tedious hand-stitching, but who's counting? Not Rose. She couldn't string enough words together to complain if she wanted to. Also she can quilt and watch soaps at the same time, so. Makes her feel useful.

Before Gabriella sits down, she says, "Oh sorry...me and my bladder! I better use the powder room first."

She enters the bathroom and closes the door, shrilly humming the *Ave Maria* from this morning's Mass. Not ten seconds later, she pounds and scratches and finally pushes the door open, running through the bedroom and down the hall with her arms in the air, screaming an opera from the shock of it. You'd think she'd never seen a snake in a toilet before, ha ha! She near about had a heart attack! Then of course Bea-bop waddles in to investigate, screeches briefly, then steps out of the bathroom shaking her finger.

"That's the snake from the tool shed," she says.

"What?!" says Rose, freezing in place. "A snake?!"

Arielle holds her breath.

"I put it there myself years ago, and forgot completely about it. But how....?" She squints suspiciously at Arielle, getting the picture. She's smarter than she looks.

At that very moment, Constance, who lives next door, sprints into the room like a gymnast in spite of her all-consuming body aches. "What's going on!" she hollers. Beatrice tells her what happened, and Constance goes into the bathroom to inspect.

Rose peeks over her shoulder. "Ohhhh," she says, "it's rubber!"

Meanwhile, they're listening to the Gab-fest in the hall whose shrieks are loud enough to wake-up King Tut and his entire family. Arielle is frozen in an eternal moment of pure potent panic mixed with manic hilarity because she has no idea if they're going to roll over laughing or throw her out in the street. *Which will it be?!* She can't take the stress.

And then all at once, Constance giggles. She drops to the bed and balls-up in a huddle with Beatrice, both of them shaking laughing. *Crying* laughing! Between the two of them, the laughing spreads into an all-out fit so intense that Arielle practically needs an oxygen mask just to watch it. Then Rose joins in, head rolling back and giggling like a gurgling brook, very musical. OMG, what a scene! *What a relief!* It was one of the best days of Arielle's life just to witness the resurrection of it all. An old box of stale raisins turned into a fresh bunch of mouth-watering grapes by a rubber snake.

Of course all this time Gemma and Mike are nowhere around. They're in some kind of evaluation meeting, or at least that was the news from the hive. But just not having them anywhere near makes it easier to enjoy the others. The hive isn't the same around Gemma and Mike—around them it's all stiff and angry and *what-are-you-going-to-do-next-to-ruin-my-day?* kind of behavior. Without Gemma and Mike, the hive is just four old broads with low social needs having a good time and loving the Lord. Arielle kind of digs it in an old auntie kind of way. Not that Arielle ever had old aunties, but that's why she digs it. It's a family.

Tonight, with all the fun memories, Arielle doesn't mind the usual 3 AM wake-up call one bit. She rolls over on her right side to face the big window, and hugs the sheet to her chest. Comforting. The room is unbelievably bright—like strobes from alien spaceships baring every corner of the room in search of whatever. She raises herself on one elbow and inhales the light like life-support—like she could live off the light instead of food and water. Big round juicy grapefruit moon. Like ET, she wants to ride a bicycle across its surface.

She's grown accustomed to the night noises too, which is a good thing since there's no air conditioning in their wing and the windows are open practically 24/7. Even though Arielle grew up in a trailer camp only 45 minutes away, this place is like a whole different planet. For one thing, it's a damn bug zoo complete with a bug-of-the-month club that you can't send back. *"Oh, no thank you—I'll skip the May spiders and millipedes this year."* Every delivery is yours to keep. The gift of June is crickets. They're all over the place chirping back and forth like a tiny orchestra minus the rhythm.

The nuns are obsessed with hunting down the pests, though crickets are great hiders. Gemma is the worst. When a cricket makes the mistake of jumping into open space, it's a guaranteed smudge if she's around. Rose tries to catch them and throw them outside. "They're good luck! Don't kill them!" But Gemma has it in for the crickets like Goliath for David. Or David for Goliath, either way. Arielle smiles at this thought because now she knows about the hero David, and not just David, but Amos and Jeremiah and Ezekiel and Moses. She's learned so much about God in six weeks she could win Bible Jeopardy. But the truth is, all the news about God is not great. Just ask Job.

Out in the hall Arielle hears Gemma still saying her prayers, " *'She was toting about on her hip...,'* " she yells, *"Him Who carries her about the universe.'* "

Arielle likes this line very much—very poetic. She's glad the saint said it so loud. It makes a great picture—*"Him Who carries her about the universe."* She visualizes Mary, (who by the way, Beatrice informed her, was the mother of Jesus, and not the wife, how embarrassing), walking around with God on her hip like an orb of the entire created universe. Inside the orb, a little Mary. A little everyone.

"Through this union of the divine nature with the human nature," says the saint, *"God was made human and humanity was made God."*

Arielle sits up. *What?!* Did she hear that correctly? Is that true? Humanity was made into God? Taking her life into her hands, she patters impulsively to the door. She can't help herself. She can't wait for morning catechism class to get the answer to this mystery. This alone could be the reason she's here.

She sticks her head out the door and reconsiders. After all, Gemma, whose patience for Arielle was near miraculous after the naked little breakdown in the salad patch, reversed quickly into nazi saint the next day. This was apparently because Arielle, who had snuck back to the swimming hole, had found a thermos there that she very innocently handed over to Mike just because Mike happened to be at the back door when she returned.

"Why is your hair wet?" was Mike's first question, followed by, "What's inside the thermos?"

Arielle just shrugged and turned over the goods, because the truth was—she had no idea! But she wishes she'd had an idea—that she'd been the least bit curious when she found it—because from Mike's reaction it was clearly either the blood of an innocent bystander or plutonium. Or something equally evil. But what?! She can't picture the saint sipping margaritas in the field. Maybe altar wine? To tell the truth, there's some relief in the margarita story, because finding out her roommate is on the sauce goes a long way to explaining her little breakdown that day and all the crazy shit that was flying out of her mouth like hornets.

Arielle scampers down the hall to Gemma and pokes her gently on the back. "Hey," she says, "sorry to interrupt you."

Of course the saint screams bloody murder, because she's forever in some kind of self-induced trance. And after all, it's the middle of the night! Even so, this is not her usual made-for-TV scream—it's a full-feature vocal apocalypse, and it makes Arielle laugh so hard she has to cross her bare-assed legs not to run a river down the hall.

"Oh my God," says the saint, "look at you again! Are you allergic to clothes? Why do you think you can just walk around naked! This is a monastery for God's sake! Who are you anyway?! Why are you even here?!"

The saint is so out-of-control she can't stop. She could be yelling the dictionary or the Bible, it wouldn't matter. Arielle is leaning hard against the railing, laughing so hard that even Gemma starts to crack, which pisses her off even more. *When was the last time she laughed!*

"It's not funny!" Gemma says. "Put some damn clothes on!"

And then one-by-one the doors start opening.

"This is a CRAZY house!" pronounces the Gab-fest, and then "Oh my God, child, where are your pajamas?!" She runs into her room and gets a robe, which she wraps around Arielle. "What in the name of God are you doing out here stark raving naked?" she asks. "For God's sake get Connie to sew you a nightgown!"

"At least we can agree on something," snaps Gemma.

Arielle wraps the robe around her and ties the belt snuggly, still laughing. "I don't know," she says, hysterical. "I made her scream…"

Bea wanders out like round-ole Tweedly Dum wearing a hilarious little Night-Before-Christmas cap on her head. "What is going on!" she says in a loud whisper, and they all hear Constance creaking across her room on crutches, *thump thump thump.*

Next, Rose, still stuck in a dream, shuffles out in her big granny gown, her wild gray curls all staticky on one side and squashed on the other. "What can I do?" she says, dazed. "Where did you put the baby?"

"The baby!" screeches Arielle, still holding her belly to keep herself together. "Ha ha ha! No!"

"For God's sake Rosie," says Gab-fest. "That's all we need is a damn baby!"

And this line gets applause from Beatrice, too. "A baby, ohhh, a baby! Ha ha ha! What the heck are you dreaming about a baby for, Rose?!"

Pretty soon they're all in the hall except Mike, and Gemma says, "People, I am *trying* to say my Matins! Do. You. Mind?!"

"Well that's the thing," says Arielle to the others as much as to Gemma. "I heard her say something that blew my mind, so I completely forgot I was naked, and waltzed right out to hear it again."

"What would that be?" says Bea, suddenly the devoted catechism teacher.

"Yes," says Constance to Gemma. "Perhaps it has value for the girl. Perhaps you should be more patient and inclusive."

Gemma looks like she wants to gather up all the crickets she's squashed, dip them in arsenic, and force feed them to the hive.

Arielle says, "Just read that last thing you were saying about us all being God."

"I don't think I said that," Gemma says. "That we are all God." She shakes her head. "In fact I said no such thing." She opens her little black book and runs her finger down the text. "What I said was, ummm...here it is: *'Through this union of the divine nature with the human nature, God was made human and humanity...'*" She looks up, stunned.

They're all leaning in, waiting.

"Humanity was made God."

Silence.

"Well, what do you know?" says Gabriella. "I don't remember ever reading that before."

"What's the reference?" says Bea.

Gemma glances down. "St. Catherine of Siena, *The Dialogue.*"

"I knew I heard you say that!" says Arielle. "I thought to myself— if that's true, it's a good enough reason to be born, even into a hellhole trailer camp."

"Let me see that," says Gabriella, and she removes the book from Gemma's limp hand. "It does say that," she confirms. "It definitely says that."

Rose blesses herself. "Maybe we should start praying again," she says. But the way her hair is flying around on the one side, it's even harder than usual to take her seriously.

"What!" says the bop. "We pray! Speak for yourself Rose Ann, if you don't even pray."

Rose looks down. "Well, I know we pray, Beatrice, but speaking for myself..."

"Can you all please go to bed?" says Gemma. "I would like to finish my prayers."

Arielle could see that they were all sort of interested in saying the prayers together, even at this insane hour, to find out more of what had been right in front of them all along. But instead, remembering that they didn't get along, they just returned the book and walked into their little bat caves, as did she. It was worth it, though, to find out humans are divine. In Arielle's experience you only notice things like that on drugs.

The next morning, Arielle learns some more trippy things about her new religion—the founders really thought things through. Right from day one, they cut up little pieces of cloth that belonged to the robes of holy saints and made them into jewelry they could wear or carry around like holy souvenirs. According to Beatrice, even splinters of the true Cross are still hidden in charms, hanging around people's necks all over the world preventing accidents and healing the sick.

And not only cloth and splinters, but also bone fragments of the actual saints, which once you get used to the idea, is very modern and Goth. These pieces of saints are called relics, and they're not just good luck—they're sacred. When you hold them, just the vibe alone can protect you from harm or even turbo-charge your prayers to God. When Arielle thinks about relics, she thinks of the hermit.

She also learned about "the seven deadly sins and contrary virtues," which is like naming her seven stepdads—Pride, Lust, Greed, Anger, Gluttony, Envy and Sloth. Not to mention her eighth stepdad, Anthony, who possessed all seven of those endearing qualities. If only she'd known about these sins then, she could have called the deadly dads up short. Defended herself. Shamed them! Although Beatrice says shame is not the point. Conversion is the point. Arielle is betting the saint would not agree with this, though. Gemma would definitely go with shame—the more the better. *Pile it on!* The saint does not rock to the softer points of view, but then, she probably has her reasons. One day Arielle will squeeze them out of her.

"You're doing so very well with your studies," beams Beatrice. "You're my very best student ever!"

Arielle doesn't ask the bop how many students she's had, but she's pretty sure the answer is one. "Thanks," she says.

"You have a very photogenic memory!" says the bop.

"Shucks," says Arielle graciously, although she's pretty sure the word is photographic.

"You remember everything I tell you! I've never seen anything like it!" She fiddles with a button on the gigantic blue and white polka-dot blouse she's wearing. You can tell the bop thinks it goes great with the denim wrap-around skirt Constance invented for her over the weekend, completely free-form—no pattern. That woman is a regular craft fair. But to Arielle, the skirt is not flattering on the bop, and also very distracting because it keeps opening at the side showing skin so blue and lumpy a shark would spit it out. She tries to safety pin it with her mind.

"I tell you what," says Beatrice, clapping. "Let's take a little break and go into the village for ice cream, what do you say? Mike owes me a pass, and I just know she'll want to reward you, too, when I tell her how much you deserve a treat!"

"Fierce," says Arielle. "I could go for a big pile of sugary fat!" She means it, too. Ever since she gave up vodka shooters and pot brownies she craves sugar, fat and grease. Oh, and bring on the salt! French fries! "And I already have a pass for my not-so-anonymous narcotics-fest this afternoon, so."

Beatrice collects her papers and shakes them down against the desk to even out the pile. "How is that going, dear? NA? We've all been praying, you know."

"Going good," says Arielle. "No worries; no cravings. Even when they describe their best high ever, I don't relate. I'm like…missing a spark plug or something."

The bop claps with glee, her mouth in a big O. "O O O, wonderful! Just wonderful! Praise the Lord! And you've earned a break! You really have! I have it all planned out—Joey's Joint has the best sundaes in the world. And sinful BLT's!" She leans in conspiratorially, "Sometimes I have my sundaes before the sandwich!"

Arielle doesn't know what comes over her, but she says, "Let's ask the saint to join us."

"Oh, ha ha ha!" says Beatrice. Though she's heard Arielle refer to Gemma as the saint many times, it always cracks her up. But when she sees Arielle is serious, she says, "Well, I'm sure she's busy. She's got quite the grueling schedule what with all her penance, prayers and sacrifices."

"That's the point," says Arielle. "To give her a break."

Beatrice purses her lips. "Well fine, then go ahead and ask her if you must, but she prefers solitary confinement, so I doubt she'll agree. I'll get the truck keys from Mike."

Arielle runs up the long, winding stairs two at a time, down the hall, and into her room where she finds Gemma on her knees next to the bed, deep in whatever.

"Um, sorry to interrupt you..."

Without turning around, the saint raises a finger in warning.

"But Bea-bop and I are going into town for some sundaes and..."

The saint shakes her finger threateningly.

"I just thought you could use a break." Arielle waits a moment. "And I would really enjoy your company."

Slowly, Gemma closes her book and rises, shaking out the creases of her skirts. Two piles of steel wool, apparently serving as kneeling pads remain on the floor. She kicks them under the bedskirt.

When she turns around to face Arielle, she says simply, "Are you going into town dressed like that?" Not the expected—"*I can't believe you interrupted me...AGAIN.*" Or better yet: "*I wouldn't be caught dead in town with you.*" Just a plain old garden-variety fashion insult—who cares? This is not a runway!

Arielle looks down at her funky little red hoodie to make sure it's all zipped up; it is. She checks the giant flea-market jeans that Gabriella bought her last week—all zipped, no skin showing. What more does Gemma want? "Ummm, what do you think I should wear?" she says.

Gemma cups her chin in thought. "Maybe that green dress you made with Constance last week. At least it represents your station."

"My station?"

"Your calling, Arielle. Your vocation."

"You think I have a vocation?" she says, surprised. She hasn't really thought about the monastery in those terms. Maybe it's about time she did.

"Well," says the saint, "if you don't, then why are you here?"

"The angel?" says Arielle. "He told me to come? And I thought, well...why not? I don't have anything else to do!"

Gemma narrows her eyes. "I saw an angel, too," she says, "but no one believes me."

"I believe you."

"You do?"

"Of course. When you think about it, who would come here without seeing an angel? It's not exactly a place you would dream up on your own."

The saint turns and stares out the window, as she is forever doing. As if she's waiting for someone to fly through the fourth dimension, reach into the window and rescue her. Her angel, maybe. Or God.

"I saw it in the river...a reflection," she says dreamily. "I can't explain it." She turns back around. "It was a genuine angelic force. And even though I'm sure your angel was more a figment of drugs..."

Arielle can't really argue with that.

"...nonetheless, I find it interesting that you and I, the two youngest candidates, were inspired by visions—one real, one imagined. But not the older ones. The older ones are lost, Arielle, in case you haven't noticed."

Arielle says, "I bet Augusta has an angel," and then instantly regrets it since, for the saint, the subject of Augusta is a weeping wound.

The saint bristles predictably. "So Mother has told you that she's seen an angel? That an angel inspired her vocation?"

Arielle shakes her head no, although she wouldn't be one bit surprised if Augusta is surrounded by choirs of angels on a daily basis. In fact she's sure she is. The trailer is practically on fire with divine sparks. Augusta is a holy circuit board.

"Because I have a hunch that Mother would understand my vision, er...angel," says the saint. "My angelic vision. That Mother and

I are more alike that she realizes. Bound by destiny. In fact, at one point you told me I could clean Mother's trailer instead of you. I'd like you to convince Mother to let me do that. It's time." She says this daringly, as if testing Arielle's loyalty. *What loyalty?!*

"She's not going to be around much longer, and I think it's only fair to share her," says the saint. "And anyway, between us, I have the seniority. You haven't even been baptized for God's sake."

Arielle says, "Well, I'll try, but I can't promise anything. The hermit's kind of a pill, and I, like...never really know where she's coming from?" *Pants on fire!* Suddenly she feels overwhelmingly compelled to grab a pad of paper and a pencil from the saint's desk and sketch a picture of her angel. She does. She works so fast it's like she isn't even doing it herself. She turns the sketch around and says, "Ta da! Figment of my imagination...or Angel of the Lord? Take your pick."

The saint's eyes bug out. "Are you kidding me?"

"What? No."

The saint looks back and forth from the picture to Arielle as if she's comparing them. "This looks exactly like the one in *The Chronicles*. Like Grace's angel. Have you seen *The Chronicles of Saint Grace*? Of course you've seen them. You must have seen them—Mother must have shown them to you! That's the only way you could possibly know what that angel looks like."

"Just a good memory of his face," says Arielle. "And what he had on—blinding!" She holds up the pencil. "I can't really do it justice without solar flares and radiation, though. It was quite the show."

The saint says, "Huh. Well, at least you're a good artist."

"Thanks," says Arielle, "probably comes from my Dad, not that I ever met him or know who he is, but it definitely doesn't come from the psychedelic momzy side. She was like, all stick figures and crayons when she could hold one—when her hands weren't spazzing out on whatever."

Gemma ignores this. "So you copied it from *The Chronicles?*"

"Whatever they are," says Arielle. "No." She offers a pinkie swear for proof.

Instead, the saint whips out her Bible. "Swear on this," she says. "On God and your soul's eternal life. Swear on something that matters."

Even though Arielle finds this a bit extreme, there's no hot air rescue balloon at the window to get her out of it, so she places her right hand on the book and raises the left like in the old movies. "Swear to God," she says.

Gemma studies Arielle closely. "I hope you haven't just put your immortal soul in jeopardy."

"No way," says Arielle solemnly. "It really happened. All those special effects, too—Angel of Elvis!" She chuckles. "Very dramatic of him. But that was before rehab, so. He had to work extra hard to get my attention."

"I see."

They just stand there. "So maybe you actually do have a vocation," says the saint. "If you really saw this particular angel."

"Really?" says Arielle.

"An angel with that *exact* face, I mean."

Gees!

She's rescued by the bop's pitchy voice rising up like helium from the hall, "Heeeeey! Arielle are you coming? I'm starved!"

"Coming!" says Arielle. She looks at Gemma. "You coming?"

"I don't know why I would," she says. "I'm a cloistered nun."

"That's not what the craft fair told me in orientation."

Gemma crinkles her forehead. "The craft fair?"

"Yeah, well, you know, the seamstress. Always making something from nothing." She shrugs. "Anyway, she says we're not cloistered one bit unless we choose to be. We're supposed to be doing charity work. That's our entire purpose. So since the bop got hold of some money, I say, let's go tip a starving waitress and make her day." She grins.

The saint slowly shuts her eyes and reopens them in a dramatic, movie star kind of way. Immediately, Arielle thinks—Jean Seberg in *St. Joan of Arc!* The truth is, once you get over the drama of the saint's wild head gear and habit, which can take months, you start to really zone-in on her crazy watercolor eyes and super-long lashes, which is surprising, because why hasn't she pulled them all out?

"Praying for others is the highest form of charity," the saint says. "And anyway, why does it matter to you if I come to town or not?"

"Because sometimes it's good to get away from yourself so you can see who you are."

Gemma cocks her head.

"Are you afraid to go out?" asks Arielle.

"Of course not!"

"Are you scared of crowds or something?"

"No!"

"Okay then, let's go."

Gemma's chin tilts upward. "Only if you wear the green dress."

Arielle smiles—a small concession. "Frog green dress with freaky pleats it is."

Satisfied, the saint exits, shaking her head and shoulders in disbelief. Or maybe she's just squirming around to disguise the fact that she slipped Arielle's angel sketch between the sleeves of her garments. Arielle definitely saw this, but doesn't care. Why should she? You can't steal an angel. They're like God. The more you try to get rid of them, the bigger they get.

GEMMA

Gemma can't imagine how she got here. What was she thinking? Ice cream at Joe's Joint? She's barely been outside the monastery in twelve months. Arielle has an effect on her that she can't pin down. It's disturbing. Gemma says *Yes* when she means—*No! Absolutely not!* How does the girl get her to change her mind like that? But there is possibly something else at play here that is even more disturbing. Or at least equally disturbing. And that's Maya.

Lately, it's as if Maya is answering for Gemma whenever she's talking to Arielle. Like down by Henry. And now this! Sundaes at Joe's Joint, of all abominations. And Gemma is having great difficulty banishing the voice, which is why she needs access to the hermit. And to make matters worse, Mike is suspicious of something—nothing specific as far as Gemma knows, which makes it even more unnerving. In spite of Mike's recent systematic probing, Gemma won't even talk to her. She can't. What will become of her if she exposes Maya?

She sips her cloudy glass of diner water, trying to ground herself. *I am here now,* she tells herself. *Be here now!* Focusing on her 3-dimensional concrete boundaries in any given moment provides her with a distinct advantage over Maya. The voice can't slip through a mental barrier that is completely focused and airtight. She imagines Maya somewhere in a vacuum, pounding her fists and gasping for air. *Suffocating!* Because right now, Gemma is simply sitting in Joe's Joint at a corner table in front of a Greek salad with Beatrice and Arielle. She is absolutely incontrovertibly front and center. In the moment. The voice is gone.

Of course, she is having a hideously unpleasant time, but that's the least of her problems. She will persevere—offer it up to God for pagan children everywhere. She'll do her best to be charitable to her fellow Sisters, but…she will never allow this to happen again. She tightens the fingers of her right hand around her rosary beads to confirm this pledge. *Ever.* Getting rid of Maya requires her full and complete attention.

"Why don't we ever serve BLT's at the monastery?" says Beatrice annoyingly. "We should make them; they're easy." She wraps her mouth around the huge sandwich, practically groaning with satisfaction.

"Or hot dogs!" sings Arielle. "What could be simpler?"

Gemma is not given to this meaningless banter, and besides, since they're backed-in at a corner table, she's the only one facing the other customers. And to her this foreign slice of secular life seems oddly curious, like viewing gorillas at a zoo. Even though she means to stay focused on her immediate surroundings, she can't stop looking around. She might recognize a few of them from Sunday Mass, but they're so out of context. Old couples barely talking—staring out the windows at passers-by. Young families feeding babies in high chairs, disciplining older siblings. Farmers and construction workers on counter stools eating sections of lemon meringue pie the size of dinner plates. Where is she?! How did she get here?

It appears as if two of the younger men at the counter are stealing looks at their table. How embarrassing. She glances down. When was the last time anyone looked at her!? *Are* they looking at her? They must be—she's the only one in the group facing them. She wonders what they're thinking. She can't imagine.

"Why aren't you eating?" Arielle says, startling her out of her daydream.

"Ohhh!" she says, "I just…" She picks up her fork to avoid the conversation.

"Is the salad ok?"

Gemma nods.

"I could live on hot dogs," Arielle says. She closes her eyes and savors the next bite. "I could order two more right now."

"Oh, yes!" says Beatrice. "So could I! Hot dogs and French fries. Delish!"

Gemma daintily samples her Greek salad. All this slovenly sucking and lip-smacking is making her nauseous.

"What could you live on?" Arielle asks her.

Gemma lays her fork down. "Very little," she says. "Almost nothing. In fact, nothing."

Beatrice pops some fries into her mouth filling her fleshy cheeks as she watches Gemma sip water. "You're not finished are you?" she says. "You've hardly touched it."

Gemma is disgusted. "To be truthful, Beatrice, it's difficult to watch you eat all this food, when…"

"When it's so bloody hot in here?!" blurts Arielle. "I totally agree. And I'm completely ready to order my sundae to cool down. What about you, Bea?" The girl jerks around in her seat like a split atom, trying to distract everyone from the obvious and uncomfortable business at hand—Beatrice's gluttony. And here she is talking Beatrice into a hot fudge sundae when what the woman really needs is a stomach pump.

"I can't possibly eat ice cream," says Gemma. She places her napkin on the table and stands. "Excuse me; I have to use the rest room."

As she moves from the table, the gawkers at the counter slide off their stools and start walking in their direction. Are they coming here? What for?! Gemma is motionless, riveted to the tall one with the sea green eyes and rakish, chin-length black hair. What is she doing?! *She's a nun!*

Her hesitation causes Arielle, who's facing the window, to glance over. When she spots the men, her jaw drops. She turns ashen. "Oh my God," she says, looking sideways. "Don't tell me…"

"What?" says Beatrice. "What?" She turns, too.

The other bearded, sandy-haired guy glides smoothly over to Arielle. "Hello, babe," he says.

Beatrice wipes her chin. "Listen here," she says.

"Nice to see you again," he says, eyes glued to Arielle.

Arielle lets all the wind out of her lungs and hangs her head. "What are you doing here, Lucky?" She can't even look at him.

"You know these gentlemen?" says Beatrice.

Arielle nods. "I used to know them." She looks at the dark-haired one. "Hello, Eli."

Eli nods.

The man, Lucky, moves in to kiss her, but she backs off and shakes her head. "Stop."

"What's with the outfit?" he says. "You turned Amish or something?"

"Ha ha," she says sarcastically.

"As a matter of fact, she's a candidate for the monastery," says Beatrice. "Keep your hands off her, young man."

He looks confused. "What? A monastery?"

"I'm becoming a nun," says Arielle matter-of-factly.

He regards her with astonishment, his head jutting forward from his neck at an unnatural angle.

Gemma has not seen an attractive young man such as Eli in so long that she just stands there gulping. She can't process any of it. Just the muscles alone! They are practically exploding through his t-shirt.

"A nun?" says Lucky.

"Ha ha, yeah," says Eli. "You have that effect on girls!"

"You can't be serious!" Lucky says. He grabs a chair from the next table and scoots it over close to Arielle. He glances at Gemma. "Oh, sorry for my rudeness," he says. He bows his head and extends his hand, "My name is Jesse." He glances at Arielle. "But my girl here calls me Lucky."

"I'm not your girl."

It takes Gemma a long time to shake the man's hand. She is

frozen. "Uh, hello," is all she can say.

Lucky pats Beatrice on the back. "Hey, Grandma," he says.

Her face and neck sprout an instant rash.

Arielle swats him. "Hellooo?!" she snaps. "She's a nun? Be respectful for God's sake!"

Lucky sizes Beatrice up. "Oh, sorry, Sister," he says. "You look all partied-up and whatnot. I couldn't tell you were a nun."

Gemma sniggers. If Beatrice would dress like a nun, she'd be treated like a nun and not someone's Hawaiian grandmother. It's her own damn fault.

Eli removes his cap and places it over his chest. "I'm Eli," he says to Gemma. "Very nice to meet you."

"What?!" she says, blinking. She feels the mercury rise from her feet to her face like a rocket. She's probably redder than Beatrice at this point. Even so, when Eli extends his hand for a shake, she somehow takes it confidently and says, "Very nice to meet you, Eli. My name is Maya. I mean Gemma!"

It instantly hits her—what she said. *What Maya said!* She turns and practically runs to the bathroom praying that no one else picked up on it. But of course they did! They had to. Her head spins like an apocalyptic sun. Spins right out of her head, spilling its plasmic guts all over the known world, pronouncing the end of all time, or at least her time. She wipes her face with a cool wet paper towel and leans against the rickety sink hyperventilating. *Lord Jesus, take me now!*

After however long—fifteen minutes anyway, in waddles Beatrice consuming all the spare space and oxygen. "Are you all right?" she asks. "You look just dreadful!" She starts removing Gemma's veil and cowl, and for some reason Gemma allows it. *Why is she allowing it?!* "We'll just cool you off," Beatrice says more kindly than she's ever said anything to Gemma before.

She helps Gemma out of her heavy scapular and outer sleeves. "There now, that's better, isn't it, hmmm? Lower your temperature a bit?"

Gemma stares at her blankly. Nods. It is better. When she gets the courage she says, "Have those men left?"

"Arielle is sending them on their way. It was a shock to the poor dear; I could see it. They'd been *involved* at some point, and it's clear that he'd like to stay in touch."

"But they don't live nearby, do they?!"

As if she could get any closer, Beatrice leans in, nose-to-nose. This woman has no concept of personal space.

"Well," she says, "the man, Lucky—or Jesse—whichever, was just released from the army. Leg injury in Afghanistan, he said, but nothing major—meniscus, I think. And now he's a fireman right here in town."

Gemma's heart pounds. "And Eli?"

"Him, too, yes." She smiles uncertainly. "A fireman. If you want to know the truth, they come across as hooligans at first…but after a while, they seem rather nice. Jesse offered to help out at the monastery for free—you know, handy man stuff. Haying. Electrical repairs and what not."

Gemma gasps. "You wouldn't permit that, though, right!"

"That's up to Mike now, isn't it? Not to worry; she'll know what to do. She always does. And anyway, it isn't as if we couldn't use the help, right?" She examines Gemma closely. "Your color is improved, Sister—not so flushed. We should get back out there in case Arielle needs us."

She covers Gemma's bare head with the cowl, but holds onto the other garments. "It's a bit warm for these anyway," she tells Gemma. "We don't want you suffering heat stroke or anything, now do we?"

All of this and …no mention of Maya! Not a word! Maybe Gemma never said it? *Maybe she imagined it.*

Mercifully, when they return to their table, the men are gone. Glancing out the window, she can see that they're outside with Arielle. All three are caught up in a heated conversation by an oak tree near the parking lot. Arielle keeps pointing her finger at Lucky in an accusatory way. Gemma wonders what went on with them—what kind of relationship they had. This girl is no end of mystery.

Finally, Lucky grabs her finger, then her wrist, spins her

effortlessly around and circles her in an embrace that is clearly not meant to be threatening. But really, how would Gemma know? No one's ever held her that way.

After a few seconds, the girl squirms out of his arms and dances backwards toward the door, talking and waving goodbye. Lucky moves with her and anyone who's watching inside or out can hear him yell, "I've changed, babe! I swear! I'm a new man, you'll see!"

Beatrice frowns. "We should go out there. See if she needs us."

But Gemma can't do it; can't go anywhere near them. *Kryptonite.* "You go if you want to," she says. "I'll order the sundaes."

Beatrice beams at this concession. "Oh! OK then! But only if you'll indulge with us?"

"Fine."

Beatrice pats Gemma's hand. "Good then. It will be worth it just to see you eat. To enjoy yourself for a change! Make mine chocolate chip mint with malt powder and extra fudge."

Gemma nods distractedly while Beatrice engages in an unseemly struggle with her chair. She finally manages to get up without ripping her skirt off, but before she's halfway to the door, Arielle storms in as fiery as the corona of hair spinning around her head.

Gemma is in awe, not only of her roommate, but of this entire experience. She has never in her life been witness to the kind of passion she has seen—*or felt*—today. She is still searching for the woman she was an hour ago—kneeling at her bedside deep in steadfast prayer. She will never allow anyone to persuade her out of the monastery again. She can't afford to. The monastery is the only real home she's ever had. She can't lose it.

"Hey!" says Arielle. She gathers her hair high in a pony tail and then drops it down across her shoulders, shaking it out like a mane. The color...*or is it the hair itself?*... Gemma isn't certain, but something about the color or the hair itself is so arresting. Other-worldly.

"Sorry about that, but like...what a shocker!" she says. "Whew!"

"Oh, don't worry, dear," says Beatrice. "Never a dull moment!"

Gemma lets this comment pass, because...*What?!* Until Arielle arrived, Beatrice's life had been nothing if not one long fat dull moment. The flattest dullest monochromatic gray there ever could be. Not that Gemma's life is a color wheel, but she has at least availed herself of the mystical realms of prayer, which after all, is the entire purpose of living in a monastery. Not that prayer is something Gemma can keep her mind on right now. She can't.

After they order their sundaes, Gemma works up the courage to say, "Was he some sort of boyfriend?" as casually as she can manage.

"You could say that," says Arielle. "But not anymore, that's for sure."

Beatrice wraps her arm around the girl. "Are you certain, dear? This is the time to discern those things—before your temporary vows."

Arielle laughs heartily. "Hell yeah!" she says. "I threw that catfish back in the river years ago!" She sticks her lips into a fish pucker and kisses Beatrice on the cheek.

Beatrice's throaty giggle turns into a laughing fit. "Oh, you're just the funniest little catechumen, you are!"

"With an intriguing history, though" says Gemma flatly.

Arielle shoots her a look. "Oh really? More intriguing than yours, Maya?"

MIKE

Mike clicks her pen repeatedly against the brown leather blotter on her desk, cursing the temperamental computer which, had it been working, might have saved her a good bit of time on the questionnaire. Not that the computer would have removed all the frustration. Okay, none. The frustration is in the thinking. In the consideration of issues she'd rather not address. Issues that she feels, rightly or wrongly, are frankly—none of the Vatican's business. Or maybe some of their business, but very little. After all, this monastery is a self-sustaining operation—no one subsidizes them unless you count their faithful parishioners. No big stipend from the corporate church, that's for sure; in fact the reverse. The slogan 'taxation without representation' springs to mind. *Give me liberty or give me death!* Not that she wants to start a revolution.

She runs her right hand repeatedly through her short, thick hair. Stops, and reaches for her mug of highly caffeinated Starbucks (espresso blend!)—fourth of the morning and she already knows, not her last. Back to the hair. To clicking the pen in and out. To the mug, almost room temperature, so…back to the carafe for a warm-up. To the desk. To the pen.

To the mug. She relishes the fresh brew while forcing herself to review her answers to the Superior General's questionnaire. Or really, her non-answers, since what she hasn't responded to in an evasive manner, she's left completely blank. The first part of the questionnaire—about

Membership, Living Arrangements and Ministries—should have been easy enough, except for the fact that to Mike's thinking the Sisters are all in a state of flux. Or possibly not so much flux as confusion. Or survival, really, when you get right down to it.

The Most Holy Order of Divine Grace is a religious order based on the holy spiritual mission—or "charism"—of charitable works to the lost and abused; she is clear on this. It's recorded right in their charter. This redundancy is probably the reason she's having so much trouble writing it down in the first place. The Vatican already has the charter. They can review it whenever they want.

But at present it seems the lost and abused mentioned in their charter are not so much from the surrounding villages and communities as they are directly in their midst. In other words, the Sisters themselves are as violated and misguided as anyone she knows. This rationale was Mike's motivation for admitting both of the younger candidates to the monastery in the first place. They had nowhere else to go. So are these girls to be counted as members of the monastery or a product of their charity?

Not that good things won't come of the girls' residencies regardless of the answer Mike supplies to the Visitator. Good things will come. For one thing, both girls are well-meaning. Gemma is already a workhorse in the field and will hopefully accept the help she needs to conduct her life with a modicum of mental stability. And Mike hasn't totally ruled out a genuine vocation there, but still. There's work to be done. And Arielle, well, Mike has no regrets there. At least the girl is stabilizing from rehab and will shortly be baptized in the faith. If that effort isn't worth its salt, what is?

Whether either one of them will fully mature in the religious life is another matter. But as far as the questionnaire is concerned, the boundaries are blurred. Will the Visitator appreciate the charity of actually boarding the lost and abused? Of inducting them in the Order? Or will they find Mike's rationale faulty and opportunistic? Or desperate? *No one else has shown up at the door!* Which brings Mike to the question about Vocation Promotion. What is the Visitator suggesting here exactly? There is no extra money. No generous benefactor. They can't travel or advertise their wares or their way of life. Short of walking around the village with sandwich signs, there is no feasible marketing opportunity. They have to rely on faith. And isn't that the point? To rely on the Holy Spirit to accomplish what they cannot?

She leans back in her swivel chair and tosses the pen across the desk. The truth is she just doesn't care. She can't afford to. The idea of Rome—or some American faction of Rome—suddenly imposing its imperialistic ego on her little farm of dysfunctional, God-fearing nuns is just so preposterous. Meaningless, even. Mike can't help it—she resents the interference. Maybe she's been in charge too long; become too autonomous.

Or maybe this little investigation of theirs has forced her to focus on the extent of deterioration in her monastery. Property deterioration as well as the deterioration of discipline and faith, hers included. And she can't get anywhere with any of it. She feels as a woman might feel on the verge of a divorce. *Is this really the life I want?* She swallows hard. This is one hell of a time for an existential crisis, she thinks.

Or maybe, a more convenient theory—she's over-thinking it. She gulps her coffee. Just the paperwork alone is enough to bury her. Maybe that's all it is. Because God, how she hates paperwork! Paperwork on top of paperwork on top of more paperwork. Paperwork from the banks, from the accountants, from Rome. This is not why she became a nun! Were it not for Augusta's uncharacteristic insistence, she would not be responding to this investigation at all. None of her friends has responded. An almost complete, across-the-board boycott from her friends! So why should she bother?

"Because we're all that's left of the Order," Augusta had rightly noted last week. "If we don't cooperate, they will surely close us down."

"And do what with us?" said Mike.

A crooked little smile cracked Augusta's leathery face. "One can only imagine," she'd said. "Such profligate heretics as we."

"But what will I say about our, uh…prospects?"

"I'm not asking you to make anything up, Michael Agnes. Just be honest."

"Really?" said Mike, raising her eyebrows. "Even about your Eucharist?"

At this, Augusta had pursed her lips and frowned. "Maybe avoid that issue as yet," she'd said. "Not forever, mind you; it must be dealt with. After all, women were not excluded from Christ's ministries! But we need not deal with all matters at once. At any rate, I don't believe there's a question in that packet about whether or not I'm consecrating my own Hosts."

Mike chuckled. "Probably not. But there are plenty of other traps. What if they don't like my answers? Isn't it best to say nothing at all?"

Stroking Assisi's flying patchwork fur, Mother said, "If they don't like your answers, so be it. Then at least we've gone down with dignity. But you know, Michael Agnes, the girl..."

Mike had nodded. "Yes, Mother...*the girl.*"

There has been no convincing Mother that the girl and St. Grace are not one and the same. Mike isn't sure where she stands on this phenomenon at present. She could go either way. Yes, the girl's looks are staggeringly similar to the young Grace represented in the portrait—fresh-faced and pretty with that signature mane of hair, and eyes like crystals into the future. Unmistakable. On the other hand...why in God's name would Grace choose such a wild card to represent her in times of monumental distress?

At any rate, as far as Mike's concerned, the questionnaire is finished. The bright morning sun is pouring through her two front windows, a perfect summer breeze casting the fragrance of cut grass and roses about the room. *Breathe it in!* She's said it before and she'll say it again—this place is worth keeping. She leaves the last tedious questions about Finances and Formation Policies completely blank, stuffs the whole mess into an envelope and scribbles the address. Maybe it will be lost in the mail. Run over by a tractor. Gnawed by woodchucks! She can only hope.

There are two knocks, and she looks up to find Gemma at the

door, fully robed in her stifling winter habit. What is wrong with this girl?!

"Come in," Mike says, forcing a smile. She isn't at all sure what she's going to say to Gemma at today's meeting, but whatever it is, with this much caffeine in her system, she'll have to rein it in. "How are you?" she asks.

Gemma flashes her usual one-second vanishing smile. "Very well, Mother," she says.

Mike blinks. "Excuse me?" she says.

"Oh sorry, I forgot you don't like to be called that."

"It's not that I don't like to be called that, Gemma. It's not my title." She is already unnerved. "Mother Augusta holds that title."

"Yes, but technically it's your job, isn't it?" says Gemma. "You're the Mother Superior, right? Not her. You're in charge."

Mike grabs the pen and clicks. "As long as Augusta is alive, she is the only one who will be called by that title."

"And your title?"

Mike taps the pen frantically. "Prioress will do if you must."

"Fine. I didn't mean to challenge you, I just…"

Mike holds up her hand. "Enough," she says. "It's ok. Let's get to the business at hand. The continuation of our, uh…dialogue." She points to the coffee station. "I don't suppose you'd like some coffee or tea?"

Gemma shakes her head, smoothes her habit, and takes a seat. She slides her hands beneath her.

Sitting on her hands could be a benign indication of nerves, Mike thinks, or—the girl could be puncturing herself repeatedly with a tack, one never knows. As a case study, this girl would have confounded Freud.

"Let's start with your mother, shall we?" says Mike. "We haven't talked much about her, and I'm not completely clear on your relationship."

Gemma frowns. "I'm sorry to question your approach, Prioress, but I don't know what possible relevance that has. I just want to take my final vows. My mother is dead."

Mike pulls on her ear. "I know you want to take your vows, Gemma. But your scrupulosity…"

"Forgive me, Moth…Prioress."

"Let's dispense with the formality, Gemma, how's that? Mike will do."

"With all due respect, during the inquiry process I'd rather address you formally."

Mike taps her pen. "This is not a formal inquiry," she says.

"Just the same."

Mike sighs. "Fine. Continue."

"My so-called 'scrupulosity' as you call it," Gemma says, "is an effort to do penance for my sins and the sins of others who have grievously offended God."

"Like your mother?"

"Maybe." She lifts her chin defiantly. "And why not? It's no secret that she was an alcoholic. You know that. You've always known that. That she slept with…whomever." She looks down at her lap. "You saved me from her neglect enough times."

Mike certainly remembers those times. The memories soften her. "I'm going to tell you something I've never shared with you before," she says.

Gemma shifts attentively.

"The truth is I have a soft spot for girls with alcoholic parents. I know their grief." She leans in. "Personally."

Gemma's spectacular eyes widen. "You do?"

"It was my father," Mike says. "He wasn't a brute, really. A good man, all in all. In any case, he never abused us physically, and was actually an affectionate drunk. And fun…at least for me, although of course I had no idea why he would suddenly become so…fun, so animated." She pauses, shakes her head. "But he was irresponsible, couldn't keep a job, and naturally my mother hated his 'sessions' as she called them. I came to feel the same way. I even hated that she hated it, because after all she was a grown-up, too. So why didn't she stop him?"

Mike pauses for a minute, reaches for her mug and takes a long sip. She continues, "He fell off the wagon every other week. He never went to AA. Years into it when I was in high school, a friend of mine told me about Al Anon. I attended a few meetings with her, and it helped a lot. Unfortunately, my mother refused to go. The meetings helped me to reconcile, more with my mother than my father. I'd been blaming it all on her, you see, since she was the one who made the fuss. She was the one who was no fun." She shrugs. "And in the end, it was the insight from the Al Anon experience that set me on the career path to counseling. Not that I do it professionally, but…let's just say it helps me in my job."

Gemma pulls her hands out from underneath her and clasps them on her lap. "I came here instead of Al Anon," she says curtly. "That is to say, I sought God first instead of man. *'But seek ye first his kingdom and his righteousness, and all these things will be given to you as well,'* " she says. "Matthew 6:33."

Mike bites her tongue.

"God will teach me all I have to know, Prioress. I understand why you needed it, but I don't need Al Anon if that's what you're implying."

"God can be sought in many ways," says Mike evenly. "Al Anon is one of them. I went to Al Anon first, and then to the monastery."

Gemma glares. "I, on the other hand, did not."

Mike pauses before returning the volley. She cannot allow herself to get sucked into this irrational morass. "You may think you went to God, Gemma, but the truth is, you can't get to God if you have no idea who you are. Knowing yourself comes first. Without knowing yourself, you cannot possibly know God's plans for you. Without knowing God's plans, you cannot possibly discern your vocation."

Gemma stiffens. "With all due respect, Sister, that may have been true for you, but it wasn't then and is not now true for me." She narrows her eyes. "I want to take my final vows," she says. "I want to take them on time."

Mike breathes deeply and stares out at the weeping cherry, now completely green and reflected in the pond as full and frilly as an antebellum ball gown. She'd like to be sitting in that tree right now. "I'm sorry," she says. "The vinegar was the last straw, Gemma. I'm sure you'll be taking your vows, but not this year. There's work to be done."

"Not this *year*?!" says Gemma. "That's totally unfair!"

Mike looks her squarely in the eyes, trying to appear compassionate while at the same time retaining some control. "I want you to agree to see Dr. Rawlins in Albany. The truth is, I feel too close to this situation, and I think you require extra help. Medication possibly. You have not been forthcoming about your medical records."

"You have no right to them," says Gemma. "There are privacy laws."

"Submission to your vows requires full disclosure, Gemma. You're not ready." She scans the room collecting her thoughts. "Dr. Rawlins is a psychiatrist," she says, "a medical doctor, so he can prescribe if necessary. Your privacy will not be an issue with him. He will be strictly *your* doctor."

"I don't need a doctor."

"There is no shame in seeking or needing medical help," says Mike. "The answers to our prayers arrive more often through natural means than supernatural. In other words, God works through people. Through doctors, nurses, and friends. Direct supernatural intervention is the monumental exception, not the rule."

"I don't need medication," she says through gritted teeth.

"Regrettably, the very ones who think they don't need medication are generally the ones who need it the most." She picks up the pen and clicks. "And there's evidence that you need medication."

"Oh really?" she says, leaning in, daring. "What evidence? When!"

Mike reaches deep for composure. "Among other things, I, as well as others have heard you, well…talking to yourself."

Gemma juts to the front of her chair and pounds her fist on the desk. "Who?! Who heard me?"

Mike is surprised at this uncharacteristic force. But in a way, it adds up. The girl's been coming undone for a few months now—since Arielle arrived, come to think of it.

"I want you to calm down," says Mike firmly. "Right now. Remember that there's a chain of authority here that warrants your respect." She breathes deeply. "And even though your initial vows were temporary, you vowed obedience."

"Sorry," she mutters.

"And suffice it to say that the conclusion I have drawn on your need for medication would be valid on my witness alone. I don't require the evidence of a single other person."

Gemma's eyes well-up.

More gently, Mike says, "I cannot in good conscience ignore this as a possible symptom of..."

"When you hear me 'talking...' " Gemma interrupts tearfully, "I am not *talking*. When you hear me doing that, I am praying. To God. I am praying to God, as we are all called to do. He is constantly with me." She pats her heart and leaves her hand there, crying. "Right here."

"Talking to God?"

"Why is that so surprising? Don't you talk to God?"

"Yes, but some of the things you say..."

Gemma flips her veil back, reaches into her outer sleeve and produces a tissue. She dabs her eyes. "You never even gave my angel any credence," she says. "I could be a bona fide mystic for all you know." She pauses. "I don't mean to be disrespectful, but...it's as if you don't even really believe Grace's story. Her angel. So how could you believe mine?"

Mike stands; she needs a stretch. Time to think. She strolls around the room. Does she believe Grace's story? She used to believe it! But this is completely beside the point, and she will not be derailed. "Across the ages many people have claimed to experience spiritual visions," she says. "And it's the job of the discerning authorities to be suspicious."

With her right hand, Gemma reaches into her left sleeve, retrieves a piece of paper, unfolds it and hands it to Mike. "I know you don't believe in them, or at least you don't believe that I've ever seen one, but this is exactly what he looked like. The angel. My angel."

Mike takes the paper and sits back down. She studies it with interest. The likeness is uncanny. *Huh.* Could Gemma be telling the truth? Not that she would lie, but…just the mental distortion. Yet this angel looks exactly like… "Why haven't you shown me this before?"

Gemma looks at the floor, shrugging. "You weren't interested. But now I need you to understand that I'm divinely guided. That my vocation is divinely guided. And stop treating me like…I don't know. A reformed addict."

Mike sighs heavily; she gets the reference. God, this is so confusing. Or maybe it's the caffeine. Just all of this at once. "Still," she says. "I want you to see Dr. Rawlins. He's accustomed to working with the clergy, and I promise you he'll respect your, uh…experiences. You needn't be afraid, ok? He'll understand your spiritual context, believe me. I'll make the appointment for Friday. If Dr. Rawlins is in agreement that you do not require treatment, we'll proceed with the vows, how's that?"

Gemma's eyes shift left to right and down. She won't look at Mike. "Fine," she says, and reaches for the picture.

Mike pulls it back. "I'll hold onto this for now," she says.

"But…"

"You're free to do your chores, Gemma," she says. "Go in peace."

Her hands in tight little fists, she retreats.

When she's at the door, Mike says, "And Gemma? You're quite the artist. I'd like to explore that talent a bit."

With her back to Mike, Gemma says, "My talent is in prayer."

"Talent like this is given by God for the good of his community. A genuine God-given talent is meant to be expressed."

Gemma mumbles something unintelligible as she closes the door.

Once Gemma has left, Mike and her espresso-charged nerves head straight for the trailer. If Augusta can't give her any relief, Mike may have to schedule a few appointments with a psychiatrist herself. For God's sake, she thinks, why can't I just put all of this into perspective? Why is Gemma so tough to handle? It's not like Mike is the girl's mother! Or maybe she is. Or maybe she should be. Representatively, at least. *Oh God, not this again!*

Mike hates this train of thought, but here it comes…charging at her like the Amtrak express while she is strapped to the tracks. *Mother! Chug-chug-chug! Mother! Zoom zoom. Whose mother are you?* Of course Mike knows she is the officially appointed Mother Superior of the Order, though she has repeatedly refused the title out of respect for Augusta. Wait. *Really?* Out of respect for Augusta? *Are you sure?*

Mike's brain nearly freezes at this latest self-conviction. Maybe she didn't repeatedly refuse the title out of respect for Augusta at all. Maybe she repeatedly refused the title of Mother Superior because she simply did not want to be anyone's mother. Because she can't be a mother. She's a nun, right?! *True, but so is Augusta.*

So maybe her repeated refusals to accept that title had nothing to do with being a nun. *Chug-chug-chug.* She can't stop the train—here it comes—*ahead of schedule or right on time?* Maybe she refuses to be anyone's mother…even a symbolic mother…because she once was someone's real mother. Someone's actual physical mother. Yes she was. And the baby died. *The baby died!*

She receives this thought like the child she never held. Owns this thought, this reality. And for the first time the familiar grief that wells up in her heart, her throat, her mouth and her eyes is not nearly as crippling as it had once been—had always been—in the past. Not even close. She takes quick inventory of her emotions—is it true? It is true! She is not going to fall apart. She is…ok! She is more than ok. She is greatly relieved at this. The train hit her full on, but this time it did not run her over. This time, she was able to look it in the eye and stop it cold—untie the straps, get up and walk away. Praise God!

She faces the sun, straightens her back, and expands her broad shoulders. A miracle? Maybe. A miracle of clarification at least. Because in truth it's all very simple. She had a baby when she should not have had a baby, and the baby was born dead. If the baby had lived, she would have given the baby up. It would be *somewhere out there!* The baby would be what—43-years-old? But there is no 43-year-old out there with

Mike's DNA. The issue was resolved by God. The baby she was not even allowed to hold, died. And it was that baby more than anyone or anything else in her life, who led her to this realization in this sunflower field in this monastery at this very moment. No regrets. All things are connected. In this moment, her baby lives.

And everyone who comes to the religious life is carried there by—or hit by—a train of her own, Mike knows. She is not alone. Most importantly, she seems to have finally forgiven herself. It's not as if she hasn't talked it to death with therapists. As if her confessors had no idea. She's never hidden anything from her superiors, but still...*why now?* Why is this thought hitting her now as she struggles to guide the young candidates? And not just the young candidates, but the entire monastery?

She reaches into her pants pocket for her army knife and saws at a ropey sunflower stem until it's thin enough to snip. She raises it up to the brilliant sun. Maybe it's time for her to stop dodging the light, she thinks. To start becoming the mother this monastery needs. She lifts her face to the noon sun, closes her eyes, and reopens them. If she can truly surrender her physical baby, she can possibly be a mother to others.

All at once waves of gold waft toward her from a crazy van Gogh sun. It's as if her new awareness was a pebble tossed into a sea of light, sending ripples through the sky. She blinks at the images...or image. *What?!* She squints then shields her eyes. What's happening here!? Too much revelation in one day is not a good thing. No, whatever this...this blinding light is...is half made-up by her. She mustn't trust it. It's a classic illusion. For all she knows, it could be the first sign of retinal detachment. She rubs her eyes, turns, and trudges up the trailer steps. If it's a real calling card from God, it will return.

Won't it?

She hesitates then knocks on the trailer door opening it slightly. "Mother? Are you there?"

ARIELLE

In the trailer Augusta stands hunched over Arielle, who is kneeling with anticipation. All Arielle can think is, *Bless me! Bless me!* On the table beside them is a charred porcelain bowl containing oily rocks of golden myrrh and a cone of frankincense sprinkled with sparkly whatnots. The rocks are very intense resin jewels with magic powers. Gemma says you shouldn't use the word magic when it comes to spiritual objects or rituals, but the relic says that's hogwash since the word magic comes straight from the word *Magi*.

"Like the Wise Men," the relic told her, "you have to know what you're doing and do it for the good of all beings. You have to be clear about your Source. It's about awareness and intention. My Source, like the Magi's, is God. God is good. God begets goodness. God is goodness itself."

For Arielle, the fact that the word magic comes from Magi is super cool. She intends to treat Gemma to this little slice of wisdom pie when the saint is more receptive and less crazy strung-out than she's been lately. *Don't hold your breath.*

In her cheerful yellow and white polka-dot house dress, the relic strikes a match, lights the myrrh, and blows on it ever so gently— *whaaa-hoooo.* She's an expert at this. The flame spreads to the frankincense and escalates; it's really steaming. Again her soft breath, *whaaa-hoooo.* It's the relic's own magic word. Her abracadabra. Arielle hopes the relic doesn't light these fires when she's alone, but she probably does. She probably does it every night. But as Arielle has said before, the relic is surrounded by angels, so.

Now the myrrh's rockin' a good smoky flame. The relic waves the whole spice bowl with its holy haze over and around Arielle's head and prays, "Lord, this child is our grace and our strength, our new life. Protect her from all harm that arises from within her spirit and all harm that she encounters from without. Complete her spirit, oh Lord, with the light of your full bounty and heal her evermore from this day forward."

"Amen to that!" says Arielle. She raises her head. "And double ditto for you!"

The relic grins approvingly. "Double ditto for me, Lord!" she says, chuckling. "St. Grace, pray for us," she adds.

Arielle gets slowly up off her knees one at a time so she doesn't startle the relic off her feet and break her. It could easily happen. She's a brittle old wish bone ready to snap in two. Arielle takes firm hold of her craggy arm and says, "Let's sit you down, little mama. Take a load off those decrepit old claws." She removes the bowl from Augusta's hands and backs her carefully into the wing chair. Easy does it! *Plop.*

"Oh ha ha—those decrepit old claws!" laughs the relic. "What a glorious day!" She gets settled in her chair, wiggling side to side. "All we need now is just the right tonic!"

Instantly, she focuses on a point far in the horizon, staring out into whatever dimension. Her brain sucks today's tea recipe like a vacuum from some poor health fanatic in Kansas, probably, who suddenly can't figure out why she opened the refrigerator door.

Snuggled deep in her cabbage-rose chintz wing chair, the relic raises her royal index finger and pronounces, "A teaspoon of minced mint!" Followed by, "A tablespoon of shaved ginger! A rosemary sprig! Pomegranate seeds!" The list goes on. Arielle's just waiting for the day she hears, "Tail of the cat!" or "Eye of the newt!" from a slightly demented relic, but hopefully that day will never come. Or hopefully if it does, by then Arielle will recognize it for what it is and know how to mix the exact tea to cancel it out. Bring the hermit right back to reality or wherever she lives. Anyway, what's true is that Arielle is learning more from the relic than she has ever learned from anyone in her entire life.

She madly scribbles the ingredients down and carries the list out to the raised herb garden behind the trailer that she planted for the hermit months ago. She picks what she's told—a little of this, a little of that. The tonic will be concocted according to the relic's instructions. Absolutely no shenanigans when it comes to recipes, Arielle is clear on that. No substitutions! No practical jokes—for instance, no diarrhea tonics or one-minute round-trip salvia hallucinations, or any other prank Arielle could easily think up to play on the hive. *Just give her five seconds!* No. This is not the trailer park.

Each tonic is an exact science created to address the precise needs of whatever. The relic may seem to be engaged in mystical mayhem, but she isn't. She's precise; you have to understand that about her. She isn't crazy. Yesterday, she prescribed a recipe to cancel out Arielle's sleepiness, which woke her right up. Last week, they made a recipe for the relic's throbbing knees, which resulted in a euphoric walk outside and around the whole entire trailer. Who knows what the recipe will be made of today, or what its purpose will be. It could be anything. High-def eyesight! Removal of toe fungus! *Out-of-body shopping mission to the Queensbury mall!* Anything at all.

In the kitchen Arielle wraps the herbs and pomegranate seeds in cheesecloth as she's been taught, ties the ends and steeps the aromatic ball in hot lemon water. Ten minutes later, Augusta pronounces the tea ready. Arielle pours it into dainty little tea cups decorated with tiny gold rosebuds and gold edging, and from there onto the chipped saucers the way the relic likes them. Like a tea party. *Where are the Oreos!* She carefully walks the cups over to Augusta and holds them out for the blessing, which the relic performs with no words, transmitting it with her hands right into the tonic. Energy. Light. Whatever. All good things. Good begets good. You can't argue with that.

Arielle, the apprentice, sits on the side bench next to her master's chair, and together they sip, relishing the minty fresh recipe of the day.

Mmmmm. "This one is yummy!" says Arielle exuberantly. "You should call it zippity-doo-dah!"

"Oh, yes, yes! Zippity-doo-dah, absolutely!" says the relic. "Write it down!"

Arielle jumps up and writes it in the little notebook in the junk drawer.

"Zippity-doo-dah!" says Augusta. "And next to it put... *Transference of Knowledge.*"

Chills run up Arielle's spine. "Transference of knowledge?" she says.

"Yes! Oh, yes!" says Augusta. "But we'll have to be very careful with this one, child. We can't have anyone misusing it." She slurps the tea. "Or any of the recipes, really. No misuse whatsoever."

"Like what?" says Arielle. "Like adding vodka and olives?"

"Oh no!" says the relic, chuckling. "No, no no!"

Arielle returns to her drink. She likes the fact that the relic laughs. That she knows Arielle would never actually add vodka and olives to any of the tonics. After all, it could be hard to trust a comment like that from a recovering addict.

"Could you make up a recipe for Constance?" asks Arielle. "For her aches and pains? She worries me sometimes."

"Oh, I don't think Constance is interested in my recipes," says the relic.

Arielle shrugs. "Well, I could get her interested. Or sneak a drink into her coffee mug or something."

"Oh no, dear, one can't sneak blessings unaware. One must drink the tea with full awareness of its divine potential. One must come to it with belief. There's no backing into truth."

Of course, Arielle would believe in this tea sight unseen. But would the craft fair believe it? In all honesty, probably not. "Oh," she says to the relic. "Well. Maybe not yet then. I'll talk to her first. Raise her awareness. But if she's willing..."

The relic nods. "If she's fully willing then she may drink of the cup, yes. And I shall give you the exact right remedy."

"And blessing," adds Arielle.

The relic widens her milky eyes as round as pennies, smiling in full agreement.

Later, when Arielle brings their empty dishes to the kitchen, she gets an idea based on something Beatrice told her in catechism class this morning. She pours olive oil into a salad bowl, grabs a hand towel and places it all on the floor by the wing chair. Kneeling, she gently removes the relic's worn felt slippers and torn knee-high stockings, nearly fainting from the sour smell.

"What are you doing, dear?" the relic says happily.

"Oh, a surprise!" says Arielle. She dips her fingers into the oil and slowly massages the relic's bent toes, one by one…anointing them as Mary of Bethany anointed the feet of Jesus, except Mary used her hair. Arielle doesn't feel like getting her hair all greasy, so.

"I learned this Gospel story from Bea-bop today," she tells Augusta. "So I thought I'd try it on you. Make your gnarly feet feel human. They really are gnarly," she says. "I don't even know how you walk on them."

Augusta leans forward. "Who?" she says.

Arielle says, "What?"

This makes the relic erupt in a volatile smile, which makes Arielle grin. *Here it comes!* Arielle loves making the relic laugh.

"Who, dear?" says Augusta on the verge of hysteria.

Arielle totally digs this lady. She's a religious rock star, or rocker like the chair, when you think about how old she is.

"Who did you say told you about the Bible story?" the relic repeats, grinning expectantly.

"Uhhh….Bea-bop?" Arielle says, realizing she's never used this nickname in front of the relic before. Will she get away with it?

Augusta places her hand on her chest in utter disbelief. "Do you mean Beatrice?"

Arielle nods uncertainly, waiting.

"Oh!" laughs the relic. "That's rich! That's a good one!" When she laughs, her feet come right off the floor.

Not ten seconds later, OMG! she is laughing so hard, she is crying, which makes Arielle cave full-bore into her snort-laugh. Eventually, she has to dart to the bathroom for a box of tissues, not that nuns wear mascara, but honestly, their eyes are so teared-up they can hardly see! On the way back, she skids on a smear of olive oil which she turns into a spontaneous little skate dance, sliding back and forth and clapping her hands. She hasn't had this much fun in a decade.

Augusta claps with her, laughing helplessly. "I beseech you!" she shouts.

Arielle doesn't even think she's that funny, but the relic's laughter is doing them both in. In between sobs of laughter, Arielle points her index finger up and yells, "Oxygen! Oxygen!!" And this just makes matters worse. Oh, is there such a thing as actually dying of laughter, she thinks? Because if there is, she and the relic are about to meet God together.

Somewhere in the background, she hears, "Mother?" followed by, "What in the name of God is going on in here!"

She whips around to see Mike carrying a single sunflower. Her face is completely confused, but with a screwy little smile. She is clearly amused. Well, who wouldn't be?! She's not made of stone. This isn't Gomorra!

Still, her presence sobers them up a bit, just because…how do you explain a little half-witted comedy? You don't.

"Oh, Michael Agnes, do come in!" says the rock star, dabbing her eyes and catching her breath.

"What in the world is so funny?" asks Mike.

You can tell she doesn't really want to smile, but.

"Sorry I missed it all," she says.

Augusta peers down at Arielle conspiratorially. "No point in trying to explain, is there, dear?"

Arielle likes this very much; she does. The fact that Augusta doesn't try to explain the unexplainable. She just lets it lie. They're like, best friends. Family. They have secrets.

Mike sits down on the bench. Her shoulders are all hunched. She looks beat, like she just lost the bonus round in a cross-country marathon.

"What's with the bowl of oil, then," she says. "Can I ask that much?"

"The little dear is anointing my 'mangled gnarly feet' as she calls them," says the relic, near about bursting into another fit. "She learned the story about Mary of Bethany from…"

She holds her chest again, which is practically spastic just from thinking about the word Bea-bop, Arielle can tell.

"…from…ha ha ha !"

"Okay okay," says Mike. She looks down at Arielle. "Who did you learn it from?"

"Beatrice," says Arielle straight-faced, and this makes Augusta start all over again, rolling around in her wing chair like a swollen tic.

Mike shakes her head. "Okay, never mind then." She looks at Augusta. "I see that I'm interrupting a solemn ritual…"

"Oh no, Michael Agnes," says Augusta, sobering. She dabs her eyes. "Arielle and I can proceed with this later, right dear?" She winks.

Arielle winks right back, but that's it because she can't take anymore hilarity, she's not kidding. She places Mike's sunflower in an old coke bottle with water, cleans up the oil spill, gives the relic a big kiss on the top of her balding head, and salutes Mike goodbye. Mike kind of ignores the salute, so Arielle knows she's wandered too far off into Slapstick City to find her way back. Time to go.

"I would have been here earlier," says Mike to Augusta, "but I was slowed down by the damn computer again. Kevin keeps promising to take a look at it, but he hasn't found his way over here for two months!"

"Good," says Augusta. "My hex is working then. Maybe he'll stay away for good!"

Mike sighs, "If you don't mind, Mother, lift the hex. At least long enough to get the computer fixed."

With her hand on the doorknob, Arielle says, "What's wrong with it?"

"Who knows?" says Mike. "I suppose I'll be forced to take it into town, though."

"I'm great with computers," says Arielle. "I can check it out if you want. Maybe save you some trouble."

Mike stares at her blankly, considering the odds of whatever. Maybe the odds of her actually fixing the computer versus breaking it. Or the odds of her actually fixing the computer versus erasing everything on the hard drive. If Mike even knows what a hard drive is. A lot of people her age don't.

"You really know what you're doing?" Mike says.

Arielle shrugs. "I was the wizard of tech in my high school. I could give it a try?"

Augusta claps excitedly. "Give her a try!" says the fan club.

Mike puckers her lips and moves them side-to-side while frowning.

Why don't you just say *Yes,* is what Arielle is thinking, and she tries to plant this thought right into Mike's brain. *Transference of knowledge,* yes!

"Yes," says Mike like pure magic. "Why not give it a try? Just promise me you won't proceed past your level of true understanding." She shakes her finger in warning. "No experimenting, Arielle."

"Okay."

"Just the obvious," says Mike.

Arielle keeps quiet and just nods because this could go on all day.

"Okay then," says Mike. "If you're absolutely sure you can do it, then go ahead. Are you?"

"I don't really know until I look at it," she says.

"Ok then, go ahead. Give it a try. I'll meet you there in 30 minutes or so. If you're absolutely sure, that is."

Arielle pastes a celebrity smile on her face, gives them both the royal hand wave, and disappears out the door before Mike has a chance to change her mind. She gallops across the field to the head office like Saul to his conversion—another great story! She just hopes she doesn't get knocked off her high horse. *Hit by lightning!* No time for screw-ups—she hasn't had access to a computer in six months and she's only got thirty minutes to fix the thing and catch-up on email.

But before she can get there, she runs into Constance who's carrying what looks like a bolt of polka dot wool designed by Betty Rubble. Her face is overly pale, so maybe she shouldn't be carrying it. Arielle hates like hell to get hung-up here, but it's the craft fair, so. "Hey, you shouldn't be carrying that heavy thing," she says.

The craft fair leans against the stair railing, huffing. "I'm okay," she says, but she sure doesn't look it.

"I have to go fix Mike's computer real fast, but just leave the fabric there and I'll bring it upstairs when I'm done. About a half-hour, okay?"

The craft fair is sweating like three fat men tied together in a sauna. "O…kay," she barely says, and drops the bolt.

"You sure you're okay?" Arielle says, frowning.

"No worse than usual, dear." *Gasp. Gasp.* "You know I have aches and pains." She swats the air. "You go on now. I'll survive. I always do." She grabs the railing and walks painstakingly upward. "I think it's my spleen this time," she says, holding her side.

Arielle watches her struggle successfully up to the first landing. "Okay then," she says, and charges into Mike's office breathless, slams the door and slides into the padded leather chair at the computer desk. Click click click click click click click like a green flash at sunset, and she has almost gotten to the bottom of it all. Click click click click. And it looks like AOL might be the culprit. The easiest thing is just to reload the program, she supposes. See if that plan works.

She roots through the cabinet and finds the AOL disk, fools around with a few passwords and then, *bingo!*—of course—"*G-r-a-c-e*"! What else would it be? While that's reloading, she checks her gmail account, and just as she suspected there's about a thousand emails from Lucky the Clown. *Helloooo? What do you want from me!? I'm practically a nun!*

Arielle still cannot believe she saw Lucky the other day, and also that he works right in town. Not that Lucky working right in town should be so surprising, since it's not so far from where they both grew up, and after all, how many firemen does a village need? You might have to travel a few towns over for a job. But just that they ran into each other the way they did, and just the whole cosmic joke of them being married for a grand total of one day, and then a hundred years later in dog years, him finding her in a diner rockin' a nun's street get-up and hanging out with other nuns. Eating a hot dog! He probably had to go back to the station and stick the hose in his ear just to extinguish the fire in his brain. Well, good! Good for him.

Email #1 from the loser: Babe, don't waste ur life. U look awful in green. I have a job. I can buy u nice things. Call me: 518-998-0468. Lucky

Email #2: Babe, don't ignore me. I'm different now. Grown up. U'll c. No more porn! JK Call me: 518-998-0468.

Emails 3-18: Blah blah blah blah, etc. etc. etc.

Arielle clicks back to AOL, which is still loading, so jumps to the internet and Googles Jesse Johnson, alias the loser. Just a little notice in the Fort Ann paper about his joining the army and going to Afghanistan and all. Not a single news flash about being picked up for pot possession, so she guesses the sheriff made good on hiding the records of a minor. She Googles herself: nothing! What a friggin' relief, but then again, it's like she doesn't even exist. Maybe she'll send the paper a press release about her jailhouse conversion. That should give the trailer trash plenty to talk about.

She quick searches her mama, Willa. Only the usual old news— arrested four times on drug charges and shipped off to rehab for three of them. Click click click, and wow, look at the picture of momzy after she got beat up by deadly sin #2: Greed. Not pretty. Arielle doesn't remember seeing that picture before, but drugs make you forget a lot, which is why you take them. Ugh, she can't look at this beat-up picture, click click. *Oh God!* Click.

She checks back on the reload, and it's almost done, so she clicks back to the internet and Googles adoption agencies, she doesn't know why. She's never really been curious about her kid, but just wondering.

The thought of that day alone can collapse her lungs, so it's not that she doesn't love the kid, but just that she doesn't know her. Or him. Not that she thinks she can search "Arielle's Baby" and an image will pop up, but whatever. She has no idea who adopted it. She quick Googles: *Adoption Agencies in Upstate New York* just to see what happens. You never know.

In comes a nice size list of agencies on the screen and right along with that comes the boss lady straight through the office door. So without giving anything away, Arielle clicks back to AOL in a split second. This is perfect timing, since Mike and her giraffe legs glide right over to Arielle's side before she can blink.

"How are we doing over here?" Mike says hopefully. *Suspiciously?*

"Cool," Arielle says, studying the screen like a librarian. "Just a glitch with AOL, I think, so I reloaded it, but you might want to ditch it completely if it gives you anymore grief, because nobody uses it anymore."

Mike raises her eyebrows. "Nobody?"

Arielle doesn't want to get into it, what with "nobody" meaning "nobody under the age of 50" or… "nobody who knows anything about computers," or whatever, so she just says, "Well, it's kind of cumbersome, stodgy, I don't know. Slooooow."

"It has my calendar," says Mike dead serious.

Arielle shifts her eyes and does an upside down smile, like: *What?!* Then she says, "Don't you have an iPhone? You should have an iPhone for your calendar. Or a Blackberry. You're the head of a business, sort of."

Mike shocks the hell out of her by saying, "Really? You think so?"

"Well, yeah. They'll probably donate one to you. The guy from the Apple store sits in the back of chapel practically every morning."

"How do you know that?"

"Just the shirt he wears." says Arielle. "The little apple logo; it's kind of obvious. You should talk to him." She doesn't know what gets into her—*this isn't the relic!*—but she says, "They probably have an app for God! For salvation!" The relic would pass-out laughing at this, but the boss isn't buying it.

"We can do without the sacrilegious humor," she says without any meanness.

"Okay, fine, but will you at least ask him?" says Arielle. "Or maybe I should since I'm more his age."

Mike goes all deep in thought again, and then says, "Well…maybe you could try. An iPhone might be…interesting, you know? Challenging."

"They have an app for tides, planting, rainfall and moon phases and I'm not kidding, they probably have one for prayers!" says Arielle. She shrugs apologetically. "It's completely possible."

"Alright then," says Mike. "Ask the young man, why not?"

The boss doesn't want Arielle to get too excited, though, so she nods at the computer screen and says, "And everything is working now?"

"Well, I did some diagnostics, and there's plenty of space…you don't need more memory or anything, so."

Mike folds her arms and nods, "That's very impressive, Arielle. Really. This little breakdown would have cost us."

Ha ha, whatever. Old people are always impressed at what you can do with computers; Arielle might as well make like it was a bunch of work. You never know where that'll get you, maybe somewhere. "Thanks, Boss," she says. *Oops!*

The boss just rolls her eyes and gives Arielle a pass. So now they're both just staring straight at the AOL Welcome screen, which is flashing stories about the latest wardrobe malfunction and the Bachelor Pad, which is a little awkward. Arielle can tell she's about to be ejected from the seat, so she says, "There are probably a couple of other things I should check out just to be sure, though." *Like emails!*

"Maybe tomorrow," says Mike. "I've got a few things to catch up on as you can imagine. I haven't been able to use this thing since last week."

"Um, okay," says Arielle reluctantly. She'd like to get rid of a few screens, though, but how is this going to happen with the boss standing right there?!

"I'm sure Constance is waiting for you, isn't she?" says Mike. "Monastic Orientation?"

Arielle shrugs. "More like sewing class at this point."

"I see. Well, that's instructive, though. Is it not? And you have a whole new wardrobe to prove it. Not to mention a new skill!"

"Yeah, I do. The craft fair's cool, and I don't mind sewing. I kind of like it, actually."

Mike frowns at whatever—too much to choose from, really. "I'm very impressed with your ability to get along with everyone," is all she says. "You're a connective force, Arielle. I hope that means you feel at home here."

Arielle is just trying to figure out how to trick her into turning around for about ten seconds so she can get rid of the buried Google screens before they pop up.

"Well, anyway..." says Mike. She sweeps her hand in an invisible line from Arielle to the door. "Time to move along."

In a stroke of genius, Arielle says, "First I have to turn it off and back on or it won't complete the updates."

"Oh, ok. Well...go ahead then."

Arielle flicks the computer right off without clearing the screens, because she can't risk it, but that's ok. More than one way to clear a computer. The main thing is to gain enough trust to be allowed access to it again. Not that she plans to play black jack or anything, but just so she can catch-up on her old life in enough time to erase it before she officially starts her new one.

"Beatrice tells me you're almost ready to be baptized," says Mike.

Arielle smiles, "Oh yeah?"

"Yes, indeed. She's very impressed with your study habits."

"Yeah," says Arielle as she steps away from the desk. "And I really enjoy Beatrice. The stories we read are awesome, like grown-up fairy tales."

"Except they're true," says Mike.

"That's what she tells me," says Arielle, "but sometimes I wonder..."

"Oh? You don't believe them?"

"No. Sometimes I wonder…if they're true then why don't you all believe them?"

Mike sits on the corner of her desk, all business-like with her same black pants and white shirt, folding her arms. "Well, of course we believe them, Arielle. That's why we're here."

For some completely insane reason, Arielle says, *"Ask and you shall receive, seek and you shall find, knock and the door shall be opened to you."* She stares at Mike. "Not to be rude, but."

"But what?"

"Well, it's just that everyone seems so confused and worried about what's going to happen to the monastery…"

The boss widens her eyes in frustration. "And?"

"Well, why not just ask?"

The boss inhales and breathes a long, deep sigh down to her toes. "We have asked, Arielle, believe me."

This makes Arielle think of something she learned from Beatrice last week, and the minute she thinks of it, it comes right out of her mouth, " *'Give and it will be given to you. In good measure, pressed down, shaken together and running over, it will be poured into your lap. For with the measure you use, it will be measured unto you.'* "

"I see," says Mike thoughtfully, stroking her chin like one of the rehab shrinks. "And what do you think that means, Arielle?"

"To be truthful? I'm not sure," she says. "I'm not even sure why I said it." She raises her hands, palms out, surrendering. "I guess, just…you know, maybe ask together for the same thing? You're good people, so. If what the book says is true, you should get what you ask for."

She inches sideways to the door and opens it. *Get me out of here!* is all she's thinking.

"Arielle?" says the boss.

Uh oh.

"Thank you," she says.

"Really?"

"Yes, really."

Arielle swallows a grin as she heads into the hall. Close call though, she thinks, because Mike could easily have gotten all pissed off—all *who do you think you are!* Arielle doesn't even know why she said half those things. Where did it all come from anyway? Maybe the tea, you never know. *Transference of Knowledge!* Not that she has any knowledge of her own, but maybe that's the point. Maybe the nuns need a fresh look at God from someone who just met him.

GEMMA

On the bus to Albany, Gemma is more than slightly unnerved and if she's completely honest, resentful as hell. How did she agree to this? As if she had a choice. Freedom from Maya is all she's ever wanted, but no shrink can give her a prescription for that. Maya has figured out how to penetrate any barrier she feels like penetrating except the hermit's. The hermit is the only one who can help, and yet Gemma is forbidden access to the trailer. Instead she is treated to this—a tedious four hour round-trip junket in a smelly bus with no ventilation. Where is the justice? This trip is a monumental waste of every resource she can think of.

But as always, and for the sake of humanity, Gemma will make good use of this godforsaken time drain. Turn a negative into a positive, because that's her nature. She won't let the devil win. She fingers the beads at her waist, one by one, digging her chewed nails into the carved cross insignias as she makes her way through all twenty mysteries of the rosary. These prayers calm her down. They put her in the company of the Lord and his mother; the only company she'll ever need. She could easily be a hermit herself; she's holy enough.

She says five each of the four mystery categories, including *The Joyful, The Sorrowful, The Glorious, and The Luminous*. Within each string of the twenty mysteries she repeats one *Our Father,* a decade of *Hail Mary's,* and a *Glory Be.* In her early days as a postulant, it seemed an endless drone just to utter a single rosary—all that repetition—but she has since progressed to the point where the entire set of twenty is no effort at all. In fact, it's one of her favorite ways to spend her precious time.

As a child, there were no *Luminous Mysteries*, of course, because they were introduced by Pope John Paul II at the turn of the century. *Let there be light!* And even though they're not ancient like the other mysteries, Gemma likes them very much. The *Sorrowfuls* are the most important, she thinks, because they depict the sufferings of Christ, sufferings that she herself cannot mimic. She would not be so arrogant. After all, pride is a capital sin of the tallest order—in fact, the root of all sin. But oh that she could mimic one of his sufferings—remove just one nail from his cross and pound it into hers! She would do it without hesitation. *Just ask!*

Instead, she does what she can without attracting attention from the other nuns, especially Mike. This includes small, everyday penances, like the rock salt hidden in the new shoes she ordered a half size too small. That and the scratchy woolen scarf that cinches the bare skin of her bony waist. It's the least she can do. And even now, on the bus, she keeps her head bowed in prayer at an uncomfortable angle as befits a woman of her holy station. So far she has successfully held it at this angle through the entire hour and a half bus ride. Her neck is sore, but so what? She's a model of sanctity, a fitting advertisement for the monastery, which God knows is sorely needed. No one else sets an example. *Follow me,* she thinks. Follow me on the rocky road to Paradise. *I will show you the way!* You will not be lost!

When Gemma becomes the Mother Superior of these women, which is her destiny, they will be forced to recite the rosary four times a day in uncomfortable positions, and every other day—they will fast. Not one of them will be allowed a spare pound of fat, especially those given to gluttony. This of course would be no issue for Gemma who could happily live off a single Host and sip of Precious Blood from morning Mass. *If they would only let her!* Not so much as a grape or a drop of water more! But of course, Mike would never be so enlightened as to allow that, now or ever. She watches Gemma like a hawk, as if

Gemma is bulimic or anorexic or otherwise diseased, which she emphatically is not. You would think Mike had never read the lives of the mystical saints. Saints starved themselves all the time. *Forty days in the desert!* It's how they got to be saints.

"World without end, Amen," she says under her breath.

There—she's finished. Good for her. She cups the beads in her hand and loops them back around her leather belt. Her neck aches. She carefully lifts her head from the odd angle, relishing the discomfort it's causing. From the window, she sees the steel buildings of Albany rising up against the powder blue sky. All this traffic! *Chaos! Mayhem!* How she wishes she were kneeling in the wildflower bed on the farm with her garden scissors and basket.

Alone.

She should never have left the village—should have hidden behind the bus shelter and wandered into the woods for the day. Visited Henry. As if last week's trip to the diner hadn't done enough damage. And now this! Is there no mercy? Of course Mike thinks the trip will do Gemma good—stimulate her mind and move her out of "the unhealthy isolation she's created." *Wait! What?!* Could this be any further from the truth?

The other bus passengers keep turning around and staring at Gemma like she's some kind of freak. Who are they to be calling her a freak?! There are five or six of them—most likely domestics and migrant workers from the looks of them. Immigrants, no doubt—not that they don't deserve a seat on a bus, but still. Why are they staring at her like they want absolution from mass murder? They're making her very nervous, and she just hopes they don't follow her off the bus. Mug her in the bushes and steal her beads.

Anxiety mounts. Her heart flips. She reaches deep down to center herself, but for whatever reason is finding this task extremely difficult. She never really felt so unnerved around the city of Manhattan, so maybe it's Albany. Some kind of negative force field around the city. Or maybe so much time on the farm has radically changed her. Tending the soil so dutifully every day, she thinks, binds you to it.

Between Henry and the soil, right there in the mountains and under the sun, she could happily live her entire life.

How hard she works! Nobody else in that place does a damn thing either. No end to the excuses! Except Beatrice, of course, though Beatrice can't complete two tasks in a row; can't even remember what they were when she's right in the middle of them. *"Where was I? Where was I?"* And Arielle, she supposes, who is cooperative enough, but highly unskilled and really, when you think about it, just plain silly. A silly girl with silly pranks who will probably never be holy. Just look at the tattoos! And here Gemma had harbored such high hopes for the urchin. But Arielle's alliance with the unholy three, well—four if you count Constance—has made a conversion to conservative practice nearly hopeless.

Gemma has worked herself up into such a froth that she has to breathe deeply to return to a prayerful state. Thinking about the other women is only riling her nerves and in that condition she won't be able to present herself to Dr. Rawlins in an authentic manner. Centered. Grounded. *Whole.* After all, that's who she truly is, and that's how she must convey her inner being. It's not an act! It's reality. It isn't she, but the other women who rob her of her bearings. Who bring out the voice.

She doesn't want to think about the voice, but there it is. The thought exists, so she won't run away from it. The more she thinks about it, the voice is just a test. What saint in the heavenly roster wasn't tormented by something or other? *Name one!* None! Joan of Arc had her own voice and it got her canonized, so there you are. Demons are to saints as hurdles to runners. They hone one's natural spiritual skills. On their own, they are nothing—*no-thing*—simply a means against which to test and constantly improve one's spiritual strength and stamina.

Most people don't know that, apparently. Because most people in this world, not to mention in this monastery, could care less about sainthood. They think demons are meant to be lustfully engaged like a steak dinner, a smoky casino, or a…"

"Handsome fireman!"

What?! Gemma turns her head quickly but discreetly, looking slyly left to right and center. Who said that?

"I did!"

But there are only six people on the bus and at this point, no one is even looking up.

"It's me! Maya! *Helllloooo!*"

This voice is as loud and clear as the Angeles bell at noon. Why can't anyone else hear it?!

Without even moving her lips, Gemma mutters, "You listen to me, you. When I walk off this bus, you do not follow me. You stay on the bus and take it all the way to hell."

The bus comes to a stop. The driver opens the door with a *whisshhh*, and turns his head to the rear. "Your stop, Sister," he says.

She nods slowly, elegantly, as if she isn't being plagued by a pit of pythons. Because today, as always, God is on her side. *Body of Christ,* she thinks. *Body of Christ.* What self-respecting demon would step up to that plate? None. Not one. "Christ crushed you!" she mutters as her feet absorb the stabbing pain of the rock salt in her shoes. "Snapped you right in half!"

"Excuse me?" says the driver.

"Oh, uh, nothing," she says. Had she spoken aloud? "Uh, when do you return to this stop?" she asks.

"There'll be another bus here at four o'clock. Reverse trip; check the signage." He points to the front of the bus.

"So be it," she says forcing a smile. "I'll be here then. God bless you."

Four blocks and six staircases up, Dr. Rawlins thinks he knows everything about the spiritual life. He's an expert. He and his sterile steel office with its glass-topped desk and absolutely no evidence whatsoever of organic life—even a fern—are going to tell her how to blaze her path to sainthood.

"I want you to feel comfortable here," he says, not unkindly, but with a hint of condescension. "I understand that you're a nun and that your belief systems are important to you. I will respect them."

"Belief *systems?*" says Gemma, agog. "By that do you mean the one true religion?"

He sits back in his leather swivel, pondering the cityscape through his transparent wall of windows. "Yes, I do," he says simply. He strokes his cliché of a pointy white beard. "We can discuss religion later, Gemma, but first I'd like you to tell me about yourself. Pre-monastery."

She has to sit on her jittery hands or they will belie the nerves. There is an earthquake inside her, and she must not cave into its fraudulent, albeit seismic, power. "Nothing to tell," she says. "Outside of religion, that is. I love God. I'm a nun."

His eyes shift; he is shifty. It is she who should be counseling him.

"For this process to work," he says, "you've got to be forthcoming. There's nothing to fear; nothing at all. Believe me. This is a safe place." He leans cloyingly forward as if they have been sharing confidences for decades. As if they are friends.

Oh really?" she says. "No one is going to get a report of your findings?"

"No," he says. "Not really. No specifics. Just a recommendation. It's actually pretty routine."

Right."I'm not hiding anything," she says. "I lived in New Jersey and held a boring job, and one day while I was jogging on the river path…"

"What river would that be?" he says.

"Henry," she says, then catches herself. "Well…actually, ha! I named the river Henry as a young girl, and it kind of stuck. It's the Hudson River. Across from New York City."

His head is a bobble doll—up, down; up, down. "I see. Charming… *Henry.* And what was the boring job?"

"Just a clerk in the church library, nothing special. But I had access to lots of information, lots of religious stories and prayers. Bible history. It was good, I guess, but not really enough to fill a life."

"So no thoughts of family? Husband and kids?"

"I don't know. Maybe. No."

He jots something down in a pad. "And did anyone guide you towards this vocation? Any particular influence or inspiration?"

"Not really. Sister Mike was a teacher of mine in grade school, so I remembered her...knew where she was. She was probably the earliest influence."

Answering this battery of endless questions wears on her, dulls her edge. What business is this of his? A complete stranger! She's not even sure what she's saying anymore. After forty-five minutes of blah blah blah blah without relief, she gathers up her skirts and rises from the chair. "I have a bus to catch," she says.

Just to show her good will, though—her magnanimity—she offers her hand for an appreciative shake, but he ignores it and instead digs into the credenza drawer behind him for a medical form. A receipt for services, which he hands her and asks her to give Mike. Maybe he's an obsessive-compulsive who can't touch anybody's hand, she thinks. Or anybody's anything. An OCD trying to make money off of some imaginary disease he's projected onto her.

But who cares? It's done. She held herself together, and that's all that matters. She really did. Not once did she allow the voice to pop in and abduct her. Rawlins even seemed rather impressed at times by her thoughtful restraint. Nothing overly emotional or really, emotional at all. *Just the facts, Ma'am!* Hooray!

He pulls out an appointment book. "I'll see you next week, then," he says. "Tuesday again."

"What? Why?" is all she can say. *Is he kidding?! I can't do this every week!*

"My arrangement with Sister Michael Agnes is for a full evaluation. That will require a minimum of six visits. I'm sorry if this is an inconvenience for you, Gemma. I really am."

"My name is *Sister* Gemma," she says pointedly. "I haven't taken my final vows, but I'm still a nun. Not that I don't want to take my final vows. I absolutely do—the sooner the better. In fact, the only hang-up with them is you. The longer it takes you to perform your little evaluation, the longer it will take Sister Michael Agnes to arrange the services. So if you don't mind, I'd like to wrap this up."

"Well then we'll try to accomplish more the next time, how's that?"

With her hand on the doorknob, she turns. "No offense, Dr. Rawlins, but there's nothing to 'be accomplished', as you say. If you must know, the women of that monastery are the dysfunctional ones. They don't know what to do with a real saint."

"Oh?" he says, tapping his pen. "A real saint?"

"Ummm. If they had one," she says. "They wouldn't know what to do with a real saint if they had one. Or someone who wished to become one, for that matter. If you're counseling women religious, I assume you're familiar with stories of the saints?" She raises her chin. "I mean, the whole concept of sainthood can't be a shock to you. It should be the goal of every religious cleric."

He scratches his forehead. "I'm familiar with saint stories, yes. Some at least. But I'm not here to psychoanalyze them, Sister Gemma."

"You're not here to psychoanalyze me either, Dr. Rawlins," she snaps. "I've been to shrinks before and…"

"You have?" He reopens her folder and squints, reaching for the reading glasses behind him. I don't see it in your medical history."

She stares out the window, thinking. "I have a bus to catch," she says. "Really. If I miss it, I'm in trouble."

"Next Tuesday at two, then," he says. "And I'd appreciate it if you could supply me with the names of your other therapists."

Gemma doesn't even respond, why should she? For all she knows, those charlatans aren't even in business anymore. They certainly didn't help her, at any rate. She slips through the doorway. On her way out, her heel strikes a piece of the rock salt at a nerve-pinching angle and shoots searing pain up her leg and spine. She has to get out of here before she passes out.

In the hallway, she shakes the salt down the shoe into the toes until she can stabilize her walk in case he watches her on the sidewalk from his office windows. He probably does watch—watches her every move, every breath, for signs of illness. Disease. Halos or horns, as if he believes in either. *He believes in nothing!* She wants to scream from the pain, but at the same time it comforts her. The pain is all hers. No one can take it away.

The pinching, searing pain that is racing up the inside of her left leg drowns out the voice which is telling her, "I'm dying, Gemma. Dying! And you haven't even given me a chance to live. Not a single day! You are so selfish!"

Gemma is angry enough to take this on. "You can't die," she tells Maya. "You don't even exist!"

"Oh, but I do; I do! But not for long!"

And this last idea is conveyed so sincerely that it truly shocks Gemma—*Maya is dying?!* At first she thinks, Praise God! But for some inexplicable reason, this same thought stabs at the very core of her being. *What?!* she thinks repeatedly. *Maya is dying?!* All at once, she is a grief-stricken wreck, practically suffering a nervous breakdown on State Street right beneath her psychiatrist's office! This can't happen. "Stop it," she tells herself. "Stop!"

She reaches for her beads and begins a rosary as she hustles to the bus stop. *Ouch! Ouch! Her feet!* Maya's death would be the best thing that ever happened to her. Wouldn't it? So why does she feel so bad?

MIKE

Mike takes her seat at the head of the long oak farm table waiting for Gabriella to deliver the last of Beatrice's family-style platters. It smells uncharacteristically aromatic tonight, which is a relief. She is so hungry. She must admit that as the mid-summer vegetables have been ripening the communal dinners have improved in taste and appearance. Not to mention the fact that Rose's cooking rotation ended last week— *thank God!* Mike doubts she'll get resistance from anybody if she ends Rose's days in the kitchen for good. Other than cleaning, that is. She's the only good cleaner in the bunch when she puts her mind to it.

Tonight's table is a bounty of reds, greens and yellows in every shade and shape. First there is what looks like pasta with vegetables and slices of roast chicken. Next, the first ears of sweet corn of the season. After that, two loaves of steamy, fresh-baked whole grain bread. A real feast! She can't help but wonder what's been inspiring Beatrice of late. She seems genuinely happy. Come to think of it, it's been at least a month since she's registered a single complaint.

When they're all seated, Mike says, "Who would like to say the blessing tonight?"

Everyone looks side-to-side, no doubt assessing who was the last to say what prayer and when. Then Gemma says, "How about Arielle?"

Generally Mike would not allow one Sister to suggest another. *Volunteer yourself!* But in this case she's rather interested in the outcome. After all, Arielle has been a member of their community for

126

several months now and has never led a service. Maybe it's time. She turns to Arielle and cocks her head. "Arielle?" she says. "Are you willing?"

The girl jumps up like a spring. She is really a sprite of a thing, dressed in an over-sized denim jumper buttoned down the front. Her neck is wrapped in a red bandana, no doubt to cover the tattoo. Her summer tan consists of a thousand connected freckles which contrast strikingly with her ocean blue eyes and firebrand hair. The total effect is endearing, minus the Frye boots she wears with everything, but after all, it is a farm. And she's not a nun yet, if ever. Flexibility is called for.

Arielle claps her hands into a steeple, and looks upward. "Well, God," she says, "I am really hungry and just...so ready to dig into this feast that Rose harvested and Beatrice cooked and Gabriella served!" She looks around at them all and grins. "And, um, I know you see everything, because I learned that in class moooonths ago..." *Pause for dramatic eye roll.* "...so seeing everything like you do, you must know how hard Gemma worked to produce these veggies. So...I want to thank you for a great looking meal here, but mostly I want to thank you for all these women, because they're..." She looks around the table again in earnest. "...they're all I've got." She clenches her jaw as her chin begins to quiver. "And...I love them."

She sits down to total silence, staring at her lap. The women are clearly tongue tied, and then, "Ohhhh ohhh ohhh," cries Beatrice. She struggles out of her chair and waddles over to Arielle. "I love you too," she wails. "We all do!"

Mike watches as Arielle disappears into Beatrice's flesh like chocolate chips into cookie dough. It's an emotional sight. Even she has to dab at a few threatening tears.

"Oh, me too, you adorable child!" cries Gabriella, who runs around the table to join the embrace.

Rose just blabbers in her chair. "You're just the sweetest...the cleverest...," etc., wiping her eyes with the cloth napkin.

Constance raises her black cane into the air, indicating her infirmity. "You're my girl!" she says choked-up with a thick rasp.

Constance doesn't sound herself, Mike thinks. Maybe she's coming down with a cold. Or maybe she's just that choked-up. Mike wonders why this display is so unfamiliar. So utterly strange. Any display of sentiment has been so…entirely absent from their lives. But why would that be? After all these years, they're family, aren't they? Well, now they are.

She raises her glass of Chablis and says, "To the Lord who provides our bounty." This should suffice, she thinks. After all she's the designated authority, not one of the intoxicated masses. At this particular point it would be insincere of her to run up and start hugging the others. Disingenuous at best. She's the grand marshal, not the parade. The bond is between the rest of them.

While sipping her wine, Mike notices that Gemma is staring at her plate like a statue. In fact, since yesterday's meeting with Dr. Rawlins, she's been a concern—exhibited more than her usual introversion. Not that Mike is about to interfere; she's not. The girl is in therapy with a competent doctor. Let the healing take its course.

Still, Mike thinks, the girl is completely and unnaturally silent. In the wake of all this contrasting emotion, it's a bit troubling. "Are you alright, Gemma?" she asks.

Gemma nods sullenly. She serves herself a teaspoon of pasta and a shred of chicken.

"Aren't you going to have your own corn!?" exudes Arielle. "You grew it yourself, Gemma! I've never known anyone who could coax so much food out of dirt! It's a regular miracle!"

Gemma pushes her tiny serving of pasta and vegetables around on her plate with a fork. Doesn't touch the chicken. "God is the one who performs the miracle," she says dully.

"Yes, but he certainly couldn't do it without your expert cooperation, could he?" Arielle prods. "Eh?!"

Mike has to hand it to Arielle, she won't let go of her sinking roommate.

Gemma turns absently, almost involuntarily, as if she's listening to something else. "What?" she says. "I didn't say that."

Mike stares, as they all do. "Say what, Gemma? What didn't you say?"

She shakes her head, confused. "What?"

"Are you alright?" says Beatrice.

Gemma looks down at her plate as if suddenly noticing she's in the dining room in the first place. "I'm fine," she says.

Arielle butters her corn liberally, salts it, and digs in lustily. "Oh my God, roomie! You are an absolute genius at corn! I've never had it this sweet before in my entire life!"

Gemma puts her fork down and pushes her chair back. She looks stunned. "May I be excused?" she says to no one in particular.

Mike frowns. "Are you sure you're okay, Gemma? Do you need help to your room? Or maybe a doctor?"

"No!" she says, clenching her fists. "I do not now, nor have I ever required a doctor. Now may I please be excused?"

Mike studies her for signs of illness—for pale flesh, cloudy eyes, weakness in the limbs. But nothing. Nothing obvious. "Go on," she says with reservation. She'll take this up later with Jim Rawlins by phone.

When Gemma is gone, the others continue as if she'd never been present at the table. This is part of the problem, Mike thinks. There is a nice sorority forming among them, and she can't help but wish that Gemma were even remotely interested in joining it. Though initially she'd put Arielle in Gemma's room so that Gemma could observe the girl for signs of drug relapse... now she's relieved that Arielle is there to keep an eye on Gemma. Interesting reversal.

"This dinner is delicious, Beatrice," says Mike, as much to divert herself as to acknowledge the cook.

Gabriella says, "You're getting great in the kitchen, Bea! You may not be much with the quilting, but..."

"Hey!" says Beatrice, laughing. "I'm a bit slow, but I try."

"A bit uncoordinated, too!" laughs Gabriella good-naturedly. "Anymore needle pricking on those squares and we'll have to call them the bloody wedding quilts!"

"Ooomph," grunts Constance, apropos nothing.

They all look over.

"What's wrong?" says Mike.

In a matter of seconds, Constance turns pale, paler, white. She tries to say something, or maybe cough. It's hard to know.

"Are you choking?" Mike says, rising.

Arielle jumps up in a flash, grabs the wall phone and dials 911. "Get over to the monastery now," she says. "Code blue heart attack, 70-something woman," and hangs up.

Constance's cheeks turn bluish, and Arielle glides over to her, moving the older nun from the chair to the ground as easily as if Arielle were made of 200 pounds of solid muscle. "Hold on, craft fair," she tells Constance, "hold on. We need you; don't go on us. Stay with us!"

"She's turning blue!" screams Gabriella, jiggling her arms nervously. "Oh my God, she's turning blue!"

Rose stands in the corner with both hands over her mouth. Tears stream down her face. Beatrice joins her.

Mike can't believe how quickly Arielle takes control. What command she has of this emergency. Mike can only stare in both horror and admiration at the situation. She doesn't want to interfere with what appears to be an area of expertise for the girl. If she did, she could jam the works.

Apparently Arielle feels that they're losing Constance, because she begins CPR—thumping the chest with her hands, trying to get her heart and lungs moving. Mike gets Beatrice's attention and points to the door. "Wait for the ambulance outside," she says. "Direct them in here as soon as you see them."

Within minutes, sirens wail in the near distance; flashing lights fly up the impossibly long driveway. Arielle is still pumping and administering breath like she knows exactly what she's doing. Mike is mesmerized, and if she admits it, afraid. She doesn't want to question the girl's actions, because at this point, it seems as if a split-second could affect the outcome.

As the sirens draw closer, Gemma comes running down the long staircase with only a simple white ankle-length gown and a thin white kerchief covering her bald head. "What's happening?!" she says, finally animated. "Who's sick? Is someone sick?!"

She looks flushed and scared; wide-eyed, like a child. Mike hasn't seen her like this since she was ten-years-old. We are all becoming something else, Mike thinks. Other people in a play.

Just as she's fixed on the nearly beatific sight of Gemma in a state of surprised innocence, Beatrice comes running into the house with two young medics in white jumpsuits who are carrying equipment.

"In here!" Beatrice says, almost pushing them, but then just as they're running into the dining room to administer to Constance, Gemma gasps and faints on the stairs, falling a few steps to the landing.

In the other room, Mike hears Arielle say, "Holy crap, Lucky, I never thought I'd be so happy to see you!"

"We've got a problem out here, too!" hollers Mike from the hallway as she rushes to Gemma's side. "Can one of the men be spared?!"

She yanks Gemma's raised skirt back down to the ankle as the girl's eyes flutter open and then closed. The dark-haired medic is dispensed to Gemma's side. He takes her pulse and checks her heart.

Barely opening her eyes, she says woozily, "What happened?" and rubs her head.

"You fainted," says Mike.

"Fainted?" she says, and with Mike's help, sits up, props herself against the wall, her skin tone fading into the beige and mauve stripes of the wallpaper. Her kerchief is askew, and the medic tenderly moves it back in place—a gesture as gentle as a glance.

For the first time, Gemma focuses and turns to look at him. Her eyes, distinct wide-open circles—the crystal blue, the topaz—drink him in. "It's you," she says, and faints again.

The man blushes, and although Mike has enough questions to fill a library, she has no time for that right now or for anything it seems but emergencies.

The young man takes a small flashlight from his pocket, opens Gemma's right lid, then left, shining the light into each eye. He turns to Mike. "I don't think it's anything acute," he says, "but we should definitely check her out. I'll just bring her in the ambulance with the other woman if that's alright."

Mike nods. "Of course," she says then rushes into the dining room where Arielle, Beatrice, and the medic named Lucky are loading Connie onto a stretcher. Beatrice is struggling, gasping; her cheeks as scarlet from the rosacea as if someone had colored her with red marker. She's in no shape for this kind of stress. Mike takes over before she loses another one.

Gabriella stands with Rose who is less than useless, although Gabriella is not far behind. In fact Gabriella cups Rose's chin, stares into her eyes, and screams hysterically, "Snap out of it, Rose! Snap out of it!"

Mike has had it with them both.

Lucky tells Arielle, "Trade places with Eli. I need help carrying this one to the truck."

"Her name is Constance," Arielle says. "She has a name."

"Fine. Constance. Now go get Eli."

Arielle obeys.

Constance is at least conscious now, though mute and clearly stunned. Mike turns to Lucky and asks, "What's your best guess?"

"A heart attack," he says. "Could be something else, but we have to treat worst case, you know? Out of my way, Sister, no disrespect."

Mike sweeps aside and follows them as they carry Connie out. "Shall I go with you?"

"No room," Lucky says. "We're taking the two patients and Ari, of course, since she's trained. We don't have room for untrained personnel."

Mike nods. She turns to Arielle who's got two fingers against Gemma's neck taking her pulse. "Arielle?" she says. "I didn't know you were trained."

"Oh yeah, well, you know," she says, shrugging. "Had to take care of momzy, so. Not that my cert's current; it's not."

"But you know what to do."

"I do my best."

When they are all loaded in the ambulance, Mike says, "Arielle, call me when you've got a fix on the problem."

"Roger that," she replies, all business.

"And also let me know when we can visit Constance," she says. "I can drive the others over, too, if you need us. If she's staying overnight."

Arielle nods as Eli shuts the doors, and the lights flash fluorescent red and blue down the hill like an alien spaceship. Mike just stands out in the fresh night air, staring at the rising moon, full as the sun, thinking that this is the kind of night you never forget. The kind of night where everything could change at the snap of God's finger. *Has changed*, really, because this whole emergency situation is a first. And not one, but two, if you count Gemma.

Enough philosophizing, she thinks. Get moving! She needs to see Augusta and explain the noise and lights. Needs to call Jim Rawlins about Gemma. She hurries to her office and leaves a message for him, then walks through the dining room to check on the other three who are consoling each other. Or really, Beatrice is the one consoling the others.

"There, there," Beatrice says, holding Rose's hand. "Connie will be alright. She was awake! If you'd taken your hands off your eyes, you'd have seen that she was wide awake. And conscious! Arielle saved her life!"

Gabriella just keeps dabbing her teary eyes behind her wire-rimmed glasses which are clouded-up.

Mike clears her throat. "Sisters," she says. "I have to report in to Mother, who is no doubt worried about all the noise and fuss. Please stay by the phone in case Arielle calls with any news, ok?"

Beatrice nods.

"When she calls, come get me," Mike says. "Oh, and also Dr. Rawlins—if he calls."

"We will," sniffles Gabriella.

"Constance will be fine," Mike says. "*They'll* be fine."

"What?" says Rose. "Is somebody else sick, oh no!"

"No no no," she says, putting up her hand to stop the waterworks. "Nothing to worry about, I'm sure. Sister Gemma had a spill on the stairs, that's all. She's being checked out. End of story." Before they have a chance to quiz her any further, she rushes into the kitchen, through the hall, out the back door, up the slate path, past the gardening shed, the pumpkin patch, and the sunflower field to the trailer. *Knock! Knock!*

Augusta actually answers the door this time as if she'd been standing there waiting, which was probably the case. She's dressed in a navy print housecoat and a heavy wool cardigan. The cardigan was Augusta's Christmas gift last year from the so-called *Craft Fair.* Connie had been working on it for half the year.

"Michael Agnes!" Mother exclaims. "What's going on around here? An ambulance, dear Lord! Thank God it wasn't you, but who...?"

"It was Constance," says Mike as she enters.

Augusta shuffles like Yoda across the abbreviated living room to the counter for her tea cup. "Is she going to be alright? My goodness!"

"I think so," says Mike. "I haven't heard anything definite yet, but hopefully soon." She can see that Augusta's knees are hurting her; she's moving like a wind-up toy. "Go sit down, Mother," she says. "I'll make a cup for myself and bring them both over."

"Oh, you can't make this," says Augusta. "This is my new Spirit tonic. I made it to strengthen myself against the troubles."

"The troubles?"

"Yes," she says.

In spite of Mike's offer, she holds the cup and saucer between her trembling hands, rattling it all the way to the wing chair. Mike holds her breath.

As she settles into the chair, Augusta says, "The coming troubles, Mike. We must be prepared. It's a very special tonic."

Mike thinks, *don't ask!* but can't help herself. "More troubles, Augusta? New ones?"

"The chaos of new birth," she says. "Is what I was told."

Mike drops slowly to the bench, her eyes on Augusta. She swallows. "You only have one cup of that tea?" she says. "None for me? I could use some strengthening, too, you know."

Augusta squirms in her chair. "None for you," she says. "I only made one cup, and without my girl, I have no one to write down the ingredients."

"I can write them down."

Augusta shakes her head. "I've already forgotten, Michael Agnes. It's too late. I need someone right with me when I'm inspired. The inspiration is ghastly strong, and then...pufff." She raises her arm. "Gone!" A sip later, she places the cup and saucer on the end table and says, "Where's Grace?"

Mike sighs. Is she dealing with a mystic genius or a senile old lady? "You mean Arielle?"

"Whichever. It's the same thing. You'd think you would know that by now."

"Augusta, the girl isn't..."

"Where is she, I said."

Her stare is penetrating, purposeful. A precision tool. She is not senile.

"She's in the ambulance," Mike says. "Probably at the hospital by now." She folds her arms and leans back against the wall. "I wish you'd seen her, Mother. You would not have believed it! She took complete command of the situation beginning to end." Mike turns her head, moves the café curtain aside and peeks out the window. To the left of the farm house, the sunset is electric. Radioactive. "I'm not sure I could have handled it without her. Things happened so fast."

"Mmmhmm," says Augusta smugly. "Exactly."

Mike ignores this. "She's actually a trained EMT; did you know that?"

Augusta holds her tea cup with both hands. "She's everything, Michael Agnes. Everything we need; a factotum. Trained and sent by God." She leans forward. "To *transform* us!"

Mike doesn't feel like resisting. "I'm sure Constance would agree with you. And oh! Gemma had a little breakdown as well. She's also at the hospital."

"Mmmhmmm," says Augusta, her head nodding up and down. "The chaos of new birth," she says. "I know all about it. I was *warned,* Michael Agnes." She sips her spiritual reinforcement. "They have the same birthdays, you know. Did you know that?"

"Who?" says Mike. "Arielle and Gemma?"

Augusta narrows her eyes and stares directly into Mike's; holds the gaze firmly. "No. Not Arielle and Gemma. Arielle and Grace."

"What?"

"That's right. Didn't you examine her paperwork? It must have mentioned her birth date!"

"I didn't…no, not really. Just to check her age. She's twenty-one."

The hermit crosses her ankles and raises her chin imperiously. "Her birthday was April 8th, days before she came to us. That was Grace's birthday, too."

"Huh."

"Another *sign,*" says Augusta. "*Numina.*" She sips her tea. "We must always heed the numina, Michael Agnes. Always."

They sit in silence for what seems like a minute, but during that time, the red hot sunset flares up, recedes, and the sky darkens to coal. Chaos certainly reigns, Mike thinks, but it's nice to know that somewhere in there is new birth.

ARIELLE

It's already 10 PM with no real news on the craft fair yet or the saint. If Arielle has to pull an all-nighter, she's going to need some java. Either that or chew on espresso beans if she can only find some. Minor stimulants. She's just happy she's not hyping for a needle or calling around for some dog breath's trailer meth. No. She's pure, holy, and rockin' God, who hasn't let her down. No urges! She hopes he's working on healing her friends right now, which he probably is since they've been nuns longer than she has. Not that she's a nun.

Lucky's wiped-out, too, not to mention a reformed speed freak, which she didn't know until tonight. Not the speed freak part; how could she not know that? It's what hooked them up and drove them apart. Her, Lucky, and their best friend, Speed, ha ha—or really any available drug—were a threesome. What she didn't know was the reformed part, which…who knows? Time will tell. For instance, why hasn't she seen him at any of the narc fests?

At any rate, she has to find them both an organic rush to head off any urges. Following some confusing signage, she eventually finds a coffee cart and orders two super grande blah blahs. It's a community hospital, so she's just glad they have a caffeine cart at all, and that it's open so late.

She pays the half-dead snack volunteer, and immediately downs two slugs from one of the cups. Ugh. Not too smooth, but. It contains energy which is the point. Part of her wouldn't mind drinking a large cup of arsenic instead, or hemlock. Not really, but what kind of a comedy karma wheel is she hitched to that's forcing her to strap-in for another roller coaster ride with the loser? Although she has to hand it to him—he's excellent in emergencies—very efficient but so what? Life is not one big emergency. Although with the loser around it sure seems like one.

She walks back to the ER waiting room and hands one of the coffee buckets to Lucky. "Here," she says. "This should keep you up for a straight week." She takes a slug. "Don't you have to get back to the station?"

He shakes his head. "Medic shift's over; fire shift tonight."

"Yeah, but in between don't you have to return the costume?"

"Nope." He takes a long sip. "You know, Ari, we make a good team."

"Whatever. It's not like there's going to be a lot of overlap. I live in a monastery."

He unzips the front of his medic uniform, revealing a blue & white checked button-down shirt that's actually ironed. So maybe there's a girlfriend in the picture, because the loser Arielle knows wouldn't plug-in an iron in exchange for a Maserati. Of course the army might have changed that, you never know.

He wiggles out of the top half of the uniform, switching his coffee cup hand-to-hand. "Can you please help me with this?" he says, all helpless.

Holding the back of his uniform seems too intimate, so she just takes the cup out of his hand and places it on the table at the end of the couch. He could easily have done it himself.

He removes his work boots so he can wiggle out of the rest of the pants part. Puts the shoes back on untied, and sits there wide-kneed and all spread out in his street clothes. He's still handsome, she grudgingly admits, as if it matters. Of course it doesn't. It couldn't matter less. She might as well be admiring a well-groomed sheep dog.

He leans to the end of the couch and retrieves his coffee. "You're only living in that hen house because your mother sold you down the river," he says. "You know that's true." He takes a long sip. The milk froth sits on his blonde moustache like a commercial. He licks it off.

Arielle shrugs like she couldn't care less, which she couldn't. "I'm living at the monastery because I was sent there by a mystical vision."

"Say what?"

"Never mind."

"Never mind is right. You shouldn't be living with a bunch of nuns and telling fibs like that."

"It's not a fib. I love those women."

He raises his eyebrows. "So now you're a woman lover?"

"What would you care?" she says. "And anyway, no, genius. Although in a way, yes."

An ER white-coat with the nametag, *Dr. Callaghan,* opens the door. It's a woman, kind of middle-aged, but who knows. All those emergencies can age you. Arielle and Lucky stand up, eager for news.

"Wassup, Doc?" says Lucky as if he's in charge of anything.

"Which one of you is related to Sister Constance?" she asks, peering from Arielle to the loser.

"I am, sort of," says Arielle. "I'm a, well…student at the monastery and they sent me to check her in and report back."

Dr. Callaghan reviews her notes. "Well, you'll be happy to know that although she's had a heart attack, it was minor. She may be advised to get a pacemaker, though. But on the whole, with a little help, she should recover nicely."

Arielle hunches down in a little victory wiggle. "Yesss!" she says happily. "Is that why she's so tired all the time? The heart?"

"Most likely," Dr. Callaghan says. "We ran some scans and it seems Sister Constance also has a small aortic aneurysm. At any rate for now, it's under control. We'll have to watch it, though."

"That's great, Doc," says Lucky like he cares.

"But we need next of kin," she says.

Arielle widens her eyes. "I don't think she has anybody blood-wise. She's never mentioned anyone to me. But I can call our boss, Sister Mike, if you want. She can come over if you need her." This gets Arielle thinking about how all the nuns are orphans in a way. At least no one ever has a visitor. But how awesome that they have each other!

The doctor checks her chart. "We're admitting her as soon as a room is ready. So we'll send the admissions counselor to her ER berth, and perhaps you can assist with the information—call your, uh, superior then if need be. I don't think she'll have to make the trip at this hour, though. Tomorrow should be sufficient. We're familiar enough with the Sisters."

"OK," says Arielle.

Running her finger down her notes, Dr. Callaghan says, "We have to consult with a specialist in Albany about the likelihood and logistics of surgery, but that won't be until tomorrow either. If the pacemaker is recommended, it will be implanted either in Albany or Syracuse, not completely sure. At any rate, it doesn't have to be done tomorrow."

"Good news," says Arielle.

"And her thyroid is off, which would also create fatigue. We're working on a few things. Thorough investigation, I promise."

"How's the other chick?" asks Lucky. "The bald one."

"Sister Gemma," says Arielle, elbowing the loser. "She has a name."

"She's not my patient," says Dr. Callaghan, "but I think she's between exams if you want to visit her. Third room down. Someone's in there with her, so when the doctor comes you'll have to leave. Not enough room." She smiles all antiseptic and professional, turns, and walks out.

When they're alone, Lucky pulls on a strand of Arielle's loose hair and drapes it behind her ear like they're a hook-up or something. She swats him like a mosquito. "Knock it off," she says.

Of course instead of being offended, he smiles as if she was all turned on and dancing naked. Same old loser—wouldn't get the hint if it was delivered on a speeding bullet. He drapes his giant paws on her shoulders and steers her into the tunnel of exam rooms. The whole time they're walking, he keeps laying his deadweight hand on her shoulder, which she practically forklifts off every time. All he does is chuckle.

"You little spitfire, you," he says. "I always loved that about you, Red."

They continue down the dimly lit hall, him grabbing her and her shooing him off. "Stop!" she complains. "I mean it!"

When they arrive at the third room, he says, "The doc said it was here," at the same time he barges in. "*Knock knock,*" he barely announces while pushing the curtains aside.

At this point Arielle is still behind him and he's a wall. She can't see yet who the berth belongs to; it could be anybody. Gemma or Jerry Lewis.

"Ohhhh, sorry, gees, whoooa," is what Lucky says. "Whoaaaa!"

Arielle peeks around his twelve-pack barricade of a torso expecting to see a naked old coot, or maybe a naked young coot, but instead she sees...

"Whoooa!" she says. *What!?*

Lucky turns, leans over her and whispers, "They don't even know we're here!"

Arielle is dumb-freaked. *What?! Holy shit!?* She just stares at the cot which contains the saint with Eli rocking and rolling on top of her. When Arielle regains her brains, she says, "Stop him, Lucky! He's raping her! Stop him!"

This thought enters Lucky's thick head like a lit grenade, because he steps inside the love canal and grabs Eli by a big chunk of his slick black hair.

"What the fuck!" Eli says, turning up on one elbow, then jumping out of the sack *fully clothed, thank God!,* but with his zipper down, *oh no!* but nothing obvious showing. As soon as he's on his feet he socks Lucky right in the face.

Lucky grabs him by the forearms and holds him at a distance. "What the fuck are you doing?" he says to Eli. "That's a nun in that bed! You're in a fucking hospital! You want to get fired? Thrown in prison? What the fuck are you doing?!"

These words are the smelling salts that raise Eli from his sex coma. Still breathing real heavy, he suddenly stops struggling and just stands there, wondering where he is and how he got there. His eyes search the room wildly for an explanation...a reason. "I just...I don't know."

Lucky drops his hold and Eli tucks in his shirt. He spins around to look at Gemma, whose bald head is exposed. Plus she's crying. Eli just doesn't seem to know what happened; how he got caught up in it. "I just...I never felt so drawn. The eyes... I don't know."

"Get him the hell out of here," says Arielle. "Beat the shit out of him out back if you want. But leave me alone with her right now." All she's thinking is, Eli's aimed for prison and the saint is aimed for an asylum. No way out of this but pure insanity.

Arielle's nerves are going galactic. Since it was Eli, friend of the loser, she feels responsible for whatever. *What really happened?* She shakes her arms all loose to get rid of the nerves; steadies herself; breathes deeply. When she's fairly in control, she pulls up a chair to the side of the cot and takes the saint's hand; strokes it.

"He didn't mean anything," she tells Gemma, though she has no idea really...what he actually intended or how far he got. *Or who he is!* Anything can happen to a person in a war zone. Maybe Eli isn't Eli anymore.

Gemma's face is wet with tears and Arielle can't stand to look at her shaved head with all its new whiskers standing straight up. She reaches for the scarf, wraps it around Gemma's head and ties it at the back of her neck.

"Do you want to report him?" she says. "I'll completely support you." She feels like she has to at least offer. She knows what it's like to be jumped, *Deadly Dad #3—Lust.* She doesn't think the saint is in any condition to deal with this alone.

"No," the saint says quietly, though something about her voice doesn't quite ring true.

Arielle examines the saint's woozy eyes—definitely drugged. "Do you remember what they gave you?" she says. "Valium...Ativan...what?"

The saint says, "What." But she's smiling. It still doesn't sound like the saint, and Arielle is worried. The saint would never make a joke, even all doped up. That sounded like a joke.

"Something, though?" Arielle asks. "Right?"

The saint looks searchingly at Arielle with her psycho-colored eyes and says, "Save me."

Save me?! "Um...okay. From what? From who? From Eli?"

She grabs Arielle's wrists and says, "From Gemma."

This takes a minute to get through. Remember she's on drugs, Arielle tells herself. "Uh...from Gemma? Um. Okay?" is what comes out of her mouth.

"I'm dying," she says. "I only have a couple months at most, and Gemma completely denies my entire existence! My entire right to live!"

Arielle bites her bottom lip. "Is that right?" she says. Her heart is beating a mile a minute because this can't be a put-on. The saint has no sense of humor; she could never pull this off. Even Arielle could barely pull off a scam like this.

"I've been trying to get through to her, but I can't," repeats whoever. "And it doesn't seem fair, since she's the one who got to survive in the first place and I can only live through her. We're only one body!" she pleads.

"Ummm."

The body snatcher tightens her grip on Arielle. "Do you understand?"

No!

"Gemma will be back before this drug is worn off and I need to know that someone understands! That someone is looking out for *me*!"

Arielle probably shouldn't, but she bites. "Who exactly are you?" she says. She has to admit that whoever it is might be an improvement.

The body snatcher's eyes seem to flip back and forth from the brown to the blue as if they are in competition with each other. They bore right through Arielle's pupils straight into her brain. "Maya," she says. "Maya Sinclair, although I was never baptized, you see, or even formally named. But our mother picked my name out before Gemma's."

"Really?" Arielle remembers the name. *Maya.* Where was it? Oh yeah, at Joe's Joint, and oh yeah, with Eli. Interesting. So whatever whacko split personality thingy is happening here, the chick locked inside the saint is definitely into Eli. So maybe he didn't start the hook-up after all. Maybe she did. Still. Arielle's not sure where to go with it. After all, the saint could show up any minute and freak the hell out of Arielle, who let's face it, is a completely innocent victim in this coven.

"My mother named me Maya first!" says the snatcher with desperation. "Before she even knew we were twins."

"Twins?!"

"Of course, twins! Can't you tell?!"

"Wellll…you do look alike," says Arielle.

All at once there's a struggle in the saint's body, especially the throat, and then whoever's in charge says, "Mom named her Gemma because she was born in Gemini and because she was surprised we weren't twins! But we were twins! *We were*!" The voice fades, which is followed by some gurgling and head thrashing and finished off with complete silence.

For a minute, Arielle wonders if this little incident was real or some kind of freakish acid flashback from the fifth century. How she handles it really depends on what happens next—whether the saint is still alive or not, and also if she remembers anything. Arielle leans over and takes the pulse of whichever occupant of Gemma's body. It's 64, so at least one of the twins isn't dead, so someone will wake up at some point. But who? Arielle decides that the best course of action is to play it completely cool. So just in case she's tempted to jump out of her own skin, which could induce a major drug craving, she takes a hike over to the hospital chapel and checks-in with God.

The chapel is dark and eerie, which is fine with Arielle. She lights a votive candle in the back and takes it in its little red glass container up the aisle so she can see where she's going. She genuflects before entering the pew as she'd been taught by the craft fair. She feels more at home in places like this now because she knows the rules. She places the candle on the seat beside her, kneels down, and gets right to work.

Looking ahead into the mist of the scattered altar light she says, "Dear God," and shakes her head. "What is going on with Gemma? And who is Maya? I'll help her, I swear, if you just tell me what to do. And keep me from completely freaking, because as you can see, the saint is a freak. At least two major personalities squeezed into one freakish body without hair. And did you see the blisters on her neck! Whatever.

"But thank you for taking care of the craft fair, because she's the greatest and she could really use a break. While you're fixing her heart, please fix everything else that's wrong with her, ok? Speaking strictly as a newcomer, she deserves a few good years without suffering. Amen.

"Oh, wait…and please bring Eli and the loser to their senses. *What was Eli doing?!* All the way up where you live, you could probably tell exactly what was happening under those sheets, but to me it looked just plain B-A-D. Maybe it was. Maybe it looked just as bad to you up there as it did to me down here. I hope not. All in all I don't think he's a bad guy, at least he didn't used to be before Iraq. So please take the Iraq out of him if that's what it is. Amen."

She takes the candle, walks to the back of the chapel and puts it in the rack, still lit. And while she's at it, she lights a half-dozen more for everyone she can think of, including Gram and Pa who she intends to look up the minute she has access to Mike's computer again. When she looks back up at the altar to sign-off, she thinks she sees something happening like light converging from all corners, separating into colors then shapes. It really does look like something is trying to form, so she stays. Sometimes God might have a hard time creating messages out of the pollution we give him to work with, you never know. You have to give him a minute. You can't be rude.

After ten or so minutes and a few eye rubs, she thinks she sees a picture of the relic sipping tea, but she's so tired she could easily be hallucinating. She walks a little closer. It's not so much that it looks like the relic, but that's the big idea planted so powerfully in Arielle's head that she can see it in her mind's eye as if the relic is right there sipping tonic like a gypsy in a cloud of cartoon smoke. It's the relic alright.

Ohhh, she thinks, grinning. *Tonic!* So maybe the relic can dream up a tonic that will help her figure this out? Wonderful! Satisfied for now, she runs off to find Connie.

GEMMA

Gemma feels like shit. Her head wants to explode and to be honest she's not even completely sure where she is. She's lying on a cot in a secluded area surrounded by a canvas curtain. She's dressed in a faded green gown. The room smells faintly antiseptic. She's obviously in a hospital, if anything is really obvious which it's not. *What happened?* Was she in a car accident? She would not have been in a car alone; she can hardly drive. So where is everybody else? She struggles to figure out who everybody would be. *Who are they?* She doesn't know.

She inches herself up to a sitting position. Her arms are sore, or maybe it's her shoulders. Her neck is stiff. Did she hurt her head? *Who am I?* She feels different; she doesn't know why. She feels different, as if something has radically changed in her core being. But what? She scratches her head and is shocked to find that there's no hair. *Where's my hair!* Did they shave it? Did I have brain surgery? A tumor?!

She slowly slides her legs off the side of the cot and, holding her gown together behind her, peeks between the curtains. It's so silent. What happened? *She feels different.* Her hand goes to her head again and then she remembers, Oh, I'm a nun! How could she have forgotten that? What's wrong with her? She *is* a nun, right? She doesn't feel like one, though. *Why not?*

She settles back onto the cot, assessing her surroundings. After a while, the curtains are spread apart by an efficient looking lady with steel-rimmed glasses, a brunette chignon, and an aqua blue smock. She carries a clipboard; pen is poised. "Gemma Sinclair?" she asks.

Gemma shrugs. "I guess so." *Sounds familiar.*

"You guess so?" She leans in. "Are you alright?"

Gemma nods, blinking, thinking. "Yes," she says uncertainly. "It's just that I can't remember exactly why I'm here."

The lady takes her hand. "You fainted," she says. "But you were given a total exam, including an MRI, and everything checked out fine. No worries. We're discharging you now. Your friend, Arielle, will take you home."

"Arielle?"

The woman cocks her head. Gemma notices that her nametag has an R.N. at the end of it. "Do you know who Arielle Santos is?" says the R.N.

Gemma rubs her forehead. "Ummm…"

"Isn't she your roommate at the monastery?"

"Oh. Um. Of course, sorry. The monastery. I'm just a little blurry…"

The nurse checks the chart. "The valium, probably," she says. "You needed it for the MRI—claustrophobia. It happens. The meds can make you fuzzy-headed for a while. Kind of a hangover effect." She hands the clipboard to Gemma. "Sign here," she says. "If you're sure you're ok."

"Oh. Yes. Sure." She scribbles her name. At least she can do that. The name comes back to her, or at least the signature does. If it's really hers.

The nurse leaves, spinning the curtain closed on the rod so Gemma can dress, but where are her clothes? She steps onto the cold linoleum floor and walks slowly, because for some reason her feet are incredibly sore and tender. She wanders outside her area and around the room, which contains three curtained cots like hers, but the curtains are all open and the beds are empty, thank God. She doesn't want to be wandering around a room with someone screaming in agony from a missing hand or God forbid, paralyzed, or convulsed at the abdomen with some sort of infectious virus. That would freak her out. She detests illness and suffering. She shivers just thinking about it. It's so awful.

At the end of the room she finds a closet and opens it. Her undergarment is hanging on a hook, but nothing else. Where's the rest of her habit? Did they take it? Is this all she wore? It's so flimsy. *Who saw her in this?* She unties the hospital gown, drops it, and slowly pulls the garment over her head. This is not easy considering her sore shoulders and neck. And what are these sores on her neck? *Ow!* She twists her head to see them in the mirror. They look like blisters—like someone had burned her or perpetually rubbed something abrasive against her neck, like sandpaper. Who would do that? Did someone abuse her? Does she have an abuser?

She returns to the bed to search the sheets for her kerchief, which she sees has fallen behind the cot. She reaches down, *ouch!* She fastens the kerchief with some difficulty and sits at the side of the bed with her hands clasped in her lap. Slips her feet into her shoes—*ouch again!* What's in these? Is someone playing a joke on her? She turns them upside down and shakes. Huge crystals of what look like salt or sand tumble out. No wonder her feet are so tender. She must have crossed a salt lick on her way to the hospital!

So many unanswered questions, she's becoming anxious. She tries to say a rosary. She's having trouble figuring out which day it is and which mystery is featured. She remembers that on Thursdays you're supposed to lead with the *Luminous* and Fridays the *Sorrowful.* But that's all she can remember. She can't pin down the names of the Mysteries themselves either. She hopes today is Friday because she remembers that Friday is *Sorrowful* and also because she's feeling very simpatico with the Cross—all this suffering. She takes a running leap into the prayers a few times, but can't recall the words to the *Apostle's Creed* which heads-up the loop. Can't get anywhere at all. *"I believe in God…"* is about it.

She waits and waits for Arielle, who finally arrives and appears to be in almost worse shape than Gemma. Maybe she fainted too. Why are they all fainting? At least she recognizes her roommate, though.

"Hey, roomie!" says Arielle. "How you feeling this morning?"

"What time is it?" says Gemma. "Where are the rest of my clothes?"

"It's 6 AM," Arielle says. "These are the clothes you came in; don't you remember?"

"No, not really." She hates to ask, but she has to. "What happened?"

Arielle's eyes are so red with so many dark circles around them, they look like targets. Her hair is screwy, like curly orange noodles, and her oversized denim jumper is a wrinkled mess. The boots are ridiculous, of course. But her knobby little knees are the only leg flesh showing, so at least it's a modest outfit.

"What happened to you?" Gemma asks. "Were we in an accident? Why did we faint?"

Arielle looks down at herself and back at Gemma, and starts to laugh. "I look like it, don't I!"

Gemma frowns. Why is she laughing? What's funny?

"But no. I'm just the caretaker in all of this," she says. Then she tells Gemma all about Constance's heart ailments and how at nearly the same time as Constance's heart attack, Gemma fainted on the staircase. Fell down a few stairs to the landing, too. "You don't remember anything?" she says.

"Well…"

"The ride in the ambulance?" she prompts. "All the commotion?"

Gemma shakes her head. "Not really." *And who is Constance?*

"Eli?" says Arielle very slowly, eyes shifting back and forth.

"What?" Gemma's entire body is paralyzed with some sort of biochemical reaction. "No. What about…? What?"

"He carried you in?" says Arielle.

Gemma is flooded with images of Eli, which feels good but also bad. Why does it feel bad? *Why does it feel good?* "No," she says. "I don't remember him. And anyway, why would anyone carry me in? Don't they have wheelchairs in this hospital?"

"He's a medic," says Arielle. "You were draped over him, so he just took you to the room."

"I thought he was a fireman." She remembers that.

"He is. They do double-duty in a squirt town like this. Lucky, alias Jesse, was there too, and he's waiting for us outside to take us home."

"No," says Gemma. "No. I can't."

"Can't what?"

"Can't go home with him. Or Eli. I'm hardly dressed."

Arielle says, "He's seen a lot worse, believe me. Totally slack old fat people, naked. He can handle it."

"That's uncharitable."

Arielle shrugs. "Seriously, compared to them you're Miss Universe. Or should I say Miss Monastery?"

"I'm not going."

"You have to! Lucky didn't get a second of sleep last night, and by the way, neither did I. We were happy to do it, believe me, but…"—she pulls strands of hair straight out on both sides of her head—"…aaaaaa get me out of here now!" She sticks her hands on her hips. "Get the picture? All-fucking-nighter. Time for bed!"

"Are you a nun?" Gemma asks.

Arielle squints. "Uh…you're putting me on, right?"

"Oh, that's right, you are," says Gemma covering her forgetfulness. "You shouldn't curse," she adds.

Arielle puckers her lips. "Uh, no? I'm not a nun…yet? Remember?"

"Oh." Gemma rubs the back of her head. *Ouch!* "Right, sorry, just kidding, but still. I'm a nun, right? So you shouldn't curse in front of me." Not that she really cares, but it feels like she should. She vaguely remembers grammar school and the big rule about not saying hell. You couldn't even say hell!

"Get up," says Arielle. "I'm not fooling. We'll lose our ride home. The loser barely has enough adrenal juice to get us up that hill before he falls asleep at the wheel." She grabs Gemma by the elbow until she stands completely up. "Come on. It'll be fine, really. We can go back to our room and get some sleep. You'll remember stuff then. After some zzz's."

"I can't. I won't. I'm almost naked." She sits back down.

Arielle sighs. "Fine." She storms out and returns five minutes later with a wheelchair and a gigantic firehouse jacket that she flings around Gemma's shoulders.

"Oh! It's so heavy," Gemma says, but Arielle ignores her—pushes her into the wheel chair, down the hall through the waiting room and out the automatic doors. Once outside, she opens the back door to a little red sedan parked in the waiting area and points at the seat. "In," she says.

Lucky jumps out of the front seat to help. "How ya doing, Sista?" he says. "I was worried about you!"

Gemma squints. He has a big black eye. "What happened to you?" she says.

He gives Arielle a panicked look. "Uh…"

"Little tussle," Arielle says. "With the uh, stretcher."

"Yeah," he says. "Getting that old nun on the stretcher."

Gemma looks confused. "An old nun?"

Arielle and Lucky jump in the front seats. Arielle turns to Gemma and says, "Constance? Remember?"

Gemma studies the car for clues. "It's hot in here," she says, shrugging the heavy jacket from her shoulders. "Where did you get this car?"

Arielle frowns. "What?"

"The car?" Gemma says. *What's wrong with these people!* "Where did you get it? I thought we came here in an ambulance."

"Oh," says Arielle smiling. "We were talking about Constance, so. Confusing."

"I had to return the truck last night," Lucky says. He pushes in the cigarette lighter and tosses a pack of Marlboros to Arielle. "Hey, Babe," he says. "Light one for me?"

"What?!" says Gemma. *Babe?!*

"I'm not your babe, asshole," Arielle says, "and you're not lighting up in the car with a nun in the back seat."

"Ha! Gotcha!" he says, winking.

"What?" Her face is a big question.

"There's a nun in the back seat," he says triumphantly. "Not the front!"

"Not yet," she says.

Gemma doesn't think she says it with much conviction, but then right at the moment, Gemma isn't even sure why she's a nun. *Why is she?!*

"Why can't you call a nun 'Babe' anyway," says Lucky. "What's wrong with it?"

"That's a ridiculous question," Arielle says, "and you know it."

But Gemma doesn't know it, although she feels as if she should. It sounds like it would be wrong to call a nun 'Babe', but she can't figure out why. *Why?*

"Why?" he says, laughing.

"You know exactly why," she says. "I'm not going to tell you."

"Then I won't take you home."

"Damn it, Lucky!" Arielle says.

Gemma is confused.

"I mean it," he says. He pulls over on a patch of grass and parks.

"Fine," says Arielle. "You can't call a nun 'Babe' because a nun is married to God."

"What!" he says genuinely shocked.

"You heard me."

"You're gonna *marry* God?" he says.

She folds her arms and turns away. Looks out her window. "I don't know. Maybe."

"Are you crazy!" he says. "Why would you do that?"

Gemma thinks, yeah, why would you? But she's a nun, so she ought to know. But she doesn't. She listens carefully.

"It's what nuns do," says Arielle. "According to Beatrice, nuns are married to God. Whatever. They're like his wives."

"Like a harem?" he says, agog.

"Shut up," she says.

"Seriously," he says, "why do you have to marry him? Why can't you just live with him?"

"Very funny."

"He can't take you on a honeymoon; give you kids…"

"Shut up," she says. "What would you know about God, anyway? How he saved someone's ass, like mine. How he blesses you with a family you never had. How he gives you people who take care of you and make clothes for you and teach you things. How he gives you your entire life back before you even know enough to ask. Before you even know what a real life is!"

This finally gets to him, because he fills his big chest with air and heaves a long sigh. Then he reaches over and cups her chin in his hand, gently turning her head to look him straight in the eye. "You'd be surprised what you learn about God in a minefield, kiddo," he says. "With your buddies blowing up one by one around you. I'd wager it's a whole lot more than you learn in a monastery."

She blinks; doesn't swat him away this time. They stare at each other for a while before he releases her. Gemma can't look. It's too personal.

After a minute of pulling on his moustache and staring out the windshield, Lucky shifts back into gear and pulls away. He doesn't say anything else for the rest of the ride. Arielle flips on the radio to a totally inappropriate song and turns the volume way up. "*Gaga-oo-la-a-a!*" But she doesn't sing along.

Gemma looks out at the passing clouds, the goldenrod hills and timothy pastures and wonders where they are and why the sign at the Monastery entrance doesn't look familiar. Did they change it? And the dirt and gravel road up the hill seems much longer than she remembers. *At least she remembers!* Even the gardens look strange. Where is she? An alternate universe? She feels as if she's been driven to a rest home or something. A retreat, perhaps. Something familiar but not home.

They pass a scattering of rustic stone buildings, a pretty pond, and a chapel connected to the main building by a portico trellis covered in morning glories. Gemma is impressed. A little rundown, but beautiful. At the turnaround, they're greeted by a committee of three badly dressed portly middle-aged women.

"You just missed Mike!" says one with messy curly gray hair and bosom-high jeans. "You must have passed her in town. She's visiting Constance!"

"Hi Rose!" Arielle says to her cheerfully.

Rose, Gemma tells herself. *Rose.*

A rotund red-faced woman in a huge flowered skirt, denim work shirt and red plastic clogs waddles toward them, "Oh Arielle dear! Tell us about Constance! How's our girl?!" She greets Arielle at the car and suffocates her with a fleshy hug. "We've been so worried!"

Why can't Gemma remember the women's names? Did she ever know their names? Do the women know Gemma? *Does Gemma know Gemma?* No one seems to be concerned about her health or wellbeing, so maybe they don't know her. Although they look vaguely familiar.

"Hey BB!" says Arielle. "The craft fair's cool; not to worry! She'll be humming along on her projects very soon and for a long time! She says hi!"

The copper-haired woman with the wire-framed glasses laughs and claps, "Oh Arielle! Hooray, she's fine! The craft fair's fine!"

"Long live the craft fair, Gabi!" says Arielle with her fist in the air.

Gemma doesn't know where this girl gets her adrenaline. She is plugged straight into Source.

Arielle continues, "She had a heart attack, but it won't do her in, believe me. She's as tough as her sewing machine! She'll never break." She puts her finger up. "Although she could definitely use a newer model!"

Gemma sits in the back of the car watching the commotion, until Lucky gallantly opens her door, wraps her in the fire jacket, zips it, and offers his hand to help her out. His actions seem so personal, she thinks, and at the same time, so foreign. Out of sheer interest, she allows him to continue. *What will he do next?* It occurs to her that allowing him to continue is probably a major lapse of judgment on her part, considering her occupation. But that thought is so distant, she can't really absorb it. Can't heed it. Because the truth is, his actions feel like plain human kindness. Not that she would know what that is.

"Oh, how rude!" says the rotund woman—*BB was it?*—as she finally notices Gemma standing there in the huge jacket. "Here we are ignoring the other patient! How are you, dear? How are you feeling after your ordeal?"

Gemma frowns. "Tired," she says. "Exhausted."

"Poor dear," says BB. "Can I make you something to eat?"

Arielle says, "She can hardly talk, Bea. She's wiped out from all the tests, the valium, and what-have-you." I'm going to take her upstairs so we can both crash. I'm living on coffee grounds myself."

The woman named Gabi runs inside and back out lickety-split (you wouldn't think she could move so fast) with a big knit sweater that she hands to Gemma. "Here dear," she says. "You can return the fire jacket now." The woman tells Lucky, "Turn around, young man. She needs some privacy."

The woman BB whispers something to Arielle, who says, "Nothing obvious," and that's it. Are they talking about her, Gemma wonders? About her condition? Is there something she doesn't know about her own condition? *Nothing obvious?* But maybe something else—something more subtle?

"Good night everybody!" Arielle says.

"Hey, Babe, wait," says Lucky, reaching out for her with his hand.

Arielle gives him the evil eye.

"Sorry," he says, "but…"

"TTYL," she says dismissively.

"What?" says Rose, "what's that?"

BB swats her gently. "It means, *Talk to You Later*," she says as if it's perfectly clear. "It's young people's talk. You have to spend time with young people to know their language, Rose."

"Yes," says Gabi. "Text talk!"

"Oh that's lovely!" says Rose. "TTYL!" she calls out to Arielle. "TTYL!"

Lucky turns toward the car and BB says, "Thank you, Jesse. For everything. For coming to our rescue so fast. For taking care of us."

He nods. "You're welcome, Sister." His shoulders are slumped from exhaustion and as far as Gemma can see, from discouragement.

"She's just tired," BB says, nodding toward Arielle.

"Yeah," he says. "What can you do?"

Arielle doesn't say anything, just lets him go, which Gemma thinks is kind of rude, so before she can edit herself, she says, "Thank you, Lucky."

Everybody stops, even Arielle. Gemma surveys the shocked looks of the bystanders. Why are they so shocked? Shouldn't they all be saying thank you!

"Yeah," he says with a salute, "no sweat. Take care of yourself, Sista!"

Arielle pushes Gemma up the stairs and inside. She supports her around the waist as they climb the wide circular staircase.

"I hate to say this," says Gemma, "but I'm confused by everybody and even by this...whole place." She grabs the railing. "It's disorienting."

"I know," Arielle says. "I can tell, and I don't want you to worry about it. We'll figure it out, I swear."

"And why didn't you say goodbye to Lucky?" Gemma says. "He really likes you."

"Yeah? Well, I've had it with him," Arielle says. "Thinks he can call me anything he wants right in front of everybody. Thinks he owns me just because of a couple of random events."

Gemma stops on the landing. "I belong to someone else," she says. "I don't belong to myself."

After a pause Arielle says, "Oh, you mean God, right? Since you're a nun?"

Gemma shakes her head, which doesn't even feel like her own head. *Whose is it?* "I don't think I belong here," she says.

"Of course you do," says Arielle. But she narrows her eyes like she might not mean it. "Let's sleep on it," she says. "We'll figure it out tomorrow."

When they get to the bedroom, Gemma walks to the back window and hugs the sweater tightly around her. Henry sparkles like a shimmery wink in the morning sun. *Oh Henry.* Glorious Henry! At least she recognizes him. By the time she turns around, Arielle is already burrowed under her covers. She's lying on her right side, facing Gemma, pillow squeezed between her hands.

Gemma sits on the edge of her bed. "Arielle?"

"Yeah?" Her eyes are closed.

"Will I ever see Eli again?"

Eyes pop open. "Uhhh…do you want to?"

Gemma shrugs. "I don't know. Maybe just one last day."

"One last day?"

"Yes. That's all. Before I die."

Arielle jolts up. Her eyes are all bleary and red, but at the same time, wide and alert. "What!? What did you say?"

"You heard me," Gemma whispers.

"Are you…? You're not…? You know, planning to do yourself in, are you?"

"No." Gemma scowls. "I don't think so." *Does anyone really plan those things?* "I have an uh…penetrating sense of doom, though. Like I *know* what's coming, although I don't." *I'm not myself!*

"News flash to Gemma," Arielle says. "You are not going to die!" She plops back down like a rag doll. "Unless it's from exhaustion, in which case I might beat you to it. Go to bed."

"Part of me is dying," Gemma says, swallowing a lump. "I fought it for a long time, but I can't fight it anymore. I don't completely understand it, either." Her eyes fill up. "It's out of my control."

"They examined you completely," Arielle says, her lips slack against the mattress.

"I know, but."

"But what?"

"I'm just very confused. It's like I'm getting mixed messages from my own brain."

Arielle rolls on her back and props up the pillow. It's clear she can't even sit up at this point, which makes Gemma feel bad, but she's desperate. "I'm sorry to keep you up," she says, "but you're the only one who can help me. You're the only one who knows what I do around here. What my routine is."

"Your routine is to stay away from everyone and to punish yourself from one end of the day to the next," Arielle says. She rolls her eyes at the ceiling. "Sorry, but you asked and I'm too tired to lie."

"Why do I punish myself so much? Does everyone? Is that what being a nun means?"

Arielle rubs her eyes. "No. Being a nun means living in a great community of people who love God and want to show it. To me it means being the happiest I've ever been, and I'm not even a nun. I just live with you all."

Gemma turns her head to hide the tears that roll down her cheeks. "I don't think I even know what happiness is," she says. "I don't have any siblings. I never knew my father, and my mother was a drunk who didn't give a crap about me."

"Join the club," says Arielle. "And just in case you forgot, that's the past. You can't live in the past; you can only live in the present. Join the living."

Gemma drags her sleeve across her face, sniveling.

"And by the way, this is the first time you've shared anything personal at all about yourself," says Arielle. "We've been roommates for almost six months."

"You don't know anything?" Gemma can't believe this. *Who am I?*

"Notta. And you don't know too much about me, either, because you're too busy praying and rubbing yourself raw with bleach and ammonia to ask."

Gemma steadies her trembling chin. *Bleach and ammonia?* "How old are you?" she asks.

Arielle smiles. "Twenty-one if you believe my fake ID. If I admit to being any younger, it might send a few people to jail, so. Oh yeah, and I'm an Aries; thus the name, Arielle. The one intentional thing my mother gave me—a meaningful name. Meaningful to her, anyway, since she grooved to the zodiac." She sighs. "But don't think I'm not grateful for crumbs. I am."

"At least your mother did one intentional thing for you," says Gemma. "That's something." She walks to the dresser and retrieves a box of tissues. "I can't name anything that wasn't completely random and accidental in my entire upbringing." She blows her nose.

Arielle leans up on her elbow. "When were you born?" she says.

She thinks for a minute. "Uh. June first."

"Well, there you are!" says Arielle. "Gemma is a Gemini! At least if you go by the zodiac the way it was when you were born. Before they invented the new one with that extra sign. But your mother wouldn't have known about the new one."

She's stunned. "Really? Do you think…?" She frowns. "No…"

"I'm sure of it," says Arielle with unmistakable conviction, even through her fatigue. "And Gemini's are twins…" she says as if she is getting at something bigger. *But what?*

"But I'm not," says Gemma. *Wait. What?* "Although…"

"Although what?"

"Although sometimes I feel like two people." She dabs her eyes, pleading. "Please don't tell anyone I said that," she says. "I think they would commit me. I think…I think I have a psychiatrist already. I can't remember his name."

Arielle closes her eyes. "I can't talk anymore," she says. "I'm like you… I don't know who I am anymore."

Gemma's chest heaves with sobs. "I think my problem is bigger than that."

"Whatever it is, we can solve it when we wake up," says Arielle, but Gemma can't tell if it's a brush-off.

"Are you sure?" she says, because if she's not sure, Gemma doesn't know if she can fall asleep.

"Uh huh," Arielle says, folding the pillow over her nodding head.

"And you'll help me?"

From under the pillow she hears a muffled, "Yes."

And this will have to do. Gemma lies down, and before she can climb under the covers, she freefalls into a welcome fog of familiar nothingness.

MIKE

Mike walks purposefully down the dirt path at the monastery with no real purpose at all except to flee from her office and every obligation she can think of. Picking up the mail seems a simple enough goal, something she could actually accomplish even in her present state of confusion.

Her mind is bombarded with questions. Questions about Gemma and that young medic, Eli. What was going on between them? *The heat!* Questions about the inquisitors. Will the monastery be investigated by resident visitors or left alone? She should be hearing any day now. Questions about Constance's health…and Gemma's! About Augusta and her new tonics. You name it. All questions; no answers. The chaos of new birth? She must be the midwife.

Augusta's words from last night still haunt her: *"We must heed the numina, Michael Agnes."* Mike shakes her head. Augusta and her numina—her signs! Mike knows Augusta's history well enough to know that when she makes an announcement of this sort, it's wise to be alert. But to what? Mike was never good at this. She's too concrete.

At the mailbox, Mike wonders at her apparent lack of transcendence. How so many of God's attempts to get her attention have no doubt floated right by until they were utterly beyond her reach. Not that she doesn't believe in divine guidance delivered in the form of visions and spiritual phenomena, of course she does. If we can make our way to heaven, God can certainly make his way to earth. It's why she joined the Most Holy Order of Divine Grace in the first place—the opportunity to witness and participate in the miraculous. But her journey has not been what she expected. And she is willing to admit that she, herself, may be blocking the light.

The truth is, her entire vocation has been spent in search of the same spiritual evidence—*inspirations*—that come so easily to Augusta, so formed. But possibly that is Augusta's singular gift. Not that Mike wants to be the Messenger, not at all. She wants to be herself. She wants to be herself recognizing the Message, that's all. For her, the transcendent world comes alive just beyond the horizon of her own deeply rooted practicality. In other words: *out of reach!* What's the solution? Should she become suddenly impractical and capricious? This is highly unlikely. And anyway, she can hardly throw caution to the wind at this point. Not with the monastery in such, well…chaos.

She retrieves the huge stack of catalogues that Mother has begun collecting thanks to Arielle and her computer skills. Harmless enough, she supposes, as long as they don't start ordering from them. What would they buy?! One can only imagine. But what's this? A small package, dear God, so maybe they have been ordering! Charged on Mother's credit card, Mike supposes—the one she keeps for identification purposes. She inspects the label. But no, this package is addressed to her—to Prioress Michael Agnes of the Most Holy Order of Divine Grace. *Huh.* She'd ordered nothing.

She carries the pile back up the path, turning over this letter—this bill—and that, as she walks. And what's this! A letter to "GEMMA" written by hand in big capital letters! She turns it over. No address or stamp—obviously hand delivered. God, she is just so…powerfully tempted to open it. She grits her teeth, *winces* at the palpable sense of righteousness with which she could *so easily* justify the act. *Gemma is in trouble. She is not herself. I must screen her mail for her own good! Etc.*

"Deliver me from temptation," she prays.

Just then, a long, slippery red and black king snake wiggles from a pile of wet leaves directly in front of her. "Aaaa!" she exclaims, wide-eyed. She studies the ground for more of its kind, but sees none. Are they poisonous? She can't remember. She steps back and waits a few minutes to make sure it's passed.

Continuing, she wonders if the snake was a coincidence or a sign. After all, it can't be taken for granted that it's a sign; it's not obvious. There are probably thousands of snakes on this property. One would certainly be confronted by a snake from time to time, because…they live here! Still. Augusta would not ponder the relevance of this; she would *know!* But Mike is sabotaged by her God-given practical nature. Or is it doubt? Does she doubt God? No, she decides. She does not doubt God. What she doubts is her own imagination.

A few feet from the house she hears the phone ring, followed by Gabriella's unmistakable screech, "Sister Mike! Sister Mike? Are you there?"

Mike debates ignoring the call; playing dead. Maybe it's the hospital calling about Constance. Or Dr. Rawlins about Gemma. Or news of the visitation. Is she really up for any of these? Oh fine. "Coming!" she calls out half-heartedly.

She climbs the porch steps and pushes the screen door open. "I'll pick it up at my desk," she calls out, making a quick right into her office. At the desk she picks up the phone and says, "That will be all, Gabriella; I've got it." And then, "Hello?" She can hear the click on Gabriella's end.

"Sister Michael? Ha! It's a fine day!"

"Kevin?" *Shit.*

"'Tis I," he says. "Sorry I'm late, but I'm on my way."

"Is this a joke, Kevin?" she says. "Because you were supposed to be here two weeks ago! You could have at least called."

"I am calling," he says, "and anyway, better late than never. I've had some trouble with my truck."

"And your phone, Kevin? Has that been broken, too?"

"As a matter of fact…"

"Bring twice as many Hosts with you," Mike interrupts. "You've been short-changing us, not to mention the parishioners."

"I've got as many as I've got," he says. "You're not my only customer."

"As far as I know there's no shortage of unleavened bread in New York State, Kevin. You've got the budget, not I."

"I would remind you that I'm the Pastor," he says.

Mike bristles. "I would remind you of the same," she says. "Although nobody around here would know it."

"Let's not make this personal."

Personal?! Are you kidding? "When will you arrive?" she says.

"Two hours or so, depending on how many goats and cows I have to move off the road."

"That's the dinner hour."

"If you insist!"

Mike hangs up, fuming. She walks to the door and calls out, "Beatrice? Gabriella?"

"In the kitchen, Mike!"

She hustles down the hall, turning left into the galley where Gabriella is husking corn and Beatrice is washing a sink full of greens.

"I'm afraid Father Kevin will be joining us for dinner tonight," she says.

Gabriella adjusts her wire-rimmed glasses. "That's wonderful news," she says.

"I'll make something special," says Bea.

"Don't go out of your way," Mike says peevishly. "The man is two weeks late and a few hundred Hosts short."

Beatrice looks over her shoulder, "Yes, but he is a priest. He deserves our respect."

Mike wants to shake her. "We deserve respect too, Beatrice. It's supposed to work both ways."

Beatrice nods uncertainly, looking to Gabriella who keeps her copper-colored head down, husking.

"By the way," Mike says, "you two can take Rose to visit Constance after dinner. It will do Connie good to see you all."

"Oh goody!" says Gabriella, finally looking up. "But when is she coming home?"

"They're not sure yet. The specialists were being consulted about the pacemaker this afternoon. I'm waiting to hear." Mike looks around. "Where is Rose, anyway?"

"She's uh, dusting the community room I think."

Mike checks her watch. "Watching *Dr. Phil*, you mean?"

No one answers, and anyway, Mike has made her point. She's pretty much given up on Rose's TV addiction, which is another worry when you consider the possible visitation.

While waiting for Kevin, Mike returns to her office and triages the pile of mail. Catalogues to the left; letters to the right. Gemma's letter on top. After staring at the large block letters for a few minutes, she holds it up to the sunlight then turns her desk lamp to its brightest setting and examines the envelope for transparency. She sees nothing. She tests the strength of the seal, which is tight, so any attempt to open it would be obvious. If she opened it and read it, she would have to throw it out. Of course, she could throw it out anyway without reading it, but...*what if it contains anthrax?!* But that's ridiculous and she knows it. *Really?* She places it in her top drawer along with the sketch of Gemma's angel.

With the drawer open, she stares at the sketch for a minute and thinks, *huh*...with all Gemma's troubles, perhaps this would be a good time to validate her miracle; acknowledge her angel. It looks so much like Grace's! For all Mike's skepticism, it could be the real thing. It looks like the real thing! After all, has Gemma even seen the *Chronicles?* Probably not—tucked away as they are in Augusta's trailer. Augusta would never have shown them to Gemma; she hides them from everyone. Unless Gemma found them on her own. But in acknowledging the likeness of the two angels, Mike would also be paying homage to Gemma's obvious artistic gifts. Such an acknowledgement may well be the ticket to drawing her out of the periphery and into the warmth of the fold. It may heal her. It's worth a try.

She decides to present the sketch to the other Sisters in a group meeting. This way she'll expose Gemma's vision at the same time praising her obvious artistic talent. Of course before entering it in the historical *Chronicle of Miraculous Events*, Mike will have to present it to Augusta first. Mike simply does not possess the sort of conviction it would take to record this on her own. *What will she do when Augusta is gone?!* She makes a mental note to schedule a meeting with all the Sisters later in the week, at which time she can also update them on the Investigation.

She turns her attention to the small package addressed to the Prioress, a formality she finds curious. Who would do that? Is it from the Visitator's office? She stabs the thick tape with her letter opener and pulls the flaps open. What's this?! She stares with pleasure. What a surprise! Arielle is a little magician! An iPhone! The card reads, *"With our compliments, Ron McGowan, Upstate Apple."* Ha! She can hardly hide her delight! She hopes the child knows how to program the thing! She spins her chair around to face the portrait. "Welcome to the 21st century, Grace!" she says gaily. "An iPhone! How about that!"

Just before dinner Mike calls Jim Rawlins to preempt a possible dinner interruption, which she would rather avoid with Kevin at the table. In truth, Kevin is like a little old lady when it comes to gossip. He's too curious, and he certainly knows Rawlins' name. Rawlins is one of the few upstate psychiatrists that specialize in the clergy. Kevin has probably been there himself more than once. She dials Rawlins' cell phone, tapping her fingers on the rim of her desk as it rings.

"Dr. Jim Rawlins," he says.

She's surprised to hear his voice. "Oh! Hello Jim," she says, "it's Michael Agnes."

"Mike!" he says. "How are you? So sorry for the delay, but my patient load is a little overwhelming at the moment. You caught me between patients."

"I'll be quick," she says. "Can you provide me with your assessment of the, uh… patient?" She is purposely vague, since she never knows who's waiting outside her door.

He pauses. "I know it would be beneficial for you to understand the full circumstances, but in this case my hands are tied."

"Oh?"

"Sister Gemma won't sign any release forms; I'm sorry. I realize you have your own protocol at the monastery, but in the end I have to honor the doctor/patient confidentiality, no way around it, and she won't release authority to you, or even any information. She's painfully careful about every response. Suspicious, actually, though I can't go so far as to say paranoid."

Mike crosses her legs at the knees, swinging her free foot back and forth as fast as her mind is spinning. "But can you tell me anything at all? I'm dealing with some issues here."

"It's too early to tell what's at the bottom of her...acute circumspection, I suppose you could call it—which is not a diagnosis, just an observation. I don't think her situation necessarily bodes for anything emergent, however, at least not that I could tell. She seemed very much in control, maybe too much. But again, I only saw her once."

Mike clears her throat. "Well, last night at the dinner table she was behaving very strangely, so I just want to make sure..."

"How strangely?"

"She was...I don't know, in another world entirely. Couldn't connect to any of us, and kept cocking her head as if to listen to...whatever she was hearing. I don't know." She searches her memory. "It was just...very strange." And she launches into the whole tedious and terrifying tale of the evening, Constance's heart attack and all.

She can hear Jim shuffling papers. "I can see her on Friday," he offers. "During my lunch hour, how's that?"

"Oh thank you," says Mike. "I'll drive her myself." But she's thinking—*that's three days away!* She can only hope that between now and then, things improve.

As soon as she hangs up with Rawlins there's a knock at her door followed immediately by, "Michael Agnes!" followed by Kevin waltzing in without an invitation.

"It's polite to wait for an answer before you barge into someone's office, Kevin."

He scowls playfully. "You'd think I'd have some wiggle room around here by now."

"Well, you don't," she says, sliding the iPhone into her top drawer and closing it.

He plops down in one of the upholstered armchairs facing her desk.

"Have a seat," she says snidely.

He frowns, pulling on his graying moustache. "You used to be so charming."

She can't tell if he means it. Was she ever charming? Even in her youth? Not really. "I'm sorry," she says anyway. "Things are a little crazy around here."

"I understand you're getting visitors," he says.

"What?"

"From the…," he sketches finger quotes, "Vatican Congregation for Institutes of Consecrated Life, etc. etc."

She drops her head in her hands. "How do you know this, Kevin?"

"Word has it."

She looks up. He's actually grinning. "Why are you grinning?" she asks. "Do you enjoy bearing bad news?"

He shrugs. "Why is it bad news? It's the Vatican's attempt to understand the quality of your life. And just, what you're…I don't know…doing out here." He grins. "What are you doing, anyway?"

She makes a fist and pops it on the desk. "It's not like that at all, Kevin, and you know it. It's the highest form of inquiry in the Church. Do you realize that? Does anybody?" She glares. "Remember the Inquisition?" She's surprised smoke isn't escaping from her nostrils. She had no idea how infuriated she'd become by this investigation. She leans toward him on the desk. "Our fearless patriarchy is also launching a doctrinal inquiry into the Leadership Conference of Women, to which, in case you don't know…we *all* belong."

He shrugs. "God has his reasons."

"God isn't the one investigating us!"

She leans back in her chair trying to temper her dragon breath. "Tell me," she says, "How is it that you know this news before I do?" She folds her arms. "And how is it that you're not being investigated, too? You and the other pastors? Who scrutinizes you?"

"I think you would agree that the priesthood has taken its shots." He runs his fingers through his salt & pepper hair. "Do you think it's easy to be a priest these days? Do you think people look up to us?" He is shaken.

"Probably not," she concedes. "Nevertheless the troubles were brought about by your own kind, not by us."

He rocks back on the hind legs of his chair. "Good will come of it," he says. "You'll see."

She has a wicked wish that his chair would tip over backwards. It would serve him right. But the way he feels entitled to rock back *on her chair* is absolutely maddening. She is about to dismiss it when she realizes she would never allow her own Sisters to get away with such infantile and inconsiderate behavior. "Stop it," she says.

He frowns. "Stop what?"

"Stop rocking my chair, Kevin. On its back legs. It's not a rocking chair. You'll crack your head open or, worse—break my chair."

He lands the chair forward on all fours and throws his hands in the air. "Good thing you're nobody's mother," he says.

This takes her breath away. She raises her back. "That was uncalled for!"

"Oh," he says. "Oh, I, uh...I wasn't referring to anything personal there, I just..."

"You're not allowed to do that," she says. She is so rattled! She takes a moment to center herself. "You're a confessor. You're not allowed to drag the confessed past into any conversation you feel like..."

"Forgive me," he says. He puts his hands up. "Please. I mean it. I'm sorry."

She nods.

"You would have made a great mom," he says.

She waves dismissively. "Enough. I've moved on." She looks down.

"Life really is a can of worms," he says. "No matter whose life it is."

They sit in silence for what seems a long time, and then Mike says, "How do you keep your faith? In the midst of all this...clerical chaos. How do you do it? You don't even have a stable community to nurture your faith. You're all over the place."

He widens his eyes. "Who says I keep my faith?"

"So you don't?"

"Well. Not every day."

"Huh." She nods. "Thanks for being honest."

"It's the least I can do."

She twirls her chair around, her back to him, and stares at Grace's portrait.

"We're soldiers on the front lines," he says. "The enemy is wily."

"Oh really?" she says. "Tell me, Kevin. Who's the enemy?" She turns to face him.

He shrugs. "Good question."

"Sometimes it's you," she says quietly. "Priests and Bishops. My own Church."

At the dinner table, only five of them are seated: Mike, Kevin, Rose, Beatrice and Gabriella. Mike isn't holding her breath for Arielle or Gemma to wake up, since both girls are difficult to explain to Kevin anyway. She's happy to leave them out of it. For instance, to Kevin, Gemma is nothing but an eccentric oddball. And even though Mike knows this is at least partially true, she resents his fast and easy conclusions. The way he simplistically discards people. Gemma is nothing if not hideously complex.

And he's been so absent from the monastery over the summer that he's only seen Arielle from a distance. To him, she's a migratory bird. Mike has done nothing to dispel this misconception, of course, because she doesn't need Kevin carrying stories about her initiates to the Bishop. It's none of his business. And anyway the child may very well be a migratory bird. Mike will keep a careful eye on her, and if need be, help her migrate. She doesn't need empty, one-dimensional advice from a priest or bishop. She's just getting further and further from any sense of belonging whatsoever to the greater patriarchy, and she blames this alienation marginally on Augusta, whose biases are becoming downright forceful. Or maybe they used to be Augusta's biases. Maybe now they're also Mike's.

Kevin pushes his chair back from the table, raises his tall shapeless body and pronounces, "Oremus!" *Let us pray.*

The other women bow their heads, but Mike's remains level. She's feeling protective of her flock. There's a wolf in their midst.

"God in his infinite grace has bestowed bounty upon us," he says. "We thank him for this wonderful dinner, created by his humble servants, Sisters Beatrice, Gabriella, and Rose."

The women grin. Mike just wishes they would desist on the completely undeserved hero worship.

"We ask the Lord to bestow upon these good women and this monastery the full light of his Being, and that they in return will remain his loyal servants through dedicated service to their Bishops and the Bishop of Rome."

"Amen," says everyone but Mike.

He raises his glass. "To the excellent Prioress," he says. "And to Connie's recovery." He sits down and sips from the elaborate crystal wine glass Beatrice and Gabriella save for favored guests, namely him.

Mike notices how his bushy head of once black hair is thinning slightly at the crown. His hair more salt than pepper. He is fading into oblivion as they all are. He was once handsome, she grudgingly admits, maybe still is, minus the widening girth and the pompous flair. She wonders why he became a priest in the first place. She's pretty sure it wasn't with the intention of being exiled as he is, deep into the Adirondack Mountains of New York serving impoverished pockets of humanity. But that could be her own cynicism. After all, this particular assignment provides him with a good bit of freedom. Who really knows what he does all day? He could be gambling at one of the reservations 24-7 for all anybody knows.

As they start digging into the chicken and roasted vegetable lasagna, Arielle slides into the doorway *Risky Busi*ness style dressed in a pair of overalls, her Madonna t-shirt, and those boots. When she spots the Roman collar, she says, "Oops," and after a moment of indecision, bows at the waist. Her hair is flying in every direction, her eyelids still sticky with sleep.

"No need to bow," Mike snaps.

Confused, Arielle's eyes seek out anyone's, and finding no hints of acceptable etiquette, she makes the Sign of the Cross. "In the name of…"

Mike slices her hand through the air. "No."

So Arielle genuflects, and Rose starts to giggle.

"Enough," says Mike. "He's a man, not a demi-god. 'Hello Father' will do."

"Oh come on, Sister," says Kevin, "a little reverence will do my wounded ego some good."

Arielle grimaces. "Should I just…?" she points upstairs. "Or I can eat…" points to the kitchen.

"No," says Mike. "Sit down. Right there in your usual seat where you belong."

The other Sisters take turns cooing and coddling her, "Such a brave girl! Why, she saved Connie's life, Father!"

"So competent!"

"Our girl!"

Arielle slips into her seat. "Shucks," she says.

Mike says, "Father Kevin, you've met Arielle Santos before, have you not?"

"Why yes," he says. "You're the summer resident, I believe. Well, good work on the vegetables. They're delicious." He narrows his eyes in a penetrating stare, as if just now noticing who she resembles.

Arielle nods mechanically as she stands to reach the platter of lasagna at the center of the table. "Glad you like them," she says, "but they're Gemma's creations not mine."

"As you can surmise, we had a couple of emergencies last night," Mike tells Kevin. "You know about Constance, of course, but also Gemma had a fall. That's why she's not here." She looks at Arielle. "I assume she's still asleep?"

Arielle blinks. "Uh…yes?" Her eyes shift left and right and her limbs get jittery.

Does Mike detect rising panic? She sips her chardonnay as her eyes sweep the table, evaluating.

"It won't be long now before Arielle's big celebration, Father!" beams Beatrice, who is dressed in glaring Tahitian colors that blind the eye and accentuate her size. Where does she buy these fabrics? Her unwieldy gray hair is slicked back and secured with what looks to be an entire package of hair pins.

"She's an excellent student!" Beatrice enthuses. "My little catechumen here!" She pats Arielle's hand. "She'll be ready for her sacraments in just a couple of months."

"Oh?" he says. "I didn't realize…" He studies Arielle closely, as if she is a very unlikely possibility for conversion. "What's the meaning of that, uh…tattoo?" he says.

Her hand flies to her neck. "Oops," she says. "I forgot…" She rolls her eyes and stretches her mouth into one of her many comical, unattractive expressions. "I usually wear a bandana right…there?"

"What does it mean to you, though?" Kevin persists. "It's a snake; is it not? Snakes are symbolic…"

"Oh for God's sake, Kevin," says Mike, "she got that tattoo years ago. Is there no redemption?"

He raises his eyes. "Of course there's redemption, Sister, but I'd like to hear from the girl herself. I'd like to know what the snake meant to her when she got it and what it means now in light of her new intentions." He zones back in on Arielle. "If I may?" he says, gesturing with an open palm. "Go on."

Arielle shrugs. "Just …"

"Don't answer him," interrupts Mike. "It's irrelevant." She glares at Kevin. "It's utterly irrelevant and I won't have another minute of this interrogation, is that clear?" She cuts into her lasagna. "This is not a confessional."

He buries his chin in his hand for a minute, stroking his moustache. "What are you so afraid of, Sister?" he finally says. "Do you think the girl can't defend herself?"

"Don't you get it, Kevin?" she says. "She shouldn't have to defend herself!"

Even though Mike's voice is clearly strained, she can hardly believe how much aggression she's actually suppressing, how little of what she's feeling is actually making its way to the surface. She has taken on more ownership of this monastery than she realized. When did it become hers? *Her family.* Not only does she resent Kevin's bombastic persecution, but she resents the interference of the entire Church! What sense does this make? They belong to the Church! *Don't they?!* Nevertheless, she feels like throwing lasagna at the man.

When he doesn't reply, she repeats more calmly, "Why should Arielle have to defend herself at all? She's made her amends." She puts her fork down pointedly. "Why should any of us be placed in such a position of interrogation by an outsider? Someone completely out of context."

He chugs his wine and pours another glass, and in this supremely awkward silence, Mike is suddenly aware of the other Sisters. Shy little Rose with her hands folded, eyes nearly closed. Gabriella's eyes open to the size of quarters, unblinking and fixed on the cuckoo clock on the opposite wall. Beatrice's rosacea blooming scarlet over her entire face as she shovels lasagna robotically into her mouth. Arielle still upright, waiting to serve herself, and shifting her weight back and forth from one foot to the other in a nervous dance. For the first time ever, Mike realizes how much she loves these women, and how much she wants Kevin to get the hell out of their home.

Kevin says, "Okay, answer this, child, 'Why is baptism necessary for the salvation of all men?'" He sits back in the chair and folds his arms defiantly. "I have a right to ask that, do I not, Michael Agnes? If I'm a priest and she's a catechumen?"

Before Mike can answer, Arielle jumps right in, "Baptism is necessary for the salvation of all men because Christ has said: "*'Unless a man be born again of water and the Spirit, he cannot enter into the kingdom of God.'*" She looks around. "And by that I suppose he also means women, because otherwise...," she rolls her eyes, "...why are we even here? I mean, why would you bother to become a nun if there was no chance for salvation to begin with? Why not become a trapeze artist or a talk show host? Something fun?"

She scoops a wedge of lasagna, slides it on her plate and sits down. "Whoever wrote that book should take another look at the pronouns," she says without even looking up. "Just a suggestion."

Mike suppresses a satisfied grin. This girl is made of something unbreakable, she thinks, yet at the same time…something delicate and intangible.

Kevin's whole face puckers-up. "The Book, young lady, was inspired by God and written down by our greatest saints and prophets. It's hardly random."

"Oops," says Arielle with only a hint of apology. "Still, it was written a long time ago when people thought slaves were a good idea too. And harems." She looks around. "Not to upset anybody."

Beatrice tries to signal Arielle into submission with wild sign language, but Arielle is the only one not watching her exaggerated motions.

Kevin clears his throat. "The job of critiquing God's Word is hardly up to a young lady with a serpent wrapped around her neck…"

"Seriously, Kevin?" Mike says, slapping the table. "Don't you dare criticize this young woman. She stayed up the entire night caring for Constance and Gemma. She's entitled to her opinion. And furthermore, she makes an excellent point."

Arielle is so completely unaffected by this conversation as to be almost absent from the room or watching it from a great distance. She is not even looking at anyone. All at once she tears a piece of garlic bread and quotes matter-of-factly, " '*The first shall be last and the last shall be first.*' "

They all turn toward her in unison, including Mike, because not only was it exactly what Mike had been thinking, but because it sounded so…unworldly. Where did that come from?

The girl just continues to eat, unaware of…anything, really, except some undetectable activity out the window. But what? Staring out in the same direction, Mike sees nothing—a blue jay, a cardinal.

Arielle stuffs a giant forkful of lasagna into her mouth and holds up a finger as she forces it down her throat in a miracle of gravity and peristalsis. "May I be excused?" she says through the remains.

Mike narrows her eyes, trying to signal Arielle to stay seated. She wants to force the meaning of *"The last shall be first"* into Kevin's thick egotistical head. Just the idea...!

"I just remembered I have to tell Gemma something very important," Arielle says. "So I have to find her. And she's probably very hungry, too, so please save her some food."

"I thought you said she was upstairs," says Mike.

But Arielle's deep azure eyes convey an ocean of data that Mike is trying very hard to read. She's afraid to ask any more questions and afraid to say no. So she nods, and Arielle darts to the hall and out the door like a greyhound.

After dinner, Kevin is remote. Mike has no idea what or if he'll report her to the Bishop. Right this minute, she doesn't really care, though she might care a lot if it actually came to pass. After all, she's over her head already. Who needs another investigation? Still, Arielle has unwittingly put Mike in touch with a root of evil within her Church that she'd been overlooking for decades. An evil that she'd refused to acknowledge even when Augusta had repeatedly presented it—the evil of exclusion, and not just women. It is so true and real that she cannot deny it any longer. She won't. Within that truth is a strength she hasn't felt in some time.

Kevin walks to the chapel where he hears the women's confessions, except for Mike who refuses. "It's been a while, Sister," he says guardedly. "You've got an investigation coming up. Good time to clean the slate."

"You'll hear my confession when I hear yours," she says, surprising herself.

He scowls. "I see. Well...there's the line in the sand, I suppose."

"There it is," she says.

"And what about Augusta?" He nods toward the trailer.

"You know how it is with her. No."

"I see. Well, I hope she's pure as a child before her God, because at her age…"

"She's pure," says Mike.

She accepts his container of Hosts and accompanies him to his old gray pickup. *Just leave!*

"I'm your confessor," he says. "I could report you both."

"Let me know if you do," she says.

He nods. "Well, good luck then."

"Good luck yourself."

"They're giving me yet another parish in my collection, so…it could be awhile." He jumps in the front seat of his truck.

"Peace, Kevin," she calls after him, meaning it.

His pickup is followed by the station wagon full of Sisters off to the hospital to visit Constance. In the far distance, she spots what looks like Arielle and Gemma on the hill overlooking the river. From here at least, it appears they're sitting companionably. Gemma is dressed in habit, so perhaps all is back to normal, whatever that is.

As Mike turns, she sees a white filmy shape looming over the hill where the girls are sitting. Blood orange light bleeds through the darkening violet sky, forming an aurora that highlights the white film. It is unmistakably *other*. She squints hard into the sun, and sees that the film is taking a familiar shape. It forms into a robed woman whose wild tendrils of curly hair are backlit by streaks of sunset orange. Although she knows it's probably her imagination, for once she's not going to leave it at that. She's going to give Grace a chance to get through to her. "If that's you, Grace," she says, "I'm listening."

ARIELLE

From their high perch on the lower east hill, Arielle and Gemma are lords of all they survey, which is basically the salad patch and the river, or as Arielle thinks of them, her lunch box and swimming hole. To their left, they watch Father Kevin's pickup truck bang its way down the pitted driveway and out the gates to the main road like a clown car. The monastery wagon is next in the caravan, driven nervously by the big, bright, colorful bop. It's the priest that unnerves the bop, Arielle knows; they're not used to men around here. Other than that she's an okay driver.

"The padre is gone," Arielle tells Gemma. "We can go back to the house now."

"I'm not ready," Gemma says, brooding.

Gemma is dressed like half a nun. The tight white head cap is missing, so her flying buttress veil is half-cocked revealing lots of new blonde puppy fuzz on the left side of her head. Arielle thinks of this side as the *brown side,* since it's the side with the hypnotizing cappuccino-colored eye, or maybe more watered-down latte since it's so pale. She wonders if the saint is growing her hair back for good or if she just thought better of taking a razor blade to her head right now. *While she's out of her mind.*

Arielle reaches up to balance the cock-eyed wimple perched so precariously on Gemma's head. "There," she says. "That's better." She tries to dream up an innocent conversation that can possibly expose the

177

identity of the current occupant of this body, or at least the identity of the current spokesperson. You never know who it might be—right when it seems obvious, it's not.

Gemma's shoulders start to tremble, shivering all over, in spite of the warm August breeze and the layers of heavy fabric covering her entire body, except for her feet which are bare and beat up from whatever. From walking on burning charcoal probably, or standing ankle deep in a tub of blood-sucking scorpions. One or the other. They're worse than Augusta's feet almost, except that the relic only has two toenails. The relic is like a little key ring troll doll and just the thought of her makes Arielle happy.

Arielle puts her arm around Gemma's shoulders. "It'll be alright," she says, although she has no idea how.

"How do YOU know?" Gemma says.

She says it in a kind of a put-downy way that sounds to Arielle like it could be the saint talking, so maybe it is. Or maybe it's a cranky five-year-old Maya, hard to tell, which brings up a good point. If Maya's just showing up now, how does anyone know what her mental age is? Should they even be listening to her? She could be thirty-two or two. Or twelve, if you go by her crush on Eli. Arielle just stares ahead thinking every which way. She's on a scavenger hunt with some pretty bad clues.

"How do you know it'll be alright?" the sort-of-saint repeats in an irritated manner. "I want to know. It doesn't FEEL alright." Her mouth moves all over the place when she talks as if she's just learning how to move her lips around the words.

"I just know," Arielle lies. "And anyway, why don't you want to go back to the house? Is there some place you'd rather be?" *In the chapel on your knees, Gemma? Or the back seat of a car, Maya?*

"I'd rather be …out there," she says, drawing a long line in the air from the river to points east. "I would go out there and LIVE!" she says, spitting the words into the air like olive pits. "Live my LIFE!" She picks a long piece of timothy grass and runs it through her fingers slowly, as if this too is something she is doing for the first time. "When I got OUT

THERE, I would do whatever I want. Whatever feels GOOD," she says.

"Like what?" says Arielle. "Because there's a long list of things that feel good for about five minutes and torture you for the rest of your life."

"How do YOU know?" she says.

"Because I've tried pretty much all of it," says Arielle. "So I don't really recommend the try-everything-approach if you can help it. It can land you in a jail cell or a cemetery just when you're expecting a parade in your honor. You have to choose carefully. To DISCERN," she says real loud just to copycat. Why not? It might get through to her.

"YOU seem happy. YOU must have had a good life so far."

"I've had less a life and more of a hallucination," says Arielle.

"But you've been FREE!"

"Freedom's just another word for whatever," Arielle says. "For screwing around so you don't do what you're supposed to do. What you came here to do." She pats the earth. "That's why I love this place right here. It's solid; can't get up and leave you. Can't walk away."

Gemma or Maya—*Gemmaya*— lifts her chin like the Queen of Everything, and in the radiant light of the gooey lava-lamp sunset, looks kind of noble like she has a big fat purpose in life. As if the only thing missing is a big operatic soundtrack building behind her like Julie Andrews in *The Sound of Music*. *"The hills are alive!!!"* Sitting there like that, Gemmaya could be anyone. Cleopatra. Beyonce.

"I need to LEAVE," Gemmaya says.

"Where do you want to go?"

"A FAIR maybe, or a CARNIVAL," she says. She stares out at the vast field that had been single-handedly planted by a more constipated version of herself. Arielle wonders if the saint even remembers planting that field. Wonders how much of Gemma is still in there getting snuffed out by her carnival-seeking twin. Knock, knock. *Who's there?* Gemma.

Gemma who?

"Do you remember planting that whole field by yourself?" Arielle says. Maybe this'll wake her up. "Every single seed of salad was laid down by you and buried in a little purse of soil."

Gemma rips the long blade of grass lengthwise. "Sort of. But it's not salad. It's cucumbers, kale, spinach, romaine, Boston lettuce, radicchio." She's calmer now, so the salad field conversation seems to have opened the hatch and lugged Gemma up the basement stairs.

"You remember the names of all those seeds, but you only *sort of* remember planting it?" Arielle says. "Don't you think that's...odd?"

"Well. I know I planted that garden, and I know what's in it. I just can't completely connect to the act of doing it. Of bending over and placing the seeds in the ground. To the actual work. I can't *feel* it. It's as if I were watching myself do it." She shrugs, picking a dandelion on her blue side. "Just like I know how to dress in the habit, but..."

And just like that she throws her hands in the air and lays back on the hill with her knees still bent, shaking her bitten-up, acid-washed feet in a little fairy dance. "I need to LIVE, Arielle! Can't you understand that? To feel the wind on my FACE!"

Then in another amazing switch she sits bolt upright, stares at Arielle with both colors—the brown and the blue—her eyes boring into Arielle's sinus cavity and back out the other side of her head. "I need to get OUT OF HERE, but I don't even know how to DRIVE. I need you to take me somewhere FUN. A carnival or a ZOO."

"A zoo? Really?" *We're in ONE!*

Or BOWLING."

Arielle shrugs. "Huh. I could go for some pins; I used to be pretty fierce at it. And there's an alley right behind the mall."

"You and ELI," says Gemmaya. "And Jesse if you want company for yourself."

"Um..."

Gemmaya nods, laughing.

Laughing?! Arielle has never seen or heard a laugh out of that mouth.

"I LOOOOVE him," she says hugging herself.

"What?!"

"Yes, why NOT? He's HEAVENLY!"

Arielle has to get this conversation under control before they run into Mike or just anybody. She has to appeal to the saint in this mythical creature, because at least the saint doesn't want to run away with Eli or double-date with the loser. The saint would perform a swan dive off a camel into a bucket of cement before she'd do either one of those things.

"I think it's time for Vespers, Gemma," Arielle says. "Prayers? GEMMA? GOD—remember him?"

"Vespers can wait," she says as she grips Arielle with her scratchy, blistered farmer's hands.

"But you always say your Vesper prayers exactly at…"

"I know. I know." She gets all in Arielle's face. "It's ME, Arielle, GEMMA." Her eyes nearly pop out of her head. "I swear!"

Uh. *I don't think so.*

"You were right last night. Now that I've had enough sleep it's clearer—what I have to do."

Wait. This actually sounds like Gemma. "It's clear?"

"Yes," she says. "I have to give in; surrender to the inevitable. My whole life has been spent keeping it at bay. My entire, ENTIRE life!" She spreads her arms at the sky, drops her head back. "If I let her go…let my tormentor have her way…I'll be free too, don't you see?"

Arielle is a big ole bass on the hook of this explanation reeled right into the trawler and ready to be filleted when all at once Gemma stands up and flaps her arms in the breeze, tears off her buttress and removes a whole bunch of clothes until she is sleeveless and spinning around in the same sheer ankle-length gown she wouldn't be caught dead in this morning.

"Wheeeee!" she yells into the wind, which catches her glee and gives it a good long ride. "Wheeee!" She stares down into Arielle's face, grinning, laughing.

Her insanity is a little contagious, Arielle has to admit. After all, Arielle herself has been known to do about anything for a good laugh. Why not? And she wouldn't mind going a little nutzo right about now either—just let go and celebrate the freedom of it all, but.

"Just for the record," Arielle says, "who exactly are you letting go OF?" She narrows her eyes, trying to reach…in. "Who? Exactly? So we both 100% understand what we're doing here. WHO exactly are you…RELEASING?"

Gemma's face lights up like a 3-way bulb against the rising moon, her one blue eye flaring brightly like the center of a gas flame. "Maya," she says sane as a CPA. "But just for a day. One single solitary day. That's it." She bends down and stares at Arielle nose-to-nose, eyeball-to-eyeball. "Maya for one day. Deal?"

Arielle thinks for a minute. This could work. "Deal," she says, nodding.

"24 hours and no more, is that clear?"

Arielle nods. "Any 24 hours in particular?"

Gemma digs deep into her brain, all thoughtful. "At the full moon. Ready or not. If I don't want to go, just shake the daylights out of me. Ok? You're the only one I can trust to do this. There might be resistance but we have to go through with it. I'm serious. I have to release this sycophant." She grabs at her heart. "She's killing me."

"Full moon's in three days, roger that."

"And I don't care if you have to put me in jail after that to keep me confined, understood? Don't let it go any further than that. 24 hours off-road. That's it. Drag me back if you have to. Commit me. I don't care."

"It's a risk," says Arielle.

"I'm releasing her, not checking her in."

"Okay. But your rival is very…"

"We have to have faith," she says, and sets her jaw tight.

They hear their names being called from a distance, and turn together in the direction of the house. Atop the main hill Mike's long figure looms in the dark like the headless horseman. Her arms are folded and she's watching them from her headless head. She might have witnessed the disrobing, not to mention the witch dance, hard to tell. In spite of the nearly full moon, it's getting darker by the second. Is it Halloween yet? It feels like it. This day is a vampire.

Gemmaya collects her various garments from the ground and brushes them off, saying, "Promise me."

"I promise, but you better crawl back into your habit fast," Arielle says, as she waves to the horseman. "If she catches wind of these plans, you can forget about ever taking your final vows."

"I have to take my vows," she says. "I'm a nun. That's my entire purpose in life."

"Then get some control over the escapee. Just a suggestion."

By the time they reach the top of the hill, the saint is back in her habit and still in charge if you can believe what you see. Arielle is trying to just go with the whacky riptide without getting sucked under and dragged out to the middle of Transylvania.

They follow Mike into the house where she hands Arielle a pile of catalogues, "I believe you ordered these?" she says.

Arielle grins angelically. *Where's the halo?* "The relic...I mean, the herm...Mother, um....Augusta likes to read magazines, so."

Mike closes her big hooded gray eyes and opens them slowly like a lizard, her eyebrows raised high. She might be amused, but on the other hand, who knows. She's hard to read.

"Uh huh," she says. "Well, just don't order anything, understand?"

Arielle bobbles her head in a googly-eyed clown nod that would give the relic a conniption, but not Mike. Arielle is so drained she can't figure out who's who anymore—who gets the googly-eyed clown nod and who doesn't.

Mike tells her to run over to the trailer real quick with the catalogues and some lasagna. "Mother hasn't eaten," she says. "She was napping at the dinner hour." Then she puts her arm around Gemma and escorts her into the office for a chat.

Because she doesn't really trust the twins with Mike, Arielle is on five alarm alert. While she's waiting in the hall to hear whatever, she jerks through the *Hammacher Schlemmer* catalogue, staring absently at some new ocean vessel rocket ship gizmo which she thinks the relic would enjoy driving around the monastery, but her attention is really tuned to the office.

"Are you feeling more at, uh, peace?" she hears Mike say, choosing her words like chess moves.

"Yes, Sister, I am," says what seems to Arielle like a kinder version of Gemma. Or maybe a more formal version of Maya, either way. Maya has definitely humanized the saint, that's for sure. Enough to get her pregnant, maybe. Not that she is. And not that a pregnancy would be funny, but. At some point you have to face facts.

"That's good, Gemma," says Mike. "Very good. Excellent. More at peace. Good. So. Let's see how it goes for the next few days, shall we? See if you can get your footing again, how's that? Make sure there's no residual injury to the brain from your fall, hmmm?" She pauses. "Then we'll go to Dr. Rawlins' office together on Friday for a quick check on the situation."

Arielle's brain alarm sounds off. *Friday?* Isn't that the day of Maya's big debut?

Arielle must have mistakenly gasped out loud, because she hears Mike's footsteps solidly hitting the oak floor of her office in rapid succession. Thud, thud, thud. Arielle creeps on her tiptoes as fast as she can down the hall and slips into the galley just as the office door slams. She just hopes that when the twins report back, they get the story straight. She has no idea which one to trust.

After all, it's not as if Arielle isn't taking any risks herself. She is. Big giant homeless ones. For instance—what if Maya runs away with Eli? *What if she really does get pregnant?!* For all Arielle knows Mike would nail Arielle's scrawny googly-eyed head on a pole in the pumpkin patch if she found out she'd been an accessory to such a thing. Red hair flying everywhere in the wind; she can see it now. Yanked out of her scalp one-by-one by a herd of magpies. *For nests!*

Well, luckily for her, the pumpkin patch is right in front of the relic's trailer, and the relic would never stand for that. The relic is her BFF!

This little story about the relic rescuing her from attacking magpies makes Arielle all glowy inside, and she dances all the way to the trailer with an epic soundtrack rising up behind and above her, *"The hills are alive…!"* She loves the relic! Sometimes she can't even stand how much she loves her! "Relic! Relic! Relic!" she chirps with the tree frog chorus. "Relic!"

She flies up the cement block steps, opens the door, and moon dances backwards right into the living room like Michael Jackson before he died. The relic is wide awake in her chair, stroking Assisi, and so happy to see her that Arielle feels like moving right in. Just playing hooky on Maya's little debut at the bowling alley—all of it! Just letting them all figure life out for themselves. Just moving right into the trailer for good. Forever! Who needs the grief when life can be so sweet!

"You just sit there in your big old chair, G-ma," she says, "and I'll warm this lasagna up for you on the stove and feed it to you spoonful by spoonful! JK—you don't need to be spoon-fed! But if you did…!" She twirls around with the dish. "And I'll massage your gnarly toes!" She lays the casserole dish and the catalogues on the counter before she drops them. She knows her limits.

The relic scoots Assisi from her lap. She pushes her tugboat body up off the chair with her rickety arms and moves herself slowly out of her nest. Slooooow—ly. Her sunken blue eyes glow in her raisin face like little chunks of uranium. She shuffles along on her slidey little boiled wool slippers, *shuffle shuffle shuffle*, right over to Arielle, wraps her decrepit little arms around her and weeping with joy, says, "Gracie, Gracie, Gracie. How I've missed you!" Her chest rattles with grief as she weeps and weeps, gripping Arielle's sleeves. "I've been heartbroken without you…" she wails. "I can't believe you're back. You're really back."

The relic isn't the only one who's heartbroken now. Arielle is too. Plus she's frozen. The blood is clotted in her veins; nothing is moving anywhere, up or down. Did the body snatcher snatch the relic, too? Is this an epidemic? It can't be happening. Maybe it isn't. Maybe she misunderstood. "I'm Arielle," she says, trying to keep the bubble of despair from popping in her throat.

Oh so gently she moves the relic back to arms-length, leans down, and stares into her ancient eyes. "It's me, Little Mama," she says softly.

"Arielle, remember? Your angel?" She halfheartedly rolls her googly eyes and sticks out her tongue sideways to shock her into recognition. *Remember me? The loopy girl? Ha ha ha!* "It's me," she says, "see?"

The relic just looks. She blinks, focusing, then runs her bent chicken-scratch fingers slowly down Arielle's cheek. "Arielle," she says softly.

Arielle wipes the tears from the relic's cheek with her hand then wipes her own. "Yes," she says gratefully. "Arielle."

"Not Grace?"

"No." But is the relic disappointed? Arielle couldn't bear to disappoint her. If the relic wants her to be Grace, she'll be Grace. Whatever. Who cares? She'll be a horn toad for the relic. *Shrek!* The important thing is the relic's happiness.

Arielle glances at the counter, judging the distance, then steps over a bit and leans to collect the catalogues. "Remember these? All these crazy catalogues you wanted?" *Please remember!*

Augusta blinks and looks up at Arielle smiling, "What shall we buy?"

Arielle grins. "We can look at aaaallll the pictures, but…"

"But what, dear?" She selects three catalogues and turns, shuffling back to her corner.

"Nothing. We can buy whatever you want," Arielle says because she loves her little mama too much to deny her anything. She'll get the loser to pay for it if she has to. She'll marry him if he agrees to take care of the relic. She'll figure something out. She's resourceful.

Augusta arrives at her armchair, turns around slowly, and says, "We can do whatever we want, Arielle. No one can stop us but God."

This remark does not give Arielle any confidence. After all, God can stop or start anything he wants—an army or an earthquake. He can raise you up or do you in. If you want anyone on your side, it's God.

When the relic is settled back into headquarters, she says, "They'll cancel my credit card unless I charge something once a year, you know." She licks her index finger and turns the page.

Arielle dials the oven temperature to 350 degrees. She opens the door to remove the big pile of pots and pans the relic hides in the oven. She's happy to be doing this one useful thing—heating up the lasagna.

She's good at heating things up. But everything else in this long bloodsucking day is confusing. For instance, does the relic even have a credit card? And if so, why? Has she ever used it? What did she buy?

"I bought a wind chime," says the relic matter-of-factly as she turns another page.

Bent over with her head in the oven, Arielle says, "What?!" *Was I talking out loud?*

"I bought a wind chime," she repeats. "It's out back I think. I haven't seen it in a while, though. You just reminded me of it. It's made of little blue and green shells. It's lovely!"

Arielle closes the oven door on the lasagna and decides to test this out—think up another question in her head and see if the relic answers. Then she'll know if it was a coincidence or not. Ok, here goes—*I wonder if Little Mama took her medication yet?*

She waits. Nothing. The relic is transfixed by the amphibious moon vessel in *Hammacher Schlemmer*. Arielle knew she would like it.

"I like this doo-hickey," says the relic. "We could escape in it when the troubles come." Then a minute later, "It might be a little pricey though."

Arielle just stands there, relieved. Phew! No mass alien possession of the monastery. The relic can't read her mind.

"By the way, I haven't taken my medication," she says. "Sorry. I didn't mean to get distracted."

"What!"

She looks up at Arielle. "I haven't taken it yet. Can you fetch my pills?"

Arielle jumps, edgy, floating around in her head like a good ganja-high just when she needs her brains in order. "How did you know what I was thinking?" she says.

The relic flips to the next page in the catalogue. "What, dear? Oh. Well, it's the Timeline Tea. I had to make it myself. I was told what to do, of course, but it wasn't easy." She brings the catalogue right to her face. "I can't read the price on this music box," she says, "but I think I'd like one. It says 'iPod', is that right? What's an iPod?"

Arielle says, "Timeline Tea?"

"Yes," she says. "Timeline. I can't remember everything at the moment, but I know there was some mint in it, and I'll think of the rest later on. You can write it down for me, how's that? I was wishing for your company very hard, but you didn't come. Constance needed you more. I hate to admit it, but it made me a little angry at Constance. She can be so demanding."

"Um, she had a heart attack?" says Arielle, because maybe the relic wasn't told.

"Yes," says Augusta, turning pages. "So dramatic."

Arielle chuckles. "So Timeline Tea makes you psychic?!" she asks, because they might as well move on.

Augusta dog-ears two pages, closes the catalogue, and looks up. "Not exactly, no. It helps you jump timelines. Then you know what's happening before everyone else, because you've already seen it. Not that you jump timelines to become psychic; you don't. It's a side effect."

It sounds tempting, but Arielle doesn't know if she wants any part of it. Could she handle the future? Another timeline? Her heart is already an ocean in a thimble for this woman. What if she knew when the relic would die? No. She can keep her Timeline Tea.

While the relic eats her dinner, she tells Arielle all about Grace. How much she loved her. How in Gracie's old age, the young relic took care of her, stayed with her. Never left her side.

Arielle sits at the relic's feet with her head against the chair cushion. "I don't want to leave you, either," she says.

And the relic strokes Arielle's hair with her chicken scratch fingers. "I know, dear," she says. "I remember how it was. You're Gracie's thank you gift. She sent you to me. I don't know how to leave you, either."

This talk is drowning Arielle, suffocating her, so she drops the conversation and instead of asking out loud, decides to play the thinking game again. Mama? If you're listening, I need some special tea for Gemma.

"You certainly do, dear," says the relic. "I've got just the thing," and she rattles off a list of herbs, oils, and flower petals that has Arielle flying all over the trailer and out back to the herb garden for half an hour.

She packages all the ingredients up in a plastic bag and zips it. "How long do I steep it?" she says.

"Twenty minutes," says the relic. "It's called Convergence..." She opens her hands, palms up. "All things will converge in God's holy wisdom. That's the message."

Arielle grabs a marker from the drawer and scribbles the name on the bag—*Convergence Tea.*

"Give it to her tonight if you can. To give her control," says the relic, her right ear turned up to the ceiling as if listening to a hovering voice. "And then three times a day until her chore is finished."

She directs Arielle to open a secret door in the bedroom bench and pull out several picture albums and one very large leather-bound gold-etched book marked *Chronicle of Miraculous Events—Most Holy Order of Divine Grace.* Arielle brings them to her.

"I want to show you pictures of Grace," she says. "You won't believe it. She could be your mother. She could be you!"

"But she's not," says Arielle.

The relic looks up. "No of course not, dear. You're you."

"And you're you," Arielle says grinning.

Augusta takes a minute to turn the heavy page of the *Chronicles* and Arielle says all bug-eyed, "What's that?"

"Why, that's Grace's angel," the relic says. "The angel that saved her life. Isn't he lovely? He's the agent of her miracles. He heralds her presence. When the angel is around, so is Grace."

"How...who..." Arielle is stunned by the resemblance. "Who drew it for her?" Because it doesn't just look like Arielle's angel...it looks like the same drawing! Not the same paper, of course—this paper is old, yellowed—but the same black sketchy lines. As if the same person drew it.

Augusta looks meaningfully into Arielle's eyes. "No one, dear. She drew it herself. Gracie was a very gifted artist."

Arielle gulps. *That's my angel,* she thinks before she can take it back.

"Yes it is, dear," says the relic. "Yes it is. You may not be Grace, Arielle, but Grace is you."

GEMMA

Gemma treads barefoot in a fairy forest along a winding fairy river lit by a glistening fairy sun. Everything is light and effortless except Gemma, who is heavy and weighed down by gravity. The wrens and warblers, dragonflies, frogs, willows—every living thing is embodied by the glistening sun, and every little thing—the mud and the river rocks—is alive. The sun is not a distant flaming orb like the sun she remembers from the lower world. Up here all matter is made from the radiant orb that illuminates its being. Everywhere she looks, there is light and lightness. The only shadow in the entire forest is cast by her.

She slogs along in dark heavy robes with her oppressive leaden headpiece, thinking she will shed this artifice when she arrives at the horizon which is so far away. One eternally long step after another she goes on forever unable to close the gap. She longs to join the light, to bury her shadow, but the process is never-ending. How will she manage? She hasn't got the patience or the focus to accomplish this task. She is sinking fast into the world of her lower nature when all at once she notices that she is not alone. Someone is with her.

Who are you?

She turns slowly to her right to face the animated companion who is skipping effortlessly beside her. "What's your name?" she asks, and the companion says, "I am Myself."

Myself is truly beautiful, and Gemma can't take her eyes off her.

Her translucent blonde hair sparkles with the sun that gives it form. It lifts in the wind like garlands as she skips along the sparkling path in a lacy white dress that bounces like a petticoat at her knees. Myself is so happy! She plucks a pink hibiscus blossom from a nearby tree and places it in Gemma's hair. The fragrance is delicate but powerful and carries a secret message. It permeates Gemma's nostrils like her mother's perfume. What is it trying to tell her?

"You won't be sorry," says Myself. "When you free me, you'll free us both."

Gemma doesn't understand Myself at the same time she understands her completely. She plucks a blossom of her own and hands it to her companion as a sign of loyalty and cooperation. *I will work with you on this. I won't let you down!*

Before Myself can accept the blossom, Gemma feels her other arm being pushed and shoved. She wants Myself to take the blossom, but this requires Gemma's complete concentration, and because of the pushing and shoving, she can't focus one bit. All she can think is, *Myself must accept the flower before I go! Take it!*

"Please take it!" she says.

She wants to hear Myself's response to her peace offering, but instead all she hears is, "Gemma, Gemma, wake up! Wake up!"

She tries to keep her eyes closed, but she can't. They pop open, startled, "What? What!" she hears herself saying in a shrill, foreign voice.

What she sees before her is Arielle sitting in the lower world on the edge of the bed with a steaming hot cup in her hand. "Sit up," she says. "Drink this."

"What? No. I don't want to." She wants to dive back into her dream before it vanishes. She wants to hear what Myself has to say. It's important! What if Myself doesn't accept the blossom? What then?

"You have to drink it," Arielle says. "Now."

"No. Go away." She swats the air. Maybe she's still in her dream, she thinks hopefully. Maybe this is part of it.

"Mother Augusta made this tea especially for you," Arielle says. "I'm not kidding. I wouldn't kid about this. Wake up."

She keeps trying to hand the cup off to Gemma, but Gemma won't take it—or can't. Her arms aren't strong; they're made of rubber. They bend and flop.

To Gemma, Arielle's ensuing stream of words sounds like a running faucet. It's impossible to identify one word from the next, just...*woooooosh,* until suddenly one word is clear: *Mother.*

"Mother?" she says as she slowly pushes herself to a sitting position supporting her back against the wall. "Mother Augusta?" The moon floods the room like a searchlight. Like fairy light. She rubs the sleep from her eyes.

"Yes, Mother Augusta..." says Arielle, pushing the cup toward Gemma. "Here. Drink it now. She wants you to drink this stuff three times a day until Friday. You're very lucky she even bothered."

Gemma wraps her hands around the warm cup and inhales the fragrant aroma. *Hibiscus!* She buries her face in the rising steam. And ginger, she thinks. "Hibiscus and ginger," she says softly.

"Bingo," says Arielle.

She sips the heavenly nectar. "And honey."

"Bing bing bing!" says Arielle. She shakes her head. "There's more in this brew than any of the others. It was the hardest to make so far."

"Others? There are others?" The hot life-giving liquid winds its way down her throat and into her belly like the fairy river.

Arielle nods. "The hermit has a recipe for everything. You name it. She could cure a war if she wanted to."

Gemma pulls her knees up to her chest and holds the warm cup on top of them. It still feels like a dream. "Why me?" she says. "What's the purpose of my recipe?"

"Um." Arielle fidgets around, flicking her fingers and readjusting her position. "I don't know. Just drink it."

"You must know something. You're over there all the time. You practically live with her!"

"To help you think better, I guess. To focus." She sighs. "I don't really know the whole story. She doesn't tell me everything."

"Mother knows everything, though, right?"

"I guess so."

"Well then, why me? What made her think of me? Why not you? Did she make a special tea for you?"

Arielle piles her three-alarm hair on her head and lets it drop. "What happens is…the hermit gets a picture of somebody who needs her help and starts flinging out the ingredients for the exact right concoction that will help them." She shrugs. "That's about it, but don't tell anybody."

Gemma can't help smiling. She knows something about the hermit that almost nobody else knows. But just to be sure she says, "Nobody else knows?"

"No one."

"Why you? Why do you know? Why not Rose, for instance? She's simple and pure. Or Mike with all her force and intelligence?" Arielle hasn't been here very long; Gemma truly wants to understand the special treatment.

"Somebody has to help her, I guess," Arielle says. "Somebody has to keep up her herb garden and run around collecting the ingredients and writing them down. No big deal."

To Gemma it's a very big deal, however, not that she wants to get caught up in the insane jealousy of it all; she doesn't. She wants to be as free as Myself. "Does Mother know about our uh…plan?" she asks.

Arielle looks surprised. Maybe she doesn't remember the plan or…maybe Gemma never told her? *Is there a plan?*

"I wasn't sure you'd remember," Arielle says. "I thought you'd…"

"Well of course I remember. We just planned it tonight."

Arielle backs into the blinding moonlight, and Gemma can only see her outline. It's unnerving. Where did she go? *Is she still in the dream?* It somehow fits—this tea made by the hermit—*the fairy hermit!* She slugs the tea down as commanded then places the cup and saucer on the end table. Arielle is still out of view. "Where are you?!" Gemma calls out in a panic.

"Right here," says Arielle. Just throwing on my pj's; I'm beat."

"I'm still a nun," says Gemma, although she doesn't know why she says it. "Right? I'm not a whore like my mother?"

At that her eyes close and her head swirls back against the pillows. The rattling of drawers is drowned out by a river of fairy light that sucks her back to the upper world. Out of the light appears Myself in white eyelet lace with her hands extended saying, "I accept your hibiscus, Gemma. Thank you. You won't be sorry."

When Gemma awakens she is more herself and less whoever has been vying for her body and mind. Right at the moment she can't even remember who that is; she doesn't want to. It's about time. She slept through Matins, but blames that on the tea. Not that she minds; she doesn't. The tea gave her more focus in the upper world and helped her concentrate on Myself long enough to get an answer. Myself accepted the flower—the agreement. That feels so significant! The tea is pure magic.

She jumps out of bed at the first light to recite today's Laudes. She walks to the window, bows to her Lord in gratitude for the day he is creating out of nothing at all. Out of air. Out of light! For just a second she watches Henry wind down the hill and over the rocks, gurgling with life. She squints at what appears to be a large white bird—an ibis?—perched atop its long stick legs on the lower west bank. Praise God!

She lifts her arms and opens her palms. "Blessed be God," she says in an appropriately raised voice. *So he'll hear her!* "Blessed be His Holy Name."

She continues in spite of the fact that the little infidel roommate has covered her head with her pillow. "Blessed be the Name of Jesus..." It feels good to be herself again. To honor God. She continues with her praises and ends with the *Magnificat: "Oh sing unto the Lord a new song; for He hath done marvelous things..."*

When she's finished, she goes to her wardrobe and selects her garments, draping each piece carefully over her left arm. Before adding each one, she genuflects and recites an exclamatory prayer, "*Jesus, imbue me with your grace!"* Thank God she recognizes the pieces, remembers their names! She is a nun again! She is something, not nothing. As she lays the cap, wimple and veil on the bed, she glances at herself in the mirror and is taken aback. Where is her hair?! She reaches up and touches the half-inch long golden down, so soft, and forces herself to remember the shaving. Goads herself—*Remember it!* She cannot.

"Hey," grumbles her roommate from under her pillow. "How you feeling after that tea last night?"

"How I'm feeling is—why don't I have any hair?"

"Oh! So." Arielle slides the pillow off her head. "Still disoriented?"

"Well, I wasn't but, yes, if that means I don't know why I have no hair."

"Don't worry about it," Arielle says. "Hair grows."

Gemma pulls on the ends trying to piece herself back together—imagining what she would look like with simple chin length hair, something modest, not elaborate. It's not as if she wants to be in a shampoo commercial. "But did they cut it in the hospital?" she asks.

"Uh, no? You mowed that scalp all by yourself, farmer."

Gemma stares in Arielle's direction. "But why?"

"Sacrificial offering maybe?" She rolls onto her back and kicks off the blanket.

Sacrifice actually makes sense to Gemma, because nuns are humble creatures or at least should be. "Spiritual poverty," she says. "Is that what you mean? An attempt to banish vanity?"

Arielle struggles to a sitting position and rubs her eyes. "News flash, roommate—if you were trying to banish vanity, the first things to go would be the cat's eyes. They're insanely huge. Not to mention two completely different colors from different palettes on different planets. Which might be illegal, I don't know. They could melt an iceberg if you actually used them."

"Is that a joke?"

"Not that I'm making any suggestions. I don't want to be blamed for any eye gouging."

Gemma doesn't know what Arielle's talking about...*melt an*

iceberg? Her eyes are hideous. The different colors are completely bizarre, not to mention the source of much bullying and shame in her younger years. Is Arielle saying they're attractive? Is she crazy? *They're not.* Arielle's wrong.

She places the cap on her head and pulls it taut. It pushes her forehead down and her cheeks forward. "This is tight," she says.

"Yeah, I don't know how you stand it." Arielle rubs her neck, spreading her wild head of hair, and groans while she stretches her arms and back. She's a tiny thing—completely lost in the blue-and-white-striped pajamas she bought with Beatrice at the Glens Falls Walmart. It's funny, Gemma thinks, how she can remember random details about Arielle's pajamas, but not other, more personal details like why she herself has no hair.

"Why don't you wear it?" Gemma says.

"Wear what?"

"This," she says pointing to the cap. "Or any of it."

"I'm not even baptized," she says. "I have a free pass."

Gemma tries to draw all the threads of lost memory into focus. "But will you?" she says. "Will you wear it after you're baptized? After you make your temporary vows?" Can someone please tell her why this girl is even here?!

Arielle yawns and shakes her head. "Not really sure that getup was designed with me in mind, but. Maybe?" She leans over and touches her toes, bends deep at the knees. "Never say never is my motto!"

"I'm Gemma," she says uncertainly.

Arielle juts her head forward quizzically. "Huh?"

"No, I mean…I am," Gemma says. "Just in case you wondered, because I would understand if you did…wonder."

"Yeah?"

She nods. "I'm more Gemma than I was yesterday, but on the whole…less."

Arielle grins. "Hold on Gemma-more-or-less. I'll throw on some clothes and we can grab breakfast."

"Chapel first," she says.

"Yes! More Gemma than yesterday for sure. Yesterday's Gemma hardly knew what a chapel was."

"But I'm not myself yet," she says. "Not completely."

Arielle throws her green gingham dress over her head and pushes her way into her boots. "Nobody is," she says. "That little job takes a lifetime."

Before chapel Arielle brews Gemma another cup of Mother's tea. She knows the tea has a name, but Arielle won't tell her what it is. At least not yet. At first Gemma is afraid that the tea will make her fall asleep again, but as they head for the chapel she's actually feeling more vibrant, more energized and assimilated. More herself.

As far as she can tell, the only difference in the pre- and post-fall Gemma is the fact that the post-fall Gemma wants to grow her hair. At least she thinks she does. Not that she remembers everything about the pre-fall Gemma. She doesn't know what she doesn't know. But she feels less afraid than yesterday to learn the details. Like why are her feet so beaten up? What is this irritation around her midriff? Why the scabs on her knees? Is it from farm work or—what? She vaguely remembers the doctors drawing the farm work conclusion. But somehow for Gemma it's more like...*or what.*

Except for Constance who is still in the hospital, the Sisters stand together in the front row of the chapel. Gemma plays it cool, but can't help wondering why she's the only one dressed in the habit. Is it because it's so clammy out? Do the others wear the habit in the cooler months? *Why am I torturing myself—I'm so hot!* Is she called by God to suffer? Maybe that's it; she wouldn't be the first. She doesn't want to let on to the others that there are things she's forgotten. She realizes it could be amnesia, but it doesn't feel like amnesia. It feels like the space between two repelling magnetic poles forcing something to the surface. But she doesn't know what. She tries to escape the polar force long enough to focus on Mike's reading of today's Gospel.

"'...*Don't ever let anyone call you Rabbi, for you have only one* teacher,'" Mike reads. "'...*and all of you are on the same level as brothers and sisters. And don't address anyone here on earth as Father...*'"

Mike hesitates here, clears her throat. She looks out at her congregation as if she's seeing them for the first time. Gemma wonders what's wrong. Maybe everybody's lost, she thinks. Maybe I'm not the only one.

Mike continues, "'...*for only God in heaven is your spiritual Father. And don't let anyone call you Master, for there is only one Master, the Messiah. The greatest among you must be a servant. But those who exalt themselves will be humbled and those who humble themselves will be exalted.*'"

She stands at the lectern for a minute, collecting herself from what seems like every corner of the room. Finally she says to the congregation of about twenty people, "I think this Gospel speaks for itself, don't you? We are all equal in God's eyes—every one of us from every walk of life." She breathes deeply as if thinking about continuing, but then says in a cracked voice, "Serve each other well," and returns to the altar.

Arielle whispers to Beatrice, "So why do we call Kevin 'Father'?"

Beatrice places her index finger firmly at her lips, which disappoints Gemma, because she too would like to know the answer to that question. She'll have to wait. One thing about her roommate is she's persistent enough to get the answers she seeks, and sometimes Gemma respects that.

After chapel they have breakfast at the big farm table in the dining room. Gemma is genuinely enjoying herself, relishing the sense of community. It's so foreign! Why don't they have meals together more often? She presents her plate to Rose who ladles some creamy scrambled eggs peppered with chives. Beatrice cuts her a slice of warm, fresh-baked sprouted wheat bread followed by a dollop of wild blueberry jam. She helps herself to the crisp maple bacon. This is a feast she can't recall sharing even once in her lifetime—her first real thanksgiving perhaps. Gratitude pumps through her veins.

Not that these women are anything like her; they're not. And this is possibly what makes Gemma's sudden appreciation that much sweeter. For one thing, with the exception of Mike, they're all dressed in unsightly clothes. But maybe like Gemma's shaved head, this is their attempt at humility. Not that Beatrice's wild magenta pant suit screams humility, it doesn't. Still, in spite of the loud color and huge buttons, it was sewn by her on the monastery sewing machine. The same with Gabriella's loose-bottomed, pinched-waist dollar store denim. Unprofessional, yes...but humble. Rose's simple gray shift is covered by a Victorian style apron featuring pink and yellow roses from top to bottom and embroidered with the name *Rose* in dark green script. Sweet. Rose is simple and sweet like her name. Gemma wonders why she doesn't really know Rose, or any of them except Arielle, who's so new. She may not know them, but the Lord is certainly giving her a heart for them, which is a start.

"It's great to have you here at breakfast for a change," says Beatrice as she serves herself.

Gemma blinks. *What?!* For a change? She just says, "Thank you," and takes her seat. There's no point in exploring it any further because after all, Arielle said it would all work out, and Arielle has access to the hermit. To the tea! So things will work out. They have to.

Arielle rushes around helping the women, and then piles her plate high with eggs, bread, sliced pineapple, mango and grapefruit. She plops happily down on the other side of the table between Rose and Beatrice as if she is their prized possession and knows it. A few seats down, Gabriella reaches out and touches the protégé, pats her hand as if to claim her share.

Mike pours a cup of coffee from the silver urn and takes her seat at the head of the table. Once settled, she says, "Praise God for our plenty," to which they all reply, "Amen."

With her mouth half-full, Arielle says, "Why do we call Kevin 'Father Kevin,'" just like that. Arielle could learn some manners from Gemma, but Gemma has the feeling she could learn a lot more than that from Arielle.

Apparently, Mike's mouthful of eggs goes down the wrong pipe, and she coughs jerkily while they push glasses of water and juice at her, until finally she speaks. "I don't know," is all she says.

Rose says, "Should we stop calling him 'Father' then?"

"We shouldn't stop," says Beatrice, "right?"

"It says we're all sisters and brothers," says Arielle. "We're all the same."

Mike sits there, pondering. "I can't solve that riddle for you, Sisters," she says. "I'm not going to lie—it's as if I saw that verse today for the first time myself. But maybe it doesn't matter. Maybe we should concentrate on ourselves instead and the impact we have on the world, how's that? Without worrying about the priests and what they call themselves."

"How do we do that?" asks Gabriella.

"I've actually been preoccupied with that exact question of late," Mike says. She pats the sides of her mouth with her napkin. "I think how we do it is by getting back to our charism. We've moved further and further away from it in the last decade, which has possibly contributed to our decline and the decline of well...the miracles that once abounded here."

"Charism?" says Arielle eagerly.

"Our reason for being here," Mike says. "Our divinely inspired mission. The charitable outreach ordained by Grace when she founded this order. In other words, people, we need to get back out to the community—our sisters and brothers in the town of Hebronville."

"But...but," Beatrice stutters, "how? There's too much to do right here!"

"I'm not sure how," says Mike. "Our resources are slim to none and the Mother House is closed. Constance isn't well, and the rest of us are certainly advancing in age. Just to take care of the farm—to work the fields alone—is too much for Gemma and Arielle. I know you all help out, but let's face it they do the brunt of it. And anyway, Arielle has been caring for Mother more than half the day, which is a gift to us all, however..." She shakes her head, looks away for a minute.

Except for Gemma, the Sisters lean in anxiously, but something tells Gemma to sit up and push back to avoid the approaching surge of bad news. She wants to derail the conversation, to run away. She wishes she had the nerve.

"I might as well tell you…" Mike continues, "that is, I suppose you should know…" She sighs deeply.

Oh God! Gemma hums a mantra in her head, *"Don't say it! Don't tell us! Keep it to yourself!"*

Mike clears her throat. "Sisters, we're going to be investigated by the Vatican committee and we have to get our act together soon or I'm afraid they'll shut us down." She opens her hands. "That's it. I don't know the exact date yet, but soon. At the very least we should all be on our knees."

"Shut us DOWN!" screeches Gabriella. "Are you KIDDING?!"

"We're being investigated?" gulps Rose. "Oh no!" She lays her face in her hands. "Investigated? What have we done?!"

Beatrice's rosacea rises visibly up her neck and cheeks.

While Mike explains the details of the investigation in general and the upcoming visitation of the monastery by the female committee, the information flows in and out of Gemma's brain completely undigested. She is stunned. How can this be? *This is her home!* This threat feels more real and dangerous than anything in her life up to now. Where will she go? What will she do? *This is her home!* She breaks into a wretched, soaking sweat that, except for her forehead, remains hidden by her voluminous habit. She dips her napkin in a glass of ice water and dabs her forehead.

The other Sisters jump in asking questions and making suggestions, but for Gemma things remain fuzzy. She hears some things clearly, such as Arielle's remark, "We can't give up! Maybe we need to bring the community here instead. You know—instead of going out? Bring them here? After all we're the charity cases now! Let them help out in exchange for food or whatever. A co-op!"

"A co-op, yes!" says Beatrice clapping excitedly. "Hooray! Ingenious! Jesse and Eli have already offered their services! They can help in the fields while Gemma and Connie are convalescing, maybe longer!"

"I'm not infirm," Gemma says, although at this exact moment she couldn't tend an ant farm. Still, if it means she can keep her home, she doesn't want to be discounted. "I can do my share."

"Or maybe the other guys," Arielle offers. "Doesn't have to be those two losers, oops—I mean firemen…medics, whatever. Parishioners can help after Mass, too." She waves her hands in the air loosely, her fingers splayed. "All those 'brothers and sisters' out there, you know, like the Gospel says."

In spite of the comedy club presentation, Mike seems to be seriously considering Arielle's proposition. She sips her coffee thoughtfully. "This has merit," she says. "At least in the short term it would help us prepare the grounds for the visitators. That is if the young men are really willing." She looks left to right, "And if we got the help we needed…we wouldn't look so, I don't know…"

"Discombobulated," Arielle says with one of her vaudeville grimaces.

Mike nods, mildly amused. "Yes, discombobulated," she says.

Rose giggles, and Gemma has to admit this word certainly describes how she's feeling so maybe they're all in the same boat—all discombobulated together.

Mike places her napkin perfunctorily on the table and stands. "Stay here, Sisters," she says. "There's something I want to show you."

In her absence, anxiety creeps into Gemma's gut and builds in intensity, migrating from her belly to her heart to her throat and out of her head like steam. She's coming apart at the seams. *And sweating! Still sweating!* She needs some of Mother's tea, but can't ask for it in front of everyone else. She tries to signal Arielle, but Arielle is too busy horsing around grinning with an orange peel over her teeth.

"Oh ha ha ha!" sings the nauseating chorus.

Gemma does not find this nonsensical behavior the least bit entertaining. Why should she? It's disruptive and makes it impossible for her to get what she needs—*her tea!* All at once she is entirely provoked and irritated at the utter childishness of it all, *uh!* And aren't these women supposed to be serving God with dignity? In solemn prayer? She's never seen a holy card saint with an orange peel for a smile. She's never seen a holy card saint with a smile period. Saints don't smile because they're incapacitated with awe and reverence for their God. Saints are dead serious about salvation.

As the anxiety escalates, her ability to think disintegrates. Her head feels like a bag of styrofoam peanuts. She needs to be working— plowing, planting, *punishing, earning—proving!*— her worthiness to her Creator, which is impossible in the midst of these spiritual ignoramuses! For relief she digs her sharp nails into her wrist and pinches until she can really feel it. Until it hurts. She pinches and twists the skin of her hand, her arm, her neck, whatever is unclothed, within reach and undetectable by others. She would stab herself with a fork if she weren't surrounded by a bunch of party clowns with no hope of understanding. The anxiety is disabling.

She doesn't even remember Mike returning to the room, but all at once there she is standing at the head of the table commanding everything—their attention, their servitude, *their souls!* She says, "I realize this is unprecedented, but in light of this morning's Gospel, I feel that I owe one of our Sisters some recognition. This Sister and co-worker of ours is a laborer of the Lord; one who has faithfully borne the most backbreaking job in this monastery." She looks around the room at each of them. "She is nearly single-handedly responsible for the food on this table.

"It's not in our tradition to distinguish one Sister over another, because after all, every job on this farm contributes to the wellbeing of each of us and our, well…tragically dwindling Order."

Beatrice gasps at this last comment, and Arielle squeezes her hand.

"However," Mike continues, "I feel that from time to time well-deserved recognition is not so much junk food for the ego as essential nutrition for the spirit. In other words, it's beneficial. Therefore, I would like us all to express our gratitude to Gemma for her dedicated hard labor in the fields. Work, I might mention, from which she has never once excused herself or even complained about." She raises her

204 REA NOLAN MARTIN

orange juice glass. "To Gemma," she says, "for the food we have been blessed to eat due to her heroic efforts."

Gemma thinks she's hallucinating. *What?!* What's happening? Is Mike talking about her? *Why?!* Why now? *What's happening?* She doesn't want this attention! This attention is the last thing she wants. Her breath is shallow and rushed. Her heart quickens. She pinches and twists the skin on her wrist to distract herself, to calm herself down, but it doesn't generate enough pain. It doesn't work.

Mike isn't finished. She pulls a square of paper from the deep pockets of her black linen suit jacket and unfolds it. She stares at it for a moment then says, "This may surprise you all, but this picture was sketched by Sister Gemma." She flips it around and extends it for them all to see. "And though many of you have not been privy to the *Chronicles* in Mother's trailer, this picture is...."

Gemma hears nothing but a cloud of *"Blah blah blah..."* There's a hole in her head and the styrofoam peanuts are tumbling out. She remembers the sketch. She remembers what she did. She remembers the lie. She can't stay. Her hot, sweaty body is telling her to go, and her belly is cramping severely. She's convulsed with this cramp. Where did it come from? She has to get out while she can still walk. She stands, "Excuse me," she says as evenly as possible. "I need air."

She barely gets to the front door before she hears Arielle's cloddy boots clomping down the hall. *Clomp, clomp, clomp.* Arielle is the last person Gemma wants to see. She feels as if Arielle is Grace, as if Grace is following her step for step. Grace and her Angel and her God. Everything belongs to Grace; nothing belongs to Gemma. Gemma is a sinkhole.

Out the front door now and across the porch, she bunches up her skirts and leaps over the steps, detouring east on high-test adrenaline in the direction of Henry. Her cramps subside, although her right lower side still throbs. She doesn't care. *She is free!* As she runs, her veil lifts so high she could fly if she wanted to! She imagines the feeling of taking off into a gust, and lifts her arms to the wind.

The running, the wind in her face, and the adrenaline ignite a spark in her awareness that converts her psyche mid-step. One step she's Gemma, the next…she's not. The poles of the magnets she lives between switch and turn, forcing a different aspect to the surface. She feels the change. She no longer wants to pinch or hurt herself; she wants only to run. *Run, run, run* with the warm sun on her face, radiating, *penetrating* her skin. Run free! If only she had long hair to catch the wind instead of a veil! What must that feel like? Long, soft hair lifting her in the wind! She longs to know.

Everything, every single sense is heightened as if she'd never felt any of them before. The fragrance of blooming lavender and fresh-mowed grass, the scorching intensity of the sun. She peels off her headdress, her cap and her bib as she runs. Without the cap over her ears she hears the crickets and the crows and the falcon caw as it sweeps the lower hill for prey. The world is enchanted and all things are possible.

She catches her foot, *oomph,* and falls on her belly. The thrust of her body against the earth is surprising. While lying there, she scratches through the tough pasture grass into the dirt and rubs it between her fingers and hands. *Soil! Earth!* Moist and soft! Were it not for the gopher hole that grabbed the stacked heel of her right black oxford, she would have gone further. Rolled down the hill, perhaps, or swung into the river from a tree vine, who knows? Escaped! But she got far enough to know what she needs. *Freedom!* What she needs is freedom. This confinement is not for her.

A minute later, Arielle catches up to her, holding her chest, huffing. "Boy can you run," she says. "I've never seen you run like that! Who are you, ha ha! Are you okay?"

"Go away," she says quietly. "I don't want your help."

"You need my help!" Arielle offers her hand. "Come on!"

"I need my freedom. I need to get out of this…" she pulls at her scapular, "…this vice."

"We'll escape on Friday," Arielle says. "I swear. This nonsense of yours will only buy you a first class ticket to the loony bin. You have to get a damn grip."

She sits up. "No," she says, "I have to get out of here." She looks at Arielle pleadingly. "Can you get me some real clothes? Please?! Meet me down by the RIVER?"

"No," Arielle says. "As much as I'd love a SWIM. Mike needs us; we can't let her down. And you need to come up with me. You need the TEA." She winks. She *knows.*

"I don't want your tea. Your tea diminishes me. It favors Gemma."

"The tea favors convergence," Arielle says firmly. "It favors sanity!" She narrows her eyes and zeros in. "Even if you don't plan to stay...and believe me, I can't stop you...you need the tea before you go."

Okay. This much makes sense, Maya thinks. *Maya?* Yes, Maya. I am almost here! Hallelujah! Encumbered by filters, still—in a blurry way—I touch, see, hear, smell and taste! *I decide!* It makes sense to drink the tea before she goes. She can still go. No one is saying she can't go. She eases her foot out of the hole, wincing.

"So you did hurt yourself!" Arielle says with what sounds like relief. "That should slow you down. Here, let me help you back and I'll make the excuses."

"Get the TEA and I'll drink it HERE," Maya says.

Arielle shoves her hands against her skinny little hips. "I'm not falling for that shit, believe me. And I'm not going back to the house alone."

Tears form in Maya's eyes. *Beautiful wet tears!* She touches them, smells them, tastes them. They're delicious. "When can I LEAVE?" she says.

"Friday," says her abductor imperiously. "As planned. No sooner. It's a promise I made to whichever one of you. I keep my promises."

She offers her arm with such authority that Maya takes it. Luckily, Maya is able to stand up and walk, however gingerly, so she isn't completely incapacitated. In her mind, she could run if she wanted to.

As they walk to the house, her gait is slightly unsteady. She realizes she couldn't get far in this condition, so maybe she'll wait. At least until tonight. She'll see how she feels. Keep her options open. "I'm less

Gemma now," she confides to Arielle.

"I know," Arielle says. "The tea will help."

"But I don't want to be Gemma."

"I don't blame you."

"She's not any fun."

Arielle guffaws. "Yeah," she says.

"And besides," Maya says earnestly, "Gemma LIED. She's a LIAR. She pretended your angel was HERS.

Arielle says, "Try not to talk to anybody until after you drink the tea, ok? TRUST me. Don't get into any conversations with anyone."

"What if they ask me a QUESTION?"

"Just nod or use sign language or something. Pretend to be deaf, whatever. Your words tumble out of your mouth like stones. They're a dead giveaway."

Maya limps along breathing the fresh farm air. *Ambrosia!!* "But what about the ANGEL?" she says. "What about the LIE?!"

Arielle pats her hand reassuringly. "That angel doesn't belong to me, roommate. He belongs to Grace. She loans him out."

MIKE

Mike waits in her office for Arielle, crossing and uncrossing her knees, playing with the rubber band from this morning's newspaper. If she had a cigarette she would smoke it. *Where is the girl?* Of course she realizes Arielle was bringing Gemma to Beatrice for a salt soak on her ankle and some godforsaken tea that Gemma was begging…nearly crying for. But why is Gemma so distraught?! She's been screaming for attention and validation since she entered the monastery. She finally gets it and she falls apart!

Suddenly Mike remembers *The Chaos of New Birth* and thinks, huh. Where's *my* tea? Which makes her wonder—what tea is Gemma drinking? It can't be from Augusta. Augusta hasn't taken Gemma under her wing. Augusta has chosen Arielle. Augusta and Arielle are a love match, grand and karmic. What they have leaves room for no one. Even Mike can only watch.

Arielle knocks on the door and slides right into the chair opposite Mike. "Hey," she says.

"So?" Mike says. "How's Gemma?"

"Fine, I guess. Aside from a little, I don't know, embarrassed by all the attention?"

Mike tosses the rubber band in the waste basket. "Just a little embarrassment? Are you sure? There's no room for a misstep at this point." At the same time she's saying this, she's thinking— *Who am I talking to?! Another child! What are you giving me to work with here,*

208

Grace?! What?!

"Yup."

"You're sure? That's all you've noticed? When you talk to her she's...okay? She's coherent?"

"My best advice about Gemma is hakuna matata," says Arielle. "You have to go with it."

"Excuse me?"

"Hakuna matata," she says, shrugging. "It's *Lion King* for don't break a sweat. It'll all work out." She leans back against the chair. "I can't believe you don't know that song. It's really great. Wart hogs sing it."

Mike massages her temples. "Look," she says, "we have a lot riding on this. I need your cooperation and full attention."

"You have it, I swear!" she says, saluting.

"Put aside the jester routine for a minute, Arielle, and become my deputy, how's that? No more wart hogs. You're all I've got. You're the only one here who can help me with this." *I'm desperate!*

Suddenly Arielle's azure eyes are pools of awareness and attention. They draw Mike in, command her faith. How does she do that, Mike wonders. Turn on that switch? *Magnetics.*

"I'm all yours," Arielle says.

Lost in the eyes, Mike forgets who she's talking to again. It could be anyone—Augusta. *Grace!* She collects herself, "Ok then," she says. "For starters, I just got a call from the hospital and Constance is scheduled for pacemaker surgery on Friday at St. Peter's in Albany."

Arielle's expression freezes. "Friday?"

"Yes why? Is that a problem? What's the significance of Friday?" Mike knows she's coming across a bit edgy, which is exactly how she feels. She can't afford to show it, though. She breathes deeply to calm herself down—doesn't mean to attack the child, for heaven's sake. The girl is her only hope.

Arielle shakes her head, "No significance to Friday."

"Gemma has a meeting with Dr. Rawlins that day, too," Mike says. "He's also in Albany, but I can't be in two places at the same time even if it's the same city. And God knows Gemma can't miss this appointment."

"She has an appointment in Albany on Friday?"

"At 10. And to tell you the truth, I don't completely trust her right now. This morning's little escape is a perfect example of why."

Arielle sucks in her cheeks. "It wasn't technically an escape, it was just..."

"Just what?"

"Just nerves sprinkled with a little shock."

"Shock?!"

"Yeah, you know."

"I'm getting the impression that something's up with you," Mike says. "And I really can't afford that right now."

Arielle raises her palms. "Nothing up but me wondering what you're going to say next—if you want me to drive Gemma or if you want me to take the craft fair to the hospital, whatever. I'll do it. Deputy reporting for duty, SIR!"

Mike considers her response for a minute and decides to lighten up. She doesn't want the girl to be afraid of her. "Alright then," she says. "I'll take the craft fair."

Arielle grins broadly. "Ha ha, good!" she says. "You take the craft fair, and I'll take the twins."

Mike's head jerks involuntarily. "The twins?"

"I mean the SAINT," she says. "All the loud prayers, the sacrifice? The shaved head? The Goliath rosary? The *saint*?"

Mike leans forward. "Why did you say twins?"

Arielle's posture stiffens. "Uh, you know...just... Gemma? For Gemini? Twins? LOL."

"Gemma for Gemini?" says Mike. "That's all?"

Arielle nods. "Gemini's can be tough. My mother was one. They just have a hard time getting over themselves, because they're like...double the trouble of other people? I wouldn't take it personally."

"That's all. You're sure."

"Yes."

They stare at each other for a moment, and then Mike slides a pad of paper and a pen across the desk. "Alright then, make a list; you're going to need it. We have to take off running and keep up the pace until the investigation is over." She crosses the room briskly to the coffee station and pours a cup. "Would you like some?"

Arielle shakes her head. "I'm pretty tanked up already. I'm surprised I'm not looking down at you from the ceiling."

"By the way, I have to thank you for your suggestion today," Mike says. "About bringing the community to us, that is." She pours milk and stirs, walks back to her desk. "Along those lines, while you were out corralling your roommate, I decided we would host our first annual volunteer day on the farm. What do you think of that?"

"Awesome!!" Arielle says, nodding. "People like to help!"

Mike takes a seat and sips her coffee. "Good. I can make an announcement from the pulpit tomorrow, but I need you to make some phone calls too. Maybe pay a visit to the fire and rescue department today, what do you think? Can you do that?"

Arielle grins broadly while she makes this notation on her pad. "Roger that, sir" she says happily.

"It's right next to the hospital, so you can visit Constance if you like. I'm sure she would appreciate it."

"Very good, sir," she says.

"Enough with the sir, Arielle, okay?" Mike opens her center drawer. "Oh and one more favor. Before you go, I need you to program this…" She removes the iPhone and holds it up, smiling.

"Hey!" says Arielle. "Look at that! Hot shit!" Her eyes widen. "Sorry," she says.

"I want to thank you for this, too" says Mike. "I would never have thought it possible, but you show me otherwise. Sometimes one simply has to ask." She gives Arielle an appreciative nod. "I'm accustomed to self-sufficiency, but I realize that at times humility is what's called for. The ability to receive gifts is a gift of its own. It opens the heart." She pulls a list from her drawer. "I'd like you to program these contacts into my phone if you don't mind."

"It's better if I get that list right from your computer," says Arielle. "Fewer mistakes, trust me. Give me a couple of hours in here and I'll take care of it."

Mike studies the girl's open face. "I suppose I can do that." She straightens her desk to make room. "I'm going to be a whirling dervish myself today, so in between setting up the phone and soliciting the volunteers I need you to bring Mother her lunch."

"Yeahhhh," she says grinning. "Little Mama! Yesss! Wednesday is mac and cheese day. She loves my mac and cheese; you should try it."

Mike stacks up a pile of bills, thinking. "You know, Arielle…there may come a time…"

Arielle covers her ears. "Don't say it," she says. "I already know. When the time comes, I'll move in with her. I'll take care of her. Whatever it takes. Just don't say it. Please. Don't."

This show of genuine adoration stops Mike in her tracks. *Could it be Grace?* It was a far flung idea—the idea of Grace orchestrating the renewal and transformation of the monastery through this street urchin. But Mike is beginning to believe it's possible. Just look at all the life in this girl! The vitality! The basic unstoppable faith in herself and everyone else. Mike wants the ruse to be over. She wants to shake the girl until Grace falls out. That way they can finally relax, assured that Grace will bring them through it.

She reaches under the desk to turn her computer on then stands. "All yours," she says. "For an hour, how's that?"

"Um…two would be better?"

Mike narrows her eyes. "Why two?"

"I have to horse around with AT&T for who knows how long to get you activated and all. Just don't count on me finishing everything in an hour."

Mike doesn't feel she has a choice. She knows nothing about these things and she has to trust somebody. It might as well be Grace.

Later in the day when Arielle is gone, Mike tears through her

paperwork energized at the idea of all the help she's going to get—
stupefied all over again by the simplicity of Arielle's suggestion to invite
the townspeople to the monastery. After all, they are not a closed
community. They never have been! Grace intended their outreach from
the start, and of course charity works both ways. How could she not
have thought of this solution herself?! She's become as petrified as
Rome—set in marble and unwelcoming of renewal, of change. But how
will they survive without change? How will anyone? Evolution itself is
change.

With her paperwork out of the way, Mike makes a dozen calls
with her new phone to register the number with the community
accountant, lawyer, suppliers, and regrettably, Kevin, who thank God
doesn't answer. She calls Rawlins and leaves a message, likewise
Constance' doctors. She fools around for a few minutes with the
weather application Arielle loaded, and finds that really…it's more
intuitive than she thought it would be. Not that she intends to be
seduced by technology, she doesn't. She can't afford that. That would
be no better than Rose and her reality shows when you think about it.
But she has to admit it is kind of fun.

At six, Mike stops to say her Vespers, "O God, come to my aid. O
Lord, make haste to help me. Glory be…" When she's finished she
thinks—we have to start saying some of this as a community. Not that
she wants to impose every manner of new rule, or really old rule, on the
Sisters at once, but still. The visitators will expect some discipline from
them, some communal prayer beyond Mass. It's a monastery. How did
she let it fall apart like this?

She arrives at the dinner table with her phone discreetly clasped at the
waist in its new leather case, also a gift. Not that the phone's a necessity,
but it's a comfort. If Rawlins calls, or Constance's doctor, it will ring right
there on her belt. It's a luxury and she's grateful for it. She's learning to
receive. Open your heart and let the gifts be made manifest!

So simple!

Mike finds Gemma improved at dinner. She's more alert and
talkative, which is not necessarily her nature, but still. It's far more

pleasant than her usual stone silence, so who's to argue? Such blessings are not to be questioned. *Receive!*

"So I got the whole fire station involved," says Arielle as she cuts her chicken parm. "Not to mention everyone at my NA meeting. The whole group!"

Beatrice raises her eyebrows. "Well, dear, of course when it comes to NA we have to be cautious, do we not?" She takes a warm roll and passes the basket. "After all everyone there is not our sweet little funny girl. Some of them are, well…"

"Charity cases?" says Arielle. "Yeah, they are, but…" she takes the basket, "so are we when you think about it."

"Inviting in all the elements, then?" says Gabriella. "Is this what it's come to?"

"Yes it has," says Mike. "We're inviting all the elements, indeed we are. That's the lovely thing about not having a choice. Things are clear."

"Beggars can't be choosers," says Arielle. "And besides when you talk about NA, you're talking about half the town. I would know. You wouldn't believe who I see there, not that I would tell you; they'd kick my butt. But just that without AA or NA the town would be half the size. There's not much to do out here."

Beatrice clears her throat. "Well then, there we are. We embrace our people, right? In sickness and in health!"

"And they embrace us," says Mike. "We have to try it."

"But what are they going to DO?" says Gemma with an odd emphasis.

Arielle rises promptly. "Excuse me for a minute," she says with a mouthful. "I just remembered Gemma asked me for the rel…" Her eyes widen. "…for some um, tea." She holds up her right index finger. "Be right back."

Mike says, "Hold on, Arielle, why can't Gemma get her own tea? You're not on table duty tonight." Something about this doesn't seem right.

Arielle halts with her back to the table on her way through the kitchen swing door. Her hair is spread out behind her like a bonfire.

"My ankle hurts," says Gemma. "I appreciate the HELP!"

"Yeah," says Arielle as she disappears through the door.

Mike frowns. She's not sure why her antennae are raised; why she questioned Arielle's kindness. After all, Gemma's ankle is sore. Of course it is. She fell in a hole. *Still.*

Arielle rushes back in with a full cup of tea and Gemma says, "Is ELI coming TOO?"

Arielle brings the tea right to her and says, "Drink up, Gemma!" She dashes over to her seat and says, "Everyone who's available will be there. That's all I know. And the fire captain is making signs. And Marjorie Culpepper from the women's auxiliary is bringing balloons for the kids. Everybody's rockin' the monastery, hallelujah!"

"Oh goody!" says Beatrice clapping. "And Gabi and I will make cupcakes for everyone, won't we, Gabi?!"

"And sell our quilts!" says Gabriella. "Will Connie be back?"

"With any luck, Constance should be back by then," says Mike, who has to admit she's looking forward to something for the first time in an exceedingly long time. A decade at least.

All at once menacing music fills the air...*doo doo doo doo.* What? Where? Mike jumps out of her chair before she realizes it's coming from her own pocket.

From her phone!

"What's that!" says Gabriella, alarmed. "Where's it coming from!"

"Oh," says Arielle, chewing. "That's the ringtone for the Apostolic Visitator."

"A phone! Mike has a cell phone now?!" says Gabriella.

Mike gives Arielle a bemused look, "What is this music?"

"Just the *Theme from Jaws?*" Arielle says as she butters her roll. "You don't have to answer it right now though. They can leave a message if you want. I recorded one for you."

Mike stares at the screen. "What? No! I think I'll just take it," she says. God only knows what the girl recorded. "Just get it over with. Excuse me." She steps out of the room, "Hello?"

"Please hold for the Superior General," says a nasal voice.

Mike hurries down the hall to her office, waiting for the Superior

General. She sits at her desk and clicks her mouse.

"Mother will be right with you," the voice repeats. "I apologize for the delay. She received an urgent call. Please hold."

"Fine," says Mike. She clicks a hidden screen that Arielle must have forgotten to exit. What's this? "Ink-B-Gone, Tattoo Removal Studio, Albany, NY." This makes her smile. But is it possible to remove a tattoo? Maybe it is. Another screen: "Stanley & Gertrude Flynn, Stockton, Vermont" and another: "New York State Adoption Agencies." Mike isn't sure what to make of this one, but decides to save them to her file. Adoption agencies?! Is Arielle adopted?

"Mother Michael Agnes?" says a crisp voice.

Mike pops out of her trance, "Oh," she says, "Yes. This is she."

ARIELLE

Arielle can't stop thinking about the big community hootenanny at the monastery. She's never been involved in a project this big. It's the bomb! The monastery will be renewed. *Saved!* She can't believe Mike agreed to it so easily, but she did. She really did. She's not the cinderblock wall Arielle thought she was. Arielle suggested that they let the community lend a hand and an hour later—wellah! You never know about people. Sometimes just below the cement surface is a pile of mush you didn't know was there. A pile of pudding that says yes to everything just when you thought they didn't know the word.

Yes! Go ahead! Let's do it!

Arielle arranged everything during yesterday's trip to the village. She was all over the place—to NA, AA, triple A—you name it. To the diner, the hospital, and finally, the fire and rescue where the loser cut her a break by not rubbing her nose in his butt while she was kissing it. You do what you have to. Arielle will do anything for her Sisters—*her family!* She'll let the loser help if that's what it takes. It won't kill her.

But the memory still bites. There she was, standing in the middle of the prefab rescue office with the loser. He was sitting back in a folding chair stroking his blonde beard while he listened to her like he was Professor Freud with a mental patient. His long legs were raised and crossed on the metal desk and she was forced to look at the bottoms of his disgusting motorcycle boots, so she moved around to the side where the view was slightly better but not by much. As sweetly as she could, she said, "I need you to buy an iPod for the relic. I'll pay for it whenever, I swear."

"Don't bother," he said. The big ugly shiner Eli gave him was in its green and yellow stage, so maybe by Friday she could stand to look at him. "Seriously, I told you, Ari—I make good money. I can afford a damn iPod for a nun. Consider it a donation."

I make good money! Gag! *Who cares?*

She said, "Here's the list of songs to load," which included everything from Benedictine chants and Sunday hymns to the relic's top secret fantasy crush, Johnny Cash, plus some Adele thrown in by Arielle because why not? It's a free country. The relic might as well know what's going on outside the trailer.

And then in walks double-shiner Eli pawing at her with his questions to learn anything at all about Gemmaya. "I need to see her, I'm serious," he said nervously, pumping his fists. "I know it looked bad, but it wasn't. We're in love!"

"You can't fall in love in five minutes," she said.

At that the loser's legs came down and he sat at full attention. "Wanna bet?" he said giving her the laser eye.

"I sent her a letter," said Eli frantically running his hands through his black hair. "I've never seen eyes like hers before. They're...I don't know...bewitching!" He glared at Arielle. "She can't be a nun! She wasn't meant to be. It's a colossal mistake!"

He sent her a letter? *What? Where is it!* But no time to sound any postal alarms and besides, with any luck it was lost in Kansas along with Toto in 1952. You have to stay focused. You can't let a letter bring you down. So while the boys were still anxious to please, *boom!*—she let it all out. "I need a little favor for Friday," she told them both, practically batting her lashes. They zeroed in like excited little baby birds waiting for their mother to feed them vomit. Arielle didn't really want this kind of power over anyone, but she can't pull off Maya's holiday without their help, so.

When she finished, the loser stood up. "Your wish is our command," he said, bending at the waist with one arm swaying kind of gracefully through the air like whatever.

At the time Arielle was confused by this comedy because Lucky is not a graceful guy. He's a trailer camp loser who learned manners from his father, Tarzan. So where this put-on polite crap came from, she'd like to know. She doubts he could keep it up for more than a day, though, or until he got what he wanted, which apparently is her, so. Never.

Meanwhile Eli stood at full attention like some kind of history dude waiting breathlessly for the first transmission from an ancient fax machine. That boy has it soooo bad for the blue eye. And he's the only bait Arielle can use to lure Maya out of hiding for her big debut. When Eli's around, the brown eye goes blind; the blue eye swings from a chandelier. Without Eli, there's no guarantee which twin will show up. Or maybe the brown and blue would battle it out and end up cross-eyed for life. It could happen. It's not like there's instructions for this.

"I need you both to meet me and Gemma at the fair outside Albany on Friday," she said. "Eleven o'clock at the main gate." And after a lot of head scratching about schedule changes, beard pulling and flying dandruff, she finally explained to them that it was Gemma's one big day out a year and they were invited. That was all. End of story. Come or don't come, who cares? *She does!* She realized she might have to explain more at some point, but best to spoon-feed the loser so he didn't take over. You can't let him think he's in charge; she's been through that. She isn't stupid. Anyway they easily agreed to the terms and conditions, why not? Just a big fun day at the fair with a couple of hot nuns, ha ha! Who wouldn't want that?

As far as the shrink appointment was concerned, well, Arielle had thought long and hard about it and decided not to ditch it, although that would definitely be the easiest way out. She doesn't want to raise any red flags too early in the day. And anyway, what harm could the doctor do? Even if he managed to lure the martyr to the surface, a single glance from Eli would slam her down like a carnival gopher. *Bam!* Maya would have her day, or at least her half-day and part of the evening. If they're a little late returning to the monastery, so what? Cars break down. People get lost. Deal with it.

But anyway, that was yesterday. Today's another day, not to mention one day closer to showtime. There's really no telling what will happen. It's pouring rain and she just hopes the sky squeezes itself dry by then. She's not a fan of roller coasters and ferris wheels in the middle of lightning and thunder. They could always go to a movie. The Rocky Horror Picture Show would be perfect, when you think about it. Or bowling, as Maya already suggested. And anyway this isn't the only thing going on in their lives. The rest of it is falling apart too.

It's true the craft fair's feeling better, but Mike's feeling worse ever since she found out the Roman army is scheduled to pillage the monastery in a week or two. They won't even give her an exact date yet. Insult to injury, Mike is responsible for their room and board. Arielle doesn't really know what this investigation means, but from the dead-serious tone of it, you'd think they were planning to gun down the nuns in the chapel and escape with their valuables. *What valuables?* Or maybe they were going to evict them from the Catholic Church altogether and send them to live wherever. If that happens, will they get unemployment? She doesn't ask. It means too much.

Hakuna matata.

Of course Mike tells them, "Just be yourselves, Sisters." *What?! Has she met Gemma?* But for Arielle, being herself means chillaxin in the trailer with the relic so no one will see her scrawny ass or her slimy snake tattoo. She doesn't have the money to erase the tattoo anyway, and she's not getting any deeper into Lucky's wallet than she has to. Where's his money coming from anyway, drugs? You never know. She still hasn't seen him at NA.

Anyway, she'll have the iPod soon, and she can fill the relic's moldy little elf ears with heavenly music. Watch her swoon to Johnny Cash's *"I Walk the Line."* They can spend investigation day dancing and singing in their Airstream cocoon while all hell breaks loose around them. End of the world! *Who cares?* How bad can it be? At some point it's over.

And to be honest, the end of the world is the least of Arielle's worries at the moment, since this entire morning has been unbelievably challenging. The twins have been Maya one minute and Gemma the next. *Gemma:Maya; Gemma:Maya; Gemma:Maya.* Arielle's brain feels like a whirligig in a hurricane. She has to be on her toes. She quizzes the twins on a regular basis to identify the occupant. A good trick question is, "Want to pray?" which sends Gemma straight to her knees on a pile of thumbtacks, and the other is, "What would you wear if you could wear anything," which if it's Maya involves a thong. It's surprising how much Maya knows about Victoria's Secret considering she's spent her entire life in the peephole of somebody else's head. *A nun's!* You just never know who's scanning a catalogue when you think they're saying prayers.

Before Arielle takes these chicks anywhere, she has to find out from the relic why the tea isn't working. For instance, shouldn't they be converged by now? She grabs the ground beef from the fridge and the taco mix from the cabinet, stuffs them in a plastic bag and heads for the door. Fiesta day with madrecita! Little Mama likes to see the food cooking, not that she can smell anything, but it feels more like home to her that way. So Arielle keeps it simple, not that she has a choice—she's not exactly a chef! But even with the two burners, she can still fry up some meat on the stovetop and heat a couple of taco shells in the oven. It's so easy Assisi could probably do it.

Assisi is a cat saint, according to the relic. His patron saint is Francis, who loved animals more than anything and gave all his riches to the poor. Not that Assisi gives anything away, plus he eats mice and birds, so. Not very saintly. Not that she points these flaws out to the relic. That would be useless. The relic worships that cat; he's her guardian avatar. Arielle grooves to Assisi, too, especially when he perches on the top of the wingchair and purrs like a Harley.

Arielle pulls off her Frye's, pushes her feet deep into Beatrice's rubber gardening boots, and darts out the screen door. She jumps through the driving rain, plopping down hard in the middle of every puddle she can find. *Plop! Plop! Plop!* On the farm, life is so much fun even when it's not.

In one minute she is so soaked she has to stop at the overhang of the tool shed to wipe her dripping forehead and catch her breath. Standing there, she catches a glimpse of Mike in the distance running down the steps of the trailer. This reminds Arielle to have a one-second heart attack about all the screens she might have left on the computer yesterday when she was interrupted. She must've had a dozen going—everything from carnivals and fairs in Albany to bowling alleys and tattoo-removal parlors to whatever. She can't even remember; there was so much going on.

She thinks she exited most of the screens, but who knows? She has to count on Mike's basic ignorance of technology, which is not far-fetched. Like most people her age, Mike only uses one screen at a time. Not to mention that in the middle of it all Arielle completed a more crucial search and destroy mission, alias Eli's letter. As soon as she found it, she slipped it into the shaft of her left Frye, which was genius. And it didn't look opened, thank God, which means Mike has more integrity than Arielle does, but then again, who stole the letter to begin with? Just saying. Not that either one of them read it; they didn't. Who would want to?

Arielle is so soaked, she can't believe it. She ducks inside the tool shed to wait it out. Sheets of rain! Oh wait, now she remembers the screens—she had a search going for her mother as usual, *Where's Willa?!*— along with one for Gram and Pa in Vermont if they're alive, and just whatever else she could think of. She was buried in her work—hypnotized!—when all at once Mike burst in with Beatrice and Gabriella to announce their surprise for the craft fair—a new sewing machine donated by a parishioner. Not that Connie doesn't deserve a new machine, but what about the screenfest?!

Arielle watches Mike take the shortcut to the other side of the farmhouse near the laundry room which is nowhere near the shed. Phew. She's in no mood for a search screen lecture. And anyway, it would be hard to have a conversation in this noisy storm which is suddenly starring thunder and lightning in hats and canes dancing like the fourth of July across the sky. Beautiful, but. Not something you want to lose an argument in.

Finally there's a let-up in the rain and Arielle makes a dash for the sunflower garden. The blossoms are huge—big as her head. She can hide underneath a cluster of them for a minute if the rain keeps up, or she can pick one for a little umbrella, LOL. It's not like Gemma would miss the seeds—she hasn't even mentioned the sunflowers since she got back from the hospital. She might just think they're outdoor decorations instead of granola snacks, you never know. Some pretty basic information was knocked off the brain shelf when she conked out on the stairs.

Arielle slides into the sunflower field on a mud slurry and ducks for cover at a giant thunder clap. The light show doesn't end, just gets closer. The bag of lunch is getting wet, so Arielle makes a mad dash for the trailer and practically throws herself through the door. "Lunchtime!" she announces all sprawled out on the floor which, even though it killed her elbows, should be good for a laugh.

No laugh.

The relic is piled in her chair with four crazy crocheted blankets and Assisi on her lap, her head bent down in a snooze, so she doesn't applaud the grand entrance. Arielle makes a lot of noise, grunting and groaning as she gets up just to make sure the relic is breathing. She's not in the mood to wonder. She has to know. Little Mama is her comfort zone—her everything zone. *Breathe!*

"What? Oh! Wonderful!" says Augusta, coming to life. She yawns and stretches. "Hello, dear girl! Taco day?"

"Fiesta…forever!" sings Arielle, snapping her fingers from side to side, keeping the beat. She should've been a mariachi. Just the fringed hats alone. She bangs around in the kitchen alcove opening packages, pulling out the frying pan and cookie sheets, and igniting the pilot light which is forever blowing out. She drops the meat into the pan and opens the sauce packet. Mild sauce for the relic, don't worry, nothing too hot. Arielle could mix the meat with a bottle of ketchup and the relic would be in heaven. The relic just grooves to festivity in general.

While Arielle's putting the water on for tea, she scans the

ingredient list for the relic's latest tea, Timeline. A little mint, a little sage, a pinch of crushed fennel seed, cardamom, on and on. How does she think of these things! Arielle combines it all very carefully in six cheesecloth balls, all the while thinking about the twins. How they're not converging and how Arielle has to find a way to tell her little magic troll that the recipe needs adjusting, while at the same time not revealing every little detail of the situation…

"The tea is perfect," says the relic.

Arielle turns. "What? What tea? I haven't given you any yet."

"The Convergence Tea, dear. The one we made for Gemma. Isn't that what you were just wondering about?"

Oh. *Right.* The relic lives in another timeline. "Whatever you say," Arielle says as she arranges the taco shells on the cookie sheet. "No secrets from you. But, Mama, the truth is Gemma's all over the place. A mess, really, and I need her converged by tomorrow."

In reply, the relic just nods off to sleep while Arielle continues to cook the taco slop and spoon it into the crispy shells. She serves it up on a plastic plate and carries it carefully over to the relic's tray table where she arranges it nicely with a napkin, some cutlery, and a cup of her tea, although the last thing Arielle needs is Augusta jumping another timeline. How many can you jump in a week? She doesn't want to lose her. She can't afford that.

When the relic smells the tea her eyes pop open. "Oh! My Timeline!" she says. "Very good, dear, thank you. You read my mind!"

"You're welcome, little Mama," says Arielle, who tucks a paper towel under the relic's chin and kisses her on the head.

She returns to the alcove for her own meal and arranges it on a snack table next to the wingchair.

"Where's your tea, dear?" says the relic.

"I don't want the Timeline, little Mama. I don't want to know the future unless you're in it."

"Oh, no indeed, child! No Timeline Tea for you!" She turns her head up and to the right where her genius lives and says, "Zippity Tea for you." She lifts her tea cup slowly with her crooked little fingers, brings it to her mouth and relishes a sip. "Mmmmm." She places it down. "You're still working on the *Transference of Knowledge*," she says. "We can't afford to have you jump timelines without the proper knowledge. That would be a disaster."

Arielle takes a big bite out of her taco. She hums *mmmmm* while the taco is in her mouth and all the way down her throat, then sips water. "I'll make my tea in a minute," she says finally, "but just a 411-on-the-verge-of-a-911—the twins…I mean Gemma…is not converging one bit. In fact she's separating."

"Well, yes, they're converging, dear. Of course they are."

Arielle doesn't want to contradict the relic, but sometimes you have to wonder how much she's really with it. No one could be less one thing than the twins. Arielle only thinks she can take them on because of the relic and her knowledge. If she thinks the relic is losing it, she might have to shoot Niagara Falls in a barrel, because she is not going to be responsible for the unconverged twins at a carnival. The unconverged twins are already a carnival.

Little Mama dabs at her wrinkly little mouth with the napkin. "Go get Assisi's mouse toy," she says. "The one on the string. It's on the bed."

What? Why? But Arielle walks over to the mattress and digs for the toy under the covers. She turns to the relic and dangles it. "This?"

"That's right, dear."

When Arielle returns, the relic takes the toy from the top of the string and swings it high from left to right in long strokes that eventually get smaller. Assisi just follows it with his gold cat eyes, biding his time. "In the beginning of convergence the spirits are further and further apart," she says. "They can retain their separate identities longer."

The mouse swings closer and closer to the middle. Arielle gets it. It's a pendulum. Eventually it stops.

"As the convergence takes place, the spirits that animate get closer and closer until they overlap in space and time. This can be confusing. They are one thing one minute and another thing the next. But at some point…"

The mouse stops.

"...convergence." Assisi pounces on the mouse and runs.

The relic's sunken blue eyes sparkle like two little fairies on the surface of still waters. Her deep pool of knowledge. She knows everything. Arielle can't help but feel safe. She's the only person in Arielle's entire life who ever shared real knowledge with her; who explained things so she would know them, too. "So we're close to the middle," Arielle says.

The relic nods. "A few more doses and she's there."

Arielle doesn't know why, but she just can't come right out and tell the relic about Eli and the carnival. Or the letter that's stuffed between her mattress and box spring. Her loyalties are torn, but. She probably knows anyway.

"Convergence isn't for a person, dear," says the relic. She bites into her taco and loses half of it on her plate.

Arielle has to fight not to interrupt or think...anything! She waits.

"Convergence is for a situation and everything related to it. Once convergence starts, it consumes everything in its path. Everything around it will be drawn to a point of conclusion. There's no escaping."

"I don't know what that means," Arielle says, but she doesn't like the sound of it.

"You will dear," says the relic. "You will."

Arielle tosses and turns the whole night. She might as well not have even bothered to get in bed. Part of it is Gemma's big holy mouth praying at the top of her Mount Sinai lungs at 2 AM, not that you can blame her. She's nervous, so. It's not that hard to understand.

"We can always bag it," she tells Gemma in the morning. "We don't have to go to any damn fair."

The minute you say it, Maya jumps out, so there. The relic is right. The mouse is close to the center. It's best to just keep the string in motion until it stops by itself. You don't want to force anything. *Convergence consumes everything in its path!* Exhausted, but as ready as she'll ever be, Arielle throws on her red plaid jumper and boots. She rolls a red bandana and ties it around her neck in case the shrink wants to see her, and who needs the grief? Then she stuffs her lilac sundress into her backpack for the twins. It's the one Maya requested, kind of a last meal. Arielle can't help feeling like she's going to her own execution.

In the same room, Gemma is selecting the pieces of her habit, genuflecting in between her selections as usual and praying this and that to the Lord. She really does love the Lord, which makes you wonder where the Lord stands on all of this. Has anyone asked? It's not up to Arielle; she's not a twin. So hopefully Gemma has had the sense to put in a request. Anyway, the saint throws Arielle a sideways glance now and then, so you know she knows. *She knows.* She's aware that this is a big day and hopefully the last battle in the epic psychic wars between Gemma and herself.

Earlier, when Maya was brushing her teeth, she told Arielle that today was her birthday and her funeral. She's very dramatic, but so what? It is what it is. She wants assurances that Arielle can't really give her, because after all, the pact was made with Gemma. You have to pick one of the twins and stick with her or you'll just be one more mentally unstable mouse on a chewed-up string.

Anyway, one day of life is better than none is how Arielle looks at it, but she could be wrong. Maybe it's a hypodermic needle into the soul. A drug you can't put down. The drug of *life*. Of freedom. It's possible. People put up with anything just to stay alive, when you think about it. The twins are trying to get along, but they're in a fight for survival. Anything could happen. In one split second Maya could bind and gag the saint and lock her up for a few years—throw away her big groovy beads and swallow the monastery key. Who could blame her? If you ask Arielle, she's saving the life of at least one person—Gemma or Maya, she can't say which. Still. You can't put a price on a life.

Downstairs, Arielle takes the MapQuest directions from the printer and hands them to Gemma. "You're the navigator," she says. "You have to stay on top of this, I mean it. Every turn. No mistakes."

At the truck, Gemma is stiff as a stick; her nerves are in a vault somewhere west of the Mississippi. Her cheeks stick out more than ever with her overly tight head cap, and it's not an attractive look. One thing though is she's allowed her hair to grow a bit. Little golden wisps are visible at the hairline, which makes her appear more human and less like a Halloween costume. Arielle just can't help thinking that this big white habit will seem very out of place at a fair. She hopes to hell Maya makes her way to the surface in time to change into the sundress. As liquid as the brown eye usually is, it's solid this morning, penetrating. *Staring.* But the blue eye twinkles merrily in the background, waiting. Biding its time.

"The appointment is at ten sharp," says Mike as she hustles into the station wagon. "Come see Constance when you're finished. St. Peter's is not that far from Rawlins' office."

"We'll see," says Arielle. She mouths to Mike in an exaggerated fashion, "WE'LL SEE HOW SHE'S DOING," as her head nods off to the truck where Gemma is seated.

"Fine," says Mike, "but try. And you have my cell number if you need to call." She grins at this because she is really enjoying her phone and all the awesome apps Arielle has loaded.

Arielle refuses to acknowledge the cell phone reference, however, because she might not call. She can't be that accountable. It's really up to Gemmaya. If Mike only knew, Arielle's sure she would understand, but. She doesn't.

"Bye now!" Arielle calls behind her as she jumps into the driver's seat. "Bye bye! Hugs to the craft fair! Tell her I love her! I really really do!"

She turns the key and they take off down the dirt path behind Mike's wagon. It's a perfect 80 degree sunny summer day. The sky is filled with popcorn clouds, wisps of cotton candy scattered across the mountain tops. Arielle wishes she felt more carefree, but she doesn't. *What's next?!* And there's Beatrice, Gabriella and Rose left to care for the entire monastery, including Augusta. The relic isn't crazy about the bea-hive, but she'll have to deal with it today. Arielle warned little mama to be pleasant. She can be such a crank when she wants to, LOL! Her crankiness cracks Arielle up, it's so funny, but it makes the hive all nervous which makes the relic crankier, etcetera, etcetera. There's no end to it.

"Goodbye, Henry!" Gemma calls out to the river like she's never going to see it again. "I love you!"

Now there's the difference between the twins right there. Gemma can only say 'I love you' to a river. Not a person in the wide world she cares enough about to utter those words to. When Arielle thinks about it, she'll be glad to see Maya. However long she'll be in custody of Gemmaya, that twin will soften their body up good. Which is a different problem, but oh well.

"Beatrice told me you'll be baptized next month," Gemma says.

Arielle smiles. "Yeah, I guess so. It's not like we set a date though."

"Well then, you should start thinking about your new name."

"A new name?" Arielle says as she hangs a sharp left off the grounds and west to the Northway. "I have a name. I like it."

"It's not a saint's name," says Gemma.

"Huh?"

"Arielle is not a saint's name. When you're baptized, you have to take on a saint's name so you have a model of righteous behavior to guide you through your new Christian life. You especially."

"Why me especially?" Arielle doesn't believe her, because why didn't the bop inform her of this little glitch by now?

"Arielle is a mermaid, not a saint." Gemma huffs into the air. "Your mother named you after a mermaid. There's no Saint Arielle."

"Hello? I told you my mother named me after a horoscope? A ram, not a mermaid. And anyway, how can there be any new saint names if we keep using the old ones? There had to be a first Saint Gemma at some point. Why did the first Saint Gemma take that name if it was against the rules?"

"You can combine your names," Gemma says. "For instance, you can be Arielle Gemma Santos and that would suffice. It doesn't have to be your first name. It can be your middle name."

Arielle grins. "That's great!" she says. "That's it!"

"Really?" says Gemma wide-eyed. "You'd do that?"

"What? Oh, no, not that! Arielle Augusta Santos! For the relic!" She's suddenly ecstatic, over-the-top happy and warm everywhere. She can hardly control herself. This solves everything! She can't wait to tell the relic! This is how she'll keep little mama alive forever, no matter how many timelines she jumps. *Arielle Augusta Santos.* Heavenly.

"It was unkind of you to lead me on like that," says Gemma. "Not that it matters. It doesn't. Why should I care?"

"Exactly." Arielle pumps the brake as she slows down on their way through town.

"Where's my dress?" Gemma says

"Huh?"

"My SUNdress. You said I could wear your lavender SUNdress."

"Um. Okay, yeah, Maya, I have it. It's in my satchel, but it's not time yet. Go back where you came from for a while. I'll let you know when to come out, ok? You have to trust me on this. I'll pull the dress out of my satchel and then you'll know."

"Know what?"

"Know that it's time to wear the uh...dress?" Suddenly Arielle feels like smoking crack for sanity, but not really. Just a pleasant thought.

The mouse swings back and forth like this, switching continuously, almost every other sentence it seems, until, by the time she pulls up to the office building in downtown Albany, Arielle wishes she were the one seeing Dr. Rawlins instead of the twins. She turns the key and searches her backpack for the bag of coins Mike gave her for parking.

"I'm not going in there," says whoever.

"You have to," says Arielle.

"I'm not. He'll know. If I go in, I'll never come out." She sticks her head out on her neck and practically into Arielle's face. "Tell me that isn't true."

Arielle sighs, defeated. Of course it's true. She'll go in and she'll never come out. People spend whole lifetimes never saying anything that true.

"I beg you," whoever says.

"Who's doing the begging?" Arielle asks.

"Me. Gemma."

Arielle blinks. "Prove it. Say a prayer."

"*'I will tell of your name to my kindred; in the midst of the congregation I will praise you; all who fear the Lord, shout praise!'*" She brings her hands together like a steeple and points them at Arielle. "Maya would never be able to pray a psalm."

It's true. Arielle has to go with that. She switches the ignition back on, reverses out of the spot, and takes off for the fair. A plan is just a plan. This is life.

You can't get in its way.

GEMMA

Sitting restlessly in the cab of the monastery truck, Gemma scratches the tender skin on the underside of her right wrist until it's raw. She wants to stop, but she can't. The surface vessels are raised in little red pinhead dots that threaten to bleed. She doesn't want to bleed. Bleeding could bring attention to her physical issues which could stop the process of banishing Maya. Stopping that process would be calamitous. Gemma forces herself to stop by sitting on her hands.

She has just told Arielle that she refuses to see Dr. Rawlins or even enter the building. How could she see that man? He'd institutionalize her, and who would blame him? If she were to enter that building, her life would follow the arc of utter and predictable destruction, which in spite of what others may think is exactly what she is trying to avoid. She knows it doesn't always look that way; she's had her destructive moments. But after her fall on the staircase, God intervened and lit a new path for her. She's seen the light. Dim, but still—*light*. Not the perennial darkness that has consumed her past.

It can't end now.

She's relieved Arielle understands this, because if Arielle didn't or if, God forbid, Arielle decided to alert Mike, which *could still happen...* it would be a devastating blow. They would no doubt hospitalize her. She would be heavily medicated and carefully observed for a long time. It would take years before she would ever conjure the courage to face Maya again, if ever. By then Mother Augusta and her remedies would be gone. After all, how long can a person live? Gemma would be doomed to a life of hiding. Of pretending. Of punishing herself to disguise her fear of being exposed. Her terrible fear of being insane would drive her straight to insanity. She would never be allowed to take her final vows.

Even with all her degrees, or maybe because of them, Mike would never understand what's happening to Gemma. But Arielle does. Arielle understands and is willing to help. Who in the wide world would have thought this messy little hobo would show Gemma the way to wholeness? To life itself? Gemma knows there's a risk, but there are also miracles. Possibilities! Her life has been an unadulterated hell. She has to give it a chance to be something else—something good.

Gemma knows it's time for Maya to make her entrance, but she's having a hard time letting go. In fact it's taking every ounce of courage she has just to begin the awkward process of making room. For one thing, her right side is sore again and her abdomen is bloated, which she hopes is just from the stress, which is not to say it isn't killing her anyway; it is. Stress kills. It's a medical fact. But at least if the pain is from stress it will exit with Maya, because the stress *is* Maya. The pain is Maya. Maya is pain.

"I know you're not a priest, but I'd like you to hear my confession," she tells Arielle. "In case things don't work out."

They're at a red light and Arielle slams down hard on the brakes. "Not only am I not a priest, I'm not even Catholic yet!" she says. "I don't want to hear your damn confession. Save it. Things are going to work out. You have to believe."

"In the name of the Father, and the Son, and the Holy Spirit," Gemma says. "It has been one week since my last confession."

"I haven't even received the Sacrament of Reconciliation," Arielle whines. "I swear if you tell me your confession I won't take you to the carnival. You can just forget about it. No cotton candy. No Eli. Nothing." Then she turns up the radio which screams, '*You may be right...I may be crazy...but it just may be a lunatic you're looking for...*' then quickly flips the dial and turns down the volume. "Sorry," she says, nodding at the radio. "It's not like I planned that."

"Since my last confession...or actually *during* my last confession..." Gemma continues.

"STOP!" Arielle screams. She pulls the truck up to the parking gate and rolls down her window. But then she does a double take. "*During* your last confession?!" she says incredulously.

The woman says, "Parking lot B," and points straight ahead. "Follow the signs."

"During my last confession I withheld sins from my confessor," she says as fast as she can, slurring her words one into the next to get it all out. "I stoleanangelsketchfrommyroommateandtoldalietomySuperior." She takes a deep breath. "I toldmySuperiorthattheangelwasmineand Iwastheonewhodrewthesketch. So two lies. Two deliberate lies."

Arielle whips into the parking space and glares at her. "I already told you it doesn't matter. That angel belongs to all of us, not to me, remember? How could an angel belong to one person? It's impossible! Angels belong to God. Don't you know your religion? Our gifts are there to be shared by all. Ask St. Paul."

Tears burn down Gemma's cheeks in streams. She can't believe this girl's generosity. "So you're not mad? You didn't tell me that," she says. "I didn't know. The guilt has consumed me."

"Oh," says Arielle quietly. She turns off the engine and pulls out the key. "I must've told Maya, sorry. It's no sweat, believe me. You can't get all possessive about an angel, Gemma. It's like thinking God belongs to only me—or to you for that matter. I don't even know much and I know that's ridiculous."

Gemma blinks. "But in a way he does," she says. "At least it feels that way. God is the most personal thing in my life."

"It's fine if he's personal," Arielle says, "but you're not the only one he got personal with, trust me. You can't be possessive. If he's personal to you he's personal to everybody—people you like and people you don't like. You have to respect that. You have to respect everyone. You can't be a righteous bitch." She cracks into her loopy grin. "Oops."

Gemma can't afford to defend the indefensible. This is a time of truth-telling, she understands that. *Is it the tea?* "I want him to be mine," she says quietly. "All mine. I've never had anything that was all mine. I want it to be God." She bends at the waist. "Oomph," she grunts.

"What's wrong?" Arielle jumps up on her knees and hovers.

Gemma shakes her head. "Nothing, sorry." This is one thing she will not confess. Arielle is fine with taking on the mental handicap, but what would she do if she thought Gemma might collapse from a physical condition? After all, Gemma is hardly in ideal shape for a day of dizzying daredevil rides, but she has no choice. This is it; today's the day. She can't afford to delay it. If she delays it, she really will go crazy! She grips her belly, thinking this must be what it's like to have a baby. *Uhhgg. Ouch!* It's exactly what she imagines labor would feel like, not that she would know. But who is she giving birth to? Maya? Well if it's Maya then she may as well get it over with so they can both feel better.

She coughs someone else's cough, which gets stuck in her throat. She can feel her eyes tearing up from the struggle. She wishes she could just go away and let Maya have the body right now, because this is just too exhausting. But she can't. Or she won't. Maya has had pieces of her before, but not her entire being. Not this. Nothing at all like this—life without filters. Without the big Gemma filter right there overseeing everything. Little did Gemma realize how good she had it when Maya was just an annoying voice in the distance. Now she is so close Gemma feels like her marionette. Who is she anymore? What has she given up already? Everything. *Everything!*

She has nothing to lose.

She shrinks back in her seat, her lap filled with the veil, cap, and wimple she has no recollection of removing. "Did you bring any tea?" she asks hopefully.

"In the thermos," Arielle says, pointing to the glove compartment.

Gemma unscrews the cap and takes a long sip of the warm, nourishing liquid. "Please work," she whispers into the cup.

"Oh, it'll work," Arielle says, "believe me. The relic has your number or I wouldn't be here. Drink up!"

"Let's say a prayer," says Gemma, bowing her head, but then she can't remember the words—or even English. She has no language.

Her heart thumps hard, so here it comes: the switch. She has to let go. Surrender. *Disappear!* She hopes Maya will take care of her body; it isn't well. She's sorry to be giving Maya a broken body, but that's all she has.

People have no idea.

MAYA

Like a pilot, Maya sits firmly in the cerebral cortex of the body that is soon to be hers. It has taken a lifetime to get here. The body and the brain are on loan of course; she knows this. Her own body, what's left of it, will soon be gone—and she with it. So she'll have to be grateful for the one day, won't she? And she will be grateful. Who wouldn't be? What the living take for granted is sinful. A single breath is eternal.

Breathe it in.

She's been nagging Gemma their entire life for a shred of recognition, a skinny slice of the big fat life Gemma got but never appreciated. Gemma is selfish, but that's not news to anyone. Her selfishness, Maya knows, is in some part caused by the confusion of never really knowing where the dividing line is; where her identity ends and Maya's begins. So instead of living her own life well, which would have satisfied Maya, she hoarded both. Confined them to a monastery, condemned them to hard labor. She has used their precious body to express nothing but pain and suffering when Maya cared only for joy and affection. *For love!* But Maya understands what others do not. She understands that Gemma has never really found herself because half of her has always been missing.

Maya zooms more clearly into focus, though she is not yet in complete control. She feels her heart thump, her pulse quicken, her chest expand and contract with the warm sensation of breath. *Breath!* Breath of her own. From the right eye, the blue one, she sees the flashing red and green carnival lights in the distance. Nothing is visible from the left eye and never has been to Maya, though from time to time she has seen flashes of light from the right. She hears the *oompapa* music loft merrily over the hum of the car engines in the parking lot. She hears car horns and voices calling out with glee. Is one of them Eli's? She can almost feel her skin. His skin. *Their skin!* But the sense of touch is the last to be manifested. She will have to wait for this until Gemma leaves completely. Maya is giving her time. She understands. This is the one unselfish act of Gemma's lifetime. It isn't easy.

Gemma drinks the tea, swallows it, and all at once here it comes—the gravity—pulling! *Wheeeewwww. Uhhhhhh.*

Touchdown!

Maya blinks from the glare of the GORGEOUS hot sun! *Gorgeous! Hot! Sun!* She can't waste a minute.

"Where's the SUNdress?" she asks Arielle. "Do you have any LIPstick?"

Sometimes talking is so difficult. She's not used to saying these words. They're hard. It's so much easier to just think things. Or to force them like a ventriloquist through Gemma's lips. But easy isn't what she came for. Easy is boring to the point of suicide when your whole life is spent stuck in somebody else's space. *Let me out! FREE me!* Now she's here. Now she's free. She breathes on her own.

"You can put the dress on at the carnival," Arielle says. "There are restrooms there. I brought you a scarf, too, for you know...your head."

"Ohh, ohh," says Maya, bending over.

"What? What?!" says Arielle.

"I have a terrible CRAMP," she says.

"Yeah, Gemma gets those, too, don't worry. Friend on the way, ha ha! If we need to hit the ladies' room we will."

"I don't know what you're talking about," Maya says.

"Yes you do; don't play dumb. If you know what Victoria's Secret is, you damn well know what a period is."

"Oh that. Ooof! Ouch!" Her whole bottom right gut is throbbing.

"Okay fine." Arielle digs through her backpack for some Midol. "Take these!"

Maya chugs the pills with what's left of the tea. In a few minutes, the cramps subside enough. She's no sissy; she can handle some pain. She flips the visor mirror down and checks her lovely ivory-skinned face, stroking it gently—*skin!* She notices the hard red indented lines caused by the tight cap that sits in her lap and the inflammation on the underside of her right wrist. Why does Gemma torture herself? Not only with the cap, but also the shoes which are excruciatingly small.

"I need new SHOES," she says. "And a WIG."

"No wig," Arielle says firmly. "Unless they're selling clown wigs at the fair—you'd make a great redhead!"

Maya can see that as much a pushover as Arielle seems at times, she has her rules. Maya wants to respect that at the same time she doesn't. Are rules really necessary when you're only alive for one day? What would the consequences be? *Annihilation?* So what.

Arielle pulls a long flowery sash from her backpack. It's pretty, like a spring garden. She wraps it around Maya's head and ties it beneath her left ear. The strings hang down softly and all the way to her elbow, which makes her feel as if she has long, flowing hair after all. She runs the tassels through her fingers. It's good.

Holding the scarf in place, she pulls the weighty scapular over her head and tosses it recklessly behind the seat in a ball. *Who cares?* She unwinds the rosary beads and unbuckles her belt. "Where's the SUNdress?" she asks.

"Hold on, Sister," says Arielle. "We'll change the rest of that costume in the ladies' room." Arielle grabs the beads and sticks them in her backpack.

Maya has her limits, too, and she isn't waiting for any restroom. She's not taking the chance that Eli will see her walking into the fairgrounds pretending to be somebody she's not. It might scare him away. She's got nothing against nuns, but she's not going to spend a precious minute of her single day on earth dressed as one. That's final. Non-negotiable. Off come the garments faster than Arielle can object.

"Okay, fine," Arielle says, and pulls the sundress out of her bag. "Put this on before anyone walks by!" She grabs one of the garments and holds it over Gemma to block the windshield view.

In the past Maya has noticed that the sundress is big on Arielle, which is the overly-modest fit the nuns seem to like. But on Maya's larger frame, it should fit perfectly. Tightly. Sexily! *Victoria-Secretly!* She wants to feel it slink all over. She wants to make Gemma feel things she's never felt before, or if not to feel exactly, then at least to watch. If Gemma is able to, that is. After all Gemma's new to this—to experiencing life from the back seat. And anyway, Maya slept half of Gemma's life away, so there's always the possibility that Gemma can't take it either, that she's sleeping too. But what a crime that would be! In missing this one day Gemma would be missing so much. She would be missing life as it was meant to be lived—full immersion. A cannonball from the prow of an ocean liner right into life.

Splash!

"My underwear is so big and UGLY," she says, snapping the high elastic waist of her plain white cotton panties.

"Tough," says Arielle. "Nobody's gonna see your underwear anyway, believe me, and if somebody does, that's your express ticket back to Rawlins' office right there. All aboard!" She claps her hands. "I mean it. Now put the damn dress on!"

Maya ignores the Rawlins comment, because who really cares? Nobody knows what this day will bring, even her, so there's no sense arguing about it. She slips the sundress over her head and slides it down her body. It fits well, snug in the boobs and the waist, slippery on the hips. "Where are my SHOES?" she says. "I can't wear these. These are UGLY and they HURT!"

"Oh no!" says Arielle. "I forgot about the shoes!" She frowns. "Wait!" and reaches under Maya's seat where she produces a pair of beat-up flip flops.

The flip flops only remind Maya of her awful underwear and how much she'd begged Gemma to buy something pretty for her only sister's one day on earth. "Pretty please!" she'd said. But there was no way Gemma was going to buy fancy underwear no matter what. Not that she had the money.

Maya takes the flip flops from Arielle and slips them on. "They're small," she complains. "And DIRTY!"

Arielle shrugs. "Oh well. They're a lot better than a pair of tie-up oxfords. And anyway we have to get going before Mike calls the National Guard."

"What's THAT?"

"Nothing, come on."

Arielle hops out of the truck, but Maya is having a bit more difficulty since this is not anything she's used to, but also because her right side is still sore, though luckily not debilitating at the moment. The medicine is working. She walks stiffly, but then loosens up as they near the gate.

"Boo!" says someone behind them and she nearly jumps out of her skin, which to Maya seems like a real possibility.

"Aaaaaaa!" she screams, which tickles her throat. It feels good. She wants to do it again—to really relish the tickling sensation—but she sees that the spook is Jesse or 'Lucky' as Arielle calls him. And *oh my God,* right behind him is ELI! Her addled brain, taut nerves, and all the blood in her arteries and veins scream his name, "*ELI!*"

He moves swiftly to her right side where she can see him. How does he know? *He knows!* He wraps his arms around her and she nuzzles into his neck, kissing him. She loves him! She wants to kiss him until she dies. She never wants to die. She wants to kiss him forever.

"Hey hey hey!" says Lucky. "Take it slow with the nun, buddy, unless you want another black eye!" He puts his arm on Arielle's shoulder and she shoves it off.

Maya has to bite her tongue to keep from saying she's not a nun, because she isn't. She is NOT a nun! But the right words are buried in a vault somewhere at the back of Gemma's vocabulary, which is the vocabulary this brain is accustomed to using. She has to let it go. She'll have to show him that she's not a nun. Her body will say more than her speech ever could.

They walk through the pay station and Lucky deals the cash. "It's on me," he says to the rest of them. Maya can see that Arielle is unimpressed. She rolls her eyes and walks ahead. Maya wonders why Arielle is so dismissive of him, but she doesn't wonder too hard. She has more interesting things to do.

"Let's go on the Thunderbird!" Eli says jubilantly.

He's so happy! He picks her up and swings her in a circle until her ugly sandals fall off. He lets her down and she retrieves them. The skin beneath his right eye is mostly yellow with thin lines running through it like little red tributaries. Lucky's left eye looks swollen, too. Maya can't remember seeing them fight, but then so much of Gemma's life has been hidden from her. She doesn't want to ask either one of them what happened. It clearly involves conflict. Today is for love. Instead she screams, "Thunderbird!" and grabs Eli's arm for ballast.

Her toes grip the band of rubber between them and she takes long strides, skipping, jumping, allowing the happiness within her to show itself off. "Let's DO that!" she says, and wraps her arms around Eli so tightly he has to pick her up and carry her, not that he minds. He obviously doesn't.

Lucky and Arielle walk ahead of them, and Maya can see Lucky trying to playfully hold her hand or really just touch her any way he can, but nothing works. She won't let it. "Stop it!" she keeps saying. "I mean it, Lucky. Stop!"

While they're waiting in line at the Thunderbird ride, she overhears Lucky tell Arielle that he needs to talk to her seriously. That there's something he's been wanting to tell her real bad, and now that they have the time he has to get to it.

Arielle says, "Well fine, just say it for crying out loud."

"Let Eli take Gemma on the ride," he says. "I'll talk to you while they're riding."

"No!" she says. "I want to go on the ride, too. It's why we came here, remember? To have fun?" She gives him a kind of one-two punch in the side which is at least playful if not romantic. But it's something. You can tell Lucky is encouraged by any contact at all. If she kicked him in the groin he'd probably be ecstatic.

When it's time to climb into the cars, Lucky and Arielle climb into the one behind Maya and Eli even though each car can easily hold four. This is fine with Maya because now she can make-out with Eli through the entire ride, which she hopes never ends. Who knows? Maybe life is a game of musical bodies and whoever occupies the body when the music stops keeps it forever. She can wish.

Listening to Lucky and Arielle now, she can tell that something upsetting is happening in their car. Just the serious way Lucky is talking and the way Arielle is responding to him, like *"What! Are you serious?!"*

Maya hopes this argument isn't about her and Eli getting all physical. After all, Lucky still thinks she's a nun, which she is not. The last thing she needs is someone getting all holy on them since that's exactly what she came here to avoid. Well, anyway, she can't tap into their whole scenario because she has her own scenario with Eli which is a good one. A GREAT one! She has to keep herself from caring about the scenario in the car behind her, and she will. She erases it with her mind. *Gone!* The ride takes off slowly climbing.

The whole crazy business of sitting in a carnival ride with someone you love is dizzying enough. She needs space to figure it all out. *To feel it!* She strokes Eli's silky black hair, memorizing the way it parts to the left and curls behind his ear. She runs her right hand down his high cheekbone; feels the scratchy stubble on his dimpled chin. She raises her chin and kisses him. She will not waste this time no matter what Lucky thinks. Screw Lucky.

Their car moves fast now, climbing a metal mountain high into the air. Their lips are locked and Eli is deep into her mouth and she into his, and the world is made of tongues and lips and teeth. She opens her eyes to see the white clouds in the powder blue sky beyond them, because she doesn't want to miss anything at all, not even the background. *It's all foreground!* Eli's strong hands against her shoulders and ribs is so distracting, she might explode! She wants to take off her clothes and lay against him. This is her one day! *Don't waste it!*

The car reaches the top, rocks back and forth for a thrilling second, and then plunges down the rails *uhhhhh* so suddenly and so fast that their teeth bump against each other and Maya feels warm blood on her chin. Eli laughs hysterically, *screams!* Throws his head back; his long arms high in the air. Maya tries to copy him, but already the gravity is too powerful. She screams from her belly, tickling everything she has. Her eyes tear-up with life!

Behind her she hears Arielle and Lucky screaming too, and it makes her feel suddenly like they are all one thing. Like she loves them all. Like she is love itself in love with everyone and everything.

This experience is more than she ever imagined it would be. Why is Gemma so miserable all the time when life is this spectacularly invigorating? When a one dollar ride on a crazy machine with a handsome man can make you lose yourself and find yourself all at once? Two-for-one! It's so simple. So obvious. *Lay down your weapons and live!*

As the car climbs another hill, she zeroes in on Arielle's voice piercing the substantial background noise. Arielle says, "What the hell are you talking about, Lucky? That baby wasn't yours! I told you that a million times. How many times do I have to say it?! That baby is not yours, Jesse Johnson. Got it? Stop thinking it is. It isn't!"

Maya turns around because she's worried about Arielle. Arielle is her only girlfriend. If it weren't for Arielle, Maya wouldn't even be here. As she turns she sees Eli's gorgeous smiling face and realizes that he's not listening to anything but the wind and the calliope music. He's just happy! She buries her face in his musky chest and in reply, he kisses her head, plants kisses down her neck and makes his way back to her mouth. She can't bear how much she wants this man. She will do anything to have him. How can this much love be bad?!

After the ride Eli says, "Hey Gemma, let's get some popcorn!"
Gemma?!

This stops her cold and she has to consider her response. She isn't Gemma. Why doesn't he know this? Calling her Gemma is like saying he's in love with someone else. "Call me Maya," she says and instantly worries that this will spoil everything.

"Ha ha, okay, Maya!" he says then grabs her hand and they run. "I like that name," he says into the wind. "*Maya.* It's beautiful like you! I'll call you that forever."

Men are so wonderfully uncomplicated, she thinks, which thrills her, too, because it really is simple when you think about it. *Today I am Maya. Or Penelope or Jasmine or Rianna. Just call me that.* No questions. Whoever expected anyone as terrific as Eli to understand that? Or really anyone at all?

"Hold on!" hollers Arielle behind them. Her fire-red hair bounces up and down as she runs, which makes Maya jealous. She wants hair like that. Long, loopy hair. Not red; she likes her own blonde hair well enough. Long and carefree, though. Hair that says, *"I can do anything I want and nobody can stop me!"* Hair that says, *"I'm free!"*

When they get to the popcorn cart, Lucky and Arielle move to the side. Arielle's straight, stiff little back is facing the concession while she looks up at Lucky. Her hands are planted firmly on her hips, and anybody watching can tell she's mad, even from the back. Maya doesn't want to be around anybody who's angry. She can't afford anyone else's anger to infect her happy spirit. She listens hard to get the gist of the argument so she can dismiss it. How bad can it be? It's probably nothing. Arielle doesn't want to marry him, so what?

"What the hell are you talking about—your aunt has the damn baby? What the hell is your aunt doing with my kid?"

What?! Maya knows she must have heard this wrong. Arielle doesn't have a baby. If she did, everyone would know it. She lives in a monastery. Maya adjusts the scarf behind her ear so she can hear better, because maybe she misheard. Maybe the scarf has been obscuring her hearing.

"Want butter?" asks Eli eagerly. "And how about a milk shake, want that?" His green eyes hypnotize.

"Sure," she says, grinning.

"I can't believe you never told me that," Arielle tells Lucky, stomping. "What the hell right did your aunt have giving my damn baby to your third fucking cousin?"

Lucky puts his finger over his lips to indicate that people are listening, but Arielle is a brushfire; she couldn't care less. Lucky whispers something to her again and she says, incredulous, "Your cousin DIED?"

Then she gets a little hysterical, her shoulders shaking, and Maya can't help it, she doesn't want to be around all this negativity. *She can't be around it!* There's no time in her life to indulge in hissy fits for any reason. "Eli," she says, "let's LEAVE!"

He brings his head close to hers. "Seriously?"

"YES!" she says, "Let's run AWAY!"

He picks her up and squeezes her. "Whatever you want, baby," he says. "I'm all yours."

While the popcorn man pumps butter into their boxes, they grab hands and sneak to the other side of the concession. The fairgrounds are so full no one would ever find them unless they wanted to be found. Which they do not. The adrenaline pumping through Maya's system is the most exciting feeling; she could hardly ask for more of life. But she will. She will ask to lie with Eli, to feel every last molecule of him again and again until she can't take anymore. And that will be her parting gift to Gemma. The joyful feeling of Eli within her and around her. And then Gemma will have the information she needs to decide which life she really wants—the empty, punishing one or the one overflowing with joy.

They run through the park laughing, running serpentine to obscure their tracks. Maya loses her flip flops—one back at the Thunderbird and the other by the exit gate. She keeps going. Who needs shoes? Her gut is throbbing a little and she wishes she had more of those pills and maybe a cup of that tea, but it's okay. It has to be.

As they run into the parking lot, Eli pulls the keys out of his pocket and beeps the fob. "Over there," he says, pointing to a green Chevy truck whose lights are blinking. Steadier on her feet, she skips easily over to the passenger side, climbs in, and clasps her seatbelt. When he turns the key, she throws her arms in the air and squeals. She is ready for this. She is ready for anything.

MIKE

In the recovery room Mike holds Constance's bony hand. She hasn't been appreciative enough of Constance in the past. Not at all. She's lived with the woman for twenty years! Only now can she see how old Constance looks and how frail. She may be seventy-five, but lying here on this cot she looks more like ninety. Seventy-five isn't the same for everyone. For some it's the end.

Like most of the others—the big exception being Arielle—Mike has allowed herself to get annoyed at Constance's apparent hypochondria, when in fact it's clear that Constance had been truly suffering. The hard reality of her heart attack and the subsequent operation has given Mike new eyes for Constance, and really for all of the Sisters. This awareness is a timely gift, of course, because it comes with renewed resolve to preserve their communal lifestyle, their monastery and their farm. She is, after all, the leader of this small band of rebels. Unlikely rebels perhaps, but rebels nonetheless—rebels who have freely elected to follow a narrow and difficult path, a path that bucks the norms of convention. It hasn't been easy. How can she abandon her Sisters when they've come this far? She can't.

As she watches Connie drift in and out of consciousness, she vows to give the Vatican visitors all the prayer, routine, and commitment to authority they're looking for. What does it matter? Whatever they want, she'll provide it. She won't allow a few Vatican stumbling blocks to destroy their lives. There's so much to be done it's dizzying—so much to whip into shape. And Gemma is key to all of it because Gemma can lead the ritual and prayer. She's ideal for it. Born to the moment! Gemma will proudly gather them all for Matins and Laudes, Vespers and Compline. It will be as it was in the old days when they followed the Way meticulously. It won't kill them. No one will know how relaxed they've become. No one will be the wiser. Mike only prays that Gemma is able to hold it together until the visit is over. Just a couple of weeks longer, that's all. From now until then she'll do everything she can to bolster Gemma's self-confidence. Gemma is key. Her purpose is finally clear.

"Why don't you get some fresh air," a nurse says to Mike. "You've been here for a while. It can take a little time for the older ones to wake up."

Mike smiles. "I could use a break," she says. She stands and stretches then steps past the cot and presses Connie's foot as she passes. "I'll grab some lunch and be right back," she says.

Down the hallway and through the lobby, she jumps when she hears loud and unfamiliar pop music pumping in from somewhere, "*I remember...I remember... when I lost my mind! Something so pleasant about that plaaaace. Even your emotions have an echo in...so much spaaaace! Does that make me craaaazy...?*"

The music screams relentlessly from somewhere nearby. Everyone's looking at Mike, but why? *Oh my God!*

The phone!

She unsnaps the case as she runs through the lobby saying, "Sorry," to everyone under her breath. What kind of ringtone is this! Who could this be? She presses the button, "Hello?" she says as she flies through the door.

"It's Jim," says Rawlins in a thick worried voice.

"Jim? My goodness, what?" she says. "What's wrong?"

"Well actually, I was hoping you could tell me. Gemma missed her appointment."

"What!" She checks her watch. It's 12:30. "Where could they be?"

"Oh. So you don't know. I was hoping you would."

"No. No, I don't. Arielle drove her in. She's the new resident."

"Yes, Gemma mentioned her in the last appointment. Her roommate."

Mike hyperventilates. She spots a free bench in a garden area on the periphery of the circular drive and rushes to it. "Jim, this is terrible news," she says. "Where could they be?"

"I...again, I don't know."

"Well, there's not much I can do, is there?" she says frantically. "They don't have a phone between them, not that they couldn't find a pay phone wherever they are." She tries to think. "Arielle knows my number for heaven's sake; she programmed my phone. Why hasn't she called?"

"I didn't mean to alarm you, Mike," he says. "Things happen. It could be a traffic tie-up or something equally innocent. A flat tire."

"It's not traffic," Mike says. Her mind is all over the place seeking easy answers and finding none. "I'm in Albany myself at the hospital with Constance. We left at the same time. There wasn't any traffic. You don't think..." *Oh my God, an accident?* "I'll check in the ER and see if anyone's been admitted!"

"I'm sure there's a reasonable explanation," he says. "Maybe she just refused to come? Not much one young woman can do to force another to keep a doctor's appointment, now is there? They could be on their way back home. At any rate, I'll stay here through the lunch hour and wait. If they show up I'll call you right away, okay?"

"I shouldn't have let them go alone," Mike says. Her stomach lurches. What if something really did happen? "If Gemma refused to keep the appointment, I'm sure Arielle would have called," she says.

"I'll touch base with you later," he says. "Keep the faith, Mike." He hangs up.

Keep the faith? Is that all there is? Faith? Okay fine, yes, she'll keep the damn faith. Her entire life has been centered around it, so why not? But why is everything so precarious right now just when it seems to be coming together? It wasn't always this fragile. In fact, it was nothing like this! Once there was firmament.

"Why is everything so precarious, Grace?" she mutters under her breath. A familiar phrase echoes in her mind: *The chaos of new birth.* Well, at least it's birth and not death, she thinks, and hopes Augusta's right because it could be both. Is it not true that new order follows the death of the old?

Stop thinking!

Mike hustles to the entrance, through the revolving doors into the lobby and over to the front desk. "Can you tell me if two young women have been recently admitted to ER due to a car accident?" she asks breathlessly. "They would have been driving a 2003 Chevy pickup with New York plates. One of them is a nun dressed in full habit from the St. Grace monastery outside Hebronville."

The receptionist puts her finger up indicating that Mike should wait, and presses a button. "Any recent ER admittances from a car crash?" she asks. "Two young women from the monastery?" She listens.

Mike taps her foot impatiently. She resists grabbing the phone from the woman.

"No?" the woman says into the phone. "Okay good, but give me a buzz if you hear anything." She hangs up. "No, Sister," she says. "I'm sorry, nothing."

"Can you give me the numbers of other hospitals in the area?" Mike asks.

The woman escorts Mike into a back office and asks one of the volunteers to assist her. "We'll do our best," she says kindly. "I've attended chapel at your monastery and enjoyed your homilies very much." She clutches Mike's elbow and whispers earnestly, "I'll say a prayer."

Beads of sweat form on Mike's forehead. She can't believe how unsettling this is. There is nothing good about this. Nothing. This is terrible! What will Augusta do if anything has...happened? What would any of them do? Only now does she realize how much Arielle has come to mean to them all. And in a different way, Gemma too. So difficult, of course, so orthodox, but still a leader in her own way—leading them back to formal prayer perhaps, or sacred ritual. Or maybe just a troubled young woman in Mike's care, it doesn't matter. She's one of them. She's family.

Mike wipes her brow with her jacket sleeve as the volunteer continues to phone emergency rooms between Fort Ann and Albany. One after the other—nothing. No news whatsoever. Which is a good thing, Mike supposes, but still. What happened? *Where are they?*

The afternoon passes into evening with no news. Mike phones Beatrice to no avail. The girls have not shown up at the monastery. They are nowhere to be found. Mike spends an uneasy afternoon with Constance, encouraging her, painting a bright picture of the monastery's future. Filling in more detail about the visitation while at the same time reassuring her that they will survive it. All the while Mike feels her insides turning out. She's surprised no one notices how fearful she is. How crazy she feels. Surprised that nobody offers to pick her up off the floor and put her back together. She feels as if she's the one who's been in an accident.

As she pats Constance's hand goodbye, she tells her, "I'll be back in the late morning, Constance. The doctors believe you'll be able to return home tomorrow. I'm hopeful."

"I can hardly wait," Constance says. "I miss everyone, especially that little girl, you know. It's hard to believe, isn't it? Such a little bit of a wild baby bird like that has me all tied up like a grandmother. It's never too late to fall in love, is it?"

Mike chokes. She blinks back tears and shakes her head. "See you tomorrow," she says, and walks out.

On her way to the car she can hardly believe that no one has called. That she has lived through this entire painful afternoon with no news whatsoever. The more silent her phone, the louder her mind. Her imagination bursts with pent-up energy conjuring scene after scene, some good and some tragic. After reviewing all conceivable possibilities it occurs to her that the worst of all is not the possibility that the girls were run off course somewhere, but that they deliberately changed course. She barely allows the thought in, but once there, it sticks. Betrayal? Thievery? Is it possible? What if Arielle...but no. What if...?

No! *Still.* She gets into her sedan and starts the car thinking she'll mow down that field of hay when she comes to it. When she gets back to the monastery she'll do what it takes—call the police, put out an APB. She'll do what she has to do. She can't stand not knowing.

By the time Mike gets halfway back to the monastery, she's reverted to her original conviction that she'll see the truck right there in the driveway. She visualizes it with the back bumper badly dented. It's there. At dinner both girls will tell a satisfying story that will give them all a laugh or at least a sigh of relief. They can't be missing, right?! They can't be. As much as Mike realizes that Gemma has not been completely stable—and also that Arielle's background is irrefutably sketchy, still—their lives in the monastery have been somewhat...well, normal. Haven't they? Mike is a trained psychologist. What has she missed? Has the abnormal become so routine that she trusted what she should not have trusted? Swept too much aside?

Up the Northway she drives at least 10 miles over the speed limit and on some stretches, when she thinks she can get away with it, as much as 15. She drives with the trucks since she believes they all have radar detectors. She's not a proponent of speeding, but the car she's driving isn't racing a fraction of the speed that her heart is. She needs to get home.

Off the highway and onto the lesser routes, she has to slow down significantly as she drives through Hebronville and its outskirts to the monastery. At every traffic light she is searching for the girls. Have they been abducted? God, let it not be so! In truth she is also searching for the young men, Eli and Jesse, to find out what they might know, if anything. They seemed upstanding; they were medics for heaven's sake! And they seemed to care a lot about Arielle. If the girls aren't home when she gets there...*they will be though.* They will. *But if they're not*— she'll call fire and rescue and let the young men take care of the search. The boys will find them. The boys will bring them home.

The tires screech as she makes a hard right past the monastery gates and up the long, dirt and gravel driveway. It's only six o'clock and already the light is getting dim. Summer is waning fast. She doesn't want night to fall without finding them. Without knowing where they are. *Where are they?*

In the hallway, she's greeted by a dour faced Beatrice dressed in a navy gingham blouse and wrap-around denim skirt, not her usual cheery colors. "Did you find them?" Bea asks eagerly, but discreetly. Quietly.

Mike shakes her head no. "I don't suppose they've called?"

"No," Beatrice says solemnly. She cocks her head in the direction of the dining room and whispers, "They don't know anything. I didn't want to get them going."

Mike appreciates this more than she can express. She takes Beatrice's plump, doughy hand and says, "Oh thank you, Beatrice. I'm not ready for full-force histrionics. And besides, I'm sure there's a perfectly good explanation," she lies.

"They'll be curious when they see the girls aren't with you," Beatrice says. "I mean at some point …"

"At some point they'll be home," Mike snaps. She lays down her wallet clutch on the hall table, sighing. "I'm sorry, Beatrice, I didn't mean that. It's been a very long day."

"I understand," she says and waddles down the hall to the dining room calling out, "Mike's home!" with forced gaiety. "Set the table, girls!"

At dinner Mike nibbles her seared scallops and pushes her corn salad around. Even though her stomach is growling, she's more anxious than hungry. She manages to drink her glass of chardonnay, however, as a means of warding off well…consciousness. Not that she means to pass out, but her brain is a traffic jam of conflicting scenarios and she has to put a red light to some of it in order to survive. Just concentrate on the meal, she tells herself. On what's right in front of you and nothing else.

"The food is delicious," she tells the Sisters.

Gabriella's faded copper-colored hair sticks out like straw from the sides of her head. She pushes the slipped nose of her wire-framed glasses up again and again, a nervous tic. "How's Constance?" she asks.

"Constance is better," Mike says. "She misses everyone, though. I'm very hopeful she'll be home tomorrow."

Gabriella, Rose and Beatrice all bless themselves as if to secure this outcome. "Amen," says Rose.

"She's very pale," Mike says. "She'll be resting for some time, I think."

"Oh we won't push her at all," says Gabriella. "We'll take good care of her—the best!" She coughs. The cough turns to hiccups.

"Drink backwards from the glass, Gabi," says Beatrice. "That a girl." Bea pats her back as she drinks.

After two attempts this technique fails and Rose shyly offers her breathing remedies. Eight tries and twenty minutes later, the hiccups finally stop. This is killing Mike—an entire dinner hour centered on middle-aged hiccups. She wonders if she were left with these three women alone, sincere as they are, if she could survive it. Not that Constance would make it any more interesting; she wouldn't. They've all become accustomed to the energy of the younger candidates. Dramatic but real. Life as it was meant to be lived, including generations of people sharing experience and life force. There's a lot of experience at this table, but no life. No force but gravity.

Mike checks her watch: 7:15. For God's sake, *where are they?!* "Has Mother eaten?" she asks evenly.

"I brought her a turkey sandwich at five," says Rose, glancing down and playing with her napkin. "But she wouldn't eat it. I left it there on the tray table. She asked me to make this complicated tea. She sent me all over the place for the ingredients." Her eyes widen, "I didn't mind though, honestly. But it took me an hour. She was nicer to me than usual."

Mike straightens her back and leans against the chair. "What, uh…what did she call the tea? Did it have a name?"

Rose concentrates. "She called it Spirit Tea," she says. "I'm pretty sure that was it. A lovely name—Spirit Tea." She reaches for a dinner roll. "It smelled good, too, but she forbade me to have any."

Spirit Tea, Mike thinks, yes. She remembers Mother saying that it *"strengthens the spirit against the coming troubles."* Mike wants some Spirit Tea right now. She needs it. She can't call the police without it. "Excuse me, Sisters," she says. "I'm going to see if Mother has eaten her dinner yet."

"Are you going to tell us anything before you go, though?" says Gabriella.

Mike sets her napkin on the table. "What did you have in mind, Gabriella?" She asks this as matter-of-factly as she can, but her veneer is thinning.

"Just, well…about Arielle? And Gemma?" she says.

"Yes," says Rose eagerly. "About where they are? Where are they? Are they staying in Albany?"

"Don't worry about them," says Mike. "They're big girls. They'll be home before we know it."

"But shall we keep the scallops warm?" asks Gabriella.

Mike nods. "Yes, keep them warm," she says, and walks swiftly down the hall to the back door and across the fields to the trailer.

Up the cement steps, she knocks on the door and opens it a sliver, pausing to collect herself. What will she say? She can't tell Mother that Arielle's missing. But she has to say something. *She needs the tea.*

"Is that you, Arielle?" says the crackling voice inside.

"It is I, Mother" says Mike as cheerfully as she can. "Michael Agnes." She walks in smiling. "You need some light in here," she says, and flicks the switch. "It's getting dark already."

Augusta reads her like the palm of a hand. "She's gone," she says to Mike.

Mike swallows.

"She's gone but she'll be back, you'll see."

Mike blinks back tears. She knows how much this means to Augusta. "I need some tea," she says. "Please don't say no."

"Yes," says Augusta. "Yes, dear, you do need the tea. It's time." She points her crooked finger in the direction of the stove. "Warm it up, Michael Agnes. Warm it up and steep the herbs for exactly three minutes."

Mike pulls a chipped teacup from the cabinet and turns on the flame under the kettle. When it whistles, she pours the water and steeps one of the cheesecloth balls of herbs marked "Spirit Tea" into her cup for exactly three minutes, up and down. With her back to Augusta, she sips the tea for courage and feels its warmth empower her as it trickles down her throat. "It's lovely, Mother," she says. "Smooth but electrifying. Thank you."

"The troubles are here," Augusta says, leaning earnestly forward.

"Yes," says Mike. "Yes they are." Three long strides and she's across the room at the long narrow window that faces the farmhouse. She sits on the cushioned bench underneath it, sipping her tea and willing herself at peace. Neither talks. Mike turns, parting the café curtains to peek outside. The hot red sun scorches the sky until it bleeds streaks of orange and violet in every direction. Mike knows she has to call the police. She also knows she's on her own and can't bother Mother with any of it. Mother won't get past her own code: *the troubles*. She can't. She can provide the tea, but this is not Augusta's test. This is Mike's.

"Would you like any of us to stay with you tonight?" Mike asks her.

"No, dear," she says, "but thank you. I appreciate that." Her sunken, baby blue eyes hold Mike's gaze like little magnets as she says, "Gracie and I will be just fine alone."

Mike crosses the sunflower patch, realizing that in spite of the ongoing conundrum of Mother's sanity, the tea has truly smoothed the rhythm of her heart. This is good. Very good. She does not feel panicked at the moment, and she's breathing steadily. There is something to that tea. It should be available to everyone, why not? Whose spirit does not need strengthening? Whose life does not have troubles? At any rate, now she feels better prepared to call the police, not that she wants to. But she will. The tea has brought clarity.

And furthermore, maybe those young medics will help her find Gemma and Arielle. Of course they will. Unless… she stops mid-step.

The young men... They couldn't, right? *No!* What kind of conspiracy theorist is she becoming? And then she remembers the letter in her drawer—the one with "GEMMA" in bold block letters on the envelope.

She steps up her pace past the sunflower field and pumpkin patch, and by the time she's reached the tool shed she breaks into a vigorous run. Rather than enter from the back door so close to the kitchen where the Sisters are no doubt huddled, instead Mike sneaks around to the front, walks up the porch steps, slips through the front door and directly into her office where she rifles through the middle desk drawer. Where is it? She checks the other drawers—*nothing!* It's here though; she knows it is. She put it there herself. Right...there! Unless... But who? *Oh no!*

ARIELLE

Arielle follows the dejected loser into his rented cottage on the river, not that she wants to be here; she doesn't. She'd rather be downriver in Sing Sing pounding bricks with a 300 ton sledge hammer until her hair bleeds. This is a day she'd like to package and shove up someone's ass. Eli would be the best ass for that since he's the one who ran off with Maya, but Lucky will have to do. She's never had a worse day in her entire life and that's saying something. She wants to go home. But she can't.

The loser sets the monastery truck keys on his kitchen table and switches the lights on. It's nine o'clock and still no sign of life or death from the traitors. If it weren't for the relic and the beahive—*her family!*—Arielle wouldn't really give a damn. The traitors are adults. Let them figure it out. But because of her family at the monastery, she does give a damn. Not a Bucky Beaver damn, a colossal Hoover damn. She probably hasn't cared about anything this much since her baby was born, which is one more Mount Everest she's expected to conquer in a day. *Convergence!* If she thought it included this, she would have screwed up the tea recipe on purpose.

Lucky checks his gigantic overly-functioned self-important watch that includes enough buttons to launch a nuclear attack. "I gotta call the boys about Eli," he says. "We gotta find out what happened. I can't hold off any longer."

It isn't as if they haven't been speed-dialing the traitor's cell phone for the last five hours; they have. Although he might've lost the phone the way Maya lost her flip-flops, but probably not. And anyway, they only found one of the flip-flops, and that was by complete accident. Other than that, nothing about this day seems accidental. Arielle has never felt so set-up.

The loser grabs a beer from the fridge, hisses it open and swigs.

"You can't call the fuzz," she says. "Eli and Ma...er...Gemma are adults." She has to remember—the loser doesn't know anything about the Maya twin.

Lucky points to the beer and then to her with a quizzical look as if beer would actually improve things for two alcoholics.

"No," she says. "And what are you doing drinking a goddamn beer anyway? Aren't you supposed to be going to NA?"

"It's alcohol free," he says, pointing to the label. "Relax. And for your information, I haven't had a narcotic for two years four months and eighteen days. I don't ever intend to have another one. The army changed me; I told you that. I meant it." He swigs. "And I go to NA every so often...whenever I need to, don't worry. I have a buddy. I pay attention."

When she doesn't say anything, because...*who cares...*he sets his big booted right foot on the chair and leans in to her. "I'm not the same guy, Ari. I was a pushy drunken cocaine-addicted asshole when we got married. I regret the hell out of that."

"You're still pushy," she says. "And you're still..."

He puts his hand up to stop her. "Maybe so, but I'm also upstanding and trustworthy."

"Yeah right."

His expression sours fast. "Look, I know you're upset about Gemma, but I didn't run off with her, Eli did. So maybe you could cut me some slack?"

"Slack? Are you kidding?" She points her finger with ultra-obnoxious emphasis like Willa the Witch would've done—mean, but effective. "Not only did I lose my roommate and probably my home today," she says, "but I also found out your damn cousin adopted my kid three years ago and then died on her! Shitty day!"

He eases into the ladder-back kitchen chair and covers her tiny hand with his Godzilla paw. She wants to slip it out, but it's trapped. "I tried to be gentle with that news, Ari, but come on! The baby needed a home then and again now. Louise adopted her, so what? She was a great mom! If you want to blame someone, blame my mom for caring. My mom arranged it. Remember her? How much you loved my mom? Blame her. She knew people at the agency. She cared about your kid."

"I would've kept her," Arielle says. "And if the damn agency wouldn't allow it they should've at least given me the final say." Her eyes tear up and she cops a hard core look to ward off the flood, but it might not work. She really feels like smoking something. A cigarette or smack. She needs a meeting.

"Look, that was three years ago," he says gently. "You were seventeen and let's face it, an addict. No seventeen-year-old addict has a right to raise a guppy, never mind a human. And for your information, Louise loved the shit out of that baby, you'll see. She's a wonderful kid! Happy!" He nods knowingly. "And smart!"

It kicks her in the ass that the loser knows anything at all about her baby. That the loser knows what her baby looks like and how smart she is. *Fuck him!* Just hearing these simple facts turns her body into a vial of unfamiliar chemicals—or maybe overly familiar like the toxic waste of her acid-washed youth. Acid that burned-out every good thing that ever started happening before it had a chance to happen. It feels like that. Like someone poured a bottle of bleach over her life.

"I gotta take a leak," the loser says, as if she cares to know what the hell he's about to do behind closed doors.

While he's gone she realizes she can't afford to go off into crazy land where drugs are the only exit. She has to ground herself. Notice where she is in space. In the "Now" as the guru—deadly Sin # 6—used to say. That was the one good thing about the guru—he was a jealous son of a bitch, but he loved Arielle and Willa; he really did. Too much. "Be in the Now…" he would say. Arielle loved that. She learned stuff from him. Too bad he was so jealous of every breath that entered

Willa's lungs without his consent as if the oxygen were having sex with her. He wanted to be her breath; to live inside her. To live in the foxhole of Willa.

In the Now Arielle notices that she is in a perky little kitchen that when you think about it, is the opposite of anything she can imagine housing the loser. In the Now there are red-checked curtains and a purple striped tablecloth—not exactly matching, but. And there on the counter, next to the iPod probably meant for the relic, is a vase with a fake daisy in it, ha ha! *What!* The loser must've had a girlfriend recently. Or an estrogen injection.

She can't really see anything outside the kitchen; it's too dark. But close by she can hear the river babbling away. *Where's Goldilocks?* And inside it actually smells good, like walnuts roasting on an open fire. Not really, but she does smell salted peanuts, which is making her hungry. If it didn't include the loser, this would be a nice place to live. She might enjoy it. Which reminds her, where is he? This is the longest pee ever.

She gets up, strolls into the next room and turns on a wall light. It's the TV room with a tweedy old burnt orange couch that smells like 1940 and a recliner chair with cigarette burns, otherwise known in the trailer park as a beer chair. Also there's a bookcase, as if the loser ever read a book, but you never know. He might've read the comics. She surveys his collection, expecting to find *Babar and Barbarella Go to Vegas*, which when you think about it could be a bestseller. But instead she finds a bunch of books by old people like Charles Dickens and Mark Twain that obviously came with the house, because. Oh, and look...*Moby Dick*. Perfect.

And here's a picture of Lucky and his deceased mom, Maggie, not that she's deceased in the picture. *Ugh*—not funny. Arielle bends in to inspect the photo, admire it really, because Maggie was the coolest lady ever, no kidding, and maybe the whole reason Arielle fell for Lucky in the first place. Maggie was a winner with a loser kid. It happens. Not that the loser was a kid when she met him; he was twenty going on ten. Statutory by legal standards maybe, and also if Arielle wasn't asking for it, which she was. She wanted to throw Deadly Sin # 3 off her scent.

Bring in another male. *Lure him in.* Some people aren't sixteen when they're sixteen. Some people are born thirty, but it's hard to prove in court. Not that the loser knew she was only sixteen. He didn't.

The fact of her pregnancy was just a blue herring. Or whatever fish, she can't remember. She's pretty sure she was already pregnant when she lured the loser, which is the reason she let it happen to begin with—so Willa wouldn't hang her from the water tower. So there would be someone else to blame it on. Not that the loser wasn't handsome then; he was. He rocked the Tim McGraw vibe—all country western musk. If he wasn't so messed up inside he could've had the trailer park version of Faith Hill or really, anybody. Anyway, Arielle refused to see him through the entire pregnancy which would've been a relief to most losers, but. Whatever. He's no ordinary loser.

A light flickers behind her and she jumps like a cricket. At the same time the light flickers and she jumps like a cricket, she spots another picture on the shelf just above eye-level. The picture catches her attention, hand-cuffs it, and puts it behind bars. She only saw it for the split second she jumped, but she knows the picture well. It's the one of her and Lucky on the day of their micro-marriage about a month after the baby was born and apparently shipped off to live with his cousin, Louise.

You could call it their wedding day or you could call it the day after Willa disappeared, or the day before their divorce—or annulment really since, on that day at least, they didn't close the deal. Take your pick. Or you could call it the day of her seventeenth birthday even though her ID said eighteen. Not that she needed a fake ID to get married, she didn't. Willa would've released her to a slave camp in the Sudan at that point. She was a swarm of gnats in her mother's eyes.

So the day of their wedding Arielle was barely seventeen and the loser was twenty-one. She got her fake ID from Deadly Dad #3's second cousin once removed from prison. Not that Lucky wondered about her age. He questioned nothing. He was too busy popping pills and smoking everything but his borrowed suit. Twenty minutes after they said "I do" he screwed the random city hall witness behind a tree in the municipal lot while Arielle was changing into her jeans. After he popped the pills and screwed the city hall witness, he passed out in the car he was driving with Arielle in it. They landed in a ditch with a few bumps and bruises and an annulment because the accident reminded Arielle that she had a brain. And her brain told her she was not intended to repeat her mother's life.

Back in the Now Lucky startles her when he walks in, still buckling his belt. "I want us to get married again," he says.

What?! "You're crazy," she says. "Out of your gourd."

She notices that his hair is suddenly all combed like he was grooming himself in the bathroom. He steps closer. "I'm not going to press you on this, Ari. And I know you think that Giselle isn't mine."

Her hand flies to her chest and her heart stops. "Giselle?"

He grins; nods. "Beautiful, right? Like her."

She finds herself smiling, speechless.

"But even if she isn't mine..." he says.

"She isn't." Giselle belonging to the loser would be against all laws of fairness, not that life has been exactly fair, but at some point shouldn't it even out?

He reaches into his back pocket and takes out his wallet, opens it.

"No," she says. "No pictures. I'm not ready to see her."

He lifts a worn picture from his wallet and checks it out, smiling. She's surprised by how happy that picture makes him. It's so wrinkled you can tell he's looked at it a million times. He slips it back into his wallet. "Take your time," he says. "But she needs a home, and with or without you I'd like to give her one."

Arielle can't believe this is happening. "I live in a monastery," she says.

"You don't have to."

"I love it there. They're my family."

"We wouldn't be far. Ten minutes tops. And I could buy this place."

"With what, box tops? Give me a break."

"With a veteran's loan and the money I've saved. We could..."

Arielle's weak, but not that weak. "No," she says. "There's no 'we' in this, Lucky. She's mine. I'm the one with the stretch marks." Which isn't exactly true, but.

He pulls his blonde moustache slowly, strokes his beard, reaches in for her gaze and holds it. "I took a DNA test," he says.

Her eyes bug out and dangle on springs. When she regains her focus, she says, "You had no right! What kind of a damn world is it when the mother doesn't even know where her kid is and some loser is taking a fake DNA test to get custody! Where's the justice in that!" She walks to the beer chair and drops down, reclines, stares at the split-beamed ceiling which is actually pretty nice. "What were the results of the fake test, not that I would believe it anyway."

He shrugs. "I took it yesterday. It takes a while."

The phone rings and he pulls it out of his pocket, mouthing, "Gotta get this" to Arielle. He turns and wanders into the kitchen as if she can't hear him there.

"They did!" he says alarmed. "What did you tell them? You can't put out an APB on adults who haven't committed a crime." He listens, hunched. "Oh geez," he says then listens for a minute. "Call it off; we've got the truck. We'll return it now."

Arielle's heart sinks like Atlantis. What should she do? Should she let the loser return the truck and walk home? Does she have a choice? Should she just fall on her sword and tell Mike everything? And what about Lucky who still doesn't know about Maya? But what good would that do? None. He would just get all righteous. Her forehead breaks out in a prickly sweat.

Lucky hangs up the phone and turns to her. "Mike called in a report to Jake," he said. "Kidnapping with stolen vehicle."

She blinks. "Did you tell them there was no kidnapping?"

"We don't really know that, do we?"

"We know there's no stolen vehicle."

"Not technically, but until you return the monastery truck, how do they know that? We need to return the truck."

"I will. Case closed."

"Not quite. Eli's already an hour late for his shift."

"Well, maybe he'll show up. Give him time. They could be driving into the station as we argue."

"The guys at the station have been calling him on the scanner all night. He's ignoring them or he's shut it down. They called his neighbor, too. No sign of Eli anywhere. And he still isn't answering his cell." He crosses his arms. "Look," he says, "why don't you let me return the truck and tell the gals you decided to visit your Aunt Lulu in Watertown, or wherever. Get you off the hook for a while. You can stay with me until we figure this out." He pleads with his stupid pleading eyes.

"They're my family," she says, standing. "And as usual, I'm not that innocent."

"What's that supposed to mean?"

"It means give me the keys and I'll live my own life, thank you."

He gives her the keys and a couple of twenties.

"I don't want money," she says. Not that she doesn't want money, but she doesn't want his.

"Keep it anyway. You never know. You should always have cash."

"They give me an allowance," she says, which is sort of true since Mike coughs up change whenever she sends Arielle into town. But Arielle always returns it because what does she really need?

They stare at each other for a dumb minute, which makes no sense. It isn't Casablanca! She snaps out of it first and grabs the iPod. "Thanks for this," she says, and races to the door.

"Wait," he says with so much authority that she stops.

"What?"

He reaches into his wallet and pulls out Giselle's picture. "Stick it in your pocket," he says. "For later. When you're ready."

Her brain performs a seek-and-find for any good reason not to, but comes up with nothing. "Fine," she says, and takes the photo upside down, stuffs it in her back pocket and leaves. She can always toss it. It isn't a tattoo.

Back in the truck Arielle drives down the gravel path through the thick woods of the cottage property and out to the paved road. Her stomach is break-dancing to the street beat of her crazy thumping heart. This is the worst convergence ever. But is she really to blame? And if so, is there no mercy? Because maybe there is. According to the bop there's mercy all over the place in a religion whose main job is to forgive sinners exactly like her. *Mercy, mercy me! Things and what they used to be.* When you think about it, the whole religion would be out of business if no one sinned, so. Might as well be her.

She can't help it—as soon as she gets into town she pulls into the parking lot of Coyote Gas Express which is conveniently located next to Coyote Liquor, not that she needs gas. She sits in the truck, staring at the Johnny Walker display on the other side of the gas pumps. Staring, wishing, wanting, and practically serenading the display. *I love you joh-ho-ny! Oh yes I dooo!*

Just then a man walks out the door and pulls a pint of whatever scotch from a paper bag. She mentally siphons it from his bottle. It's just her mind, not her mouth. Just scotch, not crack or meth! It's not illegal. And anyway scotch can kill a pain in the ass as well as anything. *And then what, genius?* Her eyes follow the bottle—she can practically taste the sharp, crackly, caramely acid—follows it up to the mouth of the man who twists the bottle top and chugs. She is the man! She is the man's mouth. His tongue. His throat.

She wants to chug the scotch with him or without him. Just a tiny little baby sample bottle. Not a goddamn quart! Or even a pint. Just enough to coax her in from the 20-story ledge she's hanging from by her chewed-up fingernails. *"Come on, baby! Come on in! We gotcha!"* She hops out of the truck, hustling toward the station where a man is capping his tank and jumping into his...

"WHAT?!"

The man is unmistakably Eli.

"Wait!" she says.

He slams the door and turns the key, and Arielle's not completely sure that he saw or heard her because the radio is blasting a Kings of

Leon tune: "*Your sex is on Fiiire!*"

A female voice calls out "Hurry UP, ELI!"

Arielle rushes over and hangs onto the outside door handle, jumping up and down from the cement island like a pogo stick. "Hey!" she yells, "Hey! It's me! Arielle! Where the hell have you two been? You've made us crazy!" She's mad, but also relieved because—they're here. She found them! Now she can inject some sense into their over-sexed heads!

Finally noticing her, Eli's eyes zero in like a zoom lens and—*click!*—take a picture. He panics; screeches the truck into reverse and then lurches it forward, taking off.

The forward momentum causes Arielle to let go of the handle and drop to the pavement. She recovers fast and runs after them. "Hey! Get back here!" she screams. "Where the hell are you going?" Did they even see her? They must have seen her! It's all so unreal.

The next minute Maya throws herself halfway out the window screaming, "We're going to Vegas, Arielle! To get MARRIED! Yaaaahoooooooooo and thanks for everything! We owe it all to you!"

Arielle runs after the truck a good fifty feet, choking on their Bonnie & Clyde dirt cloud. She made it happen—Arielle did. All by herself with the loser's help. So who's the loser now? She stands in the shop light for about ten minutes debating. Meeting or vodka? Meeting or scotch? Meeting or cognac? Can't decide.

No harm in window shopping though, so she walks inside and strolls up and down the funky aisles decorated with giant sparkly gold-foil bottles of fancy-ass champagne and jiggly rum-drinking hula dancers. Liquor stores are so much fun! But just to show she's a responsible patron and not a loitering shoplifter, she buys a plastic 12-pak of little brandy-flavored cigarillos, a six-pack of extra-caffeinated diet-whatever and oh, a bottle of Grey Goose Vodka l'Orange because why not? She's never tried the orange. And anyway vodka isn't scotch. Vodka doesn't make you mean.

Whistling to keep things light and upbeat, she strolls matter-of-factly back to the truck and climbs into her seat like she just bought a gallon of distilled water for her steam iron. Her heart is performing triple flips off an 800 foot cliff somewhere like Acapulco, somewhere tropical and worth visiting. The beat is so out-of-control that if her heart called her up right now, she'd tell it to get its cliff-diving ass home this minute. Her chest hurts. Everything does.

She rolls down the window, lights a brandy cigarillo, inhales, and coughs her head off. So what? When was the last time she smoked? Her lungs need time to adjust. Not that she has to inhale; she doesn't. She tries again, just sucking the smoke into her mouth and pushing it out before it gets into her throat. That's better. Nice! Not exactly smooth, but.

She places the cigarillo in the ashtray and slides the bottle of vodka out of the paper bag. Rolls it in her hands. She feels the smooth glass, the shiny label, the indentation on the bottom of the bottle. Alcohol isn't really her problem anyway. She was never an alchie when she thinks about it, which is why she ended-up in NA. Not AA. She was being very careful staying away from everything, but was that really necessary? What about altar wine? No harm in that. In fact…grace galore!

She takes one more tug on the cigarillo, puts it down and untwists the bottle cap. The tangy orange smell overwhelms her smell buds. Ohhh baby! But then she thinks—what? *Did I say, "baby"*? This baby thought kills the fun right there, which is the problem with babies. She still wants the vodka; she'll have the vodka, no problem. She's not an alcoholic. But first, she'll look at the baby picture. *Are you sure?* Yes, she's sure. She shouldn't be the last one to know what her kid looks like. She lifts her bony butt, pulls the picture out of her back pocket and lays it on the console upside down.

She puffs the cigar once and replaces it in the tray. Maybe she should take a wee sip before she checks out the picture. A wee sip is innocent enough in the face of impending motherhood for God's sake. When will she ever drink again? *Where will she live?* What does she know about being a mother? Nothing if you go by her childhood. Zip! But neither did Willa and Willa got to be a sort-of-mom. The back of the picture says *Giselle* in scribbly writing that might be Lucky's. Well at least Louise had great taste in names. Giselle isn't even a name Arielle would change. And look—the last part of it is the same as hers! They're both Elle's! Maybe that's why Louise picked that name. She grabs the picture and runs her fingers up and down trying to prepare herself for her daughter's image through some kind of Zen picture Braille. It doesn't work.

She sniffs the orange vodka again and swears she's getting high just by sniffing. She probably is. It works with glue so why not vodka? Maybe she should call her sponsor, but no. That would be so melodramatic. It isn't even a joint. It's orange vodka, LOL! Her sponsor would get hysterical laughing, *mocking* her! "Oh for God's sake, Arielle, call me when you're about to sniff toot! Orange vodka is way too PTA, ha ha ha!" And anyway, she doesn't have a phone, so.

Okay fine—she'll take one peek at Giselle's picture and then she'll sample the vodka. A sip; that's it. A single sip of mostly orange vodka. Orange juice, for God's sake! *Call off the Gestapo!* She settles back in the seat and flips the overhead and also the visor light so she can see every last pixel. Okay, ready.

She turns the picture over and nearly caves in, nearly implodes, because have you ever seen Cupid? Or baby angels on a Christmas card? That's exactly what she's looking at. Her baby is an angel. A tsunami of emotions rushes over and under and through her, threatening everything. Her eyes spill tears she hardly notices while she stares at the fat rosy cheeks, the big swimming pool eyes, and oh my God, the halo of fired-up curls, and the little dimpled chin that are unmistakably hers. This is her kid. *Hers.* This kid is Arielle's one thing on earth.

The knock on the back window of the truck nearly gives her a fucking heart attack! She turns, ready to pounce.

It's Lucky.

"Sorry," he says. "I just…was worried."

She stares, blinking.

He swipes his fat thumb slowly across her cheek like a windshield wiper. "If you drink that stuff you could lose her again," he says quietly, pointing to the vodka.

She nods. This suddenly makes sense.

"So. Maybe hand me the bottle?"

She inhales the stuff deeply into her sinuses one more time then twists the cap back on and hands it over. "I didn't have any," she says.

"What about the cigars?" he says. "You really want those?" He reaches in and takes the plastic case. She doesn't protest.

"Fine," she says, and squashes the one that's lit and hands it to him.

"Let me take you to a meeting?" he says.

"No. This was meeting enough. I'm done. I swear. But thanks?"

He doesn't press, which is so unlike the loser. Maybe underneath all the speedballs, dope, and unzipped pants he's a nice enough guy, not that she cares.

"I saw them," she says.

"Eli?"

She nods. "They're on their way to Vegas with a full tank."

His head bobs up and down thoughtfully. "I'll let Jake know."

"They're adults," she says defeated. "Right? They can do what they want?"

He shrugs, "We'll see. Will you tell Mike?"

"I have to."

He chucks her chin gently and returns to his car, waits a minute before he follows her truck through town and all the way to the monastery. It's dark and there are other cars around, but she knows it's him. She isn't stupid. He's a baboon's ass, but he cares about her. She'll give him that.

MIKE

In the dark kitchen, Mike dips a small ball of fragrant herbs wrapped in cheesecloth into her mug of steaming water. *Spirit Tea.* Maybe it will help her sleep. Last night she pilfered a six pack from the trailer, which may not suffice. She would pour it over her head if it would make her stronger, because if her spirit needs anything right now, it's strengthening in the face of advancing trouble. Mother's prediction is clearly manifest, and God only knows what its fullness portends. *Are the girls alive?* At this point Mike can only drink the tea, hope for the best, and strengthen her spirit against a worst case outcome. She does not want to resonate with the fear that's settling in.

Though the tea is unmistakably nourishing, she can't help wishing it were triple-espresso. But of course if it were espresso—she might never sleep. Not that she can sleep anyway; she can't. But sometime in the next half-century she'd like to give it another try. Upstairs she hears Beatrice and Gabriella chatting nervously while no doubt knitting their fifth lap blanket since Constance was taken to ER. What will Constance do with five blankets! Rose is in the den watching a late night rerun of some low-brow nonsense—*Desperate Housewives* perhaps—one of her favorites. *Desperate Nuns* would make a great reality show, Mike thinks. Make a lot of money. Maybe she'll give Hollywood a call when the Vatican evicts them.

Mike can't really hide the fact that she's been reduced to a classic nervous wreck. At this point she's really no more pulled together than any of them, even Gabriella. How did this happen? She was always such a low-key practical sort—a no-nonsense problem solver. But in this "rebirth" as Augusta so poetically calls their catastrophic unraveling, everything is up for grabs. This is no run-of-the-mill chaos, no. Pure Apocalypse. Christ in his fury at the temple overturning corrupt systems and entrenched ways. Returning them to their intended simplicity—to what really matters.

What really matters is each other, Mike knows. As furious as she is with Arielle and Gemma, she is more furious with herself for not properly evaluating the risks. After all, she's the one in charge. She should have paid more attention to what was unfolding around her. She should have known more than she apparently did. *She knew nothing!* She sips the tea, which tingles its way across her palette and down her throat, energizing her senses. She feels a bit better, like her synapses are conducting the cellular information they were intended to transmit. It's good, effective. But that could be her imagination.

She wraps her scotch plaid flannel robe tightly around her waist and walks up the corridor in her navy fleece slippers to her office which she takes apart for the umpteenth time in search of that letter. It could still be here. It has to be! It's the only evidence there is. She kneels down to open the bottom drawer of the file cabinet for another look when the pounding starts down the main staircase—the familiar thunderous stampede of Rose, Gabriella and Beatrice. It's nearly midnight for God's sake. What do they want now?

"Mike! Mike!" Beatrice calls out in her raspy voice. "The truck is back!"

Scrambling off her knees, Mike nearly knocks over the tea. She catches it by the handle, sets it squarely on the credenza and rushes to the hallway.

"Look! Look it's here!" screeches Rose.

From their reaction it's clear to Mike that Beatrice has filled her Sisters in. Otherwise why would they be so anxious? Not that any of the nuns has ever been out after nine PM without good and well-advertised reasons. From that standpoint alone, the girls' absence qualifies as a disappearance. They live in a community; they share information. They're accountable to one another. Of course it's possible that Gabriella or Rose directly overheard Mike's call to the police station. Mike was discreet but worried, nervous, and possibly even shrill, who knows? Someone could have been near her office at the time. At any rate, they're all clearly on the same frantic wavelength.

In the foyer Mike sees that the substantial wooden door of the front entrance is wide open. Only the screen door lies between her and the truth. She can't guess what's about to happen. *Arielle had her cell number! Why didn't she call?* She fights a bolus of fear and anger, because if this disappearance was the result of carelessness or inconsideration, she might explode with rage for all the grief it's caused. She pumps her fists for control.

The truck chugs up the drive and sputters to a stop near the mailbox far left of Mike's office. Notwithstanding the noisy engine, it looks to be in one piece, so no apparent accident. Mike says, "Sisters, I need to speak with the girls alone. I'm sorry." She conveys an expression stern enough to broker no compromise. After a minor stare-down, they huff and puff, and retreat mostly without protest.

"In your rooms," she says. "No eavesdropping." After all, she has no idea what to expect. She needs room to make decisions without regard for the emotions of others. Room to react! She's only human. Who knows what she'll do?

She throws open the screen door and waits at the threshold of fate itself, it seems. It was confirmed earlier tonight that the Vatican investigation will take place at some point between three and twenty-three days with little to no notice. So they have to be ready, which they are clearly not. What will it bring? Which of the Sisters will even be present? What "new news" will change everything yet again, placing them at even greater risk? In so little time, how will they ever bring the "troubles" to rest?

Or maybe the visitors will come and go between troubles, and that will be that—no one the wiser. At this point, Mike has to "let go and let Grace" because without Grace's divine intervention, they're out of business anyway.

Her stomach drops when she sees that it's not who she thought—not "Arielle and Gemma"—but one or the other. Only one. The light of the nearly full moon reveals it to be the slighter-built gamine, Arielle, her body dragging behind the reluctant lead of her hanging head. Her body tells a tale of utter dejection. Mike vows not to make matters worse for the girl, but she's not at all sure she can live up to the vow. She puts her counselor cap on, albeit a bit lopsided. After all, in such a case as this she can hardly be objective.

Arielle takes a detour toward the trailer, but then, spotting Mike under the porch light, wisely diverts back. Mike waits. As the girl approaches, her face mirrors her defeated posture. No characteristic smile. No life. No Arielle.

"Come in," Mike says. "To my office. We'll talk there." She herds the girl inside, listening for the busybodies, and when she's convinced they're down the hall in somebody or other's bedroom, she shuts the office door.

"Have you eaten?" she asks Arielle nervously. "Do you need food? Water? What?" She folds her arms.

Arielle drops into one of the straight-back office chairs facing Mike's desk. "No. Nothing."

Mike takes her seat behind the desk, allows the girl a minute or two to collect herself, then jumps in. "Are you okay? Did you get hurt? Did somebody hurt you? What? What's happened? Talk."

Arielle's chin rests on her chest. She massages her temples. In time, she slowly raises her head, puckering her lips and issuing any number of expressions that indicate she is at an utter loss to convey the information she stores. Her brain is a logjam of what appears to be terrible news.

"Arielle, whatever it is, you have to tell me. Dr. Rawlins told me Gemma skipped her appointment. I'll spare you that. Go from there."

"Um." She blinks, stares around the room, up at the ceiling, out the window.

Exasperated, Mike raises her hands, fingers splayed. "For God's sake, Arielle, is Gemma alive or not?"

"Oh," she says, shocked. "That. Sorry. I thought you meant…but yeah, she's alive. Really alive! She's uh…she ran away with Eli. They're alive together."

Mike blinks. "The paramedic?"

"Yes. We had a plan…"

Mike sits like a broomstick listening to the shocking story of Gemma's…alter ego? *Maya?!* Arielle's complicity with a plan to set this schizophrenic personality free?! To heal Gemma?! To cure her!

At a carnival!

Mike has to clamp her jaws completely shut not to interrupt. She sets herself on auto-therapy in order to listen carefully to every detail of this insane tale, because she should never have placed this much responsibility on a newly recovering addict. *A teenager!* The responsibility is all hers. All Mike's! She's complicit herself by virtue of her utter denial of the obvious psychosis that's been playing out all around her for months. Not to mention Augusta's obvious senility in undermining the seriousness of Gemma's condition by treating it with…Convergence Tea!

"I hope you're not upset with little mama?" Arielle says with concern. "I still think the tea works, but. Not that madrecita knew about Eli; she didn't." She shakes her head. "But she can read thoughts, so."

"Who can read thoughts?"

"Augusta? Did you think I meant Gemma? Gemma can't read thoughts, which is too bad, because she'll be pretty damn surprised when she finds herself all converged at a chapel in Vegas married to Eli." She clasps her hands in her lap. "Eli really loves her though, if that's any consolation. Not that he knows he's marrying twins."

Mike forces her voice down from a scream to a normal tone, which comes out more like a harsh whisper. "Where's the letter?" she says.

Arielle's head jerks up. "What? Oh! Yeah, that. Sorry. It's upstairs between the mattresses. I just…I didn't. Whatever."

"Did you read it?"

"No! That would be a sin, but I can't remember which one."

"It was a sin to steal it in the first place," Mike says. "So go get it and bring it back." She freezes her sternest expression in place.

"But what about...I mean, who took it from Gemma?" And then "...oh," she says catching Mike's icy stare.

While Arielle's gone, Mike leaves a message with Rawlins' emergency service. She hopes for a call back tonight, but what will he say? Even she knows there's very little anyone can do. Can you really blame Eli for Gemma's illness? For running off with a split-personality he has no comprehension of? Will the police apprehend a grown woman based on what? Dereliction of duty? Abandoning her profession? Abandoning her Sisters? *Being crazy?*

There are all kinds of whisperings in the upstairs hall, so obviously Arielle has run into her fan club. Mike gives up on rumor control. What harm can the visitors do at this point anyway? All that's left of their Order are two seamstresses, a TV junky, a hermit who creates magical teas and consecrates her own Eucharist, a sickly invalid, a psychotic runaway, a teenage ninja, and a lame prioress. Do any of them really belong in a monastery? It's legitimately debatable. Maybe they really should be closed down.

Arielle takes her time and Mike is ok with this because she's finished her tea, which was energizing, but still—time for coffee. Not espresso; she won't go that far, but real coffee. She makes a pot. And the girl must be hungry, no matter what she says. So Mike hurries into the kitchen and throws together a ham and cheese sandwich just in case. She's forcing herself to be thoughtful, she knows. Pretending not to be angry because she is angry. Very angry. But she knows she shouldn't be. She'd entrusted Arielle with too much, and Arielle disappointed her. And Gemma, well. At any rate, the burden of mercy is squarely upon Mike. She must be merciful.

She brings the sandwich and a glass of cola as far as the main hall where Arielle is descending the staircase in the big fluffy blue robe Constance made her months ago. She's disheveled but comfortable. Endearing. *She didn't steal the truck!* And she's dressed in her pajamas, so at least she's planning to stay. Right? At least for now. This is a good thing. She's staying, not running away, which is a relief if for no other reason than Augusta. Though there are plenty of other reasons, Mike knows. As many reasons as there are Sisters in this house. Not to mention Constance who's still in the hospital.

In the office Arielle nibbles on the sandwich like a little church mouse, tiny little nibbles, clearly just to please Mike. She pushes the plate to the side just as Mike sits down with her steaming cup of coffee.

"I'm really sorry," Arielle says, shrugging. "I should have told you everything before I left, but."

"Why didn't you?" asks Mike quietly. "Do I intimidate you, Arielle?"

She takes a minute, squirming. "Um, sometimes, but. Not really? It wasn't you, it was…" She stops squirming and stares at Mike meaningfully, "I just…to be completely honest…I believed Maya."

Mike leans back on her swivel chair. "You believed the alter ego?"

"Whoever. I believed her, and in a way…I still do. So maybe I'm crazy too, who knows? But the insane part of Gemma isn't Maya; it's Gemma. Gemma hates herself. Maya doesn't. Maya would never hurt herself. Maya loves life. She's full of it."

Mike sighs. Arielle really is a "sensitive" in the way that Augusta is and always has been. No wonder they connected. Even without the esoteric language or education, she knows things; sees right into people. Which is the reason Mike was persuaded by her in the first place. Sucked right in after Augusta. And shame on her—on Mike. Mike knows better. The girl may be a sensitive, but she's also a barely twenty-year-old recovering addict with a history of reckless behavior. The fact that she's persuasive doesn't mean she's right. It means she's persuasive.

"I know Gemma's been hard on herself," Mike says. "That she harms herself."

"She calls it penance," says Arielle.

Mike nods.

"She just wants to be a saint is all."

"Some saints practiced harsh penances," Mike says. "Not that I agree with that practice; I don't."

"She kneels on Brillo pads when she says her prayers and walks around all day in really tight shoes full of rock salt."

Mike didn't know this about the shoe fit, not that she's surprised. She's almost impressed at the innovation—at finding a penance that no one but a roommate could possibly notice—not to mention the rock salt. "Anything else?"

"She wears a burlap undershirt…" Arielle moves her lips from side to side, as if deciding how much to reveal. "I'm not a tattle tale," she says. "I hate tattlers."

Mike has to take this childishness for what it is. Her only life experience is in a trailer camp full of abusers, not to mention a jail cell or two. In that culture, tattling got you beaten-up and sometimes killed.

"You're not exactly a tattle tale," she says. "You're helping me to evaluate the situation properly. In this capacity, Arielle, I'm a psychologist and I won't reveal my sources or really even the details of this conversation, ok?"

The girl barely relaxes. "Can I have some of that coffee?" she asks.

Mike nods, and Arielle walks robotically to the coffee station, her back to Mike when the cell phone blasts, *"I remember…I remember…when I lost my mind! Something so pleasant about that plaaaace…"*

With her back still to Mike, Arielle says, "Oh, Rawlins, you better get that." She turns her head, "Sorry about the ringtone. It seemed funny at the time."

"Does that make me craaazy?" sings the phone until Mike answers it.

"Hello?" she says, flustered.

"Yes, Mike, what's up?" he says with thick-throated hoarseness.

"Sorry to wake you, Jim," she says, and explains the situation from Arielle's point of view—about Maya and her day of freedom. About Eli and Vegas. About Gemma's self-punishment.

"Fascinating case," he says, "but there's very little we can do about it until she returns. She's thirty-two years old, Mike. Older than the abductor apparently. Did you say he was twenty-seven? Not that age is a factor here."

"I don't know if he's an abductor necessarily," Mike says. "But...what if he is?"

Arielle widens her eyes, shakes her head and mouths, "Nooooo. No way! Not an abductor!"

After exploring the consequences of various actions, legal and illegal, that the monastery might take, Mike finally hangs up, defeated. "There's really nothing we can do," she tells Arielle. "If we hear from her, though, we must convince them to return." Her head shoots up, "Wait...the letter? Where is it?"

Arielle pulls it out of her big bathrobe pocket. "Here it is, but I doubt it's anything we don't already know. I've known Eli quite a few years and he's no ladies' man. He's actually kind of old-fashioned. For him to send a letter like this, well...it's pretty dramatic. He's in love, that's it. End of story."

Mike lays the envelope on her desk blotter and stares at the block letters. "Still," she says. "It could be a dangerous situation. People are not always what they appear to be. I think we need to explore every piece of evidence."

Arielle waves her hand in the air. "Be my guest, but the only perp in that truck is Maya."

Mike slits the top of the envelope with her letter opener. It's a clean tear; great, so what? She feels awful about it, because in truth she never thought Gemma was cut-out for the monastery to begin with. Which is why Mike delayed her final vows. *Let her think about it. Let her get well!* But since there clearly wasn't anything else on Gemma's horizon, well...what was the harm in helping her out for a few years? And you never know, perhaps a sincere vocation would emerge. And now this young man. Just maybe... She pushes the letter away. "I don't want to read this," she says.

"Good," says Arielle. "It doesn't seem right."

"No, it doesn't."

Arielle says, "Are you going to throw me out?" Her eyes tear up. "I just, you know…need to figure out a few things if you are."

Mike studies the girl's porcelain skin flecked with a smattering of copper freckles. Her shock of tumbling hair. She's a child! *Be kind!* "Do you want to stay?" Mike asks.

"Uhh…"

"That is to say…do you intend to become a nun, Arielle?"

Arielle clasps her hands behind her neck, elbows in the air, and stretches. "I might," she says, "but."

"But what?" Mike demands. She's slipped into a harsh voice, she knows, but the girl's pregnant pauses have become downright maddening and almost manipulative. Or maybe they're both too damn tired to have this conversation. "Never mind," she says abruptly. "Maybe we both need some sleep before we go any further with this."

Arielle raises her chin and stares. "Just one more thing," she says, and reaches into her bathrobe pocket retrieving a wallet-size picture which she slaps onto the desk and pushes toward Mike.

Mike stares at…what? A cherubic picture of what has to be…Arielle as a child? Or…she suddenly remembers the search screens Arielle left on the computer that time. The adoption agency. Her heart sinks.

"I'll spare you the suspense," Arielle says, her voice breaking. "This is my kid. She was adopted three years ago at birth by Lucky's cousin, Louise, but. Louise just died, so." All at once heavy tears plop down her cheeks like rain.

Arielle is crying and Mike is torn. She wants the whole story. She's sick of half-stories. She's got an investigation in weeks or even days— how compassionate is she expected to be?! "So…?" she prompts.

"So Lucky thinks he's the father, which is unlikely since…well." She swipes her sleeve across her face. "My mother's boyfriend…might've been my stepdad, but…there were so many."

Stunned, Mike rises and walks to the other side of the desk. She drags the other chair up to Arielle's and takes her hand. "What?" she asks gently. "What is it, Arielle? Get it all out."

"Now, I just…Lucky wants to marry me, but."

Mike steels herself. "But what? Do you love him?"

"Isn't it obvious?" she sobs. "I love this! This monastery. It's my hoooome."

Mike rubs Arielle's arm gently up and down. "Do you love Lucky?" she asks.

Arielle shakes her head. "I used to, but. Maybe not really, because there were…so many drugs. It wasn't real."

Mike hands Arielle a tissue from the box on her desk. "So you don't know if you love him, is that it? Or you know that you don't?"

Arielle blows her nose. "He wants…to….adopt Giselle," she sputters between sobs.

"Giselle?" repeats Mike, smiling. "My goodness, how lovely!"

Arielle nods, "It is, right?! But if I want her, I have to marry him or find a job so I can support her. And so the court will let me have her. And I have to prove that I'm fit. And that I can provide a home. And I've never even met her since I had her, but Lucky has. He's met her. How is that fair?!"

"Do you want her?"

Arielle buries her face in her hands, sobbing helplessly. "Yyyyes," she cries. "I do. I want her as much as I want to live he-he-herrre. I want them both."

Mike is so overwhelmed with facts and emotions that she can barely focus. Arielle can't have both. She obviously can't have both. The monastery cannot accommodate a baby for heaven's sake. If they even have a monastery by the end of the month. Children are not part of their charism, among a million other reasons. The idea is laughable. Nuns do not have babies! Although Mike did, she realizes that. She had a baby but the baby died. If the baby hadn't died, Mike would clearly not have been able to become a nun or live in a monastery. Still. What will Arielle do when she leaves? What will they do without her? Not that Mike ever thought the girl would stay forever. She didn't. She was under no such illusion. But to imagine life without her now…back to the utter blandness of life as it was before Arielle…is inconceivable.

"I can't figure it out right now," Mike says. "Let's try to get some sleep, ok? If we can. Today was long, but the way things are going, tomorrow will be longer."

After a hideous night of pop-up dreams featuring unholy visions of yelping babies and cheap tinsel weddings, Mike finally rises nearly as exhausted as she was when she laid down. Praying Laudes, she praises God a bit insincerely since today she is far more angry than exultant of his glory. She pushes forth in faith, because she's experienced enough to know that her reaction is temporary and also the result of vastly incomplete information.

She does remind God, however, that it is he who created her in all her angry imperfection. If he desires a different reaction, perhaps he should reach down with his illuminated finger and erase the smudge of original sin from her fallen nature. She hardly knows herself like this— so unapologetically arrogant and indignant. So rebellious of God. Nevertheless she's unafraid to state her case because if she's still in possession of a single virtue, it's honesty.

She dresses in her usual black linen suit and black loafers, combing her short, dense, ever-graying hair and wishing for the first time she can remember that she had something less dreary to wear. That she weren't a black and white constant adrift in a sea of colorful variables. That everything wasn't always up to her. Wishing that she was a variable, too. A variable who could count on someone else to 1) locate Gemma; 2) retrieve Constance; 3) resolve Arielle's troubles; 4) care for Mother; and 5) wow the visitators into dropping any grudge they may hold against the Sisters of the Most Holy Order of Divine Grace and their ungodly lives full of demonstrably human flaws! Not to mention all the things that could happen in the meantime. The list is overwhelming. And there isn't anyone else to help.

There's only Mike.

She hustles down the back staircase and over to the chapel to say Mass—another privilege she'd like to share with someone else, but whom? No one she can think of, since she can't abide Kevin and she doesn't know any of those renegade so-called *"womenpriests"*, though she'd like to. She really would. She'd like to be at the vanguard of something—to exhibit that much courage.

Back in the sacristy she flips through the Mass book to familiarize herself with today's readings, at the same time listening to the chirping swell of her assembling congregation. No homily today, she's afraid, unless she's surprisingly and spontaneously inspired, which under the dire circumstances is doubtful. All she could share with her parishioners today would be the blinding fog of her own confusion.

As she flips through the book to today's Gospel—*about the hypocritical Pharisees!*—she's startled by a loud and unexpected knock on the sacristy door. Anyone belonging back here doesn't knock.

"Sister?"

She turns to see the young paramedic, Jesse, or Lucky as Arielle calls him, standing at the door.

"Sorry to interrupt," he says, "but may I come in?"

His hair is combed and his beard trimmed. Mike can't remember seeing him this groomed before, not that she'd paid much attention to his appearance the night of Constance's attack. Constance's attack and oh yes, Gemma's fainting episode—a busy night. "Come in," she says. Even in her vast fatigue, she's curious. What does he want!

His jittery hands hold a navy blue and white Yankee's cap. She's touched that he knew enough to take it off.

"What is it, Jesse?" She checks her watch. "It might be better if you wait until after Mass, actually, although…I also have to make a trip to Albany this morning."

"I'll be quick," he says. "First I want you to know that fifty volunteers from town are ready to clean up your grounds tomorrow."

Her hand flies to her heart. "Oh my. Oh…oh my. I'd completely forgotten…"

He grins. "Not to worry, Sister, we haven't forgotten. We're ready. Everyone's meeting at the station and coming over together, and we're bringing our own tools. Just so someone tells me what you need done is all."

284   REA NOLAN MARTIN

"Beatrice and Arielle can familiarize you today while I'm out. You do know Beatrice?"

"Ha, yeah, Ari calls her the big colorful bop."

Mike smiles. "Yes…that would describe our Beatrice."

"And I know things are crazy here, and I realize you might even think I'm to blame," he says, "but…"

Mike narrows her eyes. "Are you?"

He shakes his head vehemently. "No! I'm not! I'm sorry about my friend, but…and he's the least of my problems right now, believe me."

She raises her hand to spare him the explanation. "It's a serious situation," she says.

"We're still trying to communicate," Jesse says. "We'll get her back, don't worry, just maybe not as, you know…a nun, ha ha."

Mike breathes in heavily. " 'A nun, ha ha'? Well, I suppose as long as she's mentally fit she can make those decisions herself. She's a grown woman."

He smiles gratefully. "Yeah, and anyway she might be better off."

"Excuse me?!" This is unexpected.

"Whoa, no, I just mean that my boy, I mean, Eli…he won't let her down. He'll stick by her no matter what. That's how he is. Super glue. There's no getting rid of him."

"What are you saying, Jesse, he's a stalker?"

"No! Sorry, no! Just a great guy from a decent family. He was like a big brother to me my whole life." He rubs his fingers together. "With bucks, you know, cuz he's smart. Straight out of high school he was flipping houses over at Lake George. He made a ton and put me through rehab. Kicked my ass…oops, sorry…into the army. Made me…grow up. I owe him, you know?" He pats his heart. "He's family to me."

Mike nods, touched. "I see. So he's not a hoodlum; that's good." She didn't know about Lucky's drug problem, though.

She stares at him with what must be obvious concern, because he jumps back wide-eyed to say, "Oh! Oh, the drugs, yeah." He throws his hands up. "I've been clean for years and I'll never do it again, believe me.

But Eli, he never did drugs. He's a stand-up guy. A mensch."

Mike says, "When you say he'll stick by her no matter what…it may include hospitalization, Jesse. Hospitalization and a lifetime of complicated medication. I doubt he understands how deeply her psychosis may run."

"Wow, I didn't…I thought she was just, you know…a runaway nun! What do you mean—psychosis? I didn't know …"

So Arielle didn't fill him in. Does she not trust him enough? Mike doesn't know what to do with this right now. She checks her watch again. "Is there something else?" she says. "Because I have to start the service."

"Oh, uh, yeah…I was just wondering, like, how long it takes to get baptized?"

"How long it takes?"

"To you know, prepare for it? To learn the rules of your religion? I just…I want us all to do it together. Me and Arielle and Giselle. Like a family."

Mike blinks, confused. "I uh…does Arielle know about this?"

He smiles. "I wanna surprise her."

"Jesse, I'm not sure Arielle…"

"If she stays with me or not," he says eagerly. "It's ok. We're still family. We should have the same God."

"You're sure?" she says. "Family?" It didn't sound like they were family last night.

"I told her I just had the test the other day, you know, because I didn't want her to know it's all I've thought about for three years. The whole time in the army; that's it. Ari and the baby; Ari and the baby. With or without them, they're my life. The truth is I had the test years ago. I'm not here by accident. I looked for her. I looked for her and I found her. And I moved here to be with her."

Mike is breathless at the shock of this history. This young man—this brand new acquaintance has more attachment to Arielle than any of them. Would Mike have become so attached to the girl? Would Mother? All Mike can think is *convergence.* Convergence from places utterly unknown, and yet...connected. How almost perfectly some pieces were moving into place while others seemed hopelessly missing. Would the puzzle converge in favor of the monastery? Or Jesse? Or neither? Is there more they don't know?

One thing Mike does know is that she'll support Arielle. But how can she not root for this young man as well? The father of Giselle! *Giselle!* Giselle who not only looks like Arielle, but also Grace! Did Arielle come to save the monastery, or was it the monastery's task to save Arielle all along? Not only Arielle, but her baby. Not only Arielle and her baby, but the baby's father, Jesse. They are all so cosmically intertwined, it seems, that the grand question of who's saving whom is nearly irrelevant.

They're saving one another.

AUGUSTA

Michael Agnes and the others think Augusta is getting senile, but she isn't. They think she's forgetful and eccentric, which may be true at times, but more often it's the mask she uses to shut them down and send them away. At her age she can only suffer so much ignorance; she has no time for it. So they think she doesn't know that Arielle has a child or that Gemma is in trouble, but she knows both of these things and so much more.

She knows things she can't convey because they're locked in her head without language. She knows things they'll never know about God and Grace and the timelines of the mystical multi-verse and the deep pockets of history that play on and on into the present because we allow it. How the past hypnotizes and warps; how the future deceives; how the present combusts with eternal infinite power. How so few people know how to use that power to really live—to be completely alive. But Augusta knows. Augusta lives in the trailer of Now.

Augusta lives in the present, but knows about the future. She knows how it appears in a hot flash of deep, pulsating violet light before it actually happens, because she's seen it. She's seen that light. How the wave of cause and effect unfolds from its pulsating center in ripples, swells and tsunamis. How you can stop it if you know how—if you've paid the least bit of attention to the numina in your life. But of course, most people don't pay attention. Most people don't know the first thing about the luminous signals provided by divine providence to point them in the direction of their intended lives. Most people step into the luminous crosswalk in the middle of rush hour against the light. Most people get hit head-on, stunned by their own ignorance, and blame it on God.

Augusta wraps herself in her crazy new black and red checkerboard afghan that was crocheted for Constance by Gabriella and borrowed by Arielle for Augusta. The girl is a regular Robin Hood! Its ratty woolen predecessor is balled up in a UPS box in the corner for Assisi who is already cuddled deep inside. The feline saint adores Arielle, who wouldn't? She might not be Grace but she resonates Grace, so in that way, she is. In the end what's left of us on this earth is our resonance, our energetic essence. Grace surrounds Arielle; emanates through her. If you watch the girl at high noon in the summer sun you can see the rainbow arc of Grace's light all about her. You just have to know what to look for. Arielle responds to it—dances to it. *She is it!*

The dear child has just left the trailer after cooking Augusta a five star breakfast of bacon and strawberry Poptarts, which both of them adore. Who wouldn't adore a toasty frosted tart full of warm jam on a brisk late summer morning ten miles away from autumn? And a savory mouthful of peppered Sunday bacon on an ordinary Friday? Who wouldn't love that?! Augusta trembles with pleasure just thinking of all the simple goodness in the wide world. All the bacon and Poptarts and wise fluffy angel cats and scintillating teas. All the star-breathing children starved for love. All the Arielles. It's almost more than she can bear—the infinite forms of God's beneficence.

A brand new recipe came to Augusta this morning while brushing her teeth. She never knows when inspiration will strike, and for years she refused the incoming celestial out of sheer inconvenience and also blatant distrust of its source. It could be God, or it could be her own ego. At the time, she couldn't tell the difference. Now she knows this fragile gift of attunement to the subtle folds of the Complex Sacred is her personal daemon—the charismatic gift she will leave behind for her Sisters and their progeny of believers. For their sake she is vigilant to the voice of Tea that whispers to her so generously along with the other prophetic voices. The teas work, is all she knows, though their true power may not be realized at first. With patience they cannot and will not disappoint. The teas focus, manifest and accelerate a sacred process. No recipe has ever been given to her that wasn't essential to someone's evolution.

Today's tea is made with rose hips, cinnamon, elderberries and among other things, the water of a boiled sunchoke root, which surprised her. Why that? A dozen other ingredients in exacting quantities were also steeped and recorded meticulously for her by her precious scribe, Arielle. Augusta was at a loss for the name of this most transcendent of teas—this tea of ascension—until Arielle provided her with the gift of song in a little magic box called an iPod.

The magic music box changes everything! Changes the very quality of life! It is infinitesimal in form, yet unimaginably filled with hundreds of hymns, sacred chants and catchy little tunes like the one she finally named the tea after—*Spirit in the Sky*. According to Arielle, this song was recorded by a man named Norman Greenbaum, a man who clearly understood God in joyful ways that most people do not. For one thing he knew how to listen to the celestial muse. To be so attuned to the celestial muse, one need be wholly present. When Norman Greenbaum wrote this song, he was wholly present. At least at that point, he lived in the trailer of Now.

Augusta can still hear the song:

"*Goin' up to the Spirit in the Sky! That's where I'm gonna go when I die! When I die and they lay me to rest...I'm gonna go to the place that's the best!*"

Before she left, Arielle plugged the magic box into a speaker and turned it up. From the very first note the music made them so deliriously happy that Augusta inched up and off her chair and began to dance in happy little fist-clenching circles. She couldn't help it! Arielle danced too—on the bench, on the chair, on the bed—everywhere, up and down—Assisi casting about playfully behind her. *Where will she go next!* They couldn't stop! As long as the song played, they danced. And for once Augusta's feet didn't feel like bones scraping rock as she moved to the beat of pure pleasure. She barely knew her feet were there! She danced on a cushion of grace.

"Prepare yourself, you know it's a must! Gotta have a friend in Jesus! So you know that when you die...He's gonna recommend you to the spirit in the sky!"

The song was so joyful it almost made her want to die then and there. *Lord, take me now in this storm of ecstasy!* Dying will not be by her whim, she knows, but His. And anyway, Augusta is essential to the coming Convergence.

All that happy dancing eventually wore her out, though. And now that Arielle's left, Augusta is curled back up in her wing chair, sipping tea and drifting in and out of dimensions as she investigates another iridescent fold in the intricate fabric of the multi-verse. She may jump timelines or not; she doesn't always know. There are multiple teas at work, not just *Spirit in the Sky*. *Timeline* is also a factor, not to mention *Convergence* and *Transference of Knowledge*. So much at play! Augusta doesn't have to be the one drinking a particular tea to feel its influence. It's not that straightforward. It could be anyone in her cluster.

Sipping the last bit of tart, cooled liquid, Augusta feels an unsettling sense of lift-off. How very queer! Although by now she's familiar with the effects of the other teas, *Spirit in the Sky* is new. She's been told only that it assists ascension. When sipped with pure intention it increases the probability that someone or something within or around the host will rise up to fulfill its purpose. It could be anyone or anything. She doesn't know who or what. There's no point in guessing, either, because once someone has sipped its essence, the process is well underway. One just waits with great expectation to observe God's mighty hand.

With this lovely thought, Augusta drifts off. After what seems like hours of flying to nether regions delivering her various teas to the unenlightened of other dominions, Augusta awakens to a buzz of great and noisy industry, the likes of which she hasn't heard since her bout with vertigo and tinnitus over a decade ago. Is it the tea? Her head is groggy, so she has to think which one she last drank—oh yes, *Spirit in the Sky*. Well, that wouldn't account for this hubbub, no. This hubbub is strictly physical. It's right here on the farm.

She slowly pushes herself off the arms of her chair until upright. This takes time and heroic effort. Time, heroic effort and careful planning. When no one's around, she uses her cane because she doesn't want to fall. But when someone's with her, she puts the cane aside and pretends not to need it so they won't pronounce her too infirm to live alone. Living alone is essential. Living alone gives her the clarity to inhale the Spirit that provides her the recipes, among other things. The same Spirit ordained her a mystical priestess over a people who lived centuries ago, and others who have not yet been born. Only Michael Agnes knows about that—about being ordained. Not that she knows the details. She's no mystic, Michael Agnes. She's time-bound. The details would crush her.

The details are difficult to explain to anybody, because so few people understand the nature of time and experience. And don't tell Augusta about the physicists—how much more they understand than mystics do. How much they can prove *or* disprove God. Scientists understand numbers and equations not experience. Experience rises out of the womb of awakening consciousness and alters all things. Were a thousand new people to awaken in the near blinding glare of true awareness today, the theories the scientists proved last night would already be false. A thousand new pairs of open eyes can change the universe. A single pair can do the same. Augusta knows the truth about truth—it's a subjective world. You make your own.

She shuffles with her cane over the vinyl floor to the bubble window where she sees Constance in the distance in a warm embrace with Beatrice, Gabriella and Rose. An encounter confirming their love. Outside of their embrace stands Michael Agnes who stands outside of all embraces, though this will soon change, Augusta knows. In time all encounters will occur and then concur. In the hot flash of deep violet light already witnessed by Augusta, the waves of convergence reach shore.

All around the Sisters' loving embrace are workers the likes of which Augusta has seen only in the early days with Grace. How glorious is the vision before her now of workers in the sunflower field and the vegetable patch and the hay fields! Workers on the roof and workers on the shed, scraping and painting and tarring! Everywhere there are workers with shovels and pitchforks and hoes! Augusta drops her cane to clap her stiff, bent hands with the divine glee infused in her by the Spirit for just this auspicious occasion. It is coming together exactly as she'd dreamed. *Exactly!*

Now if only she can bring Michael Agnes into alignment with the extraordinary grace of continuance, all will be well. Why oh why does she refuse to see the world as it is? And where will this refusal leave her? Leave them all? Although the convergence itself is known, its outcome is not. There are decisions yet to be made by everyone—especially Michael Agnes—that will affect the outcome.

Slowly, Augusta makes her way to the bathroom and back to her little kitchen when Michael Agnes raps on the door and squeaks it open. "Mother?" she says.

"Come in, dear," says Augusta with a patience she doesn't feel. Patience is hardly a virtue when time is short.

Michael Agnes enters and invites Augusta to sit outside on a lawn chair to drink in the flurry of activity from a safe distance. Such an unconventional idea, Augusta thinks, yet oddly appealing to her in the moment.

"Well, why not?" she says. "But let's walk out through the back where it's flat." Augusta cannot do stairs.

The walk outside is refreshing; the warm noon sun is her cloak. Assisi scoots out his cat door after a chipmunk and a bluebird settles on a branch of the wild dogwood. An emerald hummingbird with sapphire wings vibrates like a bee at the feeder.

"Hold my arm," says Michael Agnes. And Augusta takes it.

Out front, they settle into two old wooden Adirondack chairs with chipped paint and mildewed cushions. Michael Agnes gives Augusta the cushions from both chairs to raise her up and protect her brittle bones from the splintered wood.

"Why, this is a wonderful idea!" Augusta effuses, her spirit rising up within her and out her mouth like champagne bubbles. "I can see everyone cultivating the fields. Who are they? These kind people?"

Michael Agnes smiles. "These are our neighbors," she says, and points in particular to the one young man with the shaggy blonde hair who is supervising the others.

Michael Agnes launches into a tale of Arielle's life before the encounter with Grace's angel. A life with the young man, Jesse, who lived nearby. Augusta knows about Arielle's child, but not the particulars of this young man or his meaning in Arielle's life. Who is he? Why should she care?

She gathers enough courage to inquire, "But why is he here, Michael Agnes?" Her heart thumps loudly because this is information not yet revealed to her through the prism of tea and timelines. This information was withheld, so there are dreary lessons yet to be processed. What is known is known. What is unknown is a thicket.

Michael Agnes produces a small photograph from her pocket that she gives to Augusta. Augusta is speechless! It's a picture of Grace as a child! This picture makes Augusta's heart swell and press against her ribcage. She feels great pain and her breath becomes shallow. Her love threatens to suffocate her! This child that was clearly hers at one point in the history of Love is staring back at her in a photograph. Convergence. All things are one. There is no *Other!*

"Grace," she breathes.

Michael Agnes leans toward her so closely that Augusta can smell the morning toast on her breath. "Not Grace, Mother," she says. "Giselle. Her name is Giselle and she's the child of Arielle."

Giselle? The name captures Augusta in its chubby child hands like a firefly. "Giselle!" she chants. "Giselle." The resonance of this name comes to her from the future. Giselle the child who will replace her. "Promise," she says.

Michael Agnes cocks her head. "Promise?" she repeats.

Augusta grins so broadly and infectiously that Michael Agnes herself finally smiles. "The name Giselle means *Promise*," Augusta tells

294 REA NOLAN MARTIN

her. "That child is God's Promise."

Michael Agnes collects herself in the stiff manner of her acquired nature and says, "She's the daughter of Arielle and Jesse, Mother. She was adopted by Jesse's cousin who has since died."

Augusta listens anxiously; her hands tremble.

"That man out there…" she points to Jesse, "…wants to marry Arielle and raise Giselle."

Augusta's heart nearly stops. "Take her away from us?" She has to restart everything, her heart, her breath.

Michael Agnes nods with certainty as if there is only one solution to this dilemma. As if there is a single reality. "Or if Arielle chooses to stay at the monastery, then Jesse will raise the child himself," she says, as if she knows anything at all. As if she isn't guessing.

Augusta forces herself to reconnect to the violet center of the future and says, "They will live here, Michael Agnes. Arielle and Giselle will live here."

"That's impossible; you know that."

"All things are possible."

Michael Agnes is frustrated, obstinate. "The Vatican visitators will be here soon—that's enough to concentrate on, don't you think? When they interview us, do you think they'll be happy to hear about our plans to house an unmarried postulant with a child? This is not what they want, Mother. It's not what they're coming for."

"To hell with what they want," says Augusta.

"Excuse me?!" says Mike self-righteously.

Why is Michael Agnes so removed from reality?!

She huffs at Augusta with indignation. "Aren't you the one who encouraged me to go through with the visitation in the first place, Mother?"

"I don't know about that. It doesn't sound completely accurate." Anyway, things were different when she said that. *If she said that.* After all, it was a lower timeline. Until convergence, what's true on one timeline isn't necessarily true on another.

"Well, I do, Mother. I know about that! You said there was

nothing to be afraid of—that we should just do it!" She flaps like an injured bird.

"Well, of course just do it, Michael Agnes. Just do it and get it over with, who cares?" Augusta wrings her hands to divert shooting stabs of rheumatic pain through her fingers. "Why invite suspicion? Why not just see what happens?"

"See what happens? See them jot down their precious notes and sign us all over to a tenement in Albany or Troy? That?!"

Augusta huffs at the uncharacteristic hysteria from her friend. Michael Agnes is afraid, that's all. Fear breeds false pride. "They can't take our home away from us," she tells Michael Agnes consolingly.

"They can do whatever they want."

"I own the property," Augusta says, not because she wants to, but because the voices are urging her to. She trusts the voices.

Michael Agnes' cool gray eyes widen and spin like a color wheel, reflecting the mango sun, the periwinkle sky, and the distant forest green of the mountains. She is astonished at her apparent good fortune, and Augusta is delighted too! This is so much fun!

Were it only true!

But more important than truth is Michael Agnes' perception of truth. If she's to act with any conviction whatsoever, she must believe that the monastery is theirs! Theirs in every manner—physical and spiritual, real and seemingly unreal. In her heart, Michael Agnes must own the land! She must believe it's hers. By listening to the voices, Augusta is giving her friend the gift of *Transference*. With this gift, Michael Agnes can take title to anything! She can transform her life and act with conviction upon its future, a conviction she could never manifest if she knew they owned nothing.

"You own the property?!" she exclaims.

Augusta listens hard for the right words. "That's right," she says. "And upon my death it will become yours not theirs. It will belong to you."

"But what about our poverty?"

"Poverty is not homelessness, Michael Agnes."

"But we've been paying the Archdiocese…"

Augusta swats her hand dismissively. What can she really say? She doesn't have an answer for everything!

"So we can stay?" Michael Agnes says like a prayer.

"As you wish," says Augusta, one syllable behind her source. "As you wish in the monastic sense with due loyalty or commitment to the Vatican. Or not."

"Or not?!"

Augusta nods. "Remember the Beguines of Belgium. They were contemplatives of the Third Order who lived lives holier than the monks with no binding commitment to Rome. They lived freely in their own manner of worship, yet faithful to the Church in every way."

Augusta can tell that Michael Agnes is too astonished to speak. Of course she knows about the Beguines, but until this very moment neither of them had considered this to be a possibility. To live in their little mountain community in utter freedom of worship and lifestyle. Without reliance upon the vagrant Kevin or the visitating predators. Just them on their little farm in the glory of constant and continuing praise of the One.

Michael Agnes sits back in her chair, her long, slender hand over her open mouth, paralyzed with possibility. So much incredulous news to her—that she can own and direct her own life! That if she simply removes the fabricated shackles of debt from her mind, she will be free. To own nothing is to own it all!

"But why didn't you tell me this before?" she asks.

Augusta has no answer, so she rests her head on the back of the chair and nods off to sleep.

Whatever time later, a minute or fifteen, she lifts her head and Michael Agnes seems content to leave her alone. They sit there companionably into the afternoon mostly in silence, watching the workers plow, hay, and harvest like the noble peasants of another era. It is a richly rewarding day with the distant view of Constance reclining in a chaise on the balcony of her bedroom. Beatrice dressed like a Mardi Gras parade rotating the workers from this field to that like a union boss; Gabriella happily pruning the fragrant junipers; Rose running in and out with pitchers of lemonade and fresh baked cookies. Arielle dancing in the fields. It is a day of plenitude and promise.

Michael Agnes brings Augusta a batch of cookies, a thermos of lemonade and two tumblers from the farmhouse. She pours one for Augusta and says, "The men tell me that the crows are picking apart the greens in the lower field, Mother. Gemma's absence is a hardship I hadn't anticipated. She kept the crows and magpies away with her organic concoctions. She knew what to do." She looks up alarmed, as if realizing that she'd never told Augusta the whole story about Gemma's absence. But Augusta knows all she needs to know.

"She'll be back," Augusta says. "Don't worry."

Michael Agnes looks surprised, but doesn't press. No doubt she thinks that Arielle was the one to inform Augusta about Gemma, which is only fractionally true. Augusta has many sources.

"We'll need a scarecrow," Michael Agnes says. "If we're to expect another harvest of greens."

"Not to mention the squashes," says Augusta. "I can see the birds from my trailer. And the woodchucks, too."

Michael Agnes nods. "I'll talk to Arielle about it tonight," she says. "I'm sure she can come up with something."

Augusta chuckles. "Indeed!"

The drone of utilitarian conversation has calmed them both, returned them to terra firma. Their beloved farm, legions of crows—the ordinary foes of lettuce and zucchini—these things they can manage. Unlike magic music boxes, saintly cats, transcendent teas and prophetic voices—crows and crops are blessedly ordinary. Augusta just waits in the eye of the approaching storm allowing Michael Agnes this moment of peace before the first rains trumpet the atomic split of convergence that can no longer be kept at bay. What will it bring? Augusta can't say.

No one stands outside of it, including her.

GEMMA

Gemma wakes up naked in a heart-shaped bed in a lavish hotel room beside an equally naked, muscular man with copper-toned skin and sleek black hair who lies, snoring softly, with his back to her. As soon as she realizes this is not a dream, she sits bolt upright. Her head pounds and her heart raps wildly against her chest. This experience is so far beyond any reality she has ever known, that she has no idea how to proceed. Jumping out the window seems a real possibility when compared to anything else she can think of.

Wrapping herself tightly in the slick white satin top sheet, she scuttles across the pink shag carpet to the bathroom, which is also exceedingly, blindingly pink. She slowly...quietly...locks the door behind her, leans against it and exhales. She's not sure of anything, so must be mindful of every step. Must calculate every move precisely. Be on guard. Protect herself from everything and everyone, including apparently—herself.

She stares at her image in the mirrored wall behind the whirlpool bath.

Who are you?

Really—who is she? This is not a rhetorical question. Is she an amnesiac? Has she awakened in a different lifetime? All she knows is that her name is Gemma and that she doesn't belong in this vulgar pink palace. Where she does belong she doesn't know yet. In time she will hopefully remember.

She wipes her arm across her itchy nose to ward off a loud sneeze that could wake the man. Her arm smells musky like his. Musky like his and like the men her mother brought home. She remembers her mother. This memory of her mother and her mother's men disgusts her, because...*she's a nun!* So now she remembers that, too. The accompanying cruel reminder of her no doubt stolen purity is accompanied by a crippling belly cramp, because...*she's a nun!* And nuns don't sleep naked in heart-shaped beds with musky black-haired men.

She reaches behind the pink satin curtain and starts the shower. The sooner she can clean herself the better. While the water's warming up, she scours the room for clues of her whereabouts. An upstate Indian casino, perhaps, like Turning Stone, or some godforsaken hotel in the Poconos. The product label on a tiny bottle of shampoo reads, "*Vegas, Baby!*" But that's impossible! Las Vegas, Nevada?! No. If she'd traveled that far, she'd remember it. Vegas, Pennsylvania, maybe, if there is such a place.

She lifts a matchbox from the glass vanity shelf and reads, *Feather Boa Resort, Las Vegas, NV.* Her stomach lurches. As she tries to digest this news, she gags twice and vomits bile into one of the three pink porcelain sinks. Minutes later when she gathers her wits, she rinses the sink, brushes her teeth with a cellophane-wrapped pink toothbrush and splashes handfuls of bracing cold water on her face and neck.

As she pats her face with the pink hand towel, she thinks, Las Vegas? *Really?* It looks like Las Vegas, not that she's been here before, but it's exactly as she'd imagined—the garish pink, the glitzy excess. But how did they get here? Did they fly? If they drove, it would have taken days, maybe a week. She breathes deeply. If she wants to come out of this alive, she has to yank herself out of panic gear and throttle back to survivor mode. Where are her clothes? After all, who knows— she could have been abducted. She would never have agreed to come this far with anyone for any reason.

In the shower the pulsating stream of hot water pounds her back in a deep muscle massage. She unwraps the small loofah sponge and pours the bottle of lavender bath gel over her belly, rubbing in big scratchy circles. She wants to rub herself out, erase herself from this place. Barring that, she'll settle for exfoliating her skin and any evidence of the man who touched it.

Taking keen inventory of her body, she realizes that this man most likely did not stop at her epidermis. His mark is everywhere. That his mark is also within her is unmistakable. Her pelvis is sore and cramped. That she in some way participated in this debauchery both panics and thrills her. It panics and thrills her in ways that make her hate herself even more. She is a thousand confessionals crammed with mortal sins burning beyond redemption.

This momentary reflection on capital sin is when she remembers Maya. This is when she remembers that she loaned her body to Maya for 24 hours and that clearly, Maya took it as far as she could in every imaginable manner. *Is there anything she didn't do?* She rode the gamut from monastic purity to pitch black passion. And for how long? *What day is it?* How long has she been gone? And where is Arielle? Is Arielle here, too? At least now she remembers Arielle. That's progress.

What Gemma doesn't understand is why Maya left so suddenly and where she is right now. She would never have voluntarily left what to her would have been an ecstatic experience in a Vegas hotel room with…what's his name? Eli, yes. With Eli. Gemma is amazed that she can even think that name—*Eli*—without Maya combusting like a nascent galaxy out of the sheer nothingness of Gemma's poached brain. Bursting out of sheer nothingness to claim her share of life. Where did she go—the all powerful Maya? How could she have left Gemma alone with Eli?

Gemma washes her thick halo of new hair, rinses it, and depresses the lever. Stepping out of the pink marble grotto, her belly implodes with cramps so forceful she's nearly paralyzed with pain. She leans against the marble vanity for breath, grabs the pink towel and squeezes it until the cramps release and the pain subsides. She pushes herself back to a fully standing position, blots her face and *whoooosh*—blood gushes down her legs. *Oh no!* After a minute of indecision, she mops it up with the pink towel, feeling awful about ruining the hotel's property but what exactly are her choices?

Why is she bleeding like this?!

She ransacks the drawers and cabinets for feminine products, and finds a small sample box of pads and tampons that she quickly employs. Her head pounds from whatever they did last night—*what did they do?*—and her gut is a cramped, hot mess. Something tells her that isn't all. That it's worse than it even appears to be. She's got to get home. Suddenly overpowered with fear and fatigue, she's lost everything but her will to return to the monastery. Locked in a battle between fight and flight, she wants to run away at the same time she wants to pummel anyone she encounters. She's a rocket of hormones. If she's going to get safely back to the monastery, she's going to have to channel her adrenaline. Returning to the monastery is her driving force.

There's a solid knock on the bathroom door. She freezes. Her stomach drops like a broken elevator. *Crash!*

Another knock.

"Hey! You in there?" he says.

"I'll be out in a minute," she says. *Like hell!*

"Oh come on, baby, let your husband in!"

What?!! *Husband?!!* She looks down at her left hand—feels the weight of the ring even before she catches its glare. How had she not noticed it? It's huge! *Is it real?* What will she say to this man, her captor? Her husband? Anything she has to, she decides. Anything she has to tell him to get her home.

She lifts one of the pink terry robes off the hook and forces her damp body into it. Holds her breath. *She has no choice!* She opens the door.

Immediately she's wrapped in an embrace so powerful it disarms her emotional arsenal entirely. She's never felt anything like it—this…encasement. *He's naked! Uhhh!* "Get away!" she says pushing him.

"Hey!" he says gently, then holds her by the shoulders and bores into her brain with his penetrating sea green eyes. "You feeling any better?" He strokes her cheek tenderly.

"Any better?" she says.

"Yeah, you know?" He cocks his head. "Your girlfriend thing? Cramps?"

"Oh!" The only thing more mortifying than his nakedness is this suggestion of bodily intimacy. "Um, not really. I…" She can't keep it together; she just can't. She explodes into a flood of humiliating tears. How did she get here? How will she ever get back? How will her life ever be the same? Not that she voices those fears; she doesn't. She can't.

Eli wraps his arms around her again as if this will fix anything, and she struggles, elbows and fists, to free herself.

When he finally steps back, she beats his chest. "Get some clothes on!" she screams. "I barely know you!"

Even through her tears she can see the alarm in his eyes. How offended he is. At the same time she's disgusted by him, she's paralyzed with pity. He was duped! He was completely duped by her and Maya. A flailing ant in a spider's snare. He never had a chance. *But so what!* He's bigger than she is and more worldly. He should have known better.

But she doesn't really believe that tack.

From the doorway, she watches him walk across the room and hop his way into a pair of loose fitting farmer's jeans and a gray v-neck tee. She wants to stop watching, but she can't. She's never seen anything like him before, at least not this close—his tall, strong, easy strides and long, lean muscles. He runs his fingers through his full head of silky straight black hair, then opens the drapes and stares out the floor-to-ceiling windows at a view more than twenty stories up. Even from the bathroom she can see the cityscape of reflective deco buildings reflecting the demonic limelight of every capital and venial sin she can name, starting with lust. In the distance, red rock monoliths loom out of place like the painted backdrop of the wrong Broadway show. How did such a city get all the way out here? *To the moon?*

How did she?

Terror rises up her arms from her clenched, trembling fists. "I want to go home," she says as evenly as she can. She's afraid to specify the monastery in case he refuses. Anywhere near Albany is close enough. Let him think what he wants.

He turns toward her. The glare of the wall-length window surrounds him with a nimbus of confusing reflections and pulsing red and gold neon lights from outside. His features are obscured by the light and she can't read or even see his expression.

"Okay," he says quietly. "I'll take you home."

He doesn't ask her where that is or which home she means. *Not his!* But just the fact that he submits so easily gives her relief. They can discuss the other details on the long ride back. "Where's the car?" she says.

He shakes his head, confused by her confusion. "You don't remember?" he says, frowning. "We left the truck in Albany, babe."

"Don't." She reconsiders the chastisement. Let him call her what he wants for now.

"We got a one way to Vegas. You're the one who insisted." He locks his lips and turns back to the window. "I don't know what's pissing you off," he finally says. "I did it for you. I would've liked a real wedding."

"Nothing's… I'm not angry," she says. "I just don't feel that well."

"Yeah, you said that last night." He turns eagerly toward her. "I'm a medic, remember? If you just tell me where the pain is, I can probably help. Just don't shut me out."

Now she remembers. He'd brought her to the hospital that time. This gives her some comfort. He can take care of her if something goes wrong on the way home. "It's nothing," she says.

"Okay, good," he says nodding. "But still no…you know, honeymoon? Yesterday you wanted a honeymoon."

"No. I'd rather get back. This is just so far away. I feel too far from home." She swallows a lump. "It's panicking me."

"Can we get some breakfast first?" he asks hopefully.

Her eyes on the floor, she says, "I'd prefer to leave now." Which of course is to say that if she doesn't leave now she may spiral into inescapable insanity. She looks up and right back down again. His beautiful, sculpted face is so distracting she can barely look at him. It's too confusing. She can see why Maya wanted him. She isn't blind.

"We've gotta eat something," he pleads. "Unless you're feeling really bad. But if you're feeling that bad, maybe we should get you checked out before the plane ride."

"No! Fine, have breakfast. I'm ok. I don't need to be examined. I need to go home."

"Have you taken any of that Midol yet this morning?" he asks. "Might make a difference."

"No, uh, but I...I will."

Midol?! This Adonis is asking if she took Midol? When Gemma gets her hands on Maya again...uhhhhh. She'll just...*aaaaaaa!* Nothing, never mind. She'll do nothing; she knows it, which is why she's so damned defeated in the first place. When she gets her hands on Maya again, she'll do nothing because she's powerless in the face of Maya's constant interference. Maya makes false promises she'll never keep, so there is no trust whatsoever between them, nor will there ever be. It's a simple fact of their symbiotic existence that Maya is a bully who will never stop beating Gemma up. Even though Maya promised she would leave forever after her one day of freedom, Gemma knows it's highly unlikely she'll keep that promise now that she's married Eli. Not that she's going to stay married; she isn't. Or even that the marriage is legitimate. Still. How could Gemma have trusted so much deception? And one day soon Maya will no doubt land Gemma in an institution, because she has managed to cross every barrier Gemma has—psychological, mystical, pharmaceutical, and now, physical. There is no barrier Maya will not defy.

No matter how Gemma looks at it, her life is always reduced to its lowest common denominator. Saint versus Whore. Whore wins. Once the saint is rendered impure, there's no return to purity. How can there be? Just place a drop of black ink into a cup of clean water and see what happens. Black is black.

Eli uses the bathroom while Gemma gathers her few things—her underpants, bra, the lavender sundress she no doubt borrowed from

Arielle, and the four inch high Roman sandals that she must have stolen from a flamingo. She quickly dresses, and in the absence of any other footwear, she straps the sandals on and winces as she clomps across the room to search the closet for anything else she may have bought.

The closets are mirrored top to bottom, and she is shocked at this vision of herself dressed so unfamiliarly. Except for her hair which is almost comb-able, she looks like a young woman one might see in a magazine. Her hair is so short and shaggy it's even…chic. The image is arresting in its foreignness. Can it be her? Is it really her? She lifts her right arm to see if it really is, and yes, the corresponding arm moves in the mirror. She lifts her left. Likewise. She hasn't looked in a full-length mirror in so long she can hardly believe what she's seeing. At the monastery there is only the one ancient single-door medicine cabinet in bad need of re-silvering. Nothing else, nothing full-length. Nothing to promote vanity.

She opens the closet and sees nothing but hangers, so backtracks to the bed where she spots a few things on the end table, like…*what?!* A diamond bracelet? She picks it up gingerly and runs it through her fingers. Twenty-five or so sizable diamonds studded across the band. Can they be real? No way. The man is a medic not a Wall Street tycoon. And oh yes, she remembers that he's also a fireman.

So did they steal the bracelet? Does Maya steal? She breathes rapidly. And if Maya stole it, did he collaborate? Does he even know about the bracelet? She'll have to face this issue one way or the other—about all the diamonds—the ring and the bracelet. She drops it into her pocket and it's then she sees a pile of debris on the floor. It could be anything—receipts, pages from a magazine—so she isn't sure why she even picks it up. But she does.

She gathers it into a pile and inspects. First, there is a laminated, official looking, though clearly fake ID from New York for one Maya Sinclair residing at 9 Waverly Place in Hebronville. Whose address is that? Maybe Eli's? So the date is accurate if not the name or place. Next, a receipt from the casino which makes absolutely no sense to her. A third, the largest, is a...*oh God...*Certificate of Marriage registering the marriage of Mr. Eli Richards and Miss Maya Sinclair at the Chapel of Love, Las Vegas, Nevada. *Miss Maya Sinclair.* "Who are you, Maya Sinclair?" she mumbles. Where did you come from?

As if she could take any more, Gemma opens the fourth paper, a note written on hotel letterhead that reads:

Dear Gemma,

Don't feel sorry for me, because if I could have run away with your entire life, I would have. I nearly did. I would have stolen every last second of it without regret. I'm completely in love with the guy you are no doubt torturing right now. Be kind to him! He's exactly what we need—don't waste him! I want to thank you for the most beautiful day in a life—a real life—that you gave me. No one can ever take it away or erase it in the history of time. But as I've said before, I'm dying. My being is no longer able to sustain itself, and will have to be removed. The pain has been so great at times tonight I nearly passed out even while kissing the man I love! I'm jotting this down before I leave completely, and leave I must. I request one thing—a proper burial to honor the one day (okay, the two days...three?) of legitimate existence I squeezed out of you. And just so you know, the abdominal pain was so unbearable I couldn't consummate my marriage. So relax, virgin bride. You may find this hard to believe, but I love you, and I always will. Eli is my parting gift. Take care of him.

Your sister, Maya

Gemma reads it again, but makes no more sense out of it the second time. Maya is leaving—"will have to be removed"!? What is her claim to a burial? What is she talking about?! The door to the bathroom swings open and she stuffs the documents, receipt, and note into the deep front pocket of her dress. She's more relieved than she can say about her chastity, which gives her some room for kindness, because after all, *if it's true,* Eli didn't press. So he's a gentleman. A gentleman who will return her to her home intact.

He strolls out of the bathroom looking refreshed but sad. "Ready?" he says.

She nods.

"Got your bracelet?"

She nods again—so he knows! She attempts a weak smile.

Encouraged, he shakes his head, grinning and says, "That was some round of blackjack you played! What a whiz-kid! Whew! A natural!"

"Excuse me?"

"Maya the blackjack wizard, ha ha! Beginners' luck maybe, but still. If I let you keep going you'd have been able to buy five of those bracelets." He shakes his head again. "I should've let you keep playing."

He holds the door for her and they walk out of what is clearly marked the *Honeymoon Suite*. She ignores this. Down the hall and at the elevator she says, "And the um, the ring?"

He puts his big hand gently on her chin and raises it until she's forced to look into his insanely beautiful face. "The ring came from me," he says. "You know that. I told you I have money. *We* have money. We have a home and money enough for a happy, comfortable life. No worries."

Gemma can't speak. She is speechless. She doesn't speak in the elevator, and barely at the breakfast buffet. *No worries? Ha!* Too many worries to count! He hands her a fat wad of twenties so she can buy what she needs in the drug store, things like Midol which she's apparently been popping like peppermints. She just hopes it will suppress the pain in her lower belly long enough to get her home.

Just get me home!

On the wide roomy, half-full plane somewhere over the Colorado Rockies, he says, "I know you're not the same, but I don't know why."

Her throat goes dry. She gazes out the window at a long field of high cotton clouds interrupted by scant views of rugged purple peaks and deep black canyons. She can't find the words. Everywhere she searches, they are gone.

"Did you hear me?" he says quietly.

She turns to him slowly, explores his eyes for courage and says, "There's something I have to tell you, Eli."

"I'm listening."

As they fly across the country, the story chokes out of her from Henry to Maya and he listens heroically, embracing her every so often when she's too spent to talk. He brushes her cheek and strokes her neck. She knows she shouldn't let him touch her; shouldn't cling to him the way she is; shouldn't encourage him the tiniest bit. *She's a nun!* But on this plane she's as much his captive as he is hers, so what choice does she really have?

And at least she's breathing, and so is he. They're traveling together in the crucible of the open sky and there's no way out, but they're both breathing. If it weren't for that—for this inescapable pressure-controlled cabin—for this forced proximity, for the crippling pain in her cramped belly, for the fragile bone china of her shattered psyche—were it not for all that...she wouldn't be anywhere near him. She'd be long gone. She really would.

Somewhere over Illinois she finally admits to him and for the first time to herself, that there's something terribly wrong with her. "I'm crazy," she says. "I'm completely insane; it's that simple. I'm two people trying to live in one body. I don't know how it happened, but it's always been that way. You get used to things—terrible things. Well, not you...but me. And you just had the very bad luck of meeting us." It's the "us" that does it—that breaks her down to her barest components. She gasps for breath. "I'm so sorry," she says, because she is.

He presses her head hard against his chest and strokes the soft down of her crazy hair. "It's okay," he says. "It's okay. It really is. You'll see."

Somewhere over Pennsylvania or New Jersey she takes her fourth dose of Midol, which this time does little to relieve the pain. "It's emotional pain I think," she says. "That's why it isn't going away. It's because I feel so awful about what Maya did to you."

"Maybe," he says. "But it could also be appendicitis, and I'm not willing to take the chance. I'm taking you right to the hospital…"

"No! No hospital!" *They'll never let me out!* "I'll be fine as soon as I'm home, I swear."

He sighs. "By home you mean…"

"Eli, we can't…we're not even officially…"

He nods. "I know."

"The ID was fake," she says, and jerks the ring down her swollen finger until he stops her.

"Don't. There's still a chance, seriously. We can try, Gemma. Maya was fun, but it's you…"

"You don't know me."

He folds his arms. "I do now."

"If you spent time with me you'd hate me like everybody else."

"I don't believe that," he says, his voice cracking. "I was drawn to you from the second I met you. Even in that crazy get-up, that…that nun gear, it was love at first sight. How do you fall in love with a girl dressed like a nun except by pure fate? Don't ask me how it happened; it just did." He shakes his head. "It was physical, yes, I admit it. Especially, I don't know…at the carnival and after. But also magic—a real connection." He thumps his heart with a closed fist. "I kid you not. You can't run out on me." He looks away from her, swallowing.

Gemma can't believe this. *Fate? A magical connection?* How did she get here—on this plane with this kind, handsome man who thinks he loves her? Who thinks he loved her from the moment he set eyes on her? Who thinks they have a true connection? *What?!* How did she get here from the fields of a near-cloistered monastery? She's almost grateful for the pain—the near constant, searing pain in her gut, because if it weren't for that, she might…who knows…*kiss him.*

The next hour is a blur as the cabin lights flash in and out, her head spins, and she begs off all conversation by way of emotional exhaustion. But it's more than that, and he knows it, too. This goes on for a time—the silence, the stabbing pain in her gut, the exploding headaches, the moaning angst, the dizzying flashes of light. Sometimes it's bearable and sometimes it's not. All she remembers is being carried off the plane in Eli's arms in a heat of anguish. Curled up like an inch worm, she is placed on a stretcher, the red and white lights of the ambulance flashing and pulsing like a Vegas marquis.

ARIELLE

"I don't feel right about this," says the loser as he smacks the hammer onto the top of the ten foot pole for the ninth and hopefully last time. He rattles it to make sure it's deep enough into the soil and stable enough to withstand wind. "I just don't like it, Ari."

"It's not yours to feel right or wrong about," she says as she admires her handiwork from below. "You're just an assistant." *Who cares what you think?*

The wind is blowing softly, but picking up speed, and there are dark clouds approaching from the southeast. She wants to finish this job before the rain comes, if it comes at all, since no one seems to know how to forecast weather anymore. OMG, she's starting to sound like the hive—all about the weather! When the loser jumps down from the ladder, she climbs to the top to bind the base of the head—a hay-stuffed stocking—with a cord from one of the undergarments.

"But what about the rain?" he whines. "Won't the dress get ruined?"

"What?!" she says incredulous. "Are you a girl? Oh right, you are. I forgot about the fake daisy in your kitchen."

He shakes his head. Her ladder shimmies and he walks over to anchor it. "Be careful up there," he says.

"And anyway, you can wear these things in the rain," she says. "Gemma wore it everywhere. It's like a giant hot, sweaty raincoat. I don't know how she stands it in the summer."

He runs the serge fabric through his fingers. "It is kind of heavy," he says.

Finally they agree on *something!* So tedious dealing with a know-it-all on such an important project, not that there was a choice. She asked for another fireman, but of course the loser showed up instead. She couldn't do it alone, so.

She reaches into the front pocket of her bib overalls, pulls out a few bobby pins, and uses them to attach the headpieces to the pantyhose casing on the head. "There!" she says triumphantly. She spreads the veil over the shoulders and adjusts the coif and wimple to look exactly as Gemma wore it. "You know," she calls down, "the longer the saint's away the more I realize what a kook she was."

"That's not nice."

"Well, excuse me, Pope Lucky! And anyway I'm all for Maya, believe me. Not that I approve of her eloping with Eli; I don't, but. It's hard to live with a masochist is all I can say." She fusses with the white scapular apron and the big sleeves so they hang right. It has to be perfect; it represents the monastery.

"You don't have to live with a masochist, Ari," he says. "You could live with me."

"Which would make me the masochist," she says under her breath.

"I heard that," he says.

"Good."

He rattles the ladder. "Hey!" she screams.

A herd of giant crows swoop over the far field, or maybe it's a flock, she can't remember. Oh yeah, a murder, yuck! Here they come with their hatchets. "Hurry up," she tells the loser. "We have to fold-up the ladder and hide behind the bushes...see if this thing works."

Lucky offers his hand to help her down, but instead of taking it, she jumps right into the arugula. "Hurry!" she whispers real loud.

He lifts the ladder and takes it with him, all opened up and awkward. But he's big, so. Back in the woods, he folds it up.

"Look at that!" she says breathlessly. Six or seven crows start pecking at the romaine until the wind kicks up the skirts and sleeves of the scare nun. They run like hell on their little stick legs and then lift-off with their Halloween wings. A few more come to investigate, circling the head until the veil flutters, and *whoa!!!* "Ha ha ha!" she screeches jubilantly. "It works!!!"

She's so happy she barely notices that she's crouched all close to the loser like the old days. "Did you see that?!" she says, pushing his shoulder. "Did you?"

He nods, grinning. "Yeah. But still. Not to take any of the fun out of it, Ari, but what will Mike say? It seems kind of sacrilegious to me."

"Sacrilegious?!" she says, dumbfounded. "Are you kidding me? This just shows how much you don't know about religion!" Her jaw is practically hanging at her knees.

"It's not?" he says suspiciously.

"The whole reason it works is because of religion!" she says. The loser is a lost cause. He doesn't know anything about anything. "The scare nun represents God who's trying to protect the crops, but can't because he's invisible! The crows couldn't care less about scarecrows anymore, Lucky. After five hundred centuries, guess what? They recognize the costume! They know it's fake! They're not stupid." *Like you.* She lays her head in her hands like she can't take anymore, which she can't.

"Well...it is working," he concedes.

"I'll say it's working! It's scaring the living crap out of them! It's genius!"

He chuckles. He might believe her or not, hard to tell because he's trying so hard to be anybody but himself. But he can't fool her.

"What about Gemma?" he asks. "She'll be back at some point. Doesn't she wear that thing? Isn't that her uniform?"

Arielle flicks her wrist. "Hakuna matata," she says. If he even knows what that means, which he doesn't.

"Yeah," he says laughing, "hakuna matata!"

She smiles even though she'd rather not. "You know the Lion King?" she says, surprised. She didn't know him back then. Back then she saw him sashaying around town or school, all skinny and cool with his empty wallet attached to his belt by a long stupid chain. A long stupid chain attached to an empty wallet on one end and the loop of his ghetto pants on the other. But still…cool. Back in the day cool.

"Oh yeah," he laughs. "Me and my friends were addicted. We'd be all Mufasa…"

"And Scar!" she shouts, laughing.

"Yeah, Scar!" He shakes his head. "Virgil was Scar, all bad ass."

"What ever happened to Virgil?" she asks.

"He's in friggin' med school! He's gonna be a doctor!"

She pushes him so hard he falls over. "Doctor my ass! Doctor Pepper!"

"Yeah," he says laughing. "Doctor Pepper. He knows more about bottle rockets than medicine. I wouldn't let him examine me!"

"A bottle rocket scientist!" she squeals. "A new profession!"

And suddenly there they are all crouched up laughing about Doctor Pepper and the Lion King with the scare nun blowing in the wind and the rain clouds threatening. Next thing you know some crazy violin music will start playing in the sky and he'll make a move on her.

"I gotta go," she says, jumping up. "I promised to wash Connie's hair."

He stands slowly, brushing the long legs of his skinny faded jeans. "Wait," he says. "You have a tick."

Oh my God, she hates ticks! "Aaaaa! Get it off!!!" she screams. "Hurry up! Get it off!"

He checks her neck; picks off whatever. "Wait. There's another one," he says, lifting the hair off her neck and pinching her skin.

"Ouch!"

He flicks the tick into the parsley, *if there even was a tick,* turns her head and kisses her, which doesn't last because she goes completely auto-bitch and swats him hard. Not really planned, but. He acts all shocked like she was the one who kissed him. Like she started it.

His hand goes to his cheek. "Ouch," he says all quiet and offended, which should make her even madder, because…*when will he get the hint?!* But instead it churns up the guilt mill.

"Sorry," she says. "I didn't mean to smack you so hard."

He sticks his hands in his pockets. "I shouldn't have tried," he says. "I just…"

"Don't," she says. "Please. We already tried, for God's sake. All the way to marriage and it didn't work, and if you want to be friends you have to respect the fact that I live in a monastery."

"Giselle is mine," he says, and she freezes.

He lifts his hands out of his pockets and holds hers because she's paralyzed and can't pull away. He tips up her chin and tries to look in her eyes, but she doesn't let him. She's not that paralyzed.

"No she's not," she says.

"I've known it for some time," he says, "which is why I went looking for you in the first place. She's mine and she's yours, Ari. She's ours."

Her lips tremble. So maybe there isn't a God, because if there were this would not be happening.

"Are you okay?" he asks.

"No."

"I know you hate me right now, but the good news is that our daughter has a mother and a father."

"If I even believe you," she says.

"Believe it, Ari. A mother and a father."

"Who aren't married," she says bitterly. "Who aren't married, because."

"I can't erase the past, but I can make up for it."

"I'm not moving in with you, Lucky Johnson," she says. "And neither is Giselle. And besides, where's the proof?"

"I'll give you proof, whatever you want," he says. "I'll respect whatever you want."

Huh? "Good," she says suspiciously.

"I'll bring her by," he says. "I'll bring her by so you can visit, ok? No pressure. Whenever you're ready and you have it worked out, I'll help you through the custody process."

"Who has her now?"

"My cousins."

"Don't try anything fishy," she says. "Wait—they won't give you custody, will they? By yourself? Cuz your record's a lot worse than mine. And I'll fight it, Lucky," she says, her eyes all squinting and dukes up. "You and your fake blood test don't qualify to raise a turnip."

"I told you," he said. "I fucked up good last time, and this time I know my place. But if you don't want her...or you can't figure it out, I want you to support me. Okay? She needs her parents. She's what matters in this."

"I'll figure it out," she says, "don't worry." But she's had all she can take, so she turns and raises her hand sayonara style with her back to him so he can't stop her.

She races toward the hills and up to the house as fast as she can without looking back. For one thing, she doesn't want to see his sad sack face, as if he really gives a damn, and for another, it's time for the craft fair's big new sewing machine reveal. Arielle doesn't want to miss it. The craft fair's been through hell and she could use a good surprise. Not only a new sewing machine, but also one of Arielle's excellent shampoo and head massages to throw her off-track while the hive sets-up the surprise. Not that Arielle minds the dirty work, she doesn't. She's really, really good at everyone's hair but her own. She's aching to help out. To get away from her own life and into someone else's. She curls up her fingers and scratches the air; she can almost feel the crafty scalp beneath them.

When she bursts through the screen door and into the hallway, Mike says, "Go...go...hurry! You're late! Beatrice and Gabriella are setting up the machine already!" She claps her hands, "Chop chop!" Then she...*grins!* "Tell them I'll be up in a bit. I have to run some mail over to Mother."

Arielle has never seen Mike so juiced. What's going on? But she doesn't want to ruin it, so she just jumps the stairs two at a time ignoring every bad thing she could easily think about, including the *Jaws* ringtone circling Mike's phone this very minute. "Don't answer it!" she calls down the hall after her. "Don't ruin your day!"

But Mike does answer it as she walks down the hall and out the back door to the trailer. Could bring them all down when you think about it. So don't think about it.

In Connie's room, Arielle sets up the water bowls and towels next to the craft fair's bed and squeezes water from the washcloth onto her hair. The last of the day's dimming sun streams into the room—a giant strobe behind a drenched steel gray storm cloud delivering a sparkly crystal prism all the way from heaven to Connie's water glass. What a show-off God can be! Arielle wishes Assisi were allowed in the main house. If Assisi were here, he would paw the prism at the window, in the air, and all the way to the glass. Air attack! *Paw paw paw!* He would study it carefully like a burglar, and *yaaaa!*— attack it like the true ninja cat he pretends to be. He'd spend the whole day playing sneaky cat games with the prism.

"That feels so good, dear," says Connie as Arielle applies the melon-scented shampoo and works it in with her magic fingers.

While she works up a good lather on the craft fair's head, she thinks, humans should be more like cats. Humans think, *huh, there's a prism*—and instead of enjoying it—boom, right back to mindlessly watching the Kardashians pick their noses. Nothing makes humans stop in their tracks except the edge of a cliff. And even then...*CRASH!* Arielle should know. And just her opinion, but most humans fail to appreciate the big *little* things, which is why God gets so fed-up with us. *Just watch your doggone cats!* You'll have a better life.

Arielle rinses the shampoo from the head of the weak, shrunken craft fair and blots the infirm one's wet gray curls with a fluffy white towel while the fair purrs happily, which is almost as good as having Assisi here. She gently combs out the snarls with the big red wide-toothed comb she borrowed from Beatrice. She seriously grooves to the old folks and how amazed they are to be touched at all, never mind fussed over. If you want to feel good someday, she thinks, just go to a nursing home and hold someone's cold, wrinkly old hand. Guaranteed free trip to the moon and back.

When she's finished combing, Connie pats Arielle's knee and says,

"You're an angel, dear. My hair hasn't been washed in a week."

"It was kind of greasy," Arielle says, which cracks-up the crafty one.

Arielle edges off the middle of the bed and backs her butt onto the rocker. She has to waste some time because where's the hive with the surprise?

"Did you miss your projects when you were, you know…sick?" she asks. She hesitates because maybe it's un-PC to say sick anymore, you never know. Maybe health-challenged would be less offensive.

Connie shrugs. "Not really. I was so tired and weak. But I missed you! And I missed the girls!"

"Shucks!" says Arielle beaming.

"But at least now I know what was wrong with me this whole year, maybe longer. I think people were starting to think I was, I don't know…making it up."

"Naaaaa!" *Ha ha, definitely!* Next to sewing, the craft fair's health is her number one favorite topic.

Connie squirms back against the wall for support. "And my thyroid…" she points down. "Right there on the floor!"

"On the floor?" Arielle exclaims then jumps to the floor to look for it, why not? The craft fair goes nuts!

"Oh dear," she says, grinning. "Oh my!"

"Hooray, I found it!" says Arielle, backing out of the closet on her hands and knees with a rusty bent thimble that just happened to be on the floor.

The craft fair holds her belly for dear life. "I've forgotten how much fun it is around here since you came!" she cries.

"Well, now that your thyroid's off the floor, you can make something new for your favorite model, right?" Arielle prances around the room in her overalls on her tiptoes, sucking in her cheeks like someone special.

"Any day," says Connie, giggling. "Time to start sewing some winter clothes now!"

"Weeeelllll, as a matter of fact, Gemma's gonna need some clothes," says Arielle, barely stifling a giggle. Not that she can say why—that Gemma's clothes are hanging on a pole in the lower field scaring crows! She can't tell anyone. She wants Mike to find the scare nun all by herself. To be surprised at Arielle's out and out cleverness! And anyway, Gemma's the only one who wears that habit; it's a museum piece. And who knows if she's ever coming back.

The room is darkened by the encroaching night and the emerging threat of a storm, and Arielle runs about turning on lights. There's a rat-a-tat-tat on the door, announcing the super-duper new Brother PC-420. Project Runway at the monastery! The craft fair can open a business now. Prior Tuck! The hive rolls it in on a new sewing table covered by one of the ten new blankets created by the founding members of Knitters Anonymous, but where's Mike?

"Well now, what's this?" asks Connie with big wide eyes.

Gabriella lifts the crazy chartreuse and hot pink blanket like a magician, *presto!* Connie's hand flies up to her mouth in shock.

"It was donated," says Gabi, practically popping. "It's all yours!"

Beatrice beams behind her and Rose is just spinning uncontrollably. She might take off. It's very endearing how excited they all are at this gift, Arielle thinks. Real people equals real love equals a real home. There's nothing like it. It's what she wants for Giselle. A loving home.

Gabi elbows Rose and stares at her wide-eyed like she should know why.

"Oh!" says Rose, who jumps out of her spinning routine and says, "Oh! I forgot! The fabric store donated remainders!" She runs into the hall and rolls bolt after bolt of burned-out velvet into the craft fair's room, ha ha! Bolts of black and red burned-out velvet and two bolts of pink satin! *What?!*

Arielle rolls her inner eyeballs around the earth about a million times, because she'd like to see Mike—or any of them—in an outfit made from that fabric! And just when she thinks about Mike, she feels Mike's presence behind her—sullen. Heavy like meteors. Her dark, heavy presence and then the deadly mucus throat-clearing that precedes all bad news. Call her crazy, but if you ask Arielle, things are suddenly not okay.

"Oh, Mike," says Rose, clapping, "there you are! Connie loves it! She just loves it!"

Mike stares a deadly stare.

"Oh, Michael Agnes, I love the sewing machine!" Connie says. "I just...I just love it!!!" With a helping hand from Beatrice, Connie inches off the bed and stands there in her housedress all drawn out like a sack of skin on a suit hanger. The gabfest helps her into her robe.

"I'm very glad you like it, Constance, and you deserve it," Mike says like she's not the least bit glad. Like the monotone words were hitched to a trailer and dragged out her mouth one-by-one against her will.

Out the window, the dark sky suddenly lights up with jagged strips of lightning and a crack of thunder splits the world in half. They all look at Mike in anticipation of whatever doom. *The Absolute End of Everything.* Like Mike's in charge of that, too.

"Well, for heaven's sake, what's wrong, Mike?" asks Beatrice, her rosacea rising like mercury on her face. "You're so drawn!"

Mike hesitates. "It's just...Mother," she says. "She's not feeling well, but she refuses to see the doctor. I don't know. Maybe it's nothing."

Arielle darts past them and out the door. "I'll check on her," she calls out behind her. "If she needs to go I'll call the squad."

She travels like a laser beam down the stairs, through the house, into the drenched fields with its overhead light show, her leather Frye's filling with water as she runs. She could be hit by lightning, but probably not, so she'll take the risk. Anything for the relic.

Hang on, madrecita!

She blasts through the front door of the trailer where a candle flickers spookily in the corner on the edge of the counter. Looks precarious as hell, so she blows it out and switches on a light. *Where's little mama?* Nowhere obvious. Arielle gets a whiff of smoking myrrh, so the relic's obviously been burning her incense rocks, naughty little relic that she is! Everyone knows she's not supposed to be doing that alone, but. At least it means she's alive.

Just then the bathroom door creaks open and there she is, tiny Yoda backlit by the nightlight. "Oh there you are, dear," she says, feeling her way with a cane.

"Huh?" says Arielle. "I thought you were decrepit and here you are strutting your stuff!"

"Oh, yes dear!" she says grinning. "Strutting my stuff! I had a bit of a spell, but no. I'm fine now, not to worry, dear. I just made a fuss so Mike would send you over. She was going to keep you there for a dreadful meeting about prayers and procedure during the visitation. I thought you might prefer to be here."

Arielle's chest caves in with relief. "Well, here I am!" she says joyfully. "But don't scare the crap out of me like that again!"

"It's a spooky night," says the relic reflectively as she lifts her cane to part the gingham curtain. "Convergence, I'm afraid."

"Convergence?" Arielle says. "You mean the tea? I'll go make it."

"No, dear. No more tea. It's time. The tea has done its job."

Thunder rattles the trailer and Arielle grabs the relic so she doesn't fall. "Is this a tornado?" Arielle asks. "Is that what you mean by convergence?" A crucifix sways and drops from the wall, landing in Assisi's UPS bed box and sending him screeching under the couch.

"Convergence can certainly feel like a tornado," says the relic. She hangs onto Arielle's arm as they move toward the chair. "I want you to stay with me tonight, dear, if you don't mind."

"But maybe we should go to the farmhouse," Arielle says, although she has no idea how she'd get the relic over there in this cyclone anyway.

"Absolutely not, dear," says the relic. "I forbid it. Our place is right here." She taps her cane on the linoleum. "It's important to be in the right spot during convergence. Everyone in her place."

Arielle settles the relic into her dusty throne, replaces the crucifix on the wall, and wanders to the kitchen where she opens the fridge for survival snacks, why not? The end of the world could take a long time. *Where's the popcorn?* Another mad crash in the heavens confirms it all. It's the end of something alright. Another crash and another! A

322   REA NOLAN MARTIN

gigantic, massive whatever lands on the roof—a tree branch or a pair of oxen sucked off the ark. This storm might be scaring God.

Arielle gathers her wits like pickup stix. Just the galactic noise alone is enough to empty her bladder without notice. She has to get busy—apply herself to a task. "How 'bout some peanut butter and jelly?" she asks the relic. "I make a mean one!"

"Oh yes, you do!" says the relic as she squirms back and forth, nestling into her cushions. "Maybe later, though."

This prompts Arielle to feel the relic's forehead for fever. "You don't feel hot, but you are a little sweaty," she says. "Are you sure you're okay, little mama?"

The relic clucks her tongue. "I'm fine;" she says, "believe me. I just need your company tonight." She opens her mouth as wide as it can go and the entire universe swims into the big black hole of her yawn. "Just want to enjoy you, dear heart…"

And boom, she's out! Arielle looms over her, feeling her pulse, her breath, the holy mist of her being. It's all there. Her vitals are good. At least they seem good. Relics get tired is all. *They're old!* Not to mention all her exhausting astral sightseeing. Arielle shakes out a dusty blanket, wraps it right up to the relic's neck and kisses her gently on the top of her balding head.

For hours it seems, Arielle watches the light show outside and trembles with the trailer as it shakes on the cement slab in the howling wind. Lights flicker on and off in the farmhouse at least four times, but the trailer's backed-up by a generator and a couple of propane tanks, so. Should be good to go. She makes herself a PB&J and treats herself to some of the relic's iTunes as she manically straightens up the trailer, including snuffing out the myrrh that the relic left burning in the bathroom. While she's at it, she searches everywhere, including the pockets of the relic's housecoats for every match she can find and flushes them down the toilet so the mad mystic doesn't go all Salem on her.

Chores complete and madrecita still sleeping, Arielle rocks in the rocker listening to music until she practically wears a hole in the floor. Then she falls asleep too.

Hours later and the light show still in high gear, the relic says, "Arielle? Are you awake?"

Her eyes pop open. "Yes, little mama. Are you okay?" She has to focus hard in the relic's direction because the blinding flickering lighting inside the trailer and out is straight out of Frankenstein's laboratory. Madrecita lights up on her throne like a disco ball.

"I woke up because God told me to tell you something, dear," she says.

Arielle rubs her eyes. "What's that, Mama?"

"He said to tell you that you live in his mind," she says.

"I live in his mind?"

"Yes, dear. He told me that you live in his mind and that's where he dreamed you up. That you're his dream girl!"

Arielle's heart cracks in half like an egg and the raw love pours out all over her and the relic and Assisi and the trailer and the farm and Giselle and covers the entire world, including the loser. It's too much love for anyone; she can't bear it. It hurts.

"That's the most beautiful thing anybody ever told me," she says.

The relic shakes her knobby finger. "Remember it, dear," she says. "He wants you to remember it always. To never forget no matter what."

"I won't," she says, sniveling.

"He told me that specifically. 'Tell her never to forget,' he said. And also to tell Promise."

"Promise?"

"Yes, dear, Giselle. Giselle is heaven-speak for God's Promise. That's what it means."

Arielle's heart stops. "But..."

"I know all about her dear. She's part of his plan. She always was, and so were you. He dreamed you both."

They watch the storm in silence for a few minutes and then the relic says, "Arielle?"

"Yes, Mama."

"Be a good girl and collect all my tea recipes. Bring them to the farmhouse for safekeeping after the storm. Put them in your room for now. In the closet somewhere. I don't want anyone stealing them. They're for later."

Arielle smiles. "No one's going to steal your recipes, Mama," she says.

"But you'll do it?"

Arielle nods. This seems as good a time as any for more love, so she says, "I'll be baptized in a month, madrecita. Will you be coming?"

The relic slowly shakes her head. "No dear, I'm afraid not."

"But you have to!" she says. "I'm taking your name!"

The relic places her hand over her chest as she sucks a breath. "My name?"

"Arielle Augusta Santos," says Arielle. "I thought of it myself. After you." She walks to the chintz throne, kneels, and lays her head on the relic's bony lap. "So you see, you have to come! If you don't, we'll have the ceremony here, that's all. Right in the trailer!"

"We'll see, dear," says the relic. Then she recites the name like a prayer, "Arielle Augusta Santos," a couple of times.

Her eyes are all wet and teary, ha ha, good! Arielle knows she just gave the relic the best gift of all.

"Santos means saint," says the relic as she pats the top of Arielle's head with her gnarly paw. "Remember that, too." And she drops back off to sleep.

MIKE

Dressed in navy flannel pajamas and worn leather slippers, Mike paces back and forth on the rustic pine floors and maroon hook rugs of her sparsely decorated bedroom. She's worried about Arielle and Mother alone in the trailer in the midst of this hellacious storm. Staring out the west window of her bedroom she can see that the trailer is at least upright and the lights are on, which gives her some peace, but not much. The landlines are down, and she's upset that she never thought to give Augusta a cell phone. Although on second thought, Augusta's bent fingers can hardly manage a landline and would never be able to negotiate the size or mechanics of a cell. But still. Should she really be living out there with no means of communication? No. Not that Mike would have the last word on anything at all to do with Augusta.

From the outdoor shed light, Mike can see branches all over the fields, but there's just too much driving rain and intermittent pelting hail to see more than that. To attempt to traverse these grounds in this weather would be irresponsible of her at best, and at worst, calamitous. Without Arielle on duty, of course, she would have to. She's grateful Arielle shot over there when she did and without hesitation. The storm is a giant escalating loop—just when she thinks it's over, it powers back up.

So of course she can't sleep. Who could? It's not just the outdoor apocalypse and the vulnerability of the trailer; it's everything. *Everything!* She wanders down the back staircase to the kitchen to brew herself a fresh cup of Mother's strengthening tea. There are only three bags left. She should be using it more sparingly, perhaps, but no. She needs strength now. The earlier phone call from the Superior General's office announced that the visitators would be here at some point tomorrow, and she'd been hoping for at least another week. Why must they spring on her at the last moment! *What is their game?* She fills her mug with hot water and dunks the little bag of bound herbs up and down. She has no idea what to do with the visiting nuns, truly. It's like planning a welcoming party for invaders. *What's the etiquette?* And how will she tolerate their presence in her home? She prays for inspiration, but doesn't expect any.

If Mike is truthful, she'll admit that she doesn't know how to deal with the visitators in large part because she's so unsure of herself—of her own bearings, her own future. Unsure of where she stands relative to…everything! Relative to the Vatican, for instance, or to religion in general, and dare she think it…to God himself. This truth has been a dagger buried deep in her chest for some time, she realizes—one that she could only recently identify. *Last week!* But the minute she did, it pushed its rapier tip painfully to the surface, where it now lives in full bloody view of Mike and her conscience and no doubt Augusta who misses nothing. The last thing Mike needs now is a crisis of faith played out on a Vatican stage in front of a chorus of superiors. But there you are.

Timing is everything.

She places the tea bag in a dish to preserve it for perhaps one more cup then sips the tangy hot liquid. *Courage!* Only the fact that Augusta owns title to the farm has given Mike the blessed freedom to breathe. Because one thing Mike does know for sure is that, whatever her status, she wishes to stay on the farm. Existential crises do pass. Sooner or later everyone has one. Right? She doesn't want to land in an apartment in Troy, New York simply because she had a passing fling with Doubt. Or at least what she hopes is a passing fling.

She carries the tea back up to her room and sits on the edge of the ladder-back chair beside the east window facing the expansive fields. A deafening crack of overhead thunder sends branches everywhere in a whirlwind microburst that stuns her. She can hardly think! Or maybe it's the tea. But all of a sudden the sky over the lower field is brilliantly lit in combustive shades of chartreuse and magenta, commanding her complete attention. Lightning in the distance illuminates the giant pin oak and *uhh....*actually strikes one of the cedars sending bark in every direction. Utter chaos!

She presses her nose to the glass to discern...*what?!* Is she seeing things? It looks like...*but no*! It can't be! She places her mug on the sill and rubs her eyes. God, she needs sleep. She is so sleep-deprived! But is the tea hallucinogenic? If it isn't, then possibly Grace or God himself is speaking to her through an image of a nun in full habit blowing madly over the field! What can it mean? She chugs the rest of her tea and looks again.

The field lights up one more time with a giant strike and the flying nun whips around and bends to the earth, nearly touching the soil before popping back up in the air, skirts billowing. Good God, is Grace trying to tell Mike that she, too, should be dressing in full habit? That they all should? That this raging storm is a sign to them all to retreat to the past where women pledged themselves to full obedience? But obedience to what? She's lost track! Not obedience to God so much in her opinion, though that had been the plan. Not so much to God as to the whims of the men in power, she thinks. Of the Vatican prelates, though she could be wrong. She struggles to locate the flying nun again, but can't. It's impossible. The windows fog up inside while outside, hail pounds the glass like gravel.

Mike turns off the light and retreats unsteadily to bed, pulls the blankets to her neck, and retrieves her silver beads from the bedside drawer to begin a rosary. *"I believe in God,"* she recites, *"the Father almighty..."* And she does; she does believe in God. He clings like static to the dirty laundry of her misgivings, but he is unmistakably there. At some point, she'll be able to see what he's trying to tell her through this chaos. She has to believe that he will make *something* clear. She just saw a nun whipping in the wind like a witch on a stick! The heavens are talking! The least she can do is open her heart and listen. She continues to say the rosary as she drifts in and out of a thin, nearly hypnotic sleep.

As she finishes the last decade of the glorious mysteries—*the Coronation of Mary, Queen of Heaven*—she opens her eyes to a sight so alarming that it paralyzes her. She truly cannot move. In her very room—with eyes wide-open—all the colors of the rainbow bind together and fuse into a stream of blinding white light that reaches out and encompasses what she somehow knows to be the entire earth and everything on it and everything proximal in the universe. She is given to understand that the Light is God. The Light is God gathering every one of his belongings, disconnecting them from the possessive forces of gravity and ego…and assuming them Home. It sucks the air out of her, watching this Supreme Act, watching God gather us all, even our earth, to his breast…*taking us Home!*

In the midst of this spectacle a voice heralds, "This very thing would happen now if you would all simply forgive each other."

Mike knows she has some forgiving to do. Herself, for one—for birthing a child without breath. Did she will her baby dead—*for her own convenience!*—as she has long and secretly feared? Does she have that much power? Do we all? That was a day of sorrow and guilt buried so deeply in a festering pus-pocket of her soul that she'd long convinced herself it never happened. But it did. She lost the baby. Of course she did.

She didn't want it!

The voice continues, "This glorious day of souls' harvest cannot come until enough of you are reconciled to each other—until enough of you forgive and are forgiven. It isn't God who keeps you here in this suffering jungle," says the voice. "It isn't even God who judges. It is you who judge each other and refuse to forgive. It is you playing God."

We playing God!

Mike edges herself up on her elbows and then to a sitting position to convince herself that this is happening outside of herself. That she isn't making it up. That it's no mental concoction. It isn't. It can't be. Though she will no doubt one day convince herself that it was. She has never seen such wondrous terrifying things before; she would never have allowed it. This night blew a hole through the hard shell of her ordered beliefs. In its place is chaos. *And truth!*

With the next clap of thunder, the Light explodes like fireworks and vanishes. Mike lies in its sweaty aftermath. At some point, though, the message sinks in and she gets it. *Hallelujah!* It's that simple. Forgive as you wish to be forgiven. Attach yourself to nothing. This mess is of our own making. We did it; not God. Like a good parent, though, how much rescuing can a good God do without creating lazy, unaccountable children? Mike is suddenly crazy to forgive herself. To forgive everyone! To let go of everything else but that.

She falls into a deep, dreamless sleep and awakens in the dim light of dawn to the sound of bells ringing. She stretches her arms and slides out of bed ready to recite her Laudes when the bells ring again and again. *Oh my God! It's the doorbell!* The visitators? What in God's name would they be doing here so early?

She runs a comb through her hair, throws on her slacks and shirt and rushes downstairs barefoot. Maybe it isn't them? But even if it is, she's ready. She sees everything differently now. She sees things differently now that she's had the vision and also now that she knows the farm belongs to Augusta. What happens in this Vatican investigation is not completely black and white—there are practical issues to deal with still. Some that may shock the visitators, since Mike's vision of the future will no doubt vastly differ from theirs. Mike may shock the visitators, but the visitators won't shock her; that's the important thing. They can't. They have no more power over her. She has clarity now.

She descends the front staircase, knocking on the Sisters' doors as she passes to make sure they're up. But that's it. The rest, she's leaving to them. Who her Sisters are and what they do with their lives is a daily creation between them and the Lord. Mike will guide them, not punish them based on a false set of antiquated beliefs. She is the judge of nothing and no one.

In the main hall, her hand on the brass doorknob of the heavy front door, she freezes. She's thought so much about this moment that at this point, the moment itself is almost meaningless. How many times can you imagine something without erasing its impact? Nothing but God himself on the last day deserves the power and time she's already devoted to these visitors and their mission. God himself in communion with his creatures, individually, and then altogether, rising in the fullness of time, ascending as one—*that's meaningful!*

Not this. This is not.

She opens the door. The porch light flickers and residual thunder rolls like a giant sack of loose potatoes tumbling across the sky. "Come in! Come in!" she says generously, because she can afford to be generous. And also because forgiveness is more important than she ever knew.

"Good day," say the nuns as they hustle inside.

"Let me take your capes," Mike says cordially. She collects the black rain capes and leads the nuns, all in full habit, into the living area for some coffee and a chat. After all, they're guests in her home. The home that belongs to Augusta now, and after that, to her.

"Did you travel through this wretched weather?" she asks, and then, "Oh, sorry, I'm Michael Agnes, the uh..." She just can't think of her title. "The um..."

"The Prioress?" says one of the women. "How do you do," she says, offering her hand. "I'm Sister Johanna, and these are..."

Mike is so dizzyingly tired, or maybe still stunned from the vision, that she doesn't really hear the names, or at least has no memory of them even as they're spoken. She invites them in for coffee then runs to the back door to make sure the trailer is still standing. It is, praise God, although it was clearly pummeled by a forest of debris, including a massive chunk of wood that remains on the roof.

Assembled in the dining room, one of the Sisters says, "Shall we say our Laudes, Prioress?" She looks around. "Where do you say them? Shall we go to the chapel?"

Mike scratches her head. "We uh, we had a rough night here..." *Wait!* Who is she kidding? Honesty is either the rule or it isn't. She will not lie or put herself in a position of requiring the forgiveness of these women. "The Sisters recite their own prayers," she says. "During the day and evening…except for morning Mass, that is."

"It's not communal?" says the first one… *Johanna?*

Johanna appears to be the mouthpiece of this group. She's short and squat and somewhere in her sixties or early seventies. Gray hairs peek through her coif and wimple and she wears tiny round Ben Franklin specs across her wide-set brown eyes and broad nose. Mike tries to be kind in her observations, after all looks are meaningless in her profession. Even so, the woman is a bit churlish looking, she has to admit.

"I have an idea…," Mike says. "Why don't you all make yourselves at home and say your prayers while I make some coffee for us, hmmm?" She makes a slick exit before they can protest.

In the pantry, she arranges the percolator, fills it with coffee and water, switches it on and runs up the back stairs to brush her teeth, clean-up a bit, and ask Beatrice to manage the kitchen. There's no way Mike can throw a breakfast or even a snack together for these women. For one thing, she's exhausted, and for another, she doesn't want to be stuck in the kitchen where she can't keep an eye on them. *Why are they here so early?!*

When she thinks the visitors are finished with their prayers, she re-enters the dining room and opens the breakfront for the good china, which she places on the buffet table. She can handle that much.

"What is that noise?" asks one of the nuns.

"Yes," says another. "It was hard to concentrate on our prayers."

Mike turns; her face a question mark. She doesn't hear anything out of the ordinary.

"It sounds like people talking," says one of the younger nuns, in her late forties perhaps. "Or people singing. Is there a group in the other room?"

Mike attunes herself to a familiar drone in the background and jumps. "Oh, uh…I'll take care of that," she says, and darts to the den.

Rose has left the TV running overnight, what else is new? On the shopping channel! Some airtight little teenage figure is jumping around hawking an exercise machine. Mike clicks it off and in the corner of her eye

332   REA NOLAN MARTIN

spots Rose asleep on the couch, patches of green gingham quilting squares piled on her lap, her head tilted back snoring. Mike shakes her shoulder. "Rose!" she says in a whisper. "Wake up! Wake up! Rome has arrived!"

"Huh? What?!" blurts Rose, drooling.

"You fell asleep in front of the TV again!" says Mike. "Run up the back stairs and get cleaned-up then come down the front for breakfast."

Something in Rose's eyes makes Mike turn. Behind her at the doorjamb is Johanna, scribbling notes.

"Is this customary?" Johanna asks Mike. "A TV room? Sisters sleeping on couches in front of a television set?"

Mike simply smiles and says, "At times, yes." And she helps Rose up.

"Is it also customary to dress your scarecrow in full habit?" Johanna asks poker-faced.

Mike's stomach turns. "Excuse me?" she says.

"As we were driving up we saw a habit in one of the fields on a long pole. Soaking wet, of course, but clearly…the habit of your Order." She lifts her chin imperiously. "This can't be news to you," she says. "It's your monastery, is it not?"

"Uh. Yes? But I'll have to look into it. I just don't have an answer…" She walks past Johanna into the hall and keeps on going to the kitchen where she finds Beatrice dressed like Cinco de Mayo.

"You couldn't have toned it down a bit?" Mike whispers to her.

Beatrice pulls down plates from the cupboards and napkins from the drawers and barely looks up. "Not on your life," she says.

These women are so far ahead of me, Mike thinks. They know themselves. "Well then…"

Beatrice looks at her expectantly.

"Well then, good for you," says Mike, and they both grin.

"What will be, will be," says Beatrice. "I hope that's okay with you."

Mike pats her on the shoulder. "Yes," she says. "Of course."

There's a commotion in the hall. Mike arrives in time to find Arielle and her wild child hair, wrinkled shirt, and overalls stuffed into damp boots sliding into the hall. Mike tries to divert her from the dining room, but it's too late. She stands awestruck in front of the committee.

"Is everything okay?" asks Mike "I saw the branch on the roof."

"Hell yeah," says Arielle, then, "oops." She looks from Mike to the visitors and back.

"What do we have here?" asks one of the nuns. "This isn't...this can't be...your postulant?"

Mike leads Arielle into the room by the shoulders. "This is Arielle Santos," she says. "She's our catechumen, actually. She's helping out for the summer." She squeezes Arielle's shoulders. "Arielle," she says, "these are our visitors from the visitation office."

Arielle waves her hand impishly. "Hey!" she says.

They all nod, and Mike asks Arielle, "How did you and Mother survive the evening? We were worried."

Arielle shrugs. "It was freakish, but we did ok. The relic...I mean Madrecita...slept a lot. She's hungry now, so."

"But she feels okay?" asks Mike.

"Nothing wrong as far as I could tell," says Arielle. "I would've been the first to load her in the ambulance if she didn't."

Beatrice provides her with a basket of muffins, milk, and frozen waffles, while Mike beckons her into the pantry. She closes the swinging door to the dining room and asks Arielle if she knows anything about a nun on a stick in the lower field, which causes Beatrice to stand gawking in amusement.

"Oh, well yeah, you know. I thought it would be a good idea to let the crows know who's boss around here, what with Gemma gone and all? Cuz when she was here, the crows didn't dare raid the kitchen, so." She shrugs.

Beatrice goes to the east window to inspect and turns around to look at Mike. She rides out a giggle, which in all Mike's exhaustion is contagious. She tries hard to suppress a laugh, but can't.

"Genius, right?" asks Arielle, delighted at their reaction. "And it works!" She walks backwards to the door. "Gotta go!"

Gabriella walks gingerly downstairs with Constance on her arm. "Look who's here!" she says. "Walking all the way downstairs!"

Gabriella is dressed in her usual farmer's jeans and snug plaid shirt and Constance is swimming in a scarlet shift at least three sizes too big due to her weight loss. Rose follows a few minutes later in a fresh set of maroon sweatpants and a huge white t-shirt. What a motley group they make, Mike thinks. A year ago, this picture would have freaked her out. A year ago, she would have forced them all into summer habits just to conform to the occasion.

When they are all gathered at the table, Mike offers a blessing to the travelers, welcoming them—actually thanking them for their time and trouble. After all, one thought that had never occurred to Mike was that she might actually like the women. That she should at least give them a chance.

In response, one of the nuns says, "Will you be dressing in your habits later, Sisters?"

Gabriella takes a big bite of her muffin and shakes her head, no. "We haven't worn them in ages," she says. "It isn't required here."

"We work these fields," says Beatrice. "Try to mow a hayfield in a habit. You can't."

Mike sips her coffee and lets her Sisters talk for themselves. Augusta owns the farm. There's nothing to lose here that hasn't already been lost.

"Except for Sister Gemma," says Rose. "She works the fields in her full habit. But she's not here now."

On the other hand, Gemma is a topic Mike would rather not address.

"Oh?" says Johanna with her notebook open. "Where is she?"

The Sisters all look at Mike. "To be honest," she says, "I don't know. She's taking a break."

"A break from what?" asks the youngest one. "From her vocation?"

Mike stares ahead, realizing that in spite of all her good intentions, she is already losing patience. "I'd rather not speak for Gemma," she says, and leaves it at that. She fills her mouth with lemon poppyseed muffin so she can't talk.

Later on at Mass, Mike reads the Gospel of Matthew, *"Peter came up to the Lord and asked, "How many times should I forgive someone who does something wrong to me? Is seven times enough?" Jesus answered; not just seven times, but seventy times seven times."* This, too, she interprets as a sign of clarity—that last night's vision concurs with the Gospel of the day. That she finally understands forgiveness as not simply a begrudging or even sincere act of civility, but as a humble and true, life-affirming necessity.

Afterwards, she stands at the lectern and collects her thoughts from last night's vision. "God doesn't judge us," she hears herself saying. "We judge each other as if we were God. We have no right to do that. Our sole job on this earth is to forgive and be forgiven while we still can. Peace."

That's it. Not another word. She returns to the altar, satisfied that she has carried forth the message she was asked to proclaim in front of the appropriate audience—the visitators. She forgives them, too. After all, they were sent here. They're doing their job. The seat of the problem is not a pew; it's a throne.

Right after that, after her act of true forgiveness, there's a commotion outside that's distracting enough, but thankfully she's been well-trained to keep her attention on the altar where it belongs. At least the visitators will see that, in spite of her many faults and misgivings, she's respectful of the Eucharist.

Shortly after this, someone outside—no doubt one of the perpetually late village stragglers—calls out something that to Mike is unintelligible, but must make sense to Arielle because she hustles out of her pew and down the aisle toward the narthex. Well good, Mike thinks. There isn't an emergency the girl can't handle. And maybe it isn't even an emergency. *Why think the worst?* Maybe Gemma has returned, praise God!

She genuflects before the tabernacle on the other side of the altar, and removes the gold ciborium—the container of consecrated Hosts. As she returns to the altar she spots Gabriella rushing toward the front doors, followed ten feet behind by a waddling Beatrice. Though she's trying to maintain focus, Mike is rapidly becoming unnerved. After all, why can't the women stay put? *Why today of all days?!* Arielle is one thing—at least Arielle knows how to dish out some authority. How to get things done.

Mike focuses on her sacred task with difficulty. *The visitators are in the front pew!* She sets the ciborium down on the white linen altar cloth, keeping one eye on Gabriella, who is now at the front door, gasping, both hands covering her mouth. *But Gabriella is a hysteric,* she reminds herself, and continues with her prayers. In the distance, a haunting scream announces, "Oh no, it's spreading!"—followed immediately by sirens blaring up the driveway.

Mike tries, but just…can't! Can't continue; can't concentrate— just too much intereference. Her head spins with exhaustion and the inability to make decisions. *Enough!*

With whatever decorum she can muster, she abandons the altar, mumbling, "I'm sorry, but I have to investigate," to the bowed heads of the pious visitators.

She glides down the aisle in long, swift strides, her heart pronouncing doom while her head insists it's nothing at all—*a bloody nuisance!* A small brushfire, perhaps. A careless cigarette butt tossed by the trash collector into the rear dumpster.

"Hakuna matata," she chants like she means it. "Hakuna matata!"

Outside on the stone steps, she hurries towards an unrecognizable man's voice yelling, "Stop her! Stop her!" and another more familiar one that commands, "Not a step further, Arielle, I mean it!"

At the foot of the path by the overhead trellis connected to the house, Mike nearly trips on Assisi who is racing a jagged path tree to tree, hair on end, screeching. Mike has never seen him move this fast. Ahead, firemen block a group of spectators that includes Gabriella and Beatrice from advancing past the mailboxes. Beyond that she can make out the image of Lucky in the act of securing Arielle in a cross-chest hold as she furiously squirms and kicks, screaming, "Let go, dammit! Let go! I need to get her out of there! Let. Me. Go!"

Before Mike can process the scene, the sky behind the house—

above the western grounds of the monastery—is lit by a wild plume of red fiery light accompanied by a deafening blast that pops her eardrums, knocks her off-balance, and sends her sideways against the stone foundation of the farmhouse porch.

AUGUSTA

It's hard to imagine what it feels like—that moment of liftoff. That blinding unbearable pleasure of release from ego and gravity. But Augusta kneels on cracked, bony knees; head bowed; arms raised; hands open to receive her God. To hold and to be held by the entire uncreated universe where pure potential eternally brews, just waiting for the right signal from the right spirit to magnify matter and materialize. *Oh, if we only understood our power!*

She thinks she might have trouble rising, attached as she is to Arielle, her heart. But in a single blind flash she realizes that Arielle is as eternal as she. They are eternal together. They will never be apart. They have moved through time before, and will do so again. So as the concussive force of convergence arrives, Augusta moves into the explosion, not away. She is ready.

It happens instantaneously—the separation from time. She is here and then gone. *Oh, the gladness of her soul! The great soaring ecstasy of freedom!* Why do we fear it so?

She rises and rises beyond all earthly matters, beyond fear and pain and judgment, beyond sequential thinking, sequential action, sequential time. She lifts and lifts, expands and expands, encompassing all of it—the pain, the joy, the terror, the broken spirit of the lost and abused, the distortion of the proud, the purity of the humble, the simple elegance of existence. She contains it all, magically. Effortlessly.

Beneath her lies the remains of chaos, detritus of a bygone era.

Arielle tearing at her hair, keening, retching. The man Jesse reaching out to baby Promise as she runs to him. Arielle's stunned expression as she captures the simultaneous loss and gain of too much love at once. And beneath Augusta's celestial view, Mike hobbles forward delicately with enough sense knocked out of her to let some wisdom in. The visitators hands clasp over their collective mouth, overwhelmed by too little order, too few rules, and too much bursting life. Augusta watches as they move reluctantly into the fray, knowing they should help, but not knowing how.

They are all where they need to be, Augusta knows. Every one of them. It is all well and good. It is goodness itself. God in his mysterious ways births a new order by annihilating the old. Godspeed, she whispers into the ears of everyone there. But only Arielle looks up. Only Arielle hears.

ARIELLE

Convergence isn't a story that can be told when it's happening. It takes years to figure it out. When it's happening, all you can do is spin around and watch the blurry lines of what you thought was your life blend with everyone else's like a giant human smoothie. Or like Dorothy in the tornado dumped in a foreign country with flying monkeys and crazy singing munchkins. Like that. Like life and death and everything in between happening all at once until you don't even know who you are or why you're here.

Madness.

Rocking on the front porch of the farmhouse on a glorious late August evening at sunset, Arielle remembers the day like it was yesterday. But it wasn't. It was five years ago to the day. How fast a half-decade can go, she thinks, and how much can happen in a single day that contains barely an inch of those five years. It's unbelievable. Time is just space in your head that helps you put things in perspective. You need it to create whole new files for things you thought could never happen, but can. And do. If you don't make a place for them in your brain, you'll go crazy, because they'll haunt you until you do. Arielle built a cell in the dungeon of her imagination and shackled that day to a brick wall so it could never happen again. Not that it would.

First, there were all those visiting black and white habits trying to wrestle order out of a wildfire. Documenting it! It was years before Mike and the Sisters even found out what those poor women thought, not that anyone cared by then. Well, except for the fight over the farm ownership and Mike's confusion over the title, but that's another story.

Arielle takes a sip of iced tea and shakes her head. She still can't believe those women were there on that very day, but then…they were part of the convergence, so. That's how it works. Mike had been so worried for so long about the grand inquisitors, yet in the end they were no more than powerless passersby caught in the same cosmic snare. If she'd been listening carefully to the relic, she would have known that, even expected it. With convergence, every speck of dust in your life gets sucked right into the vacuum. Every speck of dust has a place. Nothing is forgotten.

Arielle has to hand it to Mike; she didn't lose her cool one bit. She knew who she was that day, and in the eye of the storm, so did Arielle, Bea, Rose, Gabi and Connie, rest her soul. Not that the craft fair died that day, she didn't. She died because of it. So much for the pacemaker. Even Gemma figured her life out, finally. And then there was the holy relic, little mama, who started it all. Or maybe Grace did, you never know. Arielle blots her eyes, wondering if thoughts of madrecita will ever wander through her brain without a hallelujah chorus of burning tears.

But even on this anniversary with all its difficult memories and everyone arriving at the farm in a few hours for the remembrance…still, it's heaven. Rocking on the porch after a hard day's work is the best feeling ever. Rocking on the porch after a hard day's work on a farm that belongs to you is even better. Not that she works the fields; she doesn't. The volunteers do that. But she manages the Teahouse downhill where the salad fields once were. The Teahouse where they assemble all the sacred Mystic Tea from the recipes left by the relic for posterity. They can't make enough. Everybody wants them all over the world, even London and India, the capitals of tea! Everyone wants a piece of the relic. She's almost as famous as God.

The only recipes little mama refused the public were Convergence and Timeline. Those teas can only be used by those in the know. And anybody who *knows* doesn't want them, ha ha! But the other recipes—

forty in all—are the absolute rage on and offline. They had to hire half the town to keep up with production and marketing. The relic must be clicking her heavenly heels.

But back to the farm ownership—it was no done-deal the way Augusta had apparently led Mike to believe, if she even did. Arielle wasn't there. But whatever paperwork she had blew up with the trailer, so. They were back to the beginning, which meant facing bankruptcy or placing themselves at the mercy of the Apostolic Visitator, which...if you know anything about Mike...wasn't going to happen. The official "recommendation" of the visitator was to merge the Most Holy Order of Divine Grace with another Order, which Mike was not about to do. Hell, none of the Sisters were! To be honest, at that point, none of them wanted one single thing other than to live out their years on the farm in the exact way they'd been living up to that point. Except Gemma, but. That came later.

If Eli and Lucky hadn't bailed them out with a healthy loan and even a donation in exchange for a few acres, they would never have been able to buy back the farm from the foundation. That Eli and Lucky would do that for them after the crappy way Arielle treated them is a wonder, but hey...as Mike keeps telling her, forgiveness is the lesson. Forgiveness is capital 'L' Love in action. Until you have to forgive someone, you haven't loved. You just think you have. Until somebody forgives you, you don't know humility. And anyway, the loser turned out to be a winner of a dad, so. It was worth swallowing a boxful of pride to find the prize.

The sun breaks up into a million broken crayons that melt into the sky like stained glass. It's bliss right now with the hot sticky days and cool mountain nights! Oh yeah, and here comes Giselle running up the hill screaming, "Mommy! Mommy! Look what I found!" Behind her is Mike, bursting at the seams like a real grandma. Mike has never been so happy since Giselle moved in—complete personality makeover. It's like she'd been waiting for that child her entire life.

"She found a fossil rock!" Mike shouts, grinning.

"It's from dinosaurs!" Giselle squeals, and runs breathlessly toward them. She's eight now, happy as hell, even baptized like Arielle and Lucky. Not that they're a regular family; they're not. Arielle likes things exactly the way they are at the moment. And hey, they get along great, so. You never know. But why ruin a good thing when it's good? If Lucky and Giselle never showed back up in her life, Arielle's pretty sure she would've just hung out at the farm and joined the hive. Become a nun or whatever. But they did show up and she's glad. And so is everyone else.

With Mike and the other aunties around, Giselle's life is as full as it could possibly be. An all-around Eden. Everything Arielle never had belongs to her daughter, and to her too when you think about it, because when Giselle's happy, so is Arielle. Giselle places the fossil rock in Arielle's lap, turns back around and takes off, her red hair a kite tail in the wind. Mike stands at the top of the hill, catching her breath. She stands there watching out for Giselle like her own flesh and blood. Arielle just wishes Giselle could've met the relic. It's a pile of rocks in her heart that she didn't.

On the day of convergence, Lucky and Giselle had just arrived at the farm when the trailer lit up. It still freaks Arielle out to think that ten minutes later they could all have been inside when...*kaboom!* But at the same time, it freaks her out that if she had been there, she might've prevented it. *Where did the little pyro find the matches?!* Not that she had any way of knowing propane was leaking from the storm-damaged tanks; she didn't. But whatever. How many times can you go over the same story without wearing a hole in your head?

To see Giselle that day five years ago for the very first time in the middle of the end of everything, was like landing right in the arms of God in the mosh pit of hell. Tearing her hair out in grief as she realized the relic was up in flames, Arielle nearly ran straight into the fire herself. Only Lucky held her back—restrained her with all his muscley might. While she kicked and screamed and tried to break loose, she turned and saw their daughter. And floating above their daughter was the exact same angel that saved her butt in the jail cell all those years ago, so. Fate. Or maybe Grace. Grace rules.

GEMMA

In the mirror, Gemma adjusts her pink lace collar and combs her lush mane of golden blonde hair. Eli presses her shoulders from behind. "Ready?" he asks. A few strands of his silky black hair fall over his eyebrows and she turns toward him, brushing them aside.

"You look mighty thoughtful," he says, and she nods.

"Would you rather not go this year?" he says. "We don't have to."

"It's like two funerals," she says.

"I know."

"Three if you count Constance."

"Three funerals and a rebirth?" he says hopefully.

She smiles. "Yes, a rebirth."

"Right?" he says, cocking his head and searching her eyes for affirmation.

"Right," she says. "I was nowhere. Lost."

"Tortured," he says.

She nods. "And to think that all that time…"

"Best not to," he says, steering her gently toward the foyer.

They walk together out the door of their mountaintop cabin admiring the shimmering silver of the lake's glassy surface far below them. Gemma still can't believe this is her home. This is her home and this is her man, her husband. Still, with all the abundance she has come to accept, her chin trembles with a familiar sense of profound loss.

"I was awful to her," she says, and he grabs her hand.

344

"You didn't know, Gem."

"How can a person not know she has a twin!"

He opens the passenger door of their SUV and supports her as she struggles up and into the seat. "You didn't exactly have a twin," he says. "You had a terratoma. A *tumor.*"

"You know what I mean."

He shuts her door and appears a moment later in the driver's seat. "Well, like Rawlins said, what you had was basically a psychic twin. It's incredibly rare. How could you be expected to know that? No one knew."

He's right, she knows. Not to mention that she could have died from the torsion on her right ovary had they not removed the tumor in time. But that was just physical pain. The mental anguish was almost worse. *But not quite.* At least it lasted longer. It took a good year of Rawlins explaining things to her—how the embryonic twin had stopped growing and how Gemma had absorbed the tumor of stem cells her twin had left behind. A tumor and an ovary whose DNA was completely different from the DNA throughout the rest of Gemma's body. And how for some bizarre reason, she'd continued to feel the mental presence of her twin until the terratoma was removed. A lifetime of torture in a fist-size ball.

"It's not schizophrenia," Rawlins had finally declared after a solid year of twice weekly therapy. "I've never seen anything like it. I didn't even know it could happen," which was the beginning of his study on psychic twins that will no doubt make Gemma a lifetime legend in the psychiatric community. Not that such a thing was a goal of hers, or really, anything she'd even remotely wanted. She'd have given anything for a normal childhood and young adult life.

But still, she thinks—what about Maya? A real twin, or at least a real mental presence, condemned to a corner of Gemma's mind. As Arielle would tell her, it was more a disease of the spirit than the mind, or at least that's what Augusta had said. *Before the trailer exploded!* How Gemma wished she hadn't irritated the old lady so much. She would love to have known Augusta as Arielle had known her. But then again, in those days Gemma irritated everyone, including herself.

Thank God for Augusta, though—how she continued to help Gemma with her mystical teas and rituals. And for Arielle who taught Gemma to stop condemning herself; to stop inflicting self-punishment. Arielle, who used Gemma's formal habit to scare off crows! Who would have thought Arielle would be Gemma's maid-of-honor? Who would think anyone would be! And thank God for Eli, who waited two years while she figured out her life. Eli, who patiently taught her how to love and be loved. Eli, who never gave up.

As they drive down the steep winding wooded path to the bottom of the mountain and from there over route 9 to the monastery, she pats the massive eight month mound of twins in her belly and prays that one of them will bear the soul of Maya, free at last. Maya, free to be happy and loved, to express her obvious vivacity. Free to run and be held and laugh. To live the life she deserves. If you want to know what would make Gemma the happiest of all, it would be that.

MIKE

From her office, Mike parts the curtains to see how many of the villager's cars and trucks have arrived for the ceremony. Quite a few—maybe fifty by now. As usual they park in the south acre by the entry gate and assemble on the old trailer site on the west hill. There, they gather in a circle surrounding the three headstones, the two large ones for Mother and Constance and the smaller one marking the remains of Gemma's "twin," Maya Sinclair. Maya's stone was a concession to Jim Rawlins who insisted that the commemoration was essential to Gemma's recovery. Must have been so, Mike knows, because the rapidity of Gemma's recovery from that point forward was nothing short of miraculous.

Mike returns to her desk and sits down for a last minute review, a final moment to collect herself before show time. How is it, she thinks, that five years have already passed? In those five years life at the farm has been...well, revolutionized, really! Gone are the days of confusion and discontent and utter lack of faith. Minus the gaping hole of Mother's presence, life has clarity and joy beyond Mike's imagining.

For one, there is the unmitigated joy of Giselle! Of teaching her and watching her grow! Oh, how Mike's heart overflows just thinking about that firebrand of a spirit—how happy the child makes them all! She can't help but think almost constantly about how much Mother would have adored this child. That's the part of the hole that will never be filled.

There are still many unknowns, of course. For instance, there's the obvious question of Arielle's growing affection for Jesse and Mike's certain knowledge that this association is the best thing for their child. Which is at least partially why Mike allowed Jesse to build a house on the lower field in the first place. She didn't have to allow it. The original loan from Jesse and Eli was free of encumbrance. Which reminds her...she opens the center drawer of her desk and removes the check for $250,000 made out to Jesse and Eli and signed by her as Trustee of the Saint Grace Charitable Estate. Now, they are free and clear.

Just then she hears Beatrice, Gabriella and Rose clomp down the stairs in their usual manner (some things never change) and out the door. Mike moves to the front window where she can see them from a sharp angle as they scoop up Giselle who quickly reports her earlier archaeological discovery in the lower field—her fossil rock. They predictably fawn over it.

The women are content these days, though Mike still wonders at times if she did the right thing in reclassifying the Order. Not that the Sisters had to comply; they could have remained in the clergy. Mike would have done nothing had their vote not been entirely unanimous. But it was. After all, those were rebellious days fueled by the Investigation. And so, after months of consideration, they recast themselves as Third Order lay persons devoted to the charism of St. Grace in the manner of the Beguines as Mother had suggested before her death. Once in a while Mike second guesses her actions, but what's done is done. And again, they are content. Not only content, but highly productive and profitable. Even Rose barely watches TV anymore!

Independence is a powerful catalyst. It changes everything. After Mother's death, miracle after miracle ensued, not the least of which were the forty sacred tea recipes she'd given to Arielle for safekeeping that very day. Another was the miracle of Gemma's healing, which is something Mike would never have expected and didn't quite believe for months.

So here they are now, a new family—utterly reborn, voluntarily reconnected and bound by love. The spirit of Grace is more present than ever as they faithfully attune themselves daily to her spirit, the spirit of Mother, and God. They employ the able and feed the poor. Mike tucks the check in her pocket and smiles as she slips into her smart hip-length ice-blue sweater. She enjoys her new, more colorful wardrobe, though she still won't allow the Sisters to convert her entirely to the fiesta of Beatrice's closet. Though they try!

As Mike opens the front door, Gemma and Eli's car arrives at the top of the hill. Eli helps Gemma out of the car and they all gasp. My goodness how large her belly has become this last month! Mike is nearly bursting with expectation herself. *Twins!* This vocation of quasi-grandmotherhood has been the best gift of all. Of course she is Arielle's godmother, so that gave her a certain status with Giselle. But she is secretly hoping to be a godmother to one of the twins as well. *Oh please!* All these realities and possibilities, not to mention Eli's generous spirit with respect to the farm and foundation…have overwhelmed Mike's heart. Her cup runneth over!

On the porch, Arielle lifts Assisi from the chair and signals Mike in eager expectation. Mike nods. *Begin!* There must be two hundred people in the field now. Arielle adjusts the large outdoor speakers and blasts Augusta's theme song to the wide world. Mike pulls a tissue from her pocket in anticipation. As with everyone else, the music begins in her toes, shoots right up her body and out of her mouth. It's impossible not to feel each note, each word, like the combined voice of Grace and Augusta orchestrating heaven and earth in a resounding convergence of song:

Prepare yourself you know it's a must
Gotta have a friend in Jesus!
So you know that when you die
He's gonna recommend you
To the spirit in the sky
That's where you're gonna go when you die!
When you die and they lay you to rest
You're gonna go to the place that's the best!"

THE END

ABOUT THE AUTHOR

Rea Nolan Martin lives on the shores of the Hudson River with her ridiculously handy, tool-guy husband, Tom, and their insanely cute Australian Shepherd, Spirit. She is the lucky mother of two charming, insightful, and hilarious sons, Charley and Zach. Her life has been a mystical journey, and much of what she's learned she shares in her short stories, poems, essays, blogs, and two novels: *The Sublime Transformation of Vera Wright* and *Mystic Tea*. Both books are available online at Amazon, Barnes & Noble, and other retailers in both print and digital editions. You can access author info, blogs, discussion questions, book signings and other inquiries, such as requests for signed copies at **www.reanolanmartin.com**. Blogs are also posted on Huffington Post: GPS for the Soul and/or Religion sections.

This book is dedicated to Tom, the consummate caretaker of all earthly things—for believing in me, and grounding me in the physical world.

ACKNOWLEDGEMENTS

This effort was a family affair. I would never have initiated *Mystic Tea* without the encouragement and support of my husband, Tom. I would never have entered the worlds of social media or digital publishing to the extent that I have without the assistance of our sons, Charley and Zach. Special thanks to my sister, Mary Lou, and my brother, John, who scrutinize every manuscript I give them expeditiously and respond quickly and generously without prompting. I am indebted to them for much more than that.

Deep gratitude also to Dineen Bornemann, master of the digital world, without whose help my website would definitely not be beautiful or really, even work at all. (She's laughing right now.)

To anyone in need of a cover artist, as well as formatting, you can do no better than the incredibly talented Kristy Buchanan of KN Design, whose graphics are strong and original, her work style responsive, generous, and collaborative. In the morass of online services, she stands way, way out.

A full curtsy to Marian Boyle, Leslie Wolfe-Cundiff, Karen Sirabian, Mary Ellen Palmeri, Rosemary Geisler, and Deborah Kessler who also read this book in raw, manuscript form—never easy or fun. A second shout-out to brother, John, who dragged 350 manuscript pages to the beaches of Puerto Rico on his vacation and finished it in two days. Thanks, Johnny!

READERS' REVIEWS

*I fell in love with every character. Very different! A joy to read.
It made me smile, laugh, and brought tears to my eyes.*
—Jennifer

Doesn't get any better than Mystic Tea.
The perfect blend of humor, intrigue and good reading.
—Bridget

Hilarious yet serious. Spiritual yet Real. This book did not disappoint.
—BookLoverRome

Mystic Tea *introduced people at their most trying, intense, cataclysmic
experiences, with profound sensitivity and awareness. Followed with true
forgiveness and acceptance. Yet, releasing the dogma of formal religion to
create their miracles! Women held by a tradition and reached beyond it,
even in their advanced years. We all can learn from them!
...This is a Must Read for everyone!*
—Mary G.

*What a story! I couldn't wait to see how it all turned out but I almost cried
when I came to the end as I felt I was losing an entire gaggle of hilarious,
loving, charismatic friends.*
—Magellan

I finished it last night and loved it! Right up through the end, I loved it! This book was a joy to read, the writing had me mesmerized. Divinely inspired!
—Polly M.

Mystic Tea *is a story about so many things. It is funny, sad, joyful, and thought provoking—all the things that make a great story.*
—A.L.B.

Loved, loved, loved this book, and was so sorry when it ended. I felt like I knew all of these ordinary women who did quite extraordinary things. The writing is absolutely beautiful, rich, colorful, and appropriate to each character. Cannot wait until the next one!
—M. A.

This book is a real page turner full of vivid imagery and compelling characters.
—J. N.

BOOK CLUB DISCUSSION

1. Each of the primary characters in *Mystic Tea* has a distinct literary voice and point-of-view (POV). Did you find each Voice/POV to be consistent and easily recognizable? Can you describe the different language used for each of their stories—Gemma, Arielle, Mike, Augusta and Maya? Was the language appropriate to the character?

2. Each of the primary characters is on a specific spiritual journey formed by the circumstances, belief systems and experiences of her past, as well as her goals and ideas of the future. How would you describe their journeys?

3. Do you think any of the outcomes of these characters' lives would be different if their journeys had not intertwined and converged? For instance, what would have become of Gemma without Arielle, Mike, or Augusta? Likewise for the other characters. Would any of them have fulfilled her purpose without the others?

4. This story begins with a monastic community of nuns who are confused about their allegiance to a church leadership that no longer serves or nourishes them. How do they rise above this disappointment and confusion to continue serving God and their communities?

5. What would you say are the true vocations of Gemma and Arielle?

6. Had you ever heard of psychic twins (or chimeras) before reading *Mystic Tea*? The author thought these conditions were a figment of her fertile imagination until the subsequent appearance of an article titled "DNA Double Take" in the *New York Times*, Tuesday, September 17. This extremely interesting article was published two years after she wrote the book and two months after its first digital release on Amazon KDP. Do you ever sense things before they happen? Do you think anything else in this book might be prophetic?

Articles:
http://www.nytimes.com/2013/09/17/science/dna-double-take.html
http://abcnews.go.com/Primetime/story?id=2315693

7. Many readers of the digital edition wrote that the characters were so real they felt as if they knew them. Which of them would you like to have known? Why?

8. Underlying the serious circumstances of *Mystic Tea* is a tone of humor. Did the book make you laugh or smile in places? If so, which of the characters and scenes made you smile the most? Do you feel that humor made the serious messages of the story more palatable?

9. If *Mystic Tea* were a movie, who would you cast for the major and minor roles? Where do you see it set? Share this with the author at **www.reanolanmartin.com**.

Made in United States
North Haven, CT
20 April 2023

35658931R00214